happyface

by Stephen Emond

LITTLE, BROWN AND COMPANY
New York   Boston

Little, Brown and Company

Hachette Book Group
237 Park Avenue, New York, NY 10017
Visit our website at www.lb-teens.com

Little, Brown and Company is a division of Hachette Book Group, Inc.
The Little, Brown name and logo are trademarks of Hachette Book Group, Inc.

First Edition: March 2010

Library of Congress Cataloging-in-Publication Data

Emond, Stephen.
    Happyface / by Stephen Emond. — 1st ed.
        p. cm.
    Summary: After going through traumatic times, a troubled, socially awkward
teenager moves to a new school where he tries to reinvent himself.
    ISBN 978-0-316-04100-3
    [1. Family problems—Fiction. 2. Emotional problems—Fiction. 3. Interpersonal
relations—Fiction. 4. Dating (Social customs)—Fiction. 5. High schools—Fiction.
6. Schools—Fiction. 7. Divorce—Fiction. 8. Diaries—Fiction.] I. Title.
    PZ7.E69623Hap 2009
    [Fic]—dc22

                                                                    2008047386

10 9 8 7 6 5 4 3 2

RRD-IN

Printed in the United States of America

Dedicated to my family and to Taryn

Write what you see and draw what you feel.

Be open and honest.

Love every word you write, even the mistakes.

Find truth in each moment and then move on to the next one.

Start good, get better.

Love, your father.

Merry Christmas, kiddo.

So I'm opening my Christmas present in June. Not that it was a bad present; I'm just lazy and stuck in my ways. The piles of napkins and backs of school papers I'd been using to write and draw on had gotten a little out of control, though, and I can only stand to hear Dad ask if I'm using my sketchbook so many times.

It's taken me a while; a blank page can be intimidating. I'll just have to put it to good use.

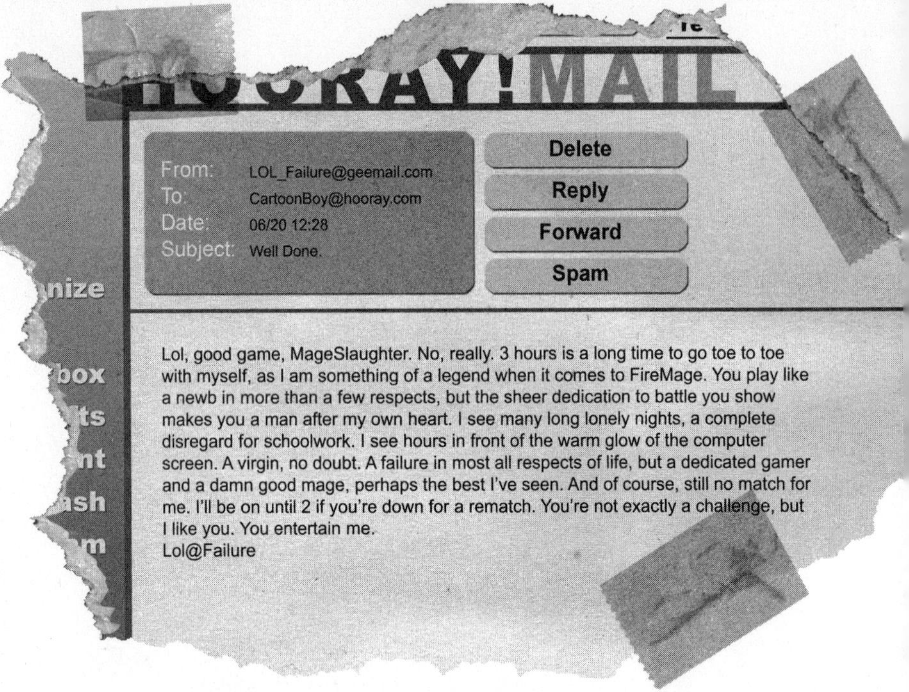

HOORAY!MAIL

From:	LOL_Failure@geemail.com	Delete
To:	CartoonBoy@hooray.com	Reply
Date:	06/20 12:28	Forward
Subject:	Well Done.	Spam

Lol, good game, MageSlaughter. No, really. 3 hours is a long time to go toe to toe with myself, as I am something of a legend when it comes to FireMage. You play like a newb in more than a few respects, but the sheer dedication to battle you show makes you a man after my own heart. I see many long lonely nights, a complete disregard for schoolwork. I see hours in front of the warm glow of the computer screen. A virgin, no doubt. A failure in most all respects of life, but a dedicated gamer and a damn good mage, perhaps the best I've seen. And of course, still no match for me. I'll be on until 2 if you're down for a rematch. You're not exactly a challenge, but I like you. You entertain me.
Lol@Failure

I'm still unsure on how to start writing in here so I figured I'd let Lol@Failure do it for me. As for capturing my life in a single paragraph, he's done a pretty handy job. Playing games online and being a virgin sums things up pretty well. I don't even know who I'm writing this for, which is why I guess I keep putting it off. I'm not writing for my family. I'm not about to let Mom, Dad, or Everett into my innermost thoughts, and certainly not Chloe, as I predict her name will pop up often.

FIRE MAGE

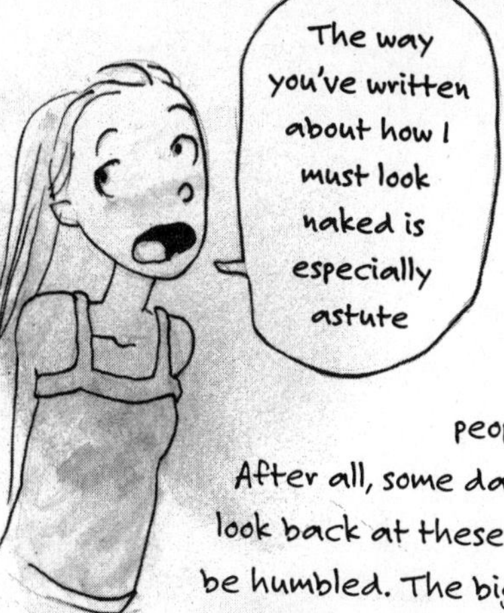
The way you've written about how I must look naked is especially astute

she'd say as I jump out the window, landing on a pillow of broken glass and the hood of my dad's '03 Honda Civic.

I don't really know a lot of other people. I guess I'm writing this for me. After all, some day when I'm rich and successful I'll look back at these tales of woe and nothingness and be humbled. The big shot, with his fancy future cars, hot chicks, and awesome job, his legions of adoring fans. He really does need to be taken down a peg.

Frankly, I'd prefer to read Future Me's journal. How'd he make it out of this town? Where'd he get the bombshell girlfriend, the books, and the gallery showings? 'Cause they sure aren't on the radar right now.

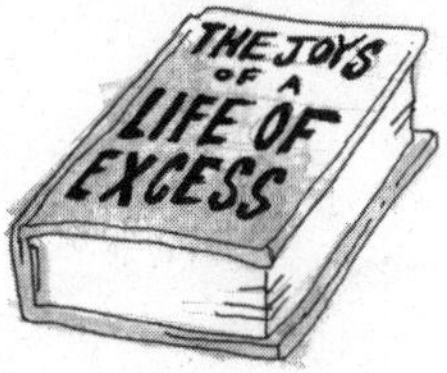
THE JOYS OF A LIFE OF EXCESS

It's not all bad. I'm a qualified loser at school and I can count the number of real-world friends I have on one hand, but maybe I like it that way. I've got my BFF Chloe, my brother's back home for the summer, I've got my art and my journal to write in, and I've got Ol' Trusty, the Internet, to keep me company. If the apocalypse strikes tomorrow, that's still a pretty good survival kit. That's a heavy load, a full schedule if you ask me. I'm not sure I could handle much more.

That said, I think I hear the movie starting downstairs. I love it when Ev's home, it's the only time my family actually does stuff together.

The rest of the night is yours, Lol@Failure. Prepare for ownage.

FAMILY PORTRAITS

Quiet fellow, but such is the life of a writer. He's even had books published. Heavy books. With lots of words. Maybe some day I'll be published, too. Dad has half of a shelf on his bookcase for just his own work. He's really smart, even when he drinks, which is kinda constant lately, but apparently it works for him. He's the ying-drunk to Mom's yang. He gets quiet and intense.

Sometimes I think he wishes I was more like my brother.

·DAD·

Mom is loud and crazy and probably insane, if she were to be diagnosed. She lives in her own world, like I do. Her world is wide open and everyone's invited, though, and mine is a padded room. Plus I think she was really popular when she was my age, so our similarities end there.

·MOM·

Everett is awesome. He's my jerky older brother sometimes, but usually he's cool. He's always with a different girl and he plays sports and is basically good with all the stuff I suck at. He'd be a good brother if it wasn't for his temper. He's always starting fights with me and winning.

· EVERETT ·

· CHLOE ·

Chloe would be the girl who never talks to me, except that she does talk to me. It's kind of a scientific anomaly. I don't know why she's on my "family portraits" wall. Maybe that's disturbing. But I like to draw her, so . . . deal with it.

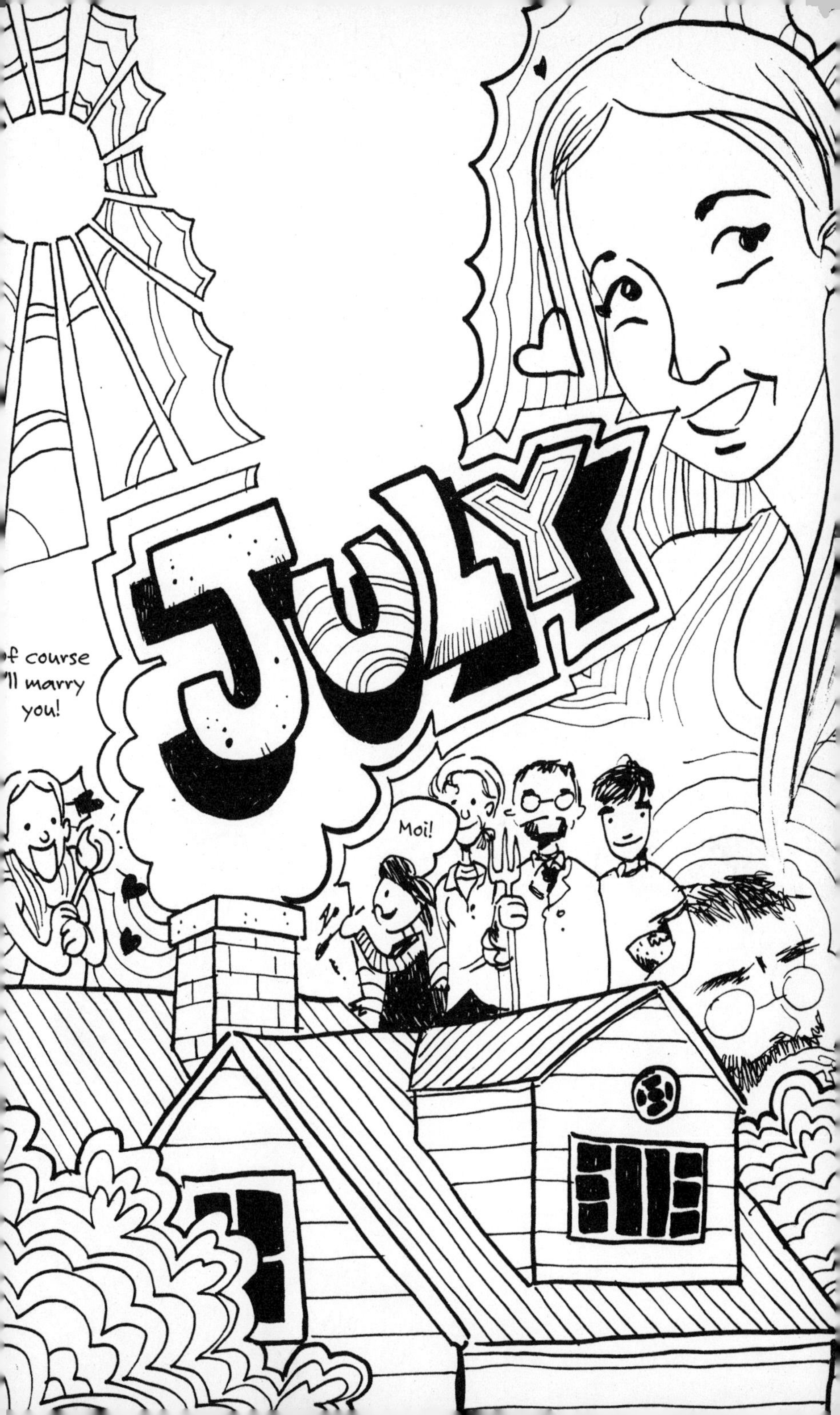
JULY
f course
'll marry
you!
Moi!

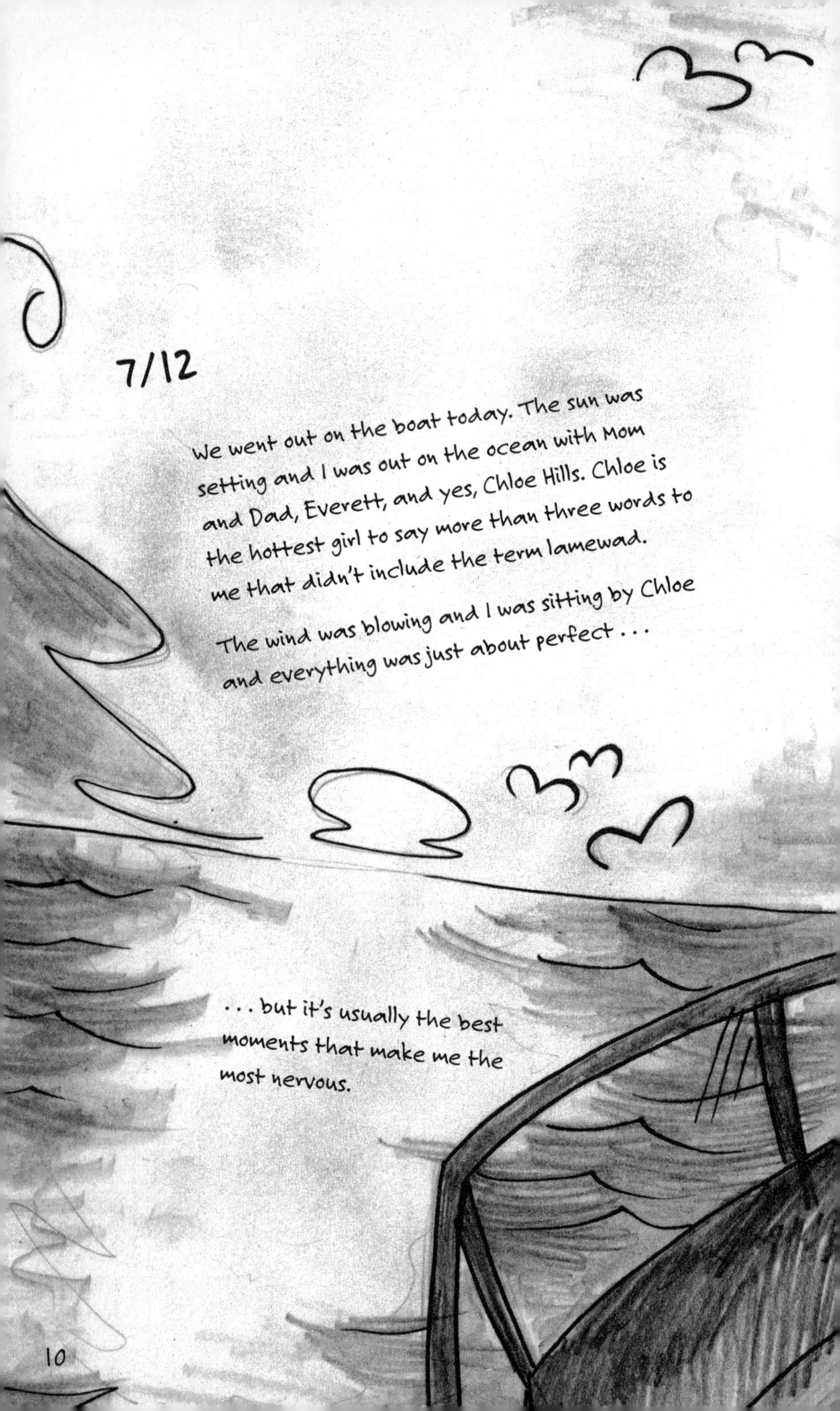
7/12
We went out on the boat today. The sun was setting and I was out on the ocean with Mom and Dad, Everett, and yes, Chloe Hills. Chloe is the hottest girl to say more than three words to me that didn't include the term lamewad.
The wind was blowing and I was sitting by Chloe and everything was just about perfect . . .
. . . but it's usually the best moments that make me the most nervous.

Chloe has been my friend for a few months now, and my family keeps pushing me to make some kind of move. I know they just want what's best for me, but that's like giving me a trampoline and expecting me to jump the Grand Canyon. They don't really understand what Chloe is and what I am. We are not of the same species. Our commingling would be illegal in most states.

Believe me, I want to ask her out, I want to tell her she's the most beautiful girl I've ever seen, I want to tell her "Sweet honey, be mine," but if I say those things, I won't even have her as a friend anymore. My macking skills are way wack. I am the least pimpin' kid in school and I'm not the slightest bit OG. MTV has failed me completely.

I didn't even want to invite her on the boat. I didn't want her seeing my family. I didn't want any of it but Mom kept pestering me, Dad was curious to meet her, and really, I shouldn't have to re-peat that Chloe is a real girl more than three times. There was no way this day could have turned out as anything but an embar-rassment. And I was not let down.

TOP 5 REASONS
I CAN'T ASK OUT
the lovely
CHLOE HILLS

5. She might cut into my wall-staring time.

4. I couldn't ask her out; the phrase "Am I going to have to get one of those restraining-order dealies?" would be too painful to hear.

3. Standing beside Chloe is sure to elicit "My God, that's a well-trained monkey" at least once.

2. Wouldn't want to have to start combing my hair or anything.

1. I'm synonymous with three words:

   Damn near invisible.

11

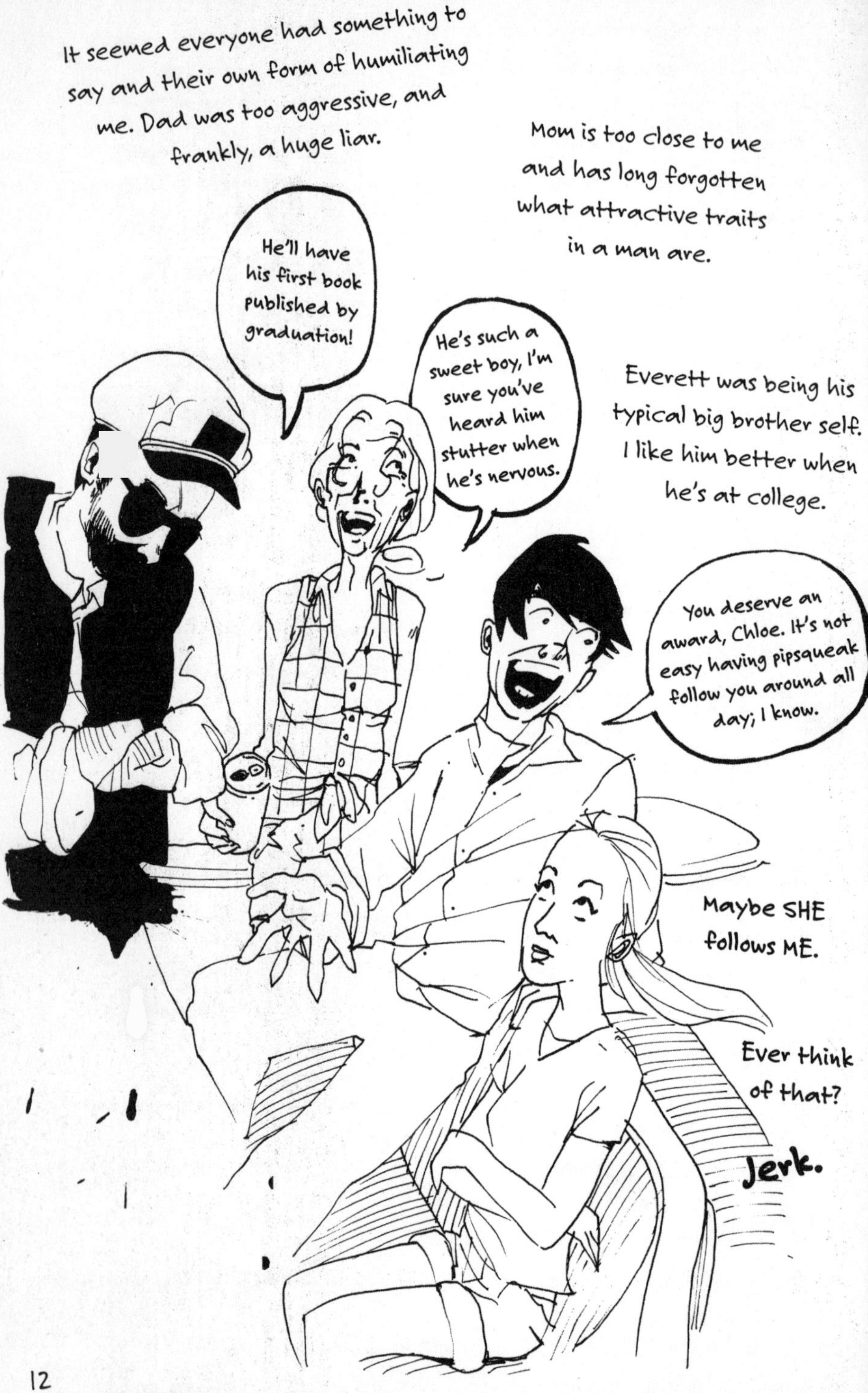

It seemed everyone had something to say and their own form of humiliating me. Dad was too aggressive, and frankly, a huge liar.
He'll have his first book published by graduation!
Mom is too close to me and has long forgotten what attractive traits in a man are.
He's such a sweet boy, I'm sure you've heard him stutter when he's nervous.
Everett was being his typical big brother self. I like him better when he's at college.
You deserve an award, Chloe. It's not easy having pipsqueak follow you around all day; I know.
Maybe SHE follows ME.
Ever think of that?
Jerk.

"I had no idea it'd be so cold," Chloe said. "I figured 'out in the sun, dress light.'" I sat there cursing myself for bringing her. She was miserable; she even had goose bumps on her arms.

Dad brought his coat over to her. "The lady's cold, show a little class, son." I think I was disappointing him.

Everyone was talking to Chloe and quickly getting to know her even better than I did. Apparently she toured the east coast with a ballet group and has been featured on TV several times. Who knew? I just looked at my feet and scratched a hole into my arm.

Dad pulled me to the side for one of our luckily infrequent father-son talks. He was looking me in the eye. It made me feel like I was in trouble. "I get it," he said. "She's too pretty; you're shy and nervous."

If he got it, we wouldn't have been out there.

"I was that way, too," he continued. "Believe it or not, you're the spitting image of me at your age." Somehow I didn't believe it. "You're gonna get older, like I did, and I know it doesn't feel like it now but it happens fast, and you're going to realize later that we're all just people. The cute ones, the not-so-cute ones, the popular people, the successful people, the rich and poor, we're all the same.

"Chloe's a girl just like any other girl. And if you don't let her know how you feel, then she's never going to know.

Hard to take a fella seriously in this get-up.

Girls may seem otherworldly, but trust me, they aren't mind readers." He even put a hand on my shoulder. He'd been drinking a bit, so that has to be part of it. "You're a sincere guy, and you have feelings. That's nothing to hide."

It was the most he'd ever said to me in one sitting. Drunk or not, I couldn't just let the guy down. I had to say something, if not for me, then for Dad. This was a lot of effort for him.

I sat by Chloe and stretched to put my arm around her. Well, I rested it behind her, which I will count as "around her." Confidence was at an all-time high, and now seemed as good a time as any to make a move. Dad smiled, Mom looked so happy. Chloe and I belonged in a picture frame in the store.

"It's so pretty out here," I said, thinking Chloe was in the zone and feeling it, too. I turned to face her. The wind pulled her hair, wrapped it around me, and I said the following: "But not as pretty as you."

I learned today that you don't say these things in front of family. Everett did a spit-take and he wasn't even drinking anything. Mom flushed red and tried her best not to laugh; even Dad cracked a smile as he turned away from me. "That didn't just happen," Everett said. Chloe was blushing when everyone finally burst into laughter. I wanted to look at the camera and shrug my shoulders as the trumpets of failure played the <u>Price Is Right</u> losing theme.

Where's an anchor when you need one?

THE BIG EVENTS

1. Fourth grade—Sitting in the library, Kerri House asks if she can take one of the empty chairs at my table as I sit alone. She feels bad and invites me to sit with her and her friends, which I decline. Still, the thought was very nice.

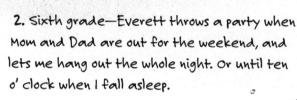

2. Sixth grade—Everett throws a party when Mom and Dad are out for the weekend, and lets me hang out the whole night. Or until ten o' clock when I fall asleep.

3. Seventh grade—I win the art award in school at the end of the year, and for some inexplicable reason, the whole auditorium cheers me.

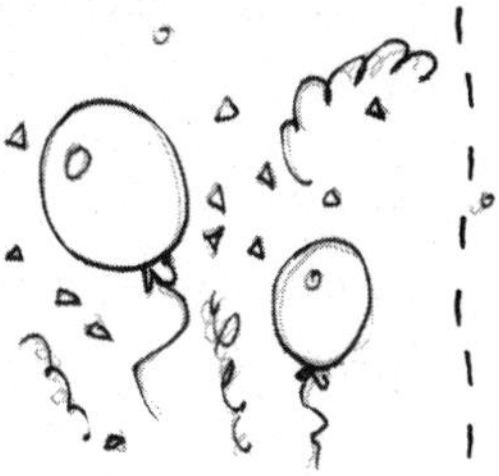

4. Eighth grade—Mom sends my cartoons in to the local paper, and they run a full-page story on me with the creepiest headline possible for what was supposed to be a fluff piece: "Kid in the Corner Might Be Drawing You."

5. And second semester, ninth grade—I meet Chloe.

POST

KID IN CORNER MIGHT BE DRAWING YOU!

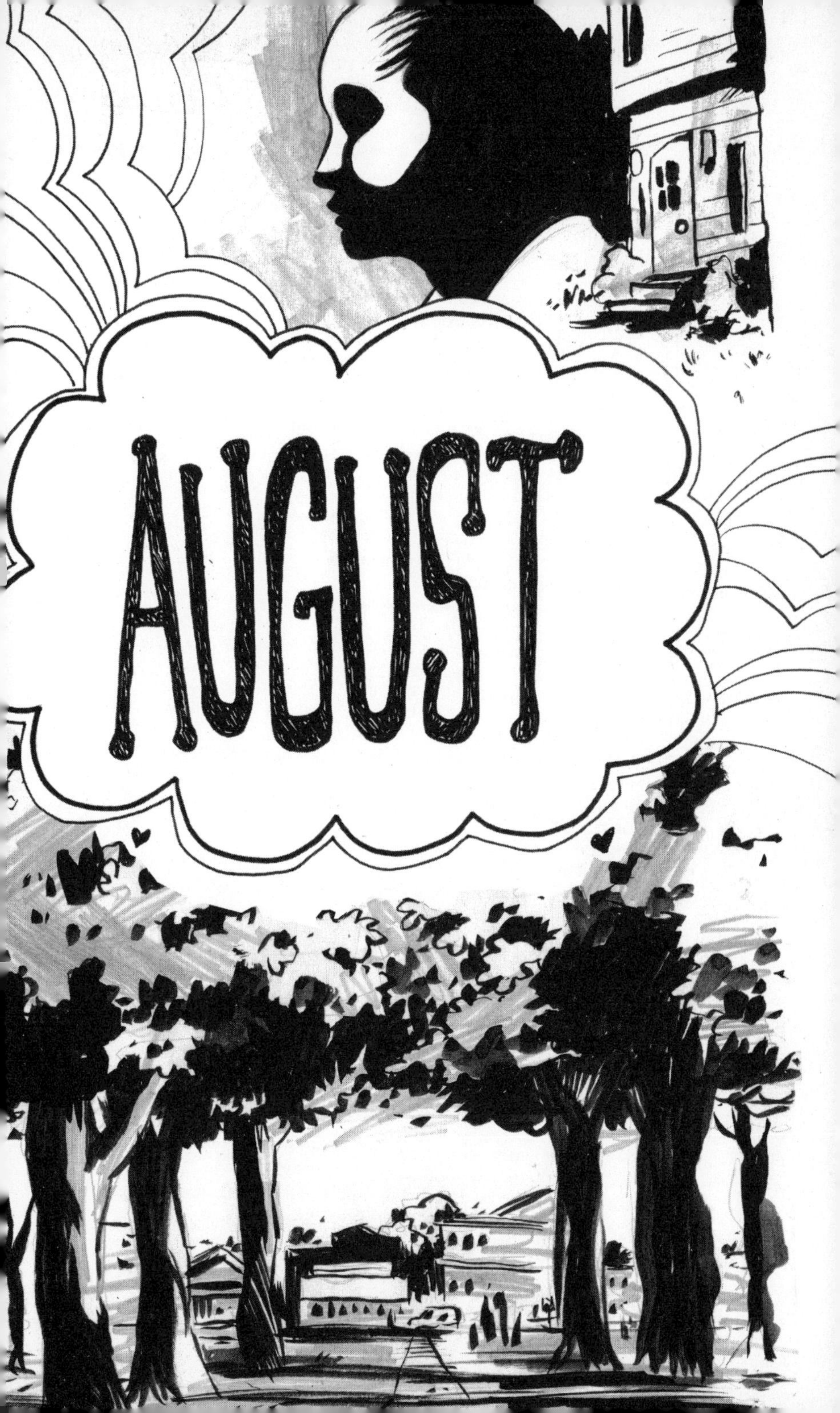
AUGUST

I.M. ♫
THE MAN WHO WILL FIGHT FOR YOUR HONOR..

Session Start (CartoonBoy:PBandFluff): Wed August 6 19:48:10
[19:48] PBandFluff: >:(
[19:48] CartoonBoy: Oh no, what's up?
[19:48] PBandFluff: You were a jerk to me.
[19:49] CartoonBoy: It was an accident, I swear, I never meant any of it! Wait, what did I do?
[19:49] PBandFluff: You ditched me in my dream.
[19:49] CartoonBoy: See this is why I hate dream-me so much. He makes me sick!
[19:49] CartoonBoy: *vomits uncontrollably*
[19:49] PBandFluff: *pole-vaults even more uncontrollably*
[19:50] CartoonBoy: Alright, enough with the pole-vaulting. What did he say to you? I'll knock him around.
[19:51] PBandFluff: We were having lunch at some fancy diner, and we're laughing and having fun, and all of a sudden, you're like "Oh I gotta go get the new 50 Cent album!"
[19:51] CartoonBoy: Hmm. I didn't know a new 50 Cent album was involved. That would be a conundrum.
[19:52] PBandFluff: I knew it. You are just like the other boys. With their 50 Cent.
[19:52] CartoonBoy: I would take you with me to go get the new 50 Cent album. Then we could get our boogie on.
[19:52] PBandFluff: Aww, you are sweet. That's what I *really* knew.
[19:52] CartoonBoy: At least you could sleep. My parents were fighting again. I wish they could at least fight in a whisper.
[19:53] PBandFluff: I wish I could help. Maybe I can slip some Tylenol PM into your lunch.
[19:53] CartoonBoy: I don't know if falling asleep in 8th period is going to be much help.
[19:54] CartoonBoy: Hey, are you busy tomorrow? If so, it's no big deal, it's nothing important.
[19:57] PBandFluff: Kinda. I can hang out after 6 but only until 8. I can talk on the phone until 9, and you can find me online any time after that.
[19:57] CartoonBoy: Oh I was just going to see if you wanted to do that drawing thing.
[19:58] PBandFluff: How about this weekend? I want to have time to look perty if you're going to be drawing me.
[19:58] CartoonBoy: You sure you still want to?
[19:58] PBandFluff: Of course, darlin'. I'd be honored for you to draw me!
[19:58] CartoonBoy: Okay, I think I can clear up my calendar for that.
[19:58] CartoonBoy: Wait Saturday or Sunday?
[19:59] PBandFluff: Which is better for you? I don't want you to have to do too much 'clearing up' of your calendar.
[19:59] CartoonBoy: It just needs a dusting; it hasn't been used in awhile.
[20:00] PBandFluff: Then let's do Saturday.
[20:00] CartoonBoy: Maybe we can get dinner or something after.
[20:00] PBandFluff: WHOA, let's not go making assumptions, here!
[20:01] CartoonBoy: Oh, jeez sorry, I didn't mean to…
[20:01] PBandFluff: Joking, sweetie.

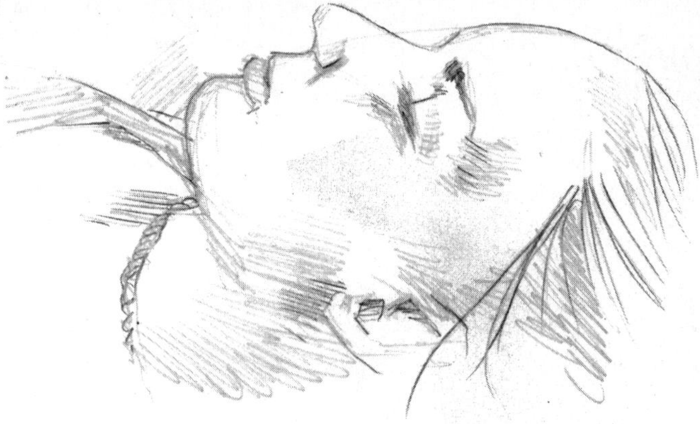

I'll be sad when summer is over . . . when Chloe's days are full of school and activities and other friends.

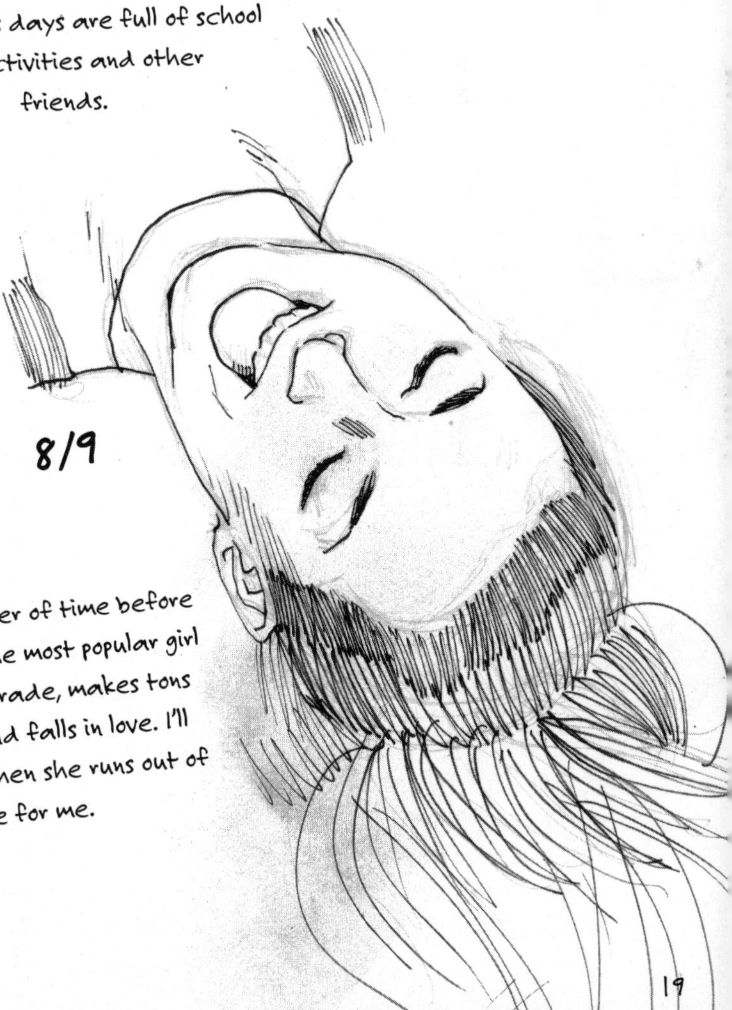

8/9

It's only a matter of time before she becomes the most popular girl in the tenth grade, makes tons of friends, and falls in love. I'll be very sad when she runs out of time for me.

SO, ABOUT CHLOE . . .

Chloe is one of those legendary relics Indiana Jones is always trying to catch. She's smart, pretty, and talented, and guys in our school would dodge poison darts and leap bottomless pits to be with her. I could only imagine their thoughts as they see her walking by with me at her side.

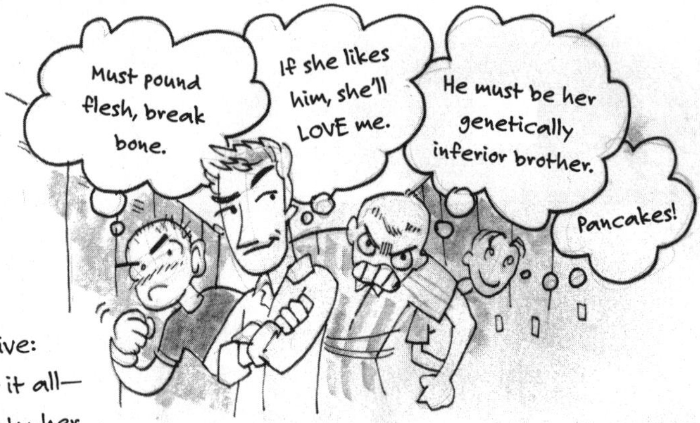
Must pound flesh, break bone.
If she likes him, she'll LOVE me.
He must be her genetically inferior brother.
Pancakes!

The positive:
She's got it all— her beauty, her huge house, her prize-winning cats, her smart family, her talents, her sense of humor, everything about her. She's even into older video games! She has an N64 from when she was a kid that she never stopped playing.

Plus, she's absolutely beautiful. Chloe showed me photographs she took for a modeling portfolio and they're incredible. She looks like she should be in magazines. She'll be super famous, I know it.

We bond over art and creativity and we both have big things we want to do in life. Most kids in school are too into themselves and trying to be cool or popular.

So, the negative: She's too good for me. Too pretty, too busy, too everything. My world is so small in comparison. Chloe takes college classes in the city on weekends, she takes dancing classes, she has her own friends in school, and that's besides her friends in other states and modeling contacts. She's busy and confident and has everything she could want already. When we're apart I must be about five percent of her life, and she's like ninety percent of mine. All I have is my drawings and her as my friend.

Sometimes I feel like maybe she does like me. It's these brief bouts of optimism that cut the sharpest. I feel these spells of hope and they make me feel like I should actually be doing something, making some kind of move, even if it flies directly in the face of my observations. I can't seem to shake either feeling: that she's too busy and too good for me, or that she's somehow waiting for me. If only I could be like Everett and just say what I'm thinking and act how I'm feeling. I can never do it, though. I get immobilized with fear and I don't even know what I'm afraid of. What's the worst that can happen?

She invited me to go swing dancing next week and I told her no. I can't dance. She'd have all her friends there and I'd be sitting in the corner by myself, dragging her down. I don't want her to see how uninteresting I really am. I don't want that to be the memory she keeps of me when school starts. I just wish things were different. I wish we could switch roles for a day and she could be me, and she'd see how hard it is to like someone so great.

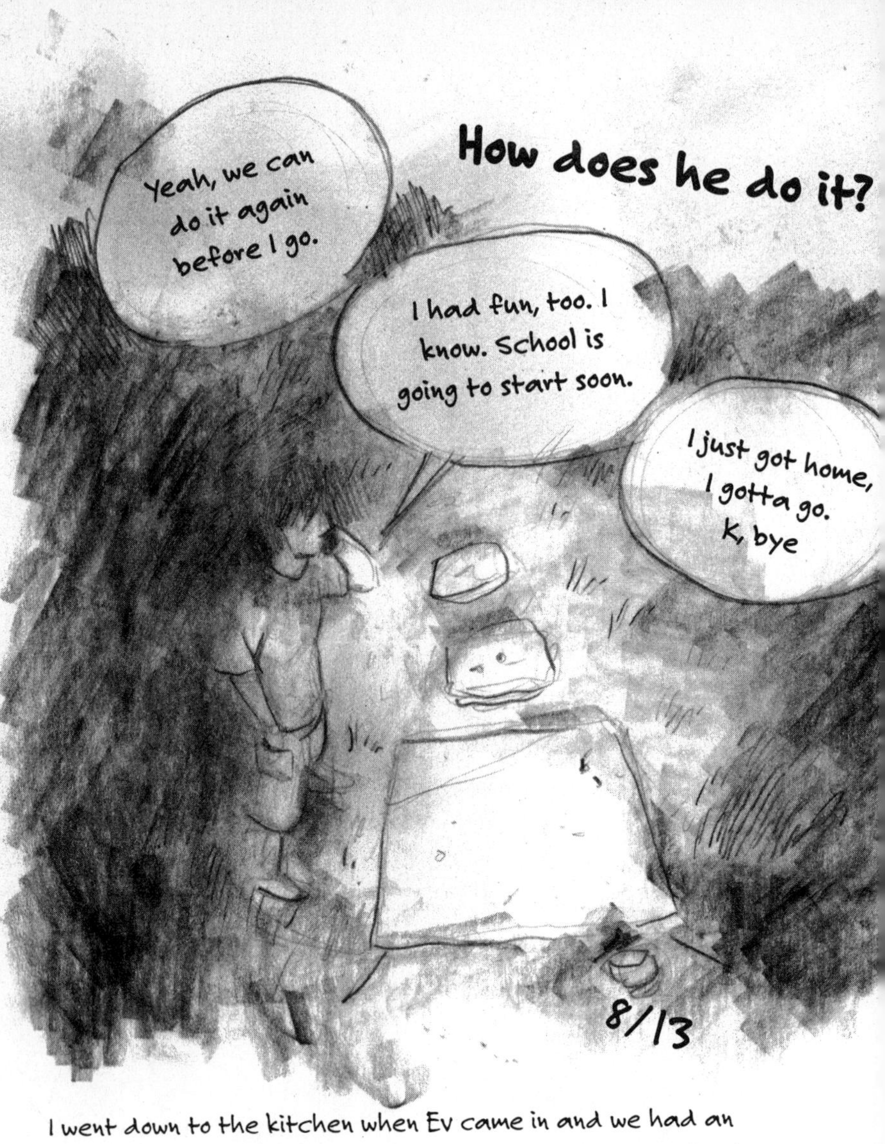
How does he do it?
Yeah, we can do it again before I go.
I had fun, too. I know. School is going to start soon.
I just got home, I gotta go. K, bye
8/13

I went down to the kitchen when Ev came in and we had an awesome talk. We talked about Mom and Dad. Ev says they're a mismatch and thinks they won't stay married. He doesn't have to worry about it now that he's at college. He's only here a few months a year and holidays and stuff. Soon he'll go back and forget about it again. I still have another few years. I heard a new story, too. Ev told me about the first time he knew Mom and Dad were in trouble. They had a St. Patrick's Day party at the house when I was too young to remember stuff like that. Ev was seven or eight.

St. Patrick's Day Massacre

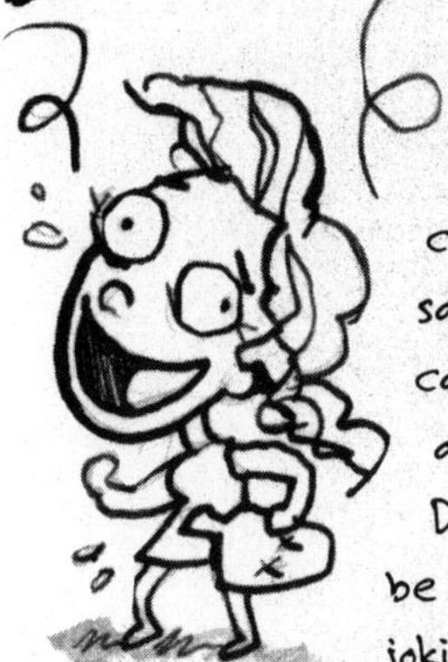

So they're having this party. They're drinking, as usual. Mom's in her stupor, Dad's just getting cranky. Some of their friends came up in conversation; I guess they couldn't make the party. Dad calls them some names or something; Mom gets all angry and defends them. Next thing you know, Dad snaps and gets it in his head that Mom must be in love with the guy friend or something. He starts joking around that she must have had sex with him, and everyone gets uncomfortable. Then he takes it further and starts asking her if she did have sex with him. Mom doesn't dignify him with an answer. Dad is so drunk and angry, he starts accusing EVERYONE at the party of sleeping with his wife. Guys, girls, everyone. The party ends right there, and Dad's just looking for someone to fight and Mom's screaming at him and calling him a crazy bastard. And that was the last party they ever had here.

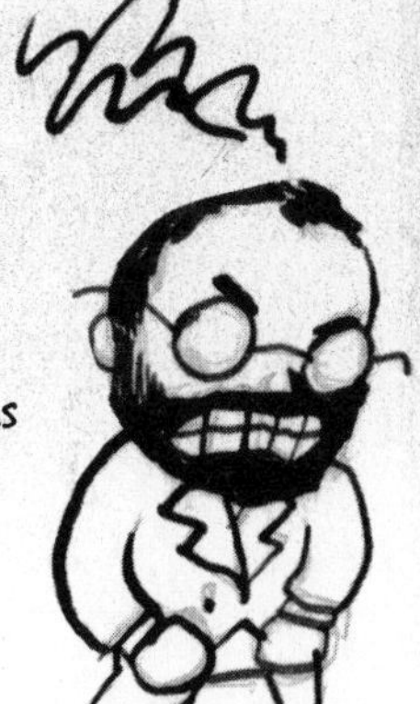

"Do you think she did it?" I asked.

Everett's always been blunt. "I don't know. Yeah, probably."

That was years ago. It can't be why they've been fighting lately.

"Do you think she did it after that?" I asked.

"I wouldn't blame her if she did."

I didn't know what Ev's problem was with Dad but I wanted to change the subject.

"Was that your girlfriend you were talking to outside?" I asked him. I was still thinking about Everett on the phone with that girl. I don't know how he ends up with so many different girlfriends. He dates someone new every month, and I can't even find someone who's single. Is he growing them on trees?

"You're spying on me now?" he asked.

"I just overheard from my room," I said.

"Not my girlfriend. She knows I'm only home for the summer." I didn't have to say anything; my face said it all. "Don't look at me like that! Why aren't you dating?" he asked me. "What about, uh, uh . . ." He snapped his fingers as he pretended not to know her name.

"Chloe?"

He smiled. "Yeah, her. She'll go out with you. You just have to be forward. She's a good catch."

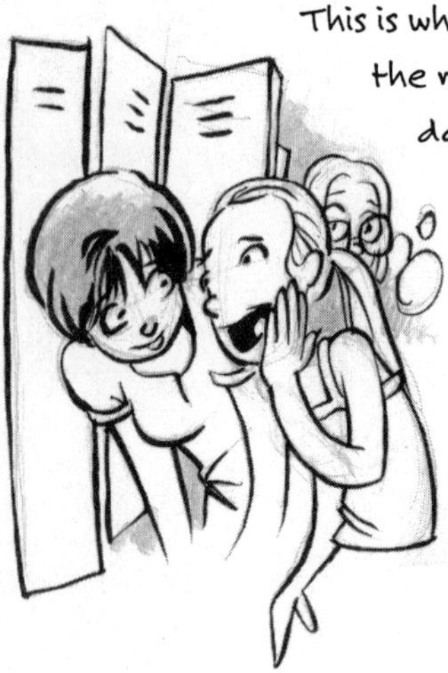

This is where most of the night went. I explained all the reasons I couldn't ask out Chloe. Why I can't date any girls, why I don't have any friends, I laid out each and every successive failure that's become me. I told him that I need friends, and she's a great one, and I don't want to ruin that. I don't want to make things awkward; I don't want her telling her friends I asked her out. I don't want to have to worry that everyone is talking about me when I see them in the halls. And Everett said:

"Her loss. And yours. You gotta put yourself out there."

I dish out my heart and my dreams in a pile on a plate, and that's what I get in return. My brother, the fortune cookie. It's easy enough for him to say. When Everett puts himself out there, he's still Everett. He's still handsome and popular and cool and the bad boy. I'm all right with school stuff and I can draw pictures. I can reach level sixty in FireMage. Everett has experience and stories and knows jokes. I have nothing to say and my few interactions with women have been traumatic.

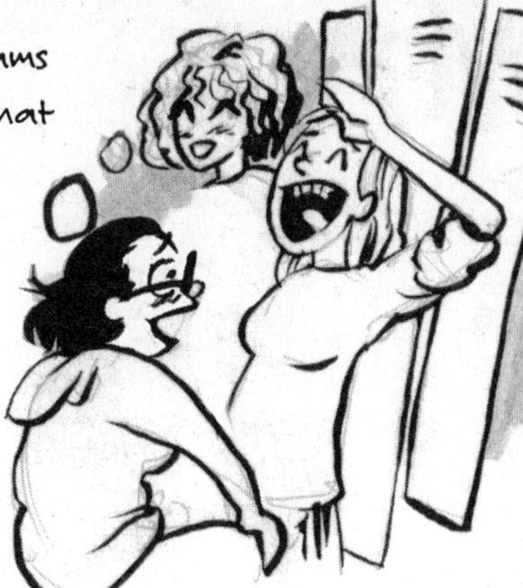

Everett should know. I'm not exactly girl-magnet material.

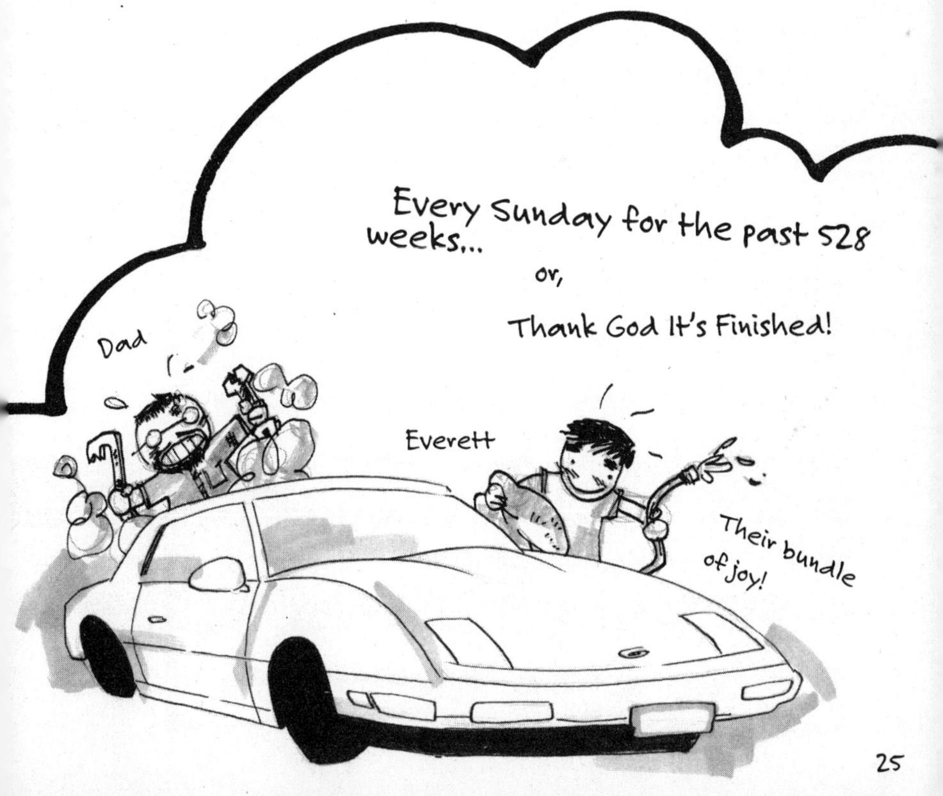

Every Sunday for the past 528 weeks...
or,
Thank God It's Finished!
Dad
Everett
Their bundle of joy!

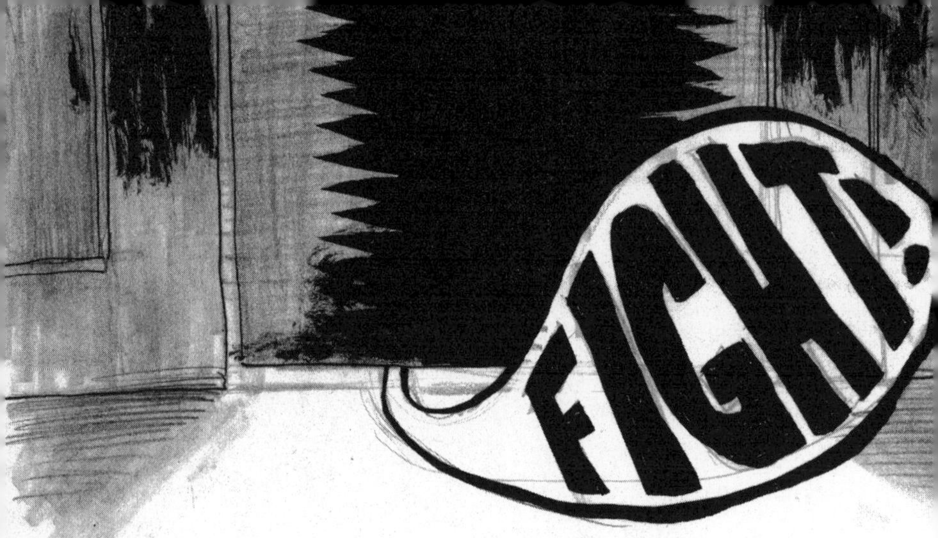
FIGHT!

Something's afoot. Mom and Dad are at it again. It's been bubbling, I suppose. Dad's been drinking, which isn't new, but he's been drinking more than normal and shutting himself off in his office. Mom's been quiet, which is cause enough for concern. They've been snapping at each other for days, but this is a new level. I actually thought they were getting along pretty well for a while, too. When Everett first came home from college this summer we were all cooking out and eating together and talking after dinner and Mom and Dad were laughing a lot, but things got back to normal pretty quick, and then got actually worse.

"Clearly you want a divorce, so that's what we'll do," I heard Dad yelling at Mom a few nights ago. Maybe Mom is cheating on Dad. Or Dad's cheating on her. They went back and forth for a while before calming down. Mom said something about a separation, which is pretty much the same as a divorce as far as I'm concerned. I'd still be down one parent and living who-knows-where.

I went out in the hall to get a better listen, but Ev took my spot already. I sat behind him for a minute but Ev told me to go back to my room. He's been a grump lately, too. He wants to go back to college, and I guess I don't blame him; there isn't much to do here. He's spent most of the summer out with his friends and girlfriends and avoiding me, anyway.

The pattern's been loud name-calling followed by quiet talking and stomping around. Those are the parts they don't want us to hear.

They're still going. I wonder if it's serious this time.

Here you go, in real time, folks:

Look at you, you're retarded. I'm married to a retarded person.

You don't know anything, you read all your dumb books but you don't have an original thought in your head.

At least I can form coherent thoughts.

How do people go from wanting to be married to being so outright cruel to each other?

I wish you'd carry yourself with some dignity.

You aren't good for anything; you have no practical use around here at all.

Now they're being quiet again. Maybe they're done. Oh, God . . . oh, God, they aren't done. Ew . . . This isn't happening. God, they're weird. I'm going to bed. Where are the earplugs?

DUMPED

Hi, Darling,

This is one of the more awkward things I've ever had to write, but I feel like I should write it because I want to be safe and I don't want to hurt you.

I am SO HAPPY I met you and you are one of my best friends and always will be, you mean SO MUCH to me, so I don't want you to feel like there are any kind of harsh feelings or like you've done anything wrong, but because you are such a good friend to me and I know you've been wondering where we stand, like, together, I wanted you to know I've been kind of seeing someone. Maybe. I mean, it's early still, but I just wanted you to know. And that we're still friends. I feel like a bitch even just writing that. That's not how I mean for it to sound. I don't want you to end up hating me, but I need to be honest.

You're a great guy and maybe someday things could be different, but right now I just want to be clear that we are just friends, and I hope this doesn't change anything in our friendship. Of course we can still hang out and we'll have a million adventures, but I just wanted to be clear on this because sometimes when boundaries aren't set up things can get awkward, and I don't ever want that for us. You are still my darling, FOREVER,

Chloe

DEAR DIARY

It's come to this, and so soon. I really didn't want to just rant about my feelings in this thing, but I don't know what else to do. So this will just have to be my first "Dear Diary" entry. I don't even know what to write. I don't have any thoughts, any feelings. My every thought these past few months has been about Chloe and me together. And now I find out she hasn't been thinking them with me. If Chloe can't be with me, then who can? I thought she got me and I got her and we got each other; I thought she was it, I thought she made sense out of all the stuff, the past stuff, so if not her, then who? Then what?

Who can blame her? It's not like I have anything going on. Let alone my messed-up family, my alcoholic parents, my rebel-without-a-clue brother. I'd stay away, too. Maybe she never even liked me. She just felt bad for the loser.

I sound like an idiot. What would Dad say? I can't even ask him. Why would I, it's not like he's in a great marriage himself or anything. I can't ask my parents anything, and Everett doesn't care about me.

He's angry and Mom is angry and Dad is angry. I had Chloe. She was it, she was my escape from all this, and she ruined it. Why did she have to ruin it? What is so much better than what we had? What we could have had. Who is she seeing? I talk to her every day, who else could it be?

What am I left with? Friendship? I have friends; I don't want anymore friends. All right, I don't have friends. I do want friends. Chloe would be a good friend; she's my best friend. But what now, she dates some other guy, some other dude hangs out with us and is all making out with her in my face? I can't do that. But what are the alternatives? What else can I do?

I think I love her. Maybe if I'd just told her . . .

Okay, I have to stop this, I sound like an ass. Whoever wrote that up there, I hate you. You suck. No, it's fine, it's whatever. It's not like I can't be alone. I have my art and my writing and my dysfunctional family and Everett's going away and he hates us all and what if Dad moves out, too? I think my whole family hates each other. And damn it, Chloe, I can't even talk to you about it. And I need to. I need you.

She flirted with me. She called me darling. I thought she wanted . . .

No, I'm done. Diary entries suck.

I just want to sleep now.

Idea for a short story:

This body lies in the street, freshly dead. Outside of its chest pops a still-beating heart with tiny legs and a mouth.

"I've never seen anything like it," says a curious female, tall and pretty, killer looks.

She calls out to the heart, which begins to run. It sees its own dead body and the heartbreaker standing next to it and puts two and two together.

The pretty woman chases the heart all around the globe, calling out to it, "I just want to touch you; you fascinate me; I can keep you warm! Don't you need a warm body?"

The heart tries to hide in New York, in Paris, in Italy, but cannot elude the female.

"Yes," he laments, "I do miss the warmth of a human body."

The woman scoops him up in her arms, which are indeed very warm. She brings him to the media, who bring him to the government, who put him to sleep, drain his blood, and slice him open with knives to figure out just what makes a heart walk and talk anyway. Results are inconclusive.

Moral: Keep it in your chest!

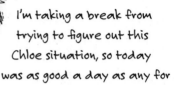

I'm taking a break from trying to figure out this Chloe situation, so today was as good a day as any for a little father/son bonding. It was definitely a little out of the ordinary, but Dad wanted "quality time" with his sons, which basically meant he had bad news to break. Mom probably put him up to taking us out. I figured we'd have a couple root beers, talk about women and how you can't live with them, can't live without them, but it wasn't really that kind of day at all. Everett came with us, for one thing. The way he's been acting toward Dad, I didn't think a divorce could come soon enough for him. He hasn't been real keen on me, either.

We ended up going bowling. At least it got my mind off of Chloe.

Ev was being an idiot from the start. Dad offered him shotgun, but he sat in the back. He wouldn't even talk. He's been on Mom's side all along with all the fighting, but he came with us so he could at least make an effort to be nice. They spent all summer on that car and they didn't ask me for any help, after all. Ev was always Dad's son. They like sports; they're both kind of macho guys. Ev gets along with Mom better than I do, too. They can talk for hours. So I don't know why suddenly I'm the only one wanting this family to stay together.

Dad said he and Mom were thinking about a trial separation as we drove to the bowling alley. He said he'll stay in the house at first, and that they have "some issues to work out."

"Seeing as the issues are your fault, I don't see how you're going to fix things staying in the house," Everett said. He was determined to make things worse at any given opportunity.

"I tried," Dad said, tossing his hands up, done with the "bad news" portion of the bonding experience.

Bowling alleys are depressing in the middle of the day. It was empty and quiet and not at all a good place to hang out with the shattered remains of your family.

The bowling itself was actually kind of fun for a while. I did all right for my first time, but it was really Dad and Ev who were competing. Ev was good but he couldn't loosen up and just have fun; he had to keep throwing the ball like he was trying to prove something, like Dad's head was affixed to the pins. And in spite of Everett's ever-present gloom, Dad was really trying to bond with him, too. He kept smiling and even offered some pointers for him. And then Everett unintentionally said the funniest thing that's still making me laugh:

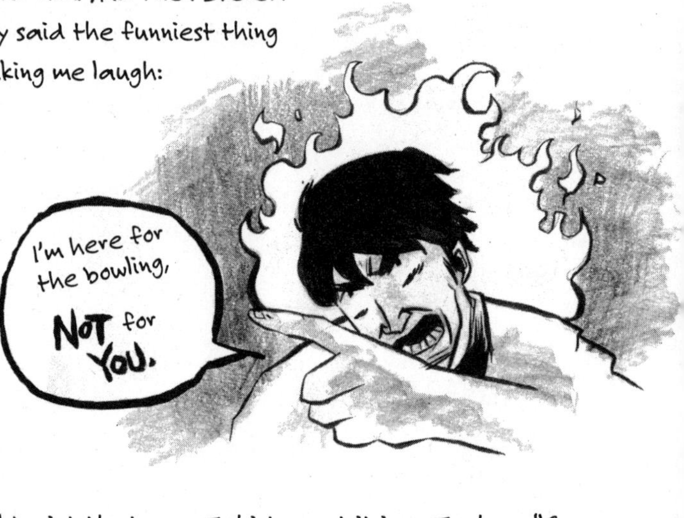
I'm here for the bowling, NOT for YOU.

Someone should print that on a T-shirt or put it in a TV show. "Grow up," I told him, with my specialty eye roll for added effect. Everett towered over me.

"Fine, you stay here and bowl, and I'll go home. I didn't want to come here, anyway."

I was getting sick of all this. Things are bad enough at home without Everett making everything ten times worse.

"What's your problem, anyway?" I asked him. I thought we were going to throw down in the bowling alley. It was embarrassing in retrospect, but I was mad enough to not care at the time.

"Don't tell me to grow up. You're just a kid; you don't know anything about the real world. You don't even know anything about your own parents!"

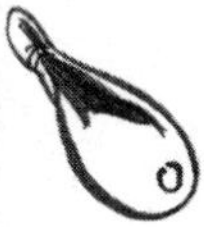

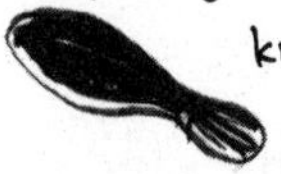

Dad got in between us. "Everett, it's your turn, go play."

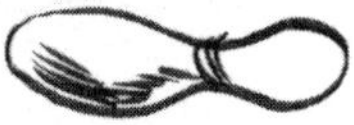

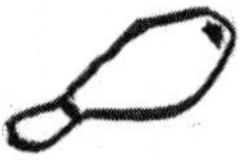

Everett stared him down, trying to act tough. He grabbed the ball and took his time with it, and then he hurled it down the alley. It sounded like rolling thunder, and lightning struck—he knocked every pin down. Ev went on to win the game, but with about as many tantrums as pins he hit. Dad still congratulated him for winning. So I say Dad won.

If things with Everett are that complicated, things with Mom must be out of control. I wonder who I stay with if they divorce. Would I have to choose?

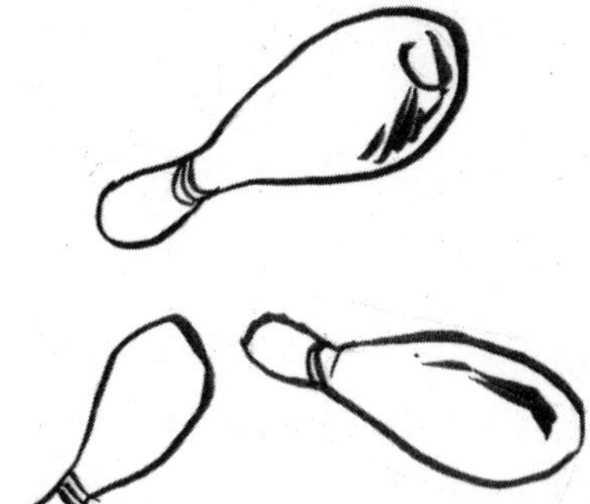

Today Is the Day the World
Changed, and that is all I will
say because I don't ever want
to think of it again.

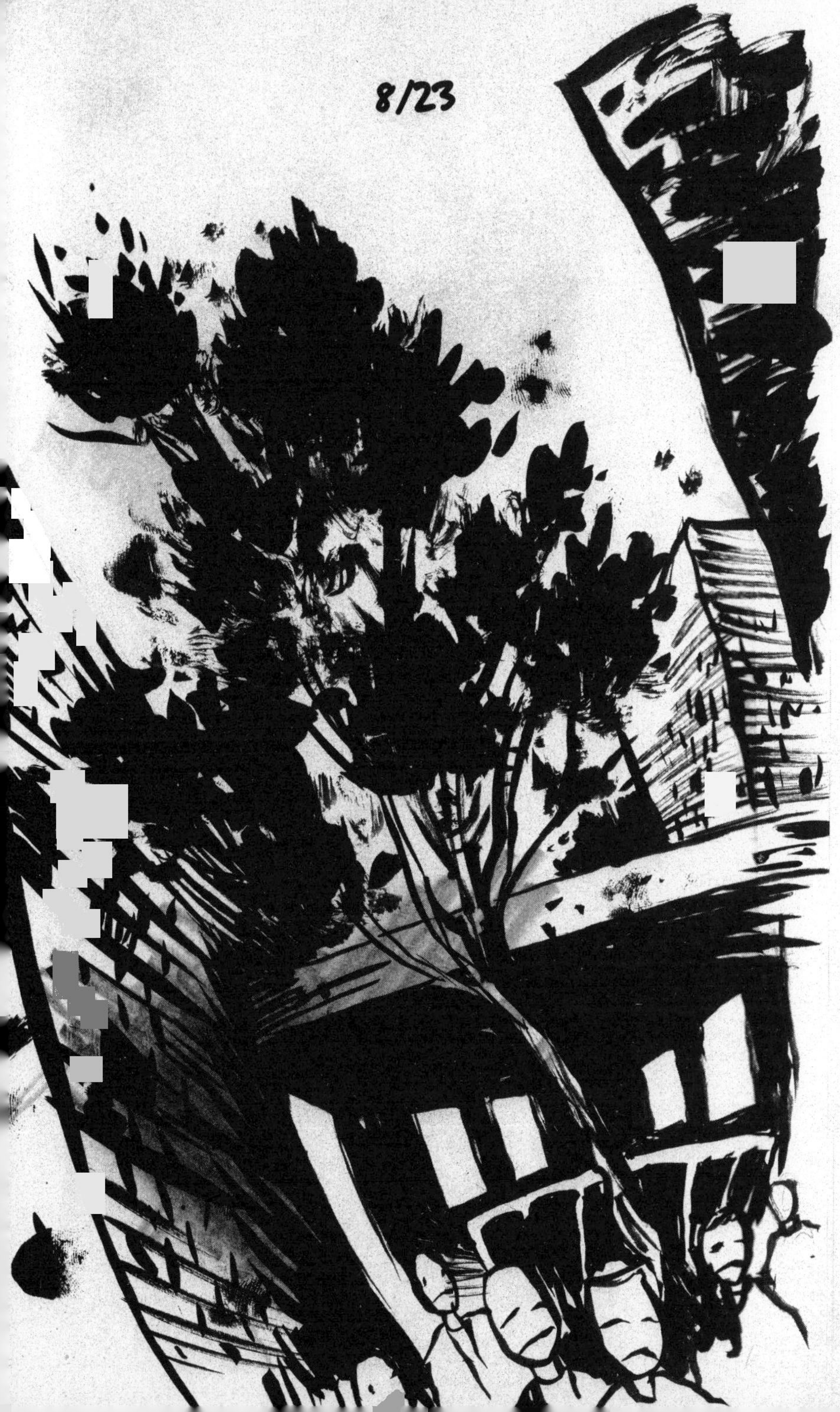
8/23

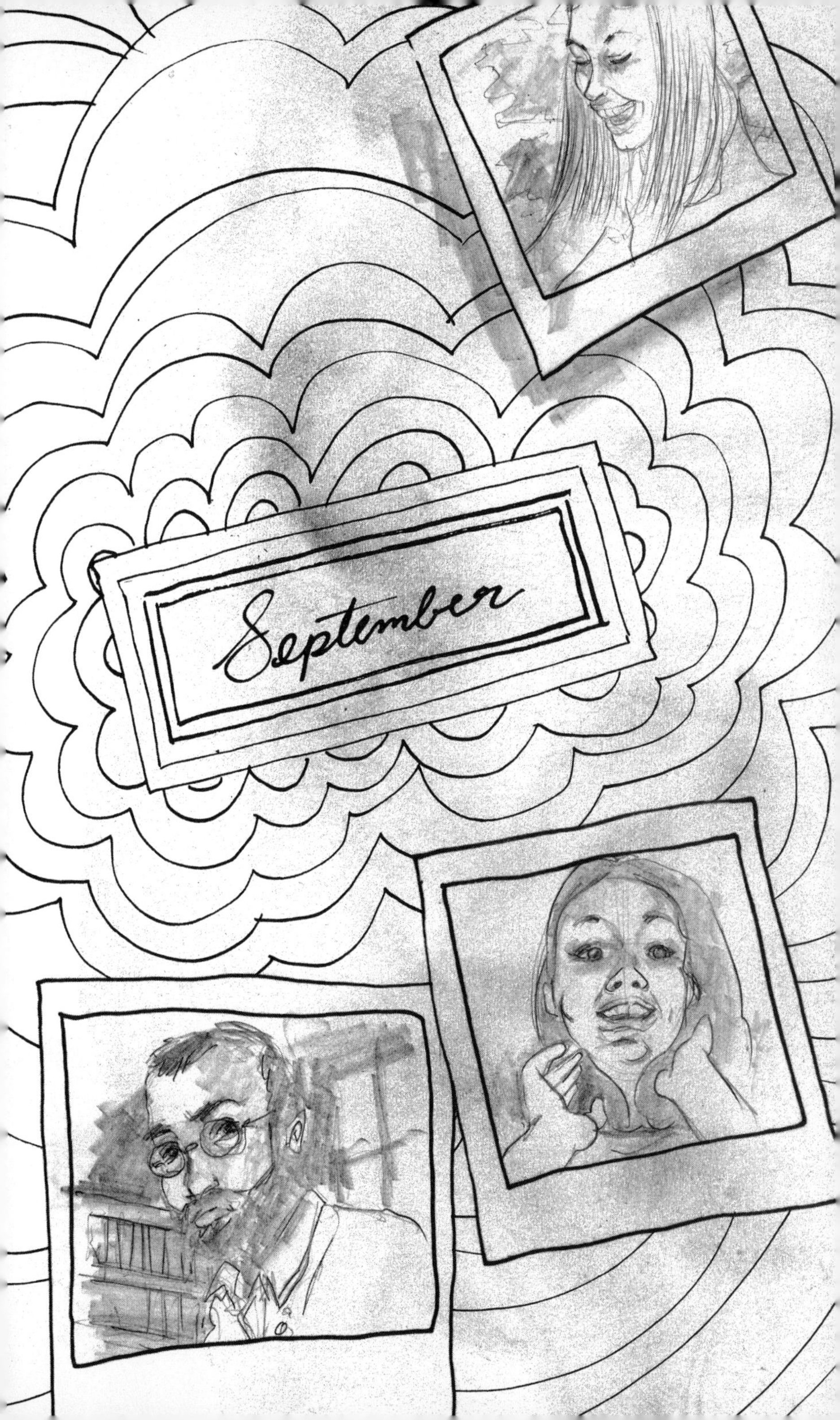
September

Today was long. Eyes watching me, voices mumbling my name. A week into September and it was my last day of school. The halls were a parade line and I was the giant float. I'd gotten used to the whispers and rumors but today it was the eyes and the handshakes and pats on the back. I kept my head down low, and my headphones covered my ears. I only walked forward, and I didn't look back. Even after I got in Mom's car and we sped away and left that school one last time. I never looked back.

My new home on Main Street — highest crime rate in Crest Falls!

MY NEW HOME

Here's the apartment. We're a quarter of this building, about the size of our old basement.

Here is the door that only two people use now. The wind blows it open so we have to dead-bolt it.

Here is the fridge, which will be much emptier. Now it's just water and soda for me. Mom quit drinking so there's no more alcohol filling up the bottom. No more of Everett's gross energy drinks.

These are the creaky boards the rats and cockroaches skitter across, eleven creaks to my room.

Here's all the same old junk. Those are the windows the monsters peek in. They don't bother me much, though. They just sit there and wait.

And there's the yard and Everett's car, two blocks from where I wait for the bus that I take to school now that I don't have a ride. School used to be a quick stop over for Mom on her way to work but not anymore.

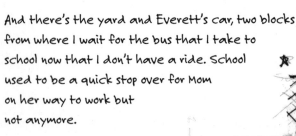

9/8 MAYBE BUSES AREN'T ALL BAD . . .

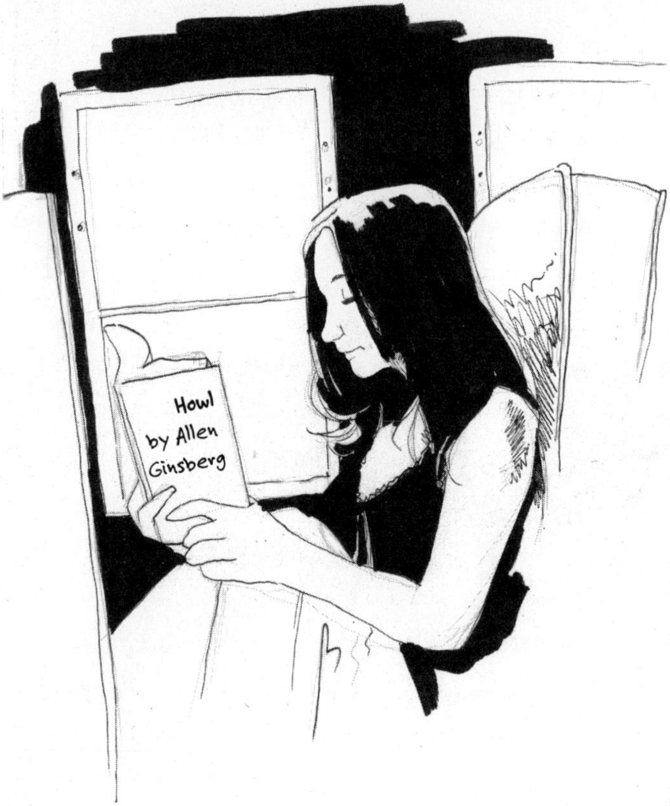
Howl
by Allen
Ginsberg

I couldn't have been more than five minutes late when my cell phone started buzzing and Mom was asking where I was. I explained that it was unintentional, that it was my first day of school here and I got on the wrong bus by accident, but honestly I didn't want to go home in the first place. There was also a girl. They tend to make me dizzy like a cat in a dryer, not that I've ever tested that. I had to follow her. I really wanted to draw her. Now I just have to find her again. And maybe even talk to her? Extreme emphasis on "?"

I guess it's not so bad. It's just different. You lose your money and then you come here, with everyone else who's lost money.

And you adapt.

9/9

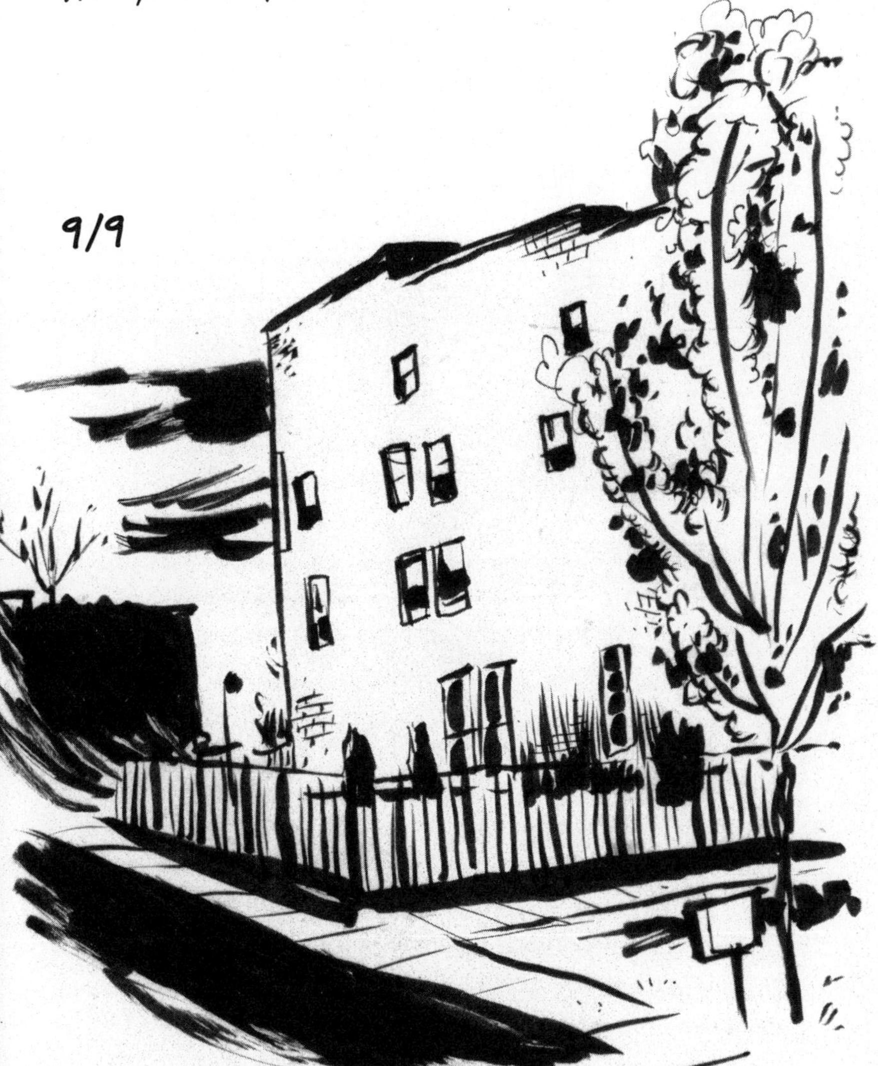

They huddle together; everyone lives on top
of each other. There's nowhere to hide so
they spend the day out on the street.

A few towns over is a world away.
It's really a whole new start.

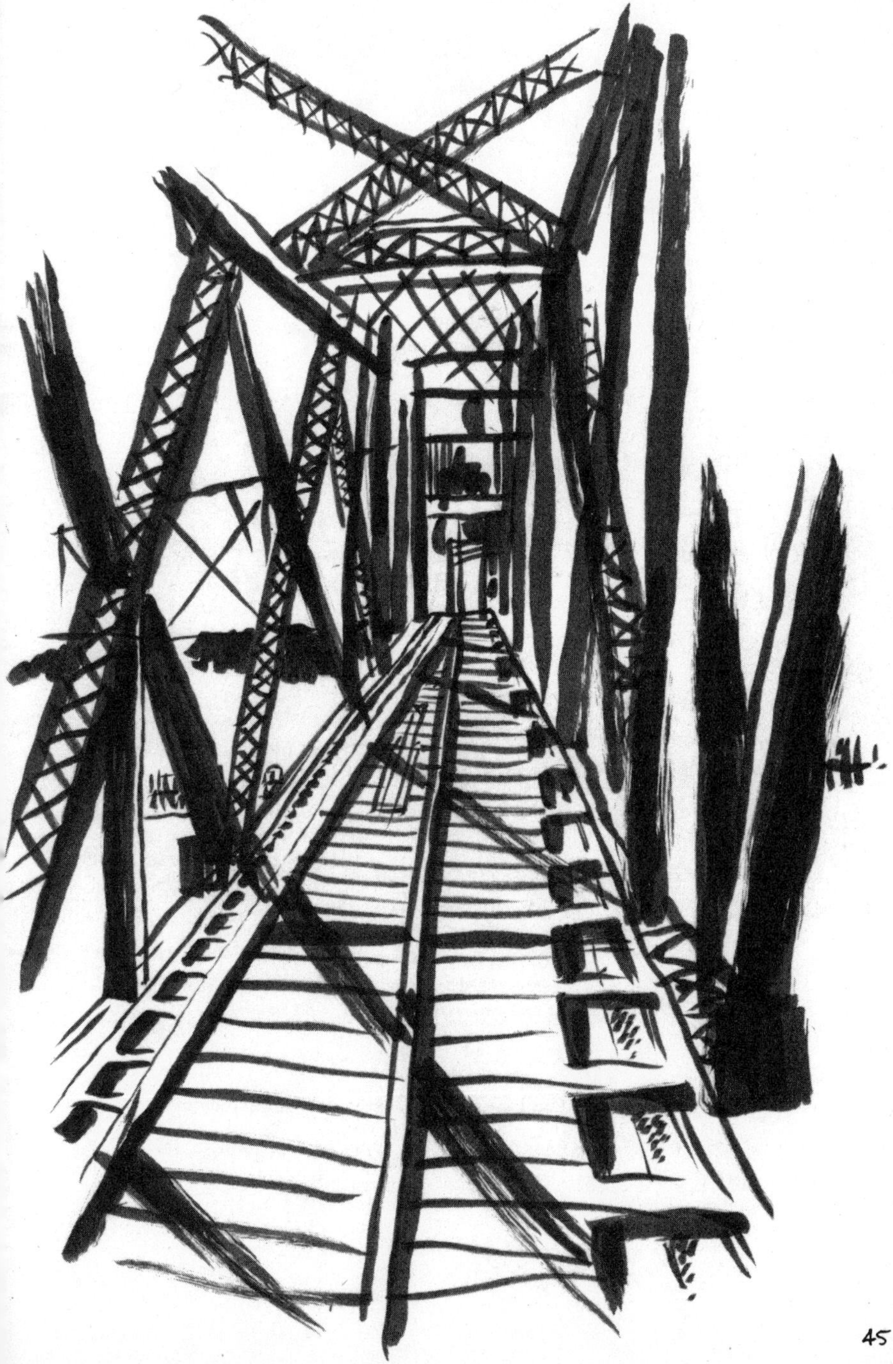

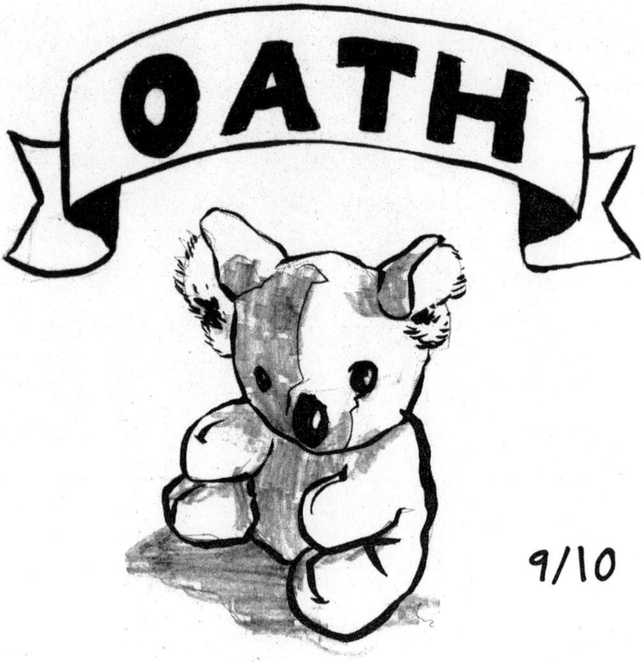
OATH

9/10

I swear, with Chloe Bear as my witness . . .

That my problems and failures will not stop me.

That I will continue to be my own person.

That I will let go of everyone and stand on my own.

That life is too short, and I will live every day
as the best person I can be.

That I will grow and that I will change.

That I will smile and hold my head high.

That my smile will mean something, and it will not crack.

That this is a new start and a new day.

That I will not stand in the piss.

That I will never stand in the piss again.

It's free period, nine a.m., the girl from the bus is three feet away, and it's time to unveil the new me.

I'd drawn her on that bus and seen her in between classes and even in English yesterday, and now she was sitting at the very next table and it was time I said something. This was clearly a sign, a new sense of purpose. She was the reason for everything that's happened to me up to this point in life, and she was where Things Got Good. Or on a less epic scale, she was a cute girl. Talking to her had to be more entertaining than doing my homework.

TALKING TO GIRLS

you should read that book outside!
Are you talking to *me*?
It's nice out!
Too bright.
We could sit in the shade ...
"We" could?
Goes back to Lonelyland to saw face off with comic books and video games
SUPER DUDE

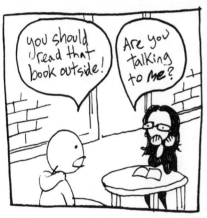

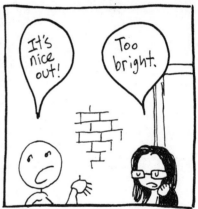

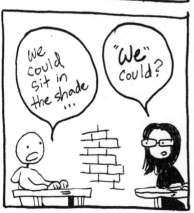

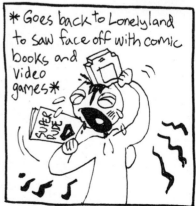

She was so pretty.

Her hair was shiny and dark, curling left and right, waves crashing on top of each other, but still so smooth. Her skin looked soft. Those cute little dimples when she smiled . . .

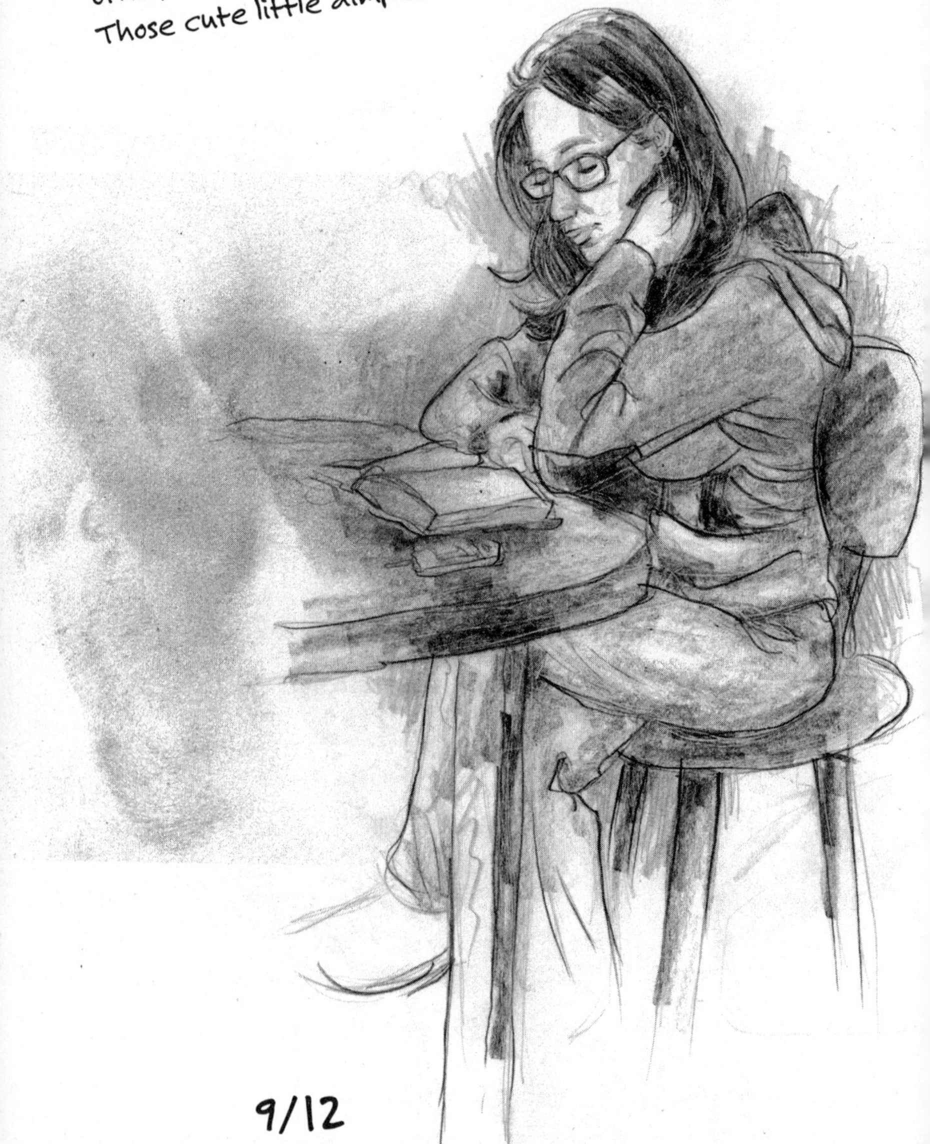

9/12

Maybe I hadn't blown it quite one hundred percent yet. "Can I sit with you?" I asked. "The lighting is all wrong over here."

I was nervous but I tried to smile. Mr. Confidence. She shrugged her shoulders in a cute way. "Free world, Happyface." She sat straight. Moved cute. Her legs were crossed. Now she was reading *On the Road* by Jack Kerouac.

I moved my bag over, and my books, journal, and pen. I grabbed the chair to her side because it was closer than the one across from her. I fell into the seat and smiled. She kept reading and didn't notice my staring.

I picked up my journal, pretending to do home-work. I was sketching her, keeping the book tilted toward myself. I was drawing her but I didn't want her to see that. I didn't want to box myself in as the "art boy," but I had to keep draw-ing. Sometimes there's an image I just can't bear to lose. I took frequent glances while I scribbled away but she never looked up to notice me, if she remembered I was there at all. I was looking for details.

The curves of her eyes . . .   the way she smiled . . .

ṅ she held her book . . .

"Kid in the corner might be drawing you," indeed.

She smelled like fruit. Raspberries, shampoo, and pheromones. She smelled so good I wanted to put my face right next to hers. I wanted to press my cheek to hers and breathe her in. I wanted to inhale her whole, she smelled so good.

The bell interrupted my silent admiration. Game over. She got up to leave in a hurry. I tried to grab my things and keep up, as the classrooms opened and bodies multiplied, spilling into our once-quiet hallway.

I was losing her in the sea:

Anyone ever tell you you're beautiful?

Like every boy EVER.

Random Guy sez:

Lame, Sonny, lame.—

Voicing sincerity equates to cliché.

I put on a charming smile and told her, "I really mean it, though."

That's when she said with a look of exhaustion and complete disbelief:

"Have you EVER talked to a girl?"

"Of course," I said. My charming smile devolved into a nervous smile. I hoped some variation could work in my favor.

"WELL, Happyface," she said, head cocked to the side.

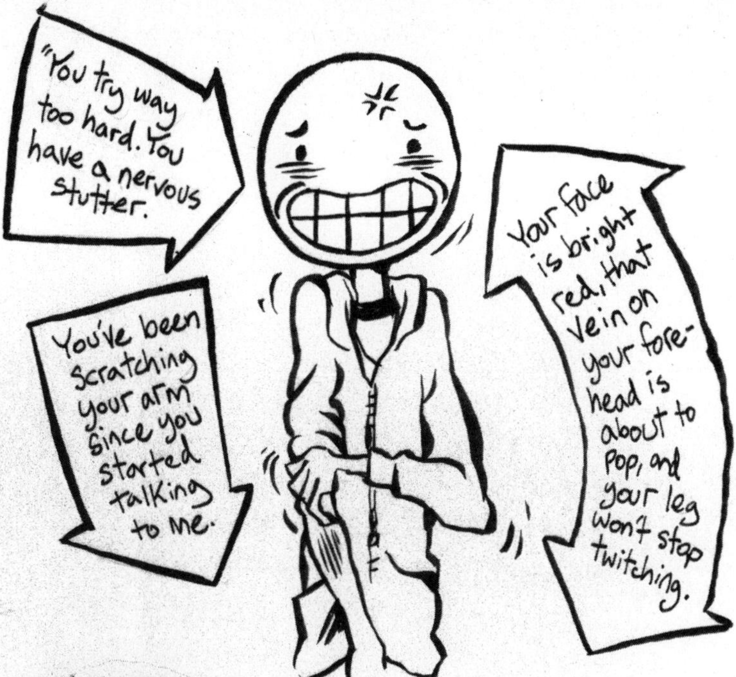
"You try way too hard. You have a nervous stutter.
You've been scratching your arm since you started talking to me.
Your face is bright red, that vein on your fore-head is about to pop, and your leg won't stop twitching.

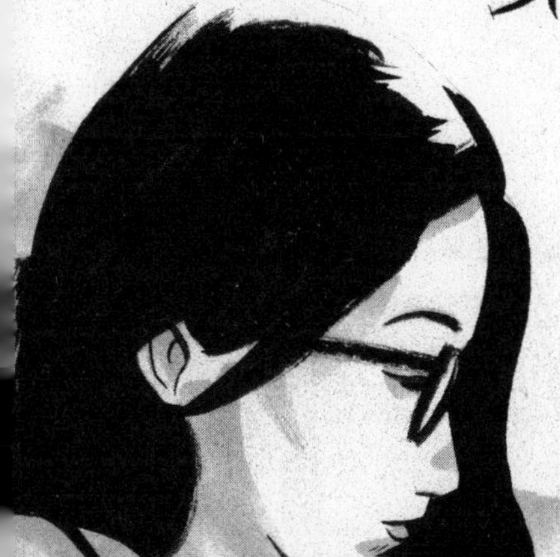

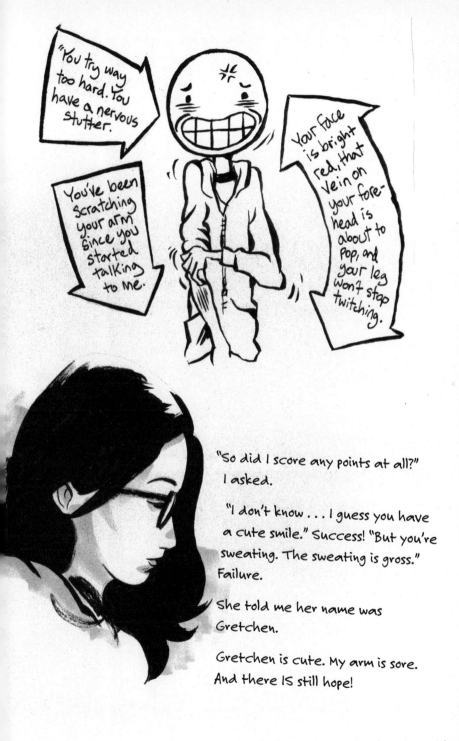

"So did I score any points at all?" I asked.

"I don't know . . . I guess you have a cute smile." Success! "But you're sweating. The sweating is gross." Failure.

She told me her name was Gretchen.

Gretchen is cute. My arm is sore. And there IS still hope!

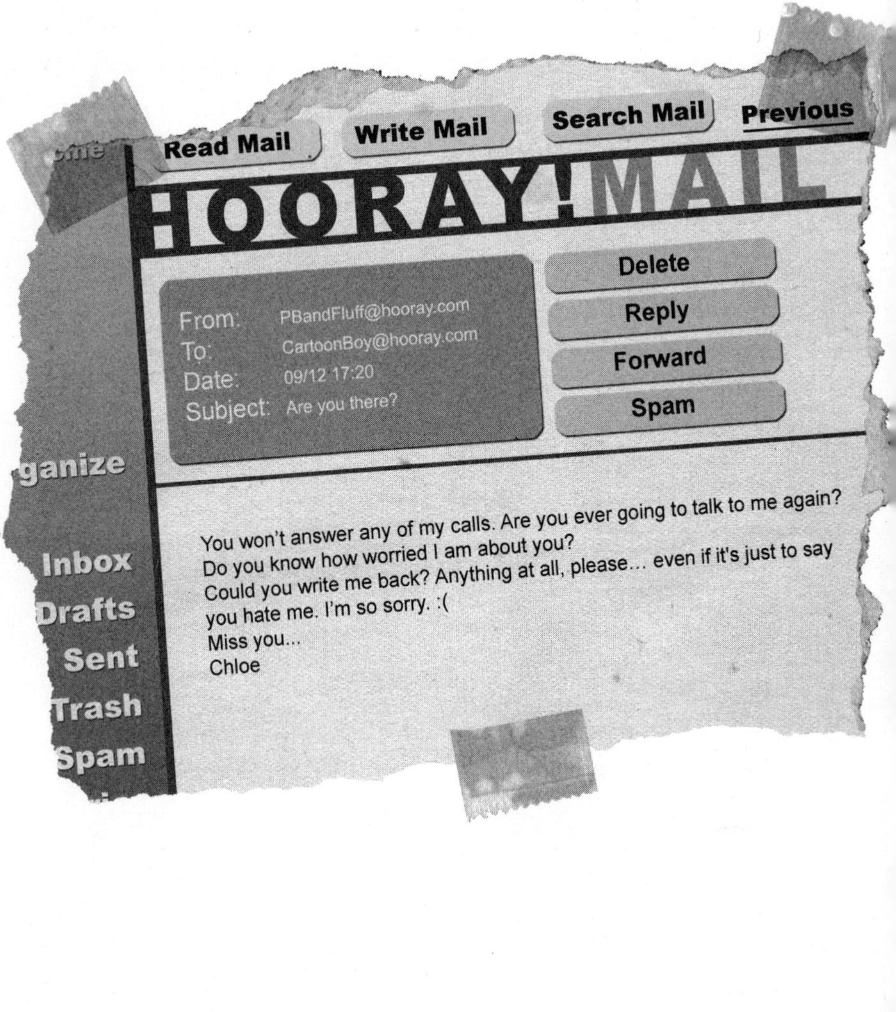
Read Mail
Write Mail
Search Mail
Previous
HOORAY!MAIL
From: PBandFluff@hooray.com
To: CartoonBoy@hooray.com
Date: 09/12 17:20
Subject: Are you there?
Delete
Reply
Forward
Spam
ganize
Inbox
Drafts
Sent
Trash
Spam
You won't answer any of my calls. Are you ever going to talk to me again?
Do you know how worried I am about you?
Could you write me back? Anything at all, please… even if it's just to say
you hate me. I'm so sorry. :(
Miss you...
Chloe

Mean Mr. Molly.

Last period I have English with Mr. Molly. Molly is a tour T-Shirt from a crappy band, a reminder of where you've been that's better left in the closet. I had Mr. Molly a year ago, before I moved. I took his class, as did my brother and probably my father and grandfather and maybe my great-great-grandfather as well. He moved here, and I moved here. He's like my shadow, if the sun was positioned just right to stretch my shadow out three or four times its size sideways. Yes, there he stands, here as in there, fat and tall as ever at the head of the class, wearing a red sweater vest, with a red face, like a creepy, clean-shaven Santa Claus. It's not that he's a bad guy, but he's the one person who really knows anything about me here, which I really don't like. It defeats the "starting new" that I'm supposed to be allowed. He can look at me and see the weak and quiet kid who got picked on in school. If he sees me like that and if he treats me like that, then so will everyone else. I also have to wonder how much he knows about why I'm here, and that makes him the enemy as far as I'm concerned. I thought of transferring to a different teacher, but honestly, this is the one class besides my free period that I have with Gretchen, and I'd like to keep it.

Gretchen sits a few seats away so I don't really get to talk to her. I speak out whenever I can, though, and I get everyone to laugh, and Gretchen laughs, too. So I joke some more. She looks over at me and smiles even when no one else gets my admittedly dry jokes and random babblings.

Mr. Molly gave us journals today. The little composition ones, with the black-and-white marble covers. We're supposed to freewrite on any given topic whenever he asks us to. Today was our first entry and we wrote about what we think of writing in our journals.

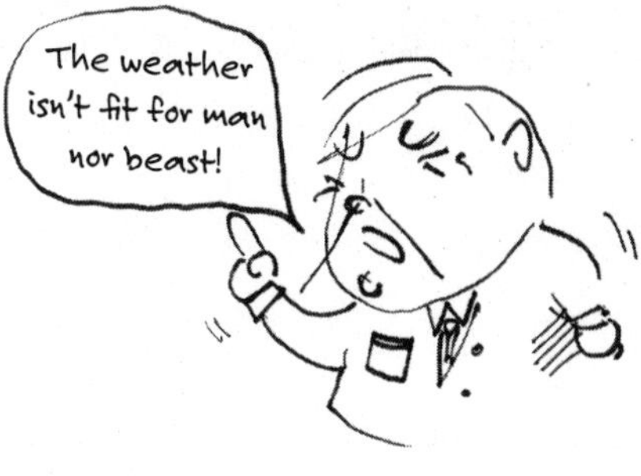
The weather isn't fit for man nor beast!
Mr.

How I Feel About My Journal   10 minutes

I'm not sure yet how I feel about this journal. It's still so new to me. It gives me a sense of déjà vu, familiarity. This may stem from the fact that I already have a journal that I recently started writing in. It gives this journal a sad sense of redundancy. Redundant, like writing in our journals about the act of writing in our journals. In fact, the act of writing in a journal is, in itself, a bit redundant. I mean, we already lived what we write about. If we didn't live it, we've thought it. Many things I write I have both lived and thought about. I live, I think, I write it in my journal. Now I will come to school and write it again, here in my second journal. I will know my thoughts inside and out, which, mind you, can only be good. To be in touch with your true innermost self, that is divine. To write, to capture life in all its detail, that is to live twice. But to have two journals . . . to have two journals is to be infinite. I hope to include in this journal only the truest of truths. To filter life, and thought (and journal #1), to only the rarest gems of ideas; to polish them and expose them as hard to read text, ink, and paper. I will accomplish much this semester, and I will give it all great thought. I hope to turn these accomplishments into wonderful ideas and great text, into beautiful prose and poetic images. And then I hope to write about all of that here in journal #2. This is a very special book you are now holding. These are very special words. They've made it this far, after all.

It's tough to stay tongue-in-cheek that long.
Try and keep an open mind, you might surprise yourself.

M

"HAPPYFACE," PERV

retchen's "Happyface" nickname for me is really taking off. I AM Happyface. I'm a happy guy, I smile in class, I spread the joy. I'm the life of the party! Why not Happyface? It took off quick because as French class was ending today, these two girls called me Happyface, so I knew they were friends of Gretchen's. I was concerned, though, that I was brought up at all, let alone by my new nickname. Why is she talking about me? Is she saying good things? Bad? They seemed friendly, at least, and I was glad to make new friends, which is the goal.

I should point out that neither of them are like cool, sexy girls or anything.

One wore a lot of black and had dyed black hair and a button nose.

The other one had blond hair with black streaks, and she wore more colorful clothing. She had braces.

They were both kinda short.

"Why ya so happy, Happyface?" the button-nosed one asked as we walked out to the hall. My knees wobbled as I carried my French book, my bag of gym clothes, and about thirty pounds of etcetera slung over my shoulder.

Normally anyone in my French class would call me Jean-Luc. That was the name I chose because there's no French version of my real name and "Jean-Luc" just seemed very French and fun to say. Plus it's one letter away from "luck," and I could always use a little of that.

"I'm happy to see you two," I flirted. I should be flirty.

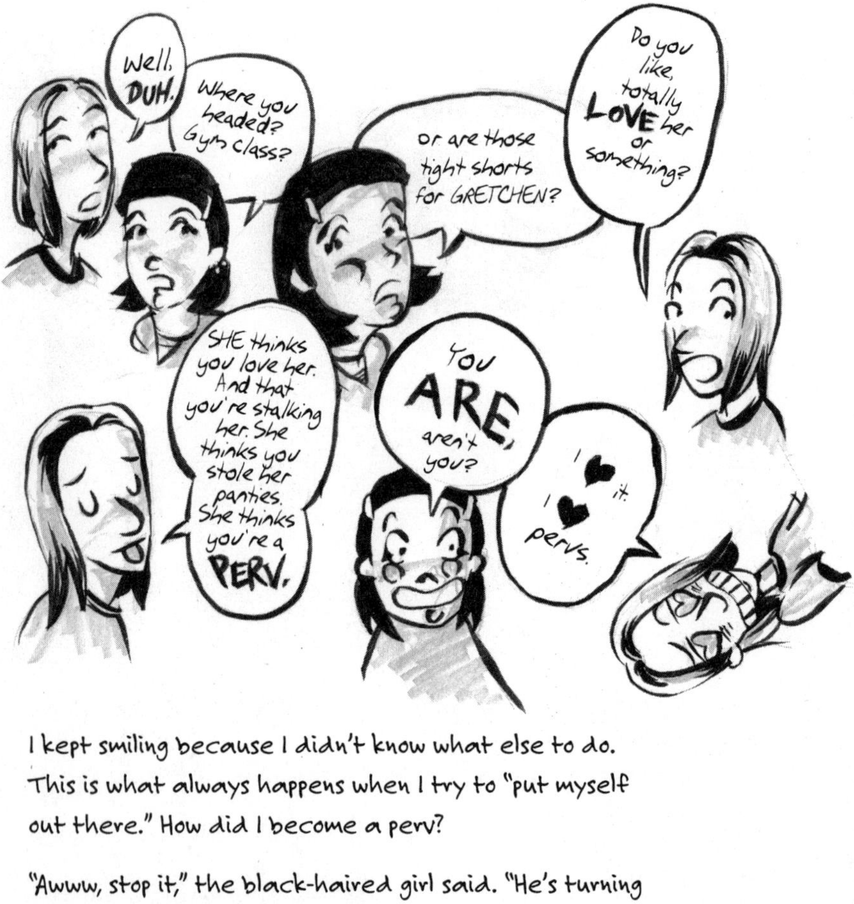
Well, DUH.
Where you headed? Gym class?
Or are those tight shorts for GRETCHEN?
Do you like, totally LOVE her or something?
SHE thinks you love her. And that you're stalking her. She thinks you stole her panties. She thinks you're a PERV.
You ARE, aren't you?
I ♥ it.
I ♥ pervs.

I kept smiling because I didn't know what else to do. This is what always happens when I try to "put myself out there." How did I become a perv?

"Awww, stop it," the black-haired girl said. "He's turning red, leave him alone, Karm!"

They started laughing. They were most definitely laughing at me and not with me, although I laughed with them. Once upon a time I'd have found the nearest locker to hide in and I'd be the butt of everyone's jokes, but this little experiment seemed to be working. I was standing there laughing with two girls, after all.

"Aw, that's so cute. We're just joking. She didn't say anything about you. Gretchen's awesome."

It was more attention than I was used to. The hall felt darker and my head was spinning but those are the best feelings. When I'm red and laughing; when I'm alive and I don't care about anything at all. When I'm seeing stars and I cease to think completely.

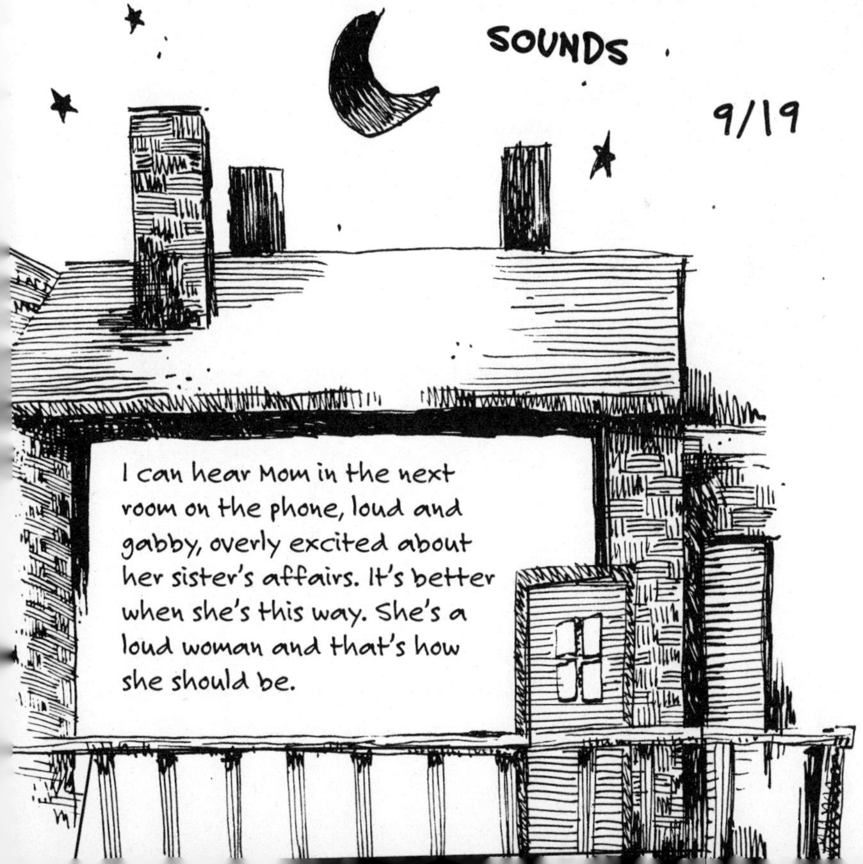

SOUNDS

9/19

I can hear Mom in the next room on the phone, loud and gabby, overly excited about her sister's affairs. It's better when she's this way. She's a loud woman and that's how she should be.

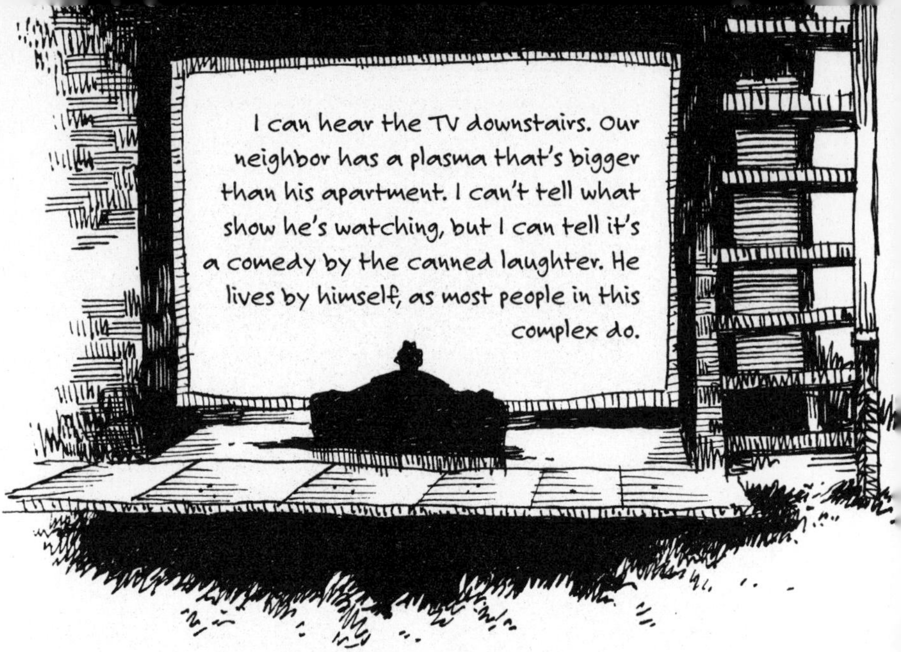
I can hear the TV downstairs. Our neighbor has a plasma that's bigger than his apartment. I can't tell what show he's watching, but I can tell it's a comedy by the canned laughter. He lives by himself, as most people in this complex do.

I can hear cars and the occasional conversation outside my window. Usually it's just bits and pieces: "Better not tell ME what to do," "hold up, hold up," and assorted laughter and catcalls.

Of course none of those sounds keep me awake as much as the constantly blinking red light outside my window.

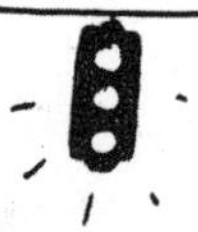

I've met Gretchen and the girls in French class, but I've still been eating by myself at lunch. I even went to the library to eat. It's too much pressure, being the new kid and being seen sitting alone in the cafeteria. It makes people even less inclined to get to know me. I need more than just a smile to make friends, it seems. This week I made an effort to find someone to have lunch with, and met Mike. I don't know what to make of him. In some ways, he's just like me. And in others he is my opposite.

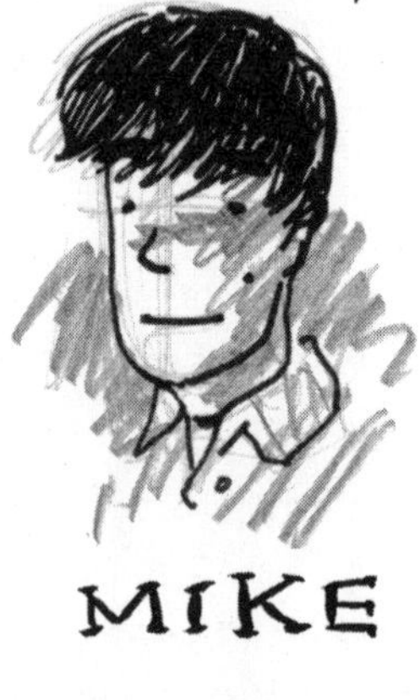

MIKE

9/22

I sat with him originally because he ate alone and because I didn't know anyone and the rest of the cafeteria was crowded. He was glad to have me sit with him and we bonded pretty quickly. Mike likes TV. We talked about a lot of TV shows, and how it's better to watch them on DVD now because you don't have to wait weeks at a time to see a new episode for shows you really like.

If I had to wait a week for every Lost episode, I'd kill myself.

Watch Conan tonight, or at least the first ten minutes. I'll recite the monologue for you word for word tomorrow.

Cable's fine but it's easier to just stream from a computer.

Mike is the kind of kid who watches old sitcoms on Nick at Night. He seems to have at least a passing knowledge of every decade of TV. Of all this encyclopedic television knowledge he has, of all the DVDs he owns and shows he can recite, he especially likes <u>Married with Children</u>.

Four touch-downs in one game!

SINGLE WITH TOO MUCH TIME

He watches it every night on cable and can quote almost everything Al Bundy has said.

The show seems a lot funnier when he quotes it than it ever did the few times I saw it, but I guess things just seem funnier when you're sit-ting at the lunch table with a friend and you've been locked in classes all day.

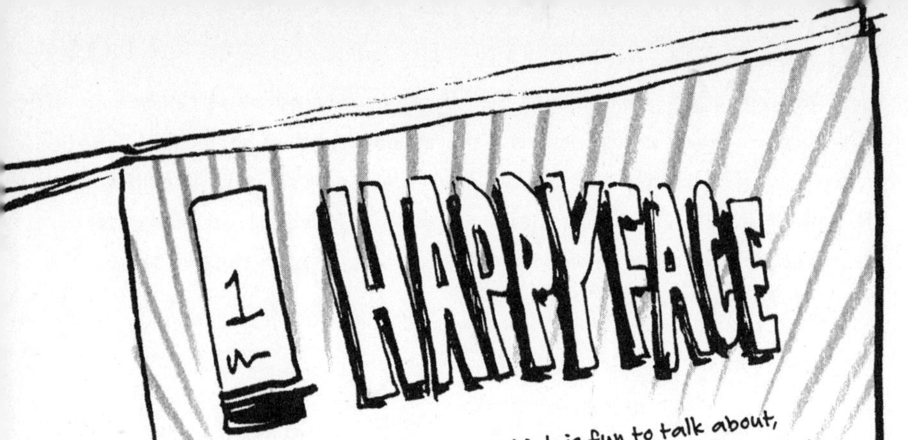
1
HAPPYFACE

Mike is into comic books, too, which is fun to talk about, because even though I don't read them anymore, I used to want to draw superhero comics. I would draw stupid pictures of myself as a hero, with a silly costume and villains to fight, and classmates I'd never spoken to would be love interests and other superheroes.

I've thought about showing Mike some of my old artwork but I shouldn't even really doodle as much as I do at school. It gives my hands and my head something to do, though.

Mike's the first person I could be placed next to and considered the cool one. In gym class today, we were running laps around the gym (admittedly slower than anyone else) to get warmed up, when this annoying kid ran up to Mike and me.

"Hey, lovebirds, save the long walks for the beach," he said.

"Yeah? Save your long walks for short piers," I said, just loud enough for the bully to possibly hear if he was really listening. Guess not everyone here is cool.

"Not bad," Mike said. "Not bad at all." It was quite the compliment.

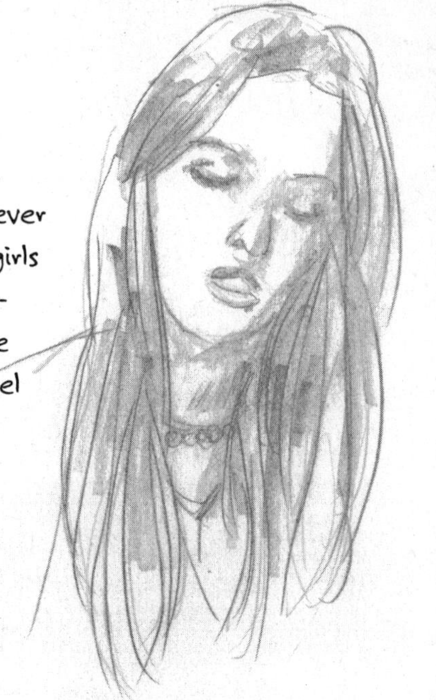

Sometimes, though, Mike goes on and on about some show I've never seen and never plan to, and I look around at boys and girls sitting together and flirting and cute girls by the soda machine, and I feel like a kid.

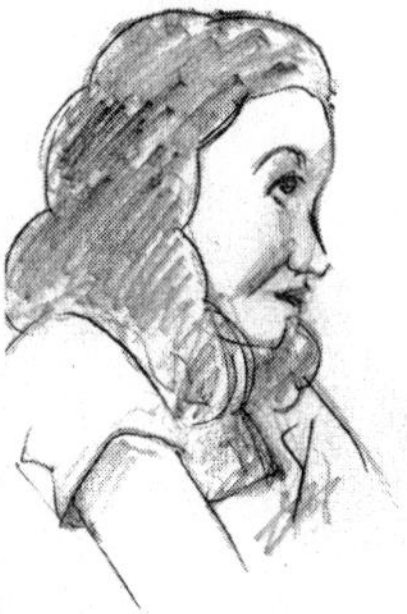

Then I just want him to shut up.

But he's a nice guy and we laugh a lot.

That's the other thing I think about . . . I'd like to have a girl that could like me in the same way that I like her. I'd kind of like someone to share little things with, like when the sky melts into fifteen different colors and the air feels just right. Maybe the pep squad could use a Happyface and I could date a cheerleader. There are the theater girls, though they tend to stick to their own. As do the Voltron girls; you know—individual girls who only really work as one huge wad of walking popularity. See, I'm getting used to this town.

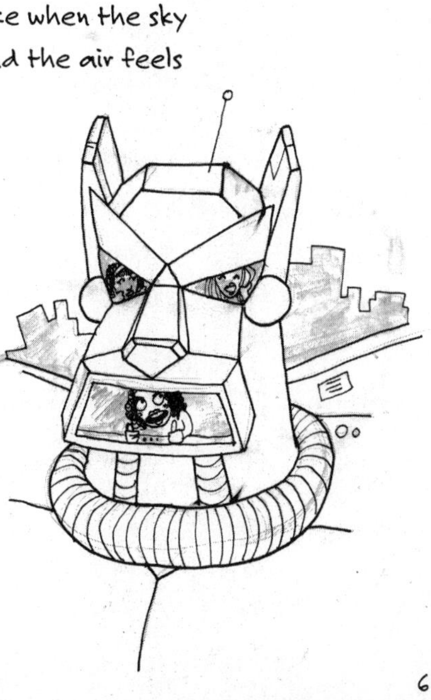

ON MOMENTS

Dad told me he was my age when he started writing. I think he'd be happy to see me using this book so much. Of course I really start to use it when he's not around anymore. He said it's good to document the things that happen, the big stuff and the small things, and that he wished he'd done it more when he was a teenager. I understand because there are things that happen almost every day, little moments . . .

There's all these little moments I wish I could **trap** and keep with me like a

9/24

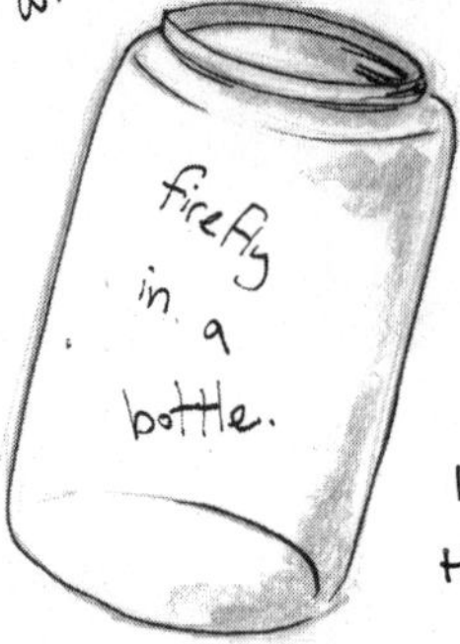
firefly in a bottle.

(of course there's little need for that when you have your very own traffic light outside your window). I'm going to make an effort to trap those moments here so I can come back and look at them whenever I want to.

Some moments are good. Mom took me out Sunday to get new clothes for school. She's insistent on not using any of Dad's money, determined, even, which is lame since he actually has money. I'm not about to go to school with paper bags on my feet so she can be stubborn.

Mom has all kinds of ideas for what I should wear. She went on and on with the magazines and ads, but I'd been paying attention to what the other kids here are wearing, and had already pieced together what I wanted to get in my mind:

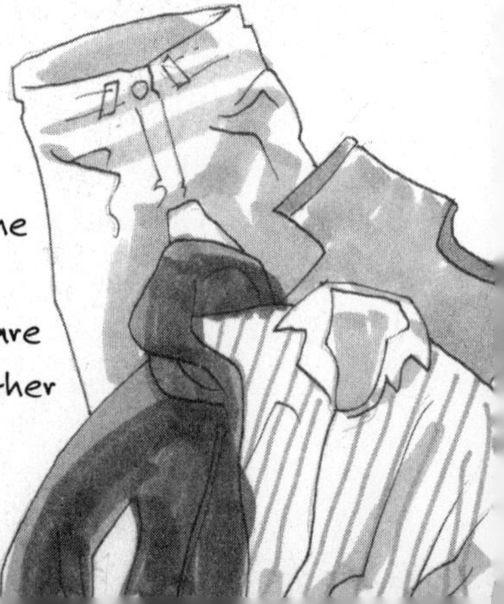

We checked out a few stores at the mall and weren't finding much, until Gretchen turned up at American Eagle with the girls I met from French class.

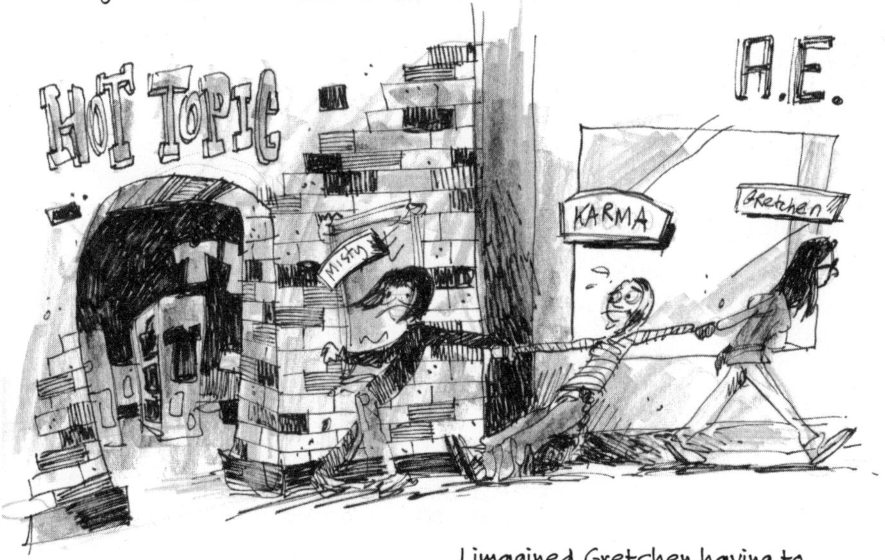
HOT TOPIC
A.E.
KARMA
Gretchen
Misty

I imagined Gretchen having to con the girls over there, or lure them with promises of visiting Hot Topic next. I talked to them for a few seconds and learned that Karma and Misty are sisters. Karma and Misty Moon.

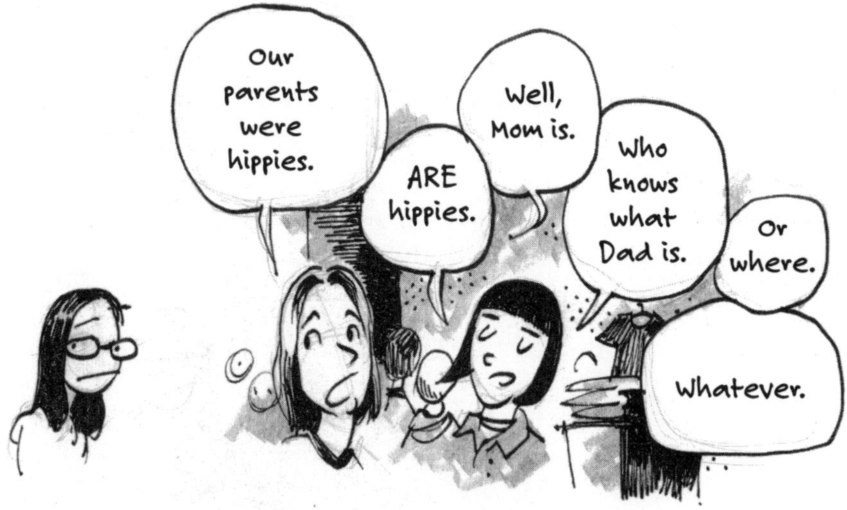
Our parents were hippies.
ARE hippies.
Well, Mom is.
Who knows what Dad is.
Or where.
Whatever.

I ran my Mr. Molly = creepy Santa Claus bit by Gretchen to decent reaction before Mom reminded me we were looking for clothes. I asked her if I could look around with my friends for a bit and she agreed. Mom browsed around by herself. She HAD to understand; after all, when have I ever walked around with three cool girls? Before Chloe, there hadn't been even one. I tried to make small talk, tried to stretch things out, but we were looking at clothes and Mom was staring into space and the fun was quickly dwindling. Misty took Karma and Gretchen out for ice cream and left the two of us to ourselves. Once Gretchen and the Moons left, I didn't have much to say and I wasn't really hungry, either. Mom took me to dinner. "It's all right that you didn't introduce me to your friends," she said. "They're real cute and you were so red."

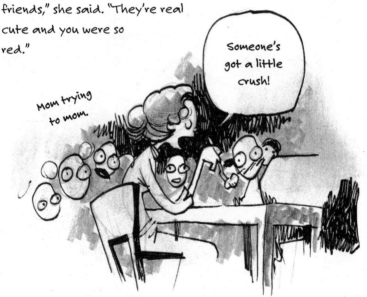

Someone's got a little crush!
Mom trying to mom.

I felt like being quiet though and Mom noticed because she got quiet, too. And she's a roller coaster, two minutes of silence, and she becomes depressed and on the verge of tears. Why do we always have to talk? I was pretty sure some of the kids nearby were from my school. I didn't feel like smiling anymore. I felt like getting away, so I left, and I waited in the car. Mom finished her dinner. We didn't talk on the way home.

Some moments are bad.

9/25

DOGGIN' IT

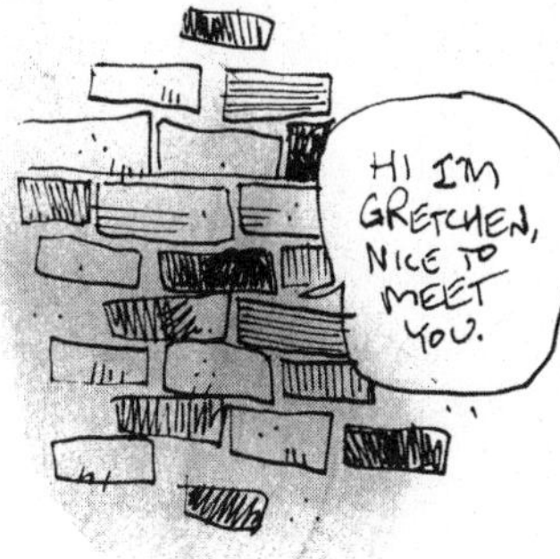
HI I'M GRETCHEN, NICE TO MEET YOU.

This morning I sat by Gretchen in the hall while she read, same as I do every day on our free period. It's just us usually and we don't say much, though she doesn't seem to mind my company. I like it because it's quiet and I can write and be alone with Gretchen for a full forty-five minutes. Yesterday I thought to ask her about herself: music, movies, family. It was like talking to a brick wall. I like that, though; she's like a mystery to solve. She has that librarian look with the glasses and the gentle, patient smile. Every week she's reading a new book. She seems observant, like she knows more than she lets on, like she watches more than she talks, like me. Today I came in with a non-personal topic to discuss, but before I could get to "There sure are a lot of mysteries in outer space" and my opinions on negative matter, she suggested we get breakfast in the cafeteria.

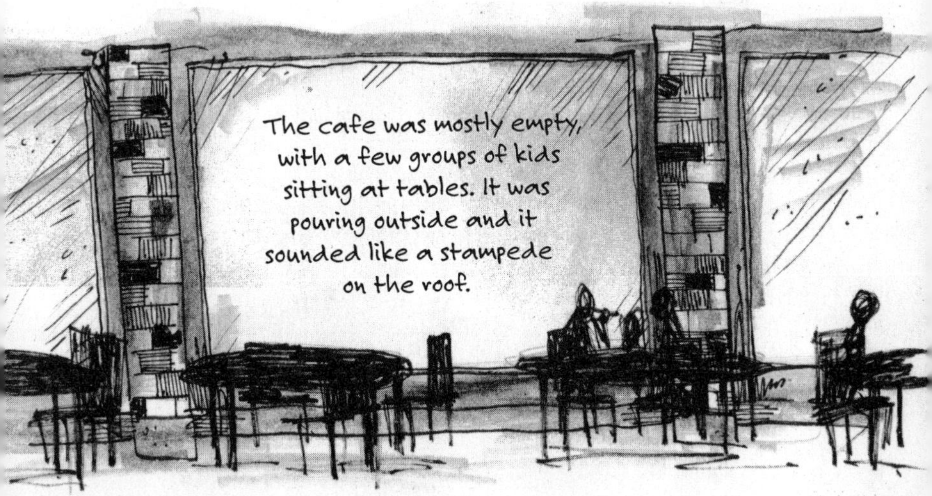
The cafe was mostly empty, with a few groups of kids sitting at tables. It was pouring outside and it sounded like a stampede on the roof.

Gretchen scolded me as I reached for a soda. "Are you serious? You'll rot your teeth. Find something healthy!" I pulled back as she added, "Or at LEAST something appropriate for breakfast." We looked at muffins. I eyed the chocolate chip before thinking better of it. I went with blueberry. "Good choice," she confirmed. I handed my two dollars to the lunch lady, who said, "Really doggin' it, today."

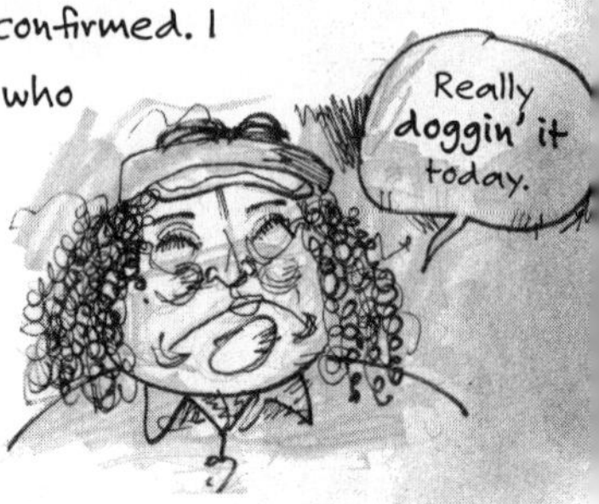
Really doggin' it today.

I looked to Gretchen to see if she had any idea what that meant, but I don't think she did, either.

We sat at the nearest table and ate our muffins in awkward silence.

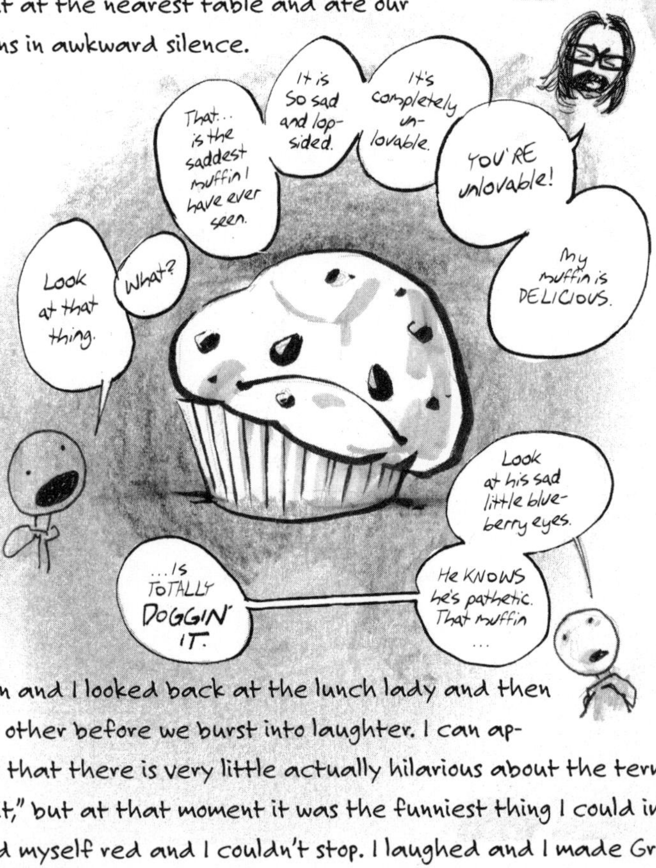
Look at that thing.
What?
That... is the saddest muffin I have ever seen.
It is so sad and lop-sided.
It's completely un-lovable.
YOU'RE unlovable!
My muffin is DELICIOUS.
Look at his sad little blue-berry eyes.
He KNOWS he's pathetic. That muffin ...
...Is TOTALLY DOGGIN' IT.

Gretchen and I looked back at the lunch lady and then at each other before we burst into laughter. I can appreciate that there is very little actually hilarious about the term "doggin' it," but at that moment it was the funniest thing I could imagine. I laughed myself red and I couldn't stop. I laughed and I made Gretchen laugh and with her by my side at that cafeteria table, I felt ridiculous and giant, taller than the clouds and rain. Silly, lost, and very happy.

MOM
9/27

Have you ever met a
smoker who doesn't
smoke? That's what
my mom is. She's tense,
always stressed, and
constantly on edge. She's
always been that way,
although she actually is a
smoker who doesn't smoke—she quit when she
met my father, a steadfast nonsmoker. Maybe that's always in the
background, maybe that's why she is the way she is. My mom is loud,
competitive, aggressive, a control freak, impulsive, and the last person
I wanted teaching me how to drive.

I don't think she likes it any more than I do. It was supposed to be
Dad's job, and he was actually looking forward to it. That's all
changed. He and Everett spent most of the last year working on Ev's
Corvette. It was old and junky at first but they made it really nice.
And while that car was sitting in our parking lot, begging to be taken
out, today I was driving the family's crappy old '92 Subaru Legacy
while Mom yelled out various non sequiturs and made me want to
never sit behind a wheel of any kind ever again.

"Why do I have to drive such an old car?" I asked.

"It was new when we bought it," Mom said.
"They didn't tell us it'd get old."

Her hair was bright in the September sun as we circled
the K-Mart parking lot. My mom is pretty if not
slightly worn down from yell-
ing and stressing all the
time. She is very thin
and has bright red
curly hair.

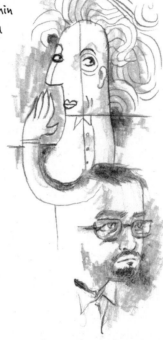

She is loose
and messy like a
painting, like art.

She is very much
the opposite of Dad,
who is bookish, studied,
groomed, and dark.
Dark hair, dark
beard, thick glasses.

Mom provided the audio for our trip, alternating between, "Slow down,
steer clear of cars!" and a detailed synopsis of my aunt's latest
fight with my uncle. On and on with the family.

I saved,
she doesn't
save.

she can't
afford her
own place.

She's not
going to
have any
money,

I don't
know what she
plans on doing if she
leaves him, she can't
stay with us.

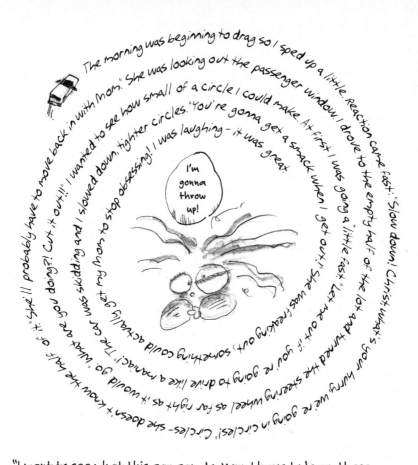

The morning was beginning to drag so I sped up a little. Reaction came fast: "Slow down! Christ what's your hurry we're going in circles!" "Circles - she doesn't know the half of it." "She'll probably have to move back in with mom." She was looking out the passenger window. I wanted to see how small of a circle I could make. I drove to the empty half of the lot and turned the steering wheel as far right as it would go. "What are you doing?! Cut it out!!" At first I was going a little fast. "Let me out!" She was freaking out, something could actually get my mom to stop obsessing! The car was skidding and I slowed down, tighter circles. "You're gonna get a smack when I get out if you're going to drive like a maniac!" I was laughing - it was great.

"I want to see what this car can do, Mom, I have to learn these things!"

I stopped the car with a screech, smoke rising off the ground. Several spectators cheered me on. "Thank you!" I waved out the window. Mom was not as thrilled.

"What the hell has gotten into you?" She kept looking out the window. "We are going to have a nice long talk when we get home. I promise you that." She was jittery with anger. We switched seats and drove home. We walked inside and Mom got back on the phone.

On Writing

When thinking of writing, the word phooey always comes to mind. I mean, really, writing is a bunch of phooey. It's what we do when we should be living, and doing. It's kind of a waste of time. Writers are so up in their heads. They're so full of themselves. I mean, the ego it takes to write and really think you have anything to say at all, let alone anything new, is a conceited notion. And generally it's written with the idea that OTHER people will actually want to read your ideas and they'll all be better off for it. Any meaningful writing is just depressing anyway. The further we get to know our own human nature, the uglier it is. That's why all the famous writers are notorious drunks and drug addicts. They shelter themselves off in a cabin in the woods, isolated and delirious. And then there are the Sylvia Plaths and Anne Sextons.

That's why the best writing is popular fiction; your crime novels and airplane books. A quick formula, a decent concept, and make a million bucks off it. That's smart writing. The rest of it is phooey. It's all an exercise in destroying from within.

I'm still unsure of how truthful you are being in these journal entries, but these are some interesting points and an emotional stance. Please, feel free to talk to me anytime.

9/27

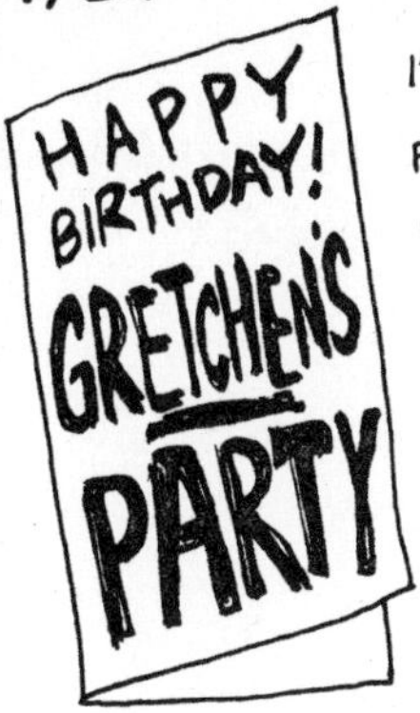
HAPPY BIRTHDAY!
GRETCHEN'S PARTY

I'm pretty sure she only invited me because I was present while she talked about it, but I got a last-minute invite to Gretchen's birthday party, and last night I went. Her birthday is actually in two weeks but last night her parents were out of town so that's why she had the party early. Mom let me take the car there since she was home for the night and too tired to drop me off. I'm still learning how to drive and Mom said we weren't making a practice of this, but Gretchen doesn't live too far away, really only two street turns, about a three-minute drive. I should be able to handle that if I'm going to be getting my license this year.

I showed up and smiled and hugged everyone (when I got there, only Karma and Misty had arrived).

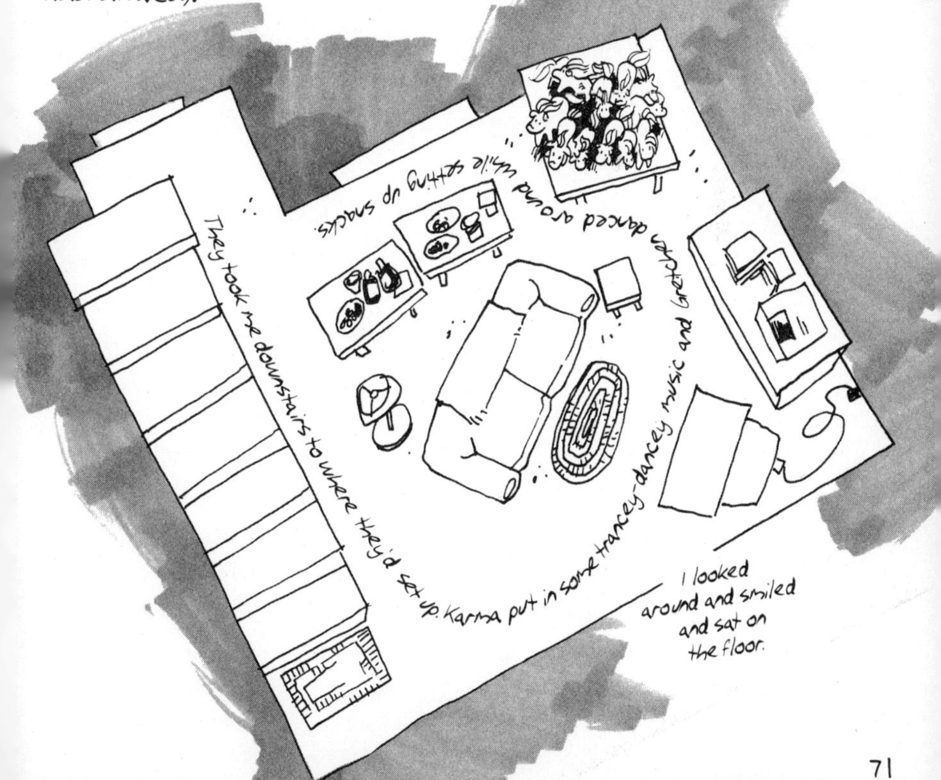
They took me downstairs to where they'd set up. Karma put in some trancey-dancey music and Gretchen danced around while setting up snacks.
I looked around and smiled and sat on the floor.

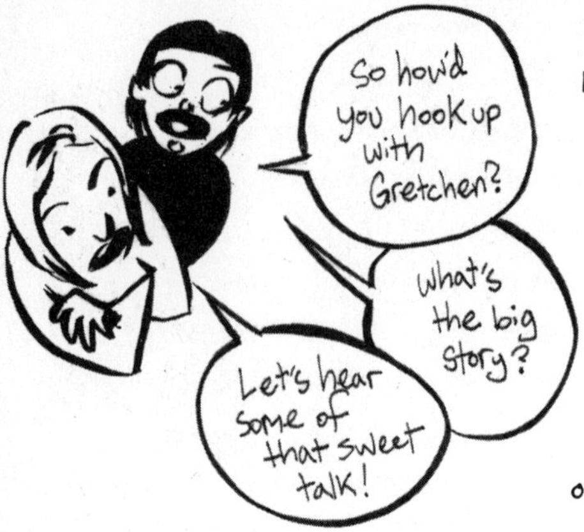
So how'd you hookup with Gretchen?
what's the big story?
Let's hear some of that sweet talk!

I fumbled out an answer: "Uh, hook up? Well, we have free period and I saw her . . ."

"That's so sweet. Come on, you can do better than that," Karma said.

"I don't know, I didn't know anyone yet so I introduced myself . . ."

Karma interrupts: "Misty, how did Happyface here meet Gretchen?"

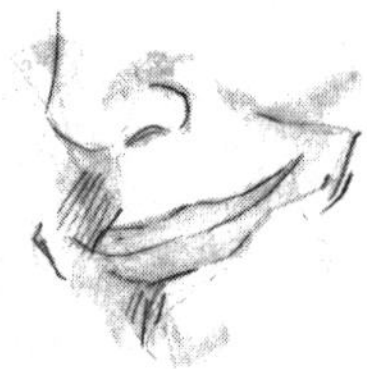

Gretchen was smiling at the exchange.

Misty didn't miss a beat. "Gretchen found him wandering the streets, completely off his rocker after a few too many shots at the Dopey Smile Convention. She took him in, potty trained him, gave him a chew toy and a filled-up food dish, and here he is, cleaned up and ready to party."

I joined in on the joke: "I'm the Snoopy to her Charlie Brown."

"Good grief," Gretchen said.

"So do we start calling you Joe Cool now?" Karma asked.

"No way," Gretchen said, "Happyface STICKS!"

The party kept growing, people started coming in as we were laughing downstairs. Josiah came first, with a large bottle of God-knows-what. Josiah was a tall guy with dark hair and a goatee. Gretchen was happy to see him and she took a swig from the bottle. Then he grabbed a guitar sitting in the corner of the basement and started playing. He was really good. I was pretty impressed but I guess maybe everyone else was used to it because they didn't gawk like I did.

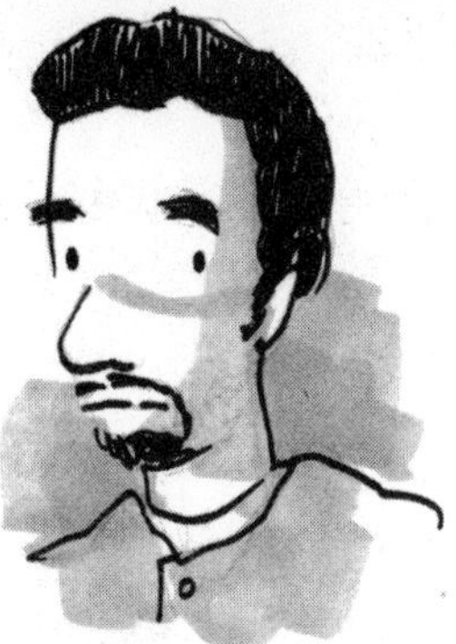

Josiah

Next down the stairs was Trevor, who I guess is an ex-boyfriend of Gretchen's, from what I could tell.

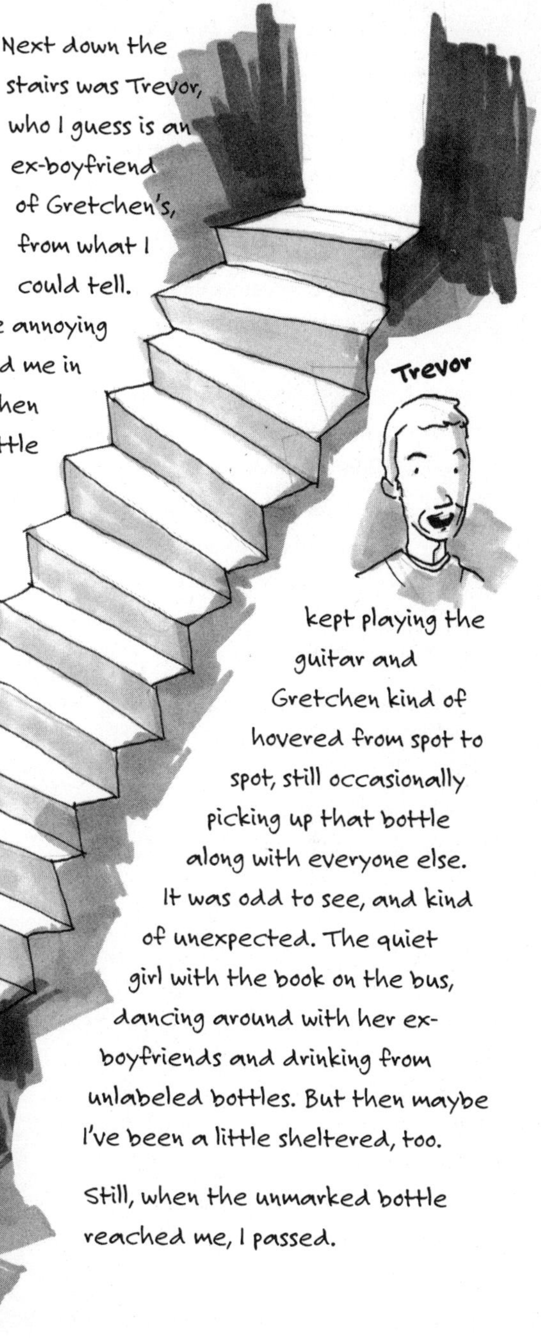

He's the annoying kid who teased Mike and me in gym class. What did Gretchen see in him? I mean, he's a little funny, in that over-the-top kind of way. The louder = funnier kind of funny. He took control once he got there, and everyone was laughing and listening to his stories.

Trevor

Josiah kept playing the guitar and Gretchen kind of hovered from spot to spot, still occasionally picking up that bottle along with everyone else. It was odd to see, and kind of unexpected. The quiet girl with the book on the bus, dancing around with her ex-boyfriends and drinking from unlabeled bottles. But then maybe I've been a little sheltered, too.

Still, when the unmarked bottle reached me, I passed.

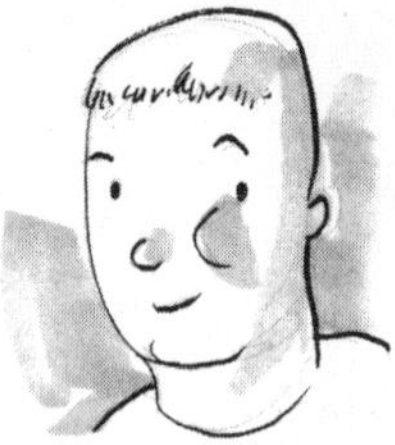

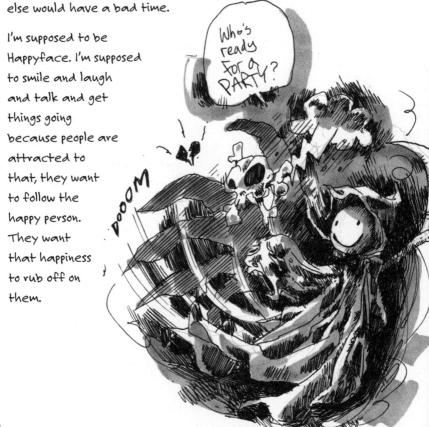

Random Pillsbury Doughboy Guy

"I've had bad experiences," I said, and left it at that.

Another guy came in; I forget his name but he looked kind of like the Pillsbury Doughboy. I was kind of hoping some more girls would show up. . . .

It wasn't long before I felt like a wallflower, watching everyone else and feeling sorry for myself. I wasn't sure what to say or who to talk to, so I just smiled like a dope. I wanted to be the life of the party, but there I was actually at a party and I was the Grim Reaper. Wishing everyone else would have a bad time.

I'm supposed to be Happyface. I'm supposed to smile and laugh and talk and get things going because people are attracted to that, they want to follow the happy person. They want that happiness to rub off on them.

Who's ready for a PARTY?
DOOOM

Gretchen put some old-timey swing record into the CD player. "Let's go, Happyface."

"I don't know how to dance!"

"Good, it's more fun that way!"

This is how I should be thinking. And if I suck and step on people then we'll laugh; we'll all laugh together. And we'll laugh if I don't suck, and we'll dance around and have fun. It took a minute to get into the groove but we swung around and I tried to copy what she was doing. Trevor took over but then I danced with Misty, and then with Karma. I kept going and I kept smiling. We were having a blast and I finally felt like I belonged and as the night went on, I felt like part of the family.

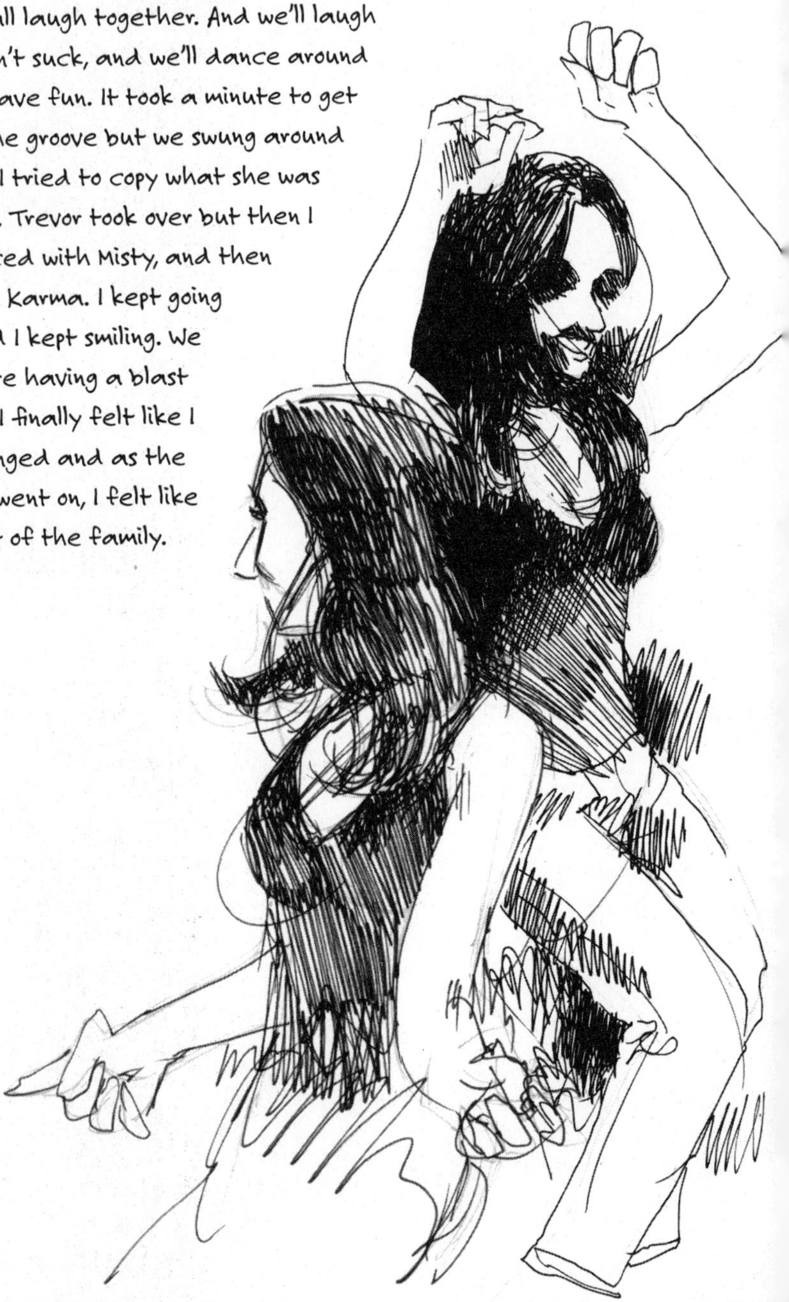

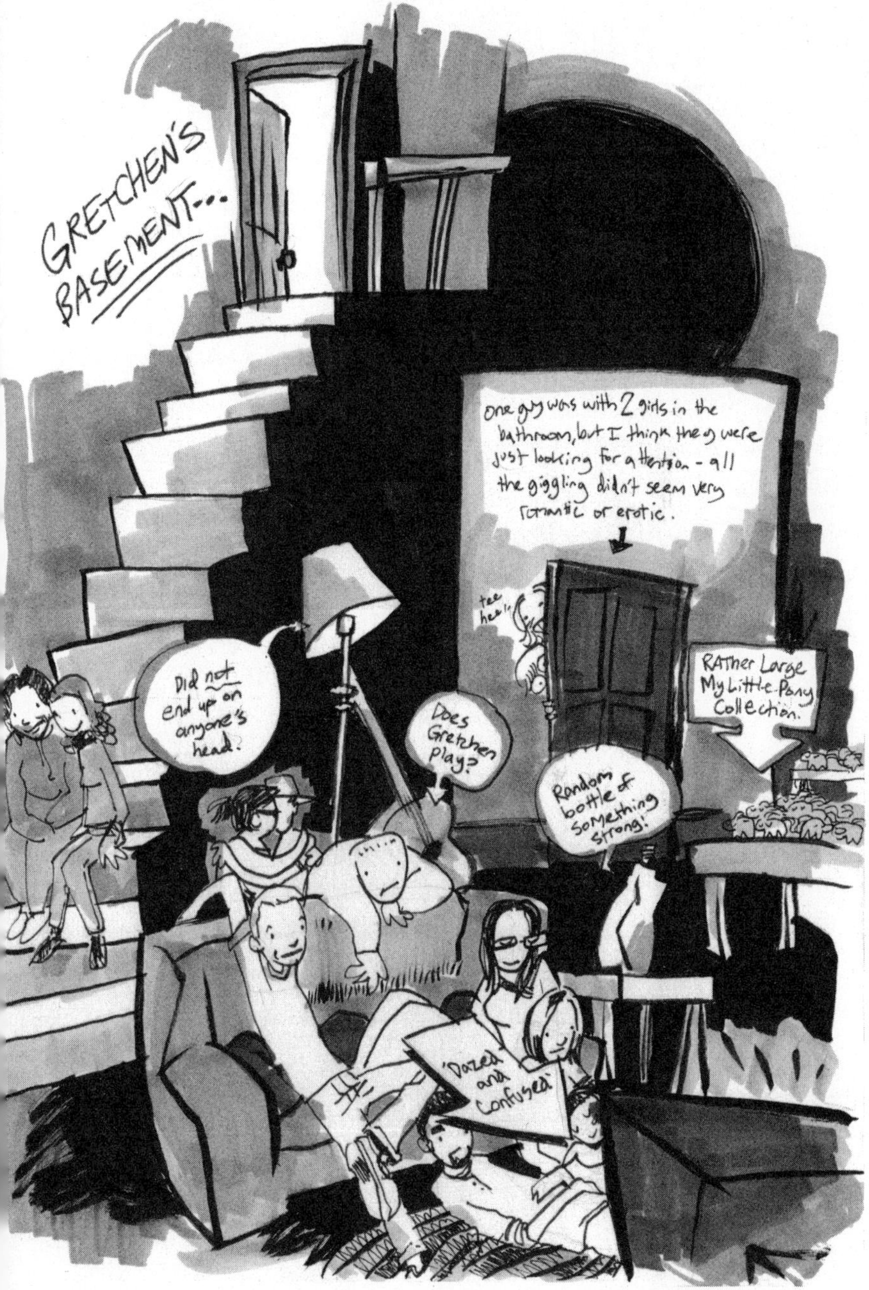
GRETCHEN'S BASEMENT...
one guy was with 2 girls in the bathroom, but I think they were just looking for attention - all the giggling didn't seem very romantic or erotic.
tee hee!
RAther Large My Little Pony Collection.
Did not end up on anyone's head.
Does Gretchen play?
Random bottle of something strong!
'Dazed and Confused'

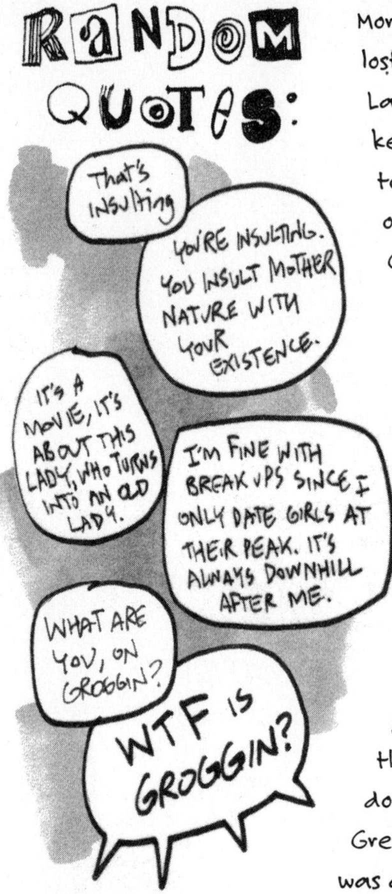
RANDOM QUOTES:
That's insulting
YOU'RE INSULTING. YOU INSULT MOTHER NATURE WITH YOUR EXISTENCE.
IT'S A MOVIE, IT'S ABOUT THIS LADY, WHO TURNS INTO AN OLD LADY.
I'M FINE WITH BREAKUPS SINCE I ONLY DATE GIRLS AT THEIR PEAK. IT'S ALWAYS DOWNHILL AFTER ME.
WHAT ARE YOU, ON GROGGIN?
WTF IS GROGGIN?

More people (girls included!) came and I lost track of time. We played "Make Me Laugh," where someone has to try and keep a straight face while people try to, well, make them laugh. It was kind of silly and I wasn't very good at it. Gretchen kept stopping by and checking in on me and telling me how drunk she was. I wasn't sure who was drinking and who wasn't; really, they didn't seem that off to me. My mom used to drink, and she was a REAL drunk.

It was getting late. Josiah brought over Harold and Maude, which he was telling Gretchen she needed to see. It was really good, though I don't think Gretchen was as into it as Josiah had expected. We were all sitting around, some passing out, others flirting in the corner, but most of us stayed through the movie. I was busy trying to figure out who everyone was in relation to Gretchen, and why I'd never seen most of them before. Some guys had clearly dated her. Others clearly liked her. She was so close to so many guys, but seemingly she wasn't actually dating any of them. I wondered if this was the in-between period, or if she was waiting for Mr. Right, or if she was just burned out on boys. Or was she dating someone else secretly?

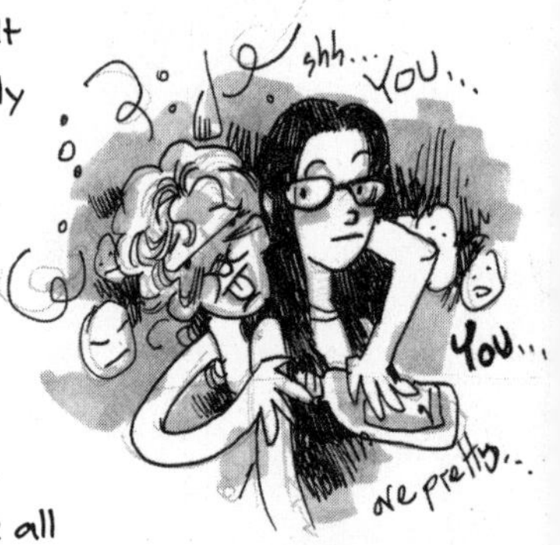
shh...
YOU...
YOU...
are pretty...

(TREVOR WAS A KNACK FOR MAKING UP WORDS)

Trevor was camped out on the couch as people began to trickle out. Once the movie ended a bunch of others left. I was curious as to who was staying, and why. It was back down to me, Misty, Karma, Trevor, and Josiah around one thirty. We sat around talking about people I didn't know and everyone was sleepy. We sat in a little circle. My phone buzzed around then when Mom called but I turned it off because I didn't want to change the mood. I was enjoying everything.

"Past my bedtime, Gretchen. Happy birthday." Josiah gave her a big hug and was on his way. Two a.m. Two thirty. Trevor still wasn't leaving. Gretchen was half asleep. Misty was tuckered out on Karma's shoulder.

"How did you guys become friends with Gretchen?" I asked.

Gretchen was awake enough to mumble an answer: "They helped me through some tough times. They've been my best friends ever since." Barely awake.

Best friends! Yesssssss!

79

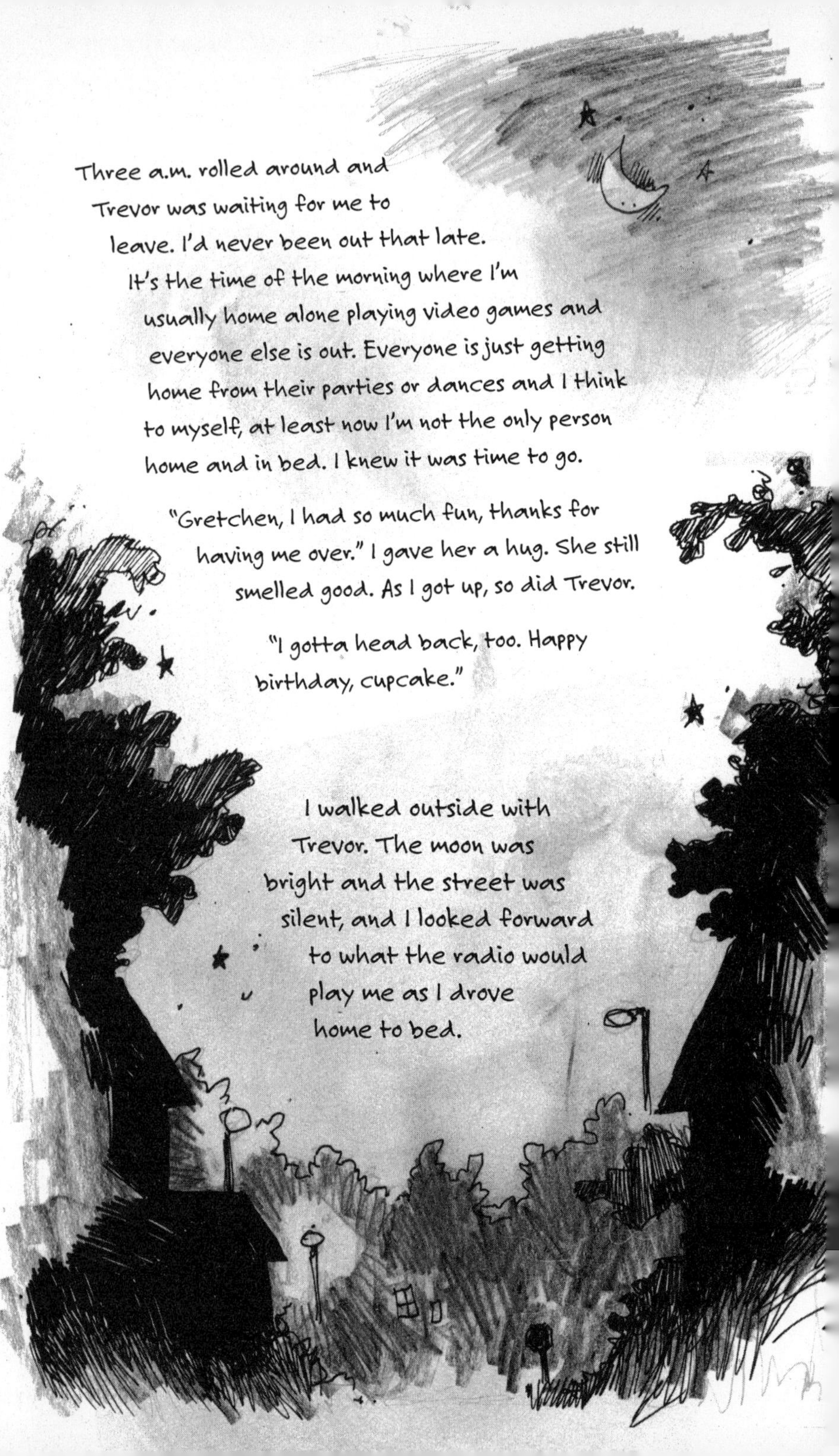

Three a.m. rolled around and Trevor was waiting for me to leave. I'd never been out that late. It's the time of the morning where I'm usually home alone playing video games and everyone else is out. Everyone is just getting home from their parties or dances and I think to myself, at least now I'm not the only person home and in bed. I knew it was time to go.

"Gretchen, I had so much fun, thanks for having me over." I gave her a hug. She still smelled good. As I got up, so did Trevor.

"I gotta head back, too. Happy birthday, cupcake."

I walked outside with Trevor. The moon was bright and the street was silent, and I looked forward to what the radio would play me as I drove home to bed.

3:30 AM...

I came home late. Mom was used to me not really going out at all. I expected I'd hear something about it but I knew it was really bad when I saw she was still awake. She'd been awake for hours, and she was furious.

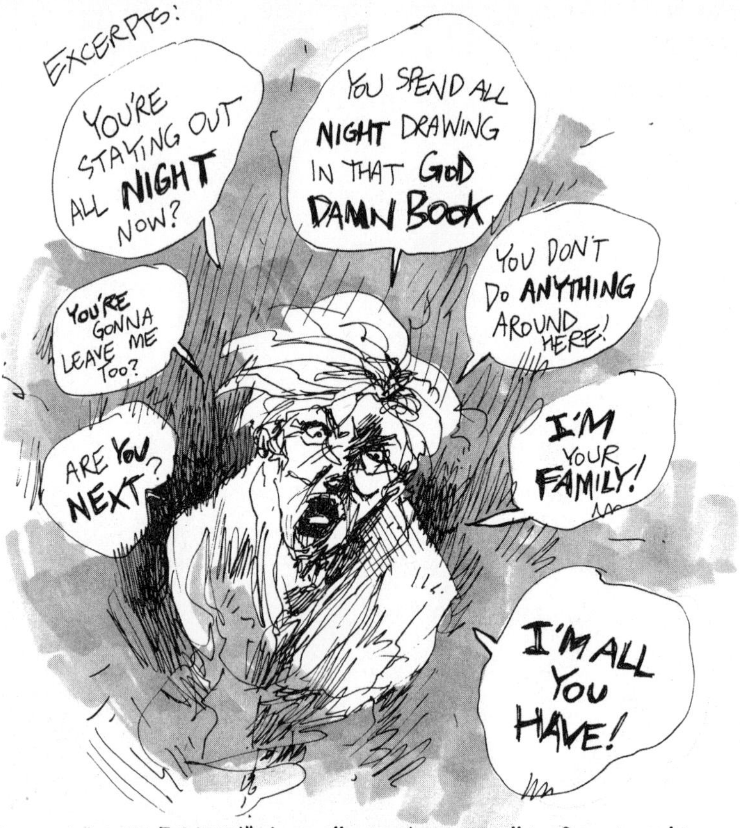
EXCERPTS:
YOU'RE STAYING OUT ALL NIGHT NOW?
YOU SPEND ALL NIGHT DRAWING IN THAT GOD DAMN BOOK
YOU DON'T DO ANYTHING AROUND HERE!
YOU'RE GONNA LEAVE ME TOO?
ARE YOU NEXT?
I'M YOUR FAMILY!
I'M ALL YOU HAVE!

"I let you drive ILLEGALLY!" she yelled. This was all before I could get the door closed. "I was worried to death and you don't have the common sense to call or even pick up your phone! I've been up all night! I almost called the police! No more driving, that's it!"

I hugged her tight and told her I was sorry, I told her I was fine and I was sorry and I smiled. It was the same smile I used when answering my teacher's questions. It was the same smile that plastered my face as I danced with Gretchen and Karma and Misty earlier in the evening. It was the smile that changed so many things and it worked again, my mom was sobbing, but calmer, and she was smiling, too. It was the smile that said, "Everything is okay."

And everything was.

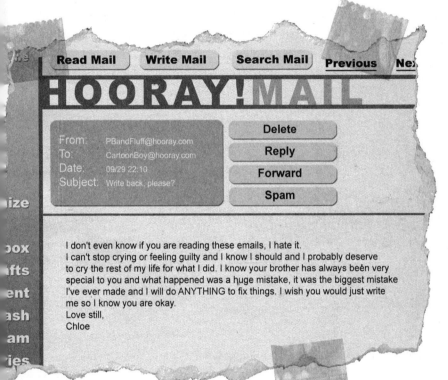

HOORAY!MAIL

From: PBandFluff@hooray.com
To: CartoonBoy@hooray.com
Date: 09/29 22:10
Subject: Write back, please?

Delete

Reply

Forward

Spam

ize

ox

fts

ent

ash

am

ies

I don't even know if you are reading these emails, I hate it.
I can't stop crying or feeling guilty and I know I should and I probably deserve
to cry the rest of my life for what I did. I know your brother has always been very
special to you and what happened was a huge mistake, it was the biggest mistake
I've ever made and I will do ANYTHING to fix things. I wish you would just write
me so I know you are okay.
Love still,
Chloe

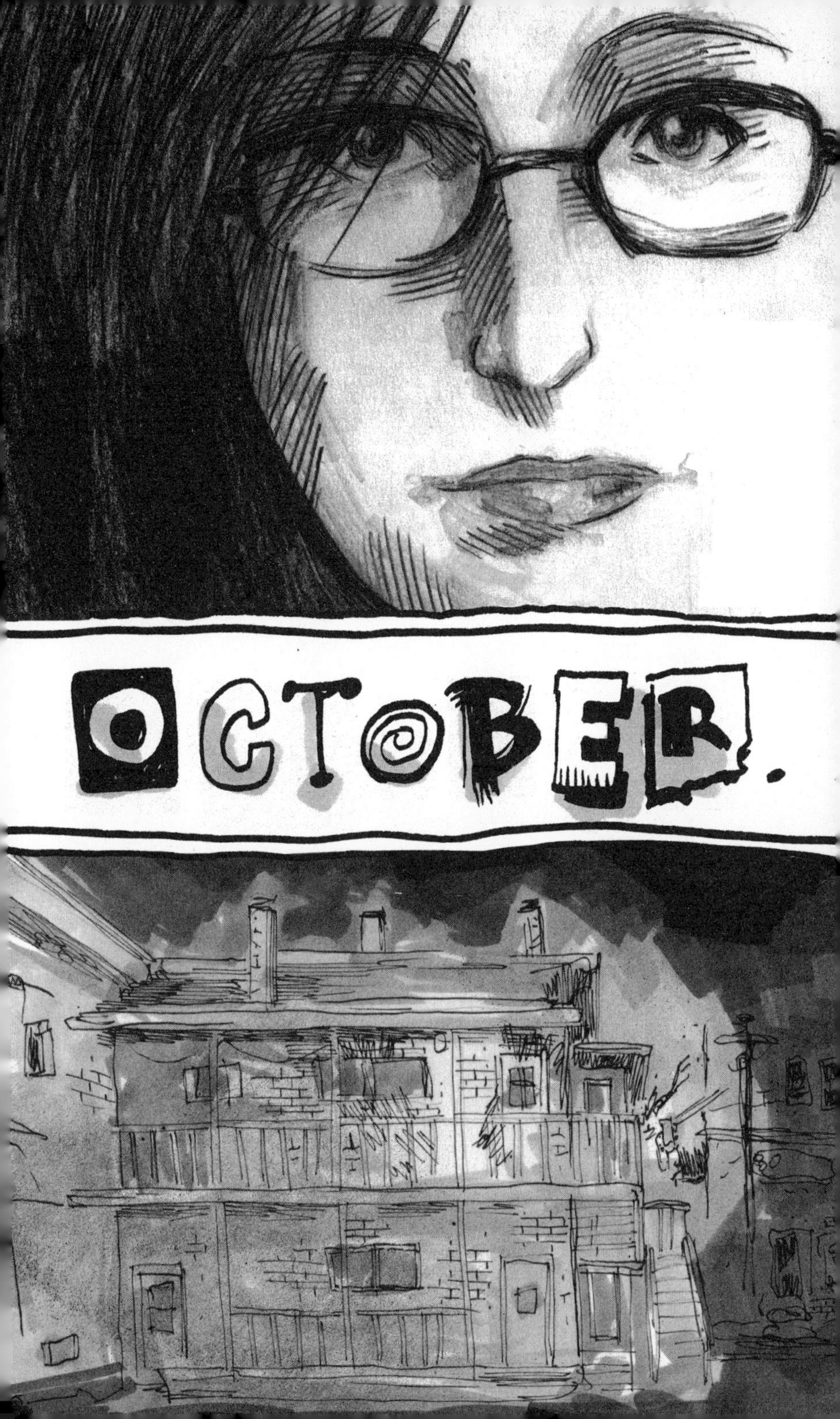
OCTOBER.

One of the Many Sordid Love Affairs of Happyface...

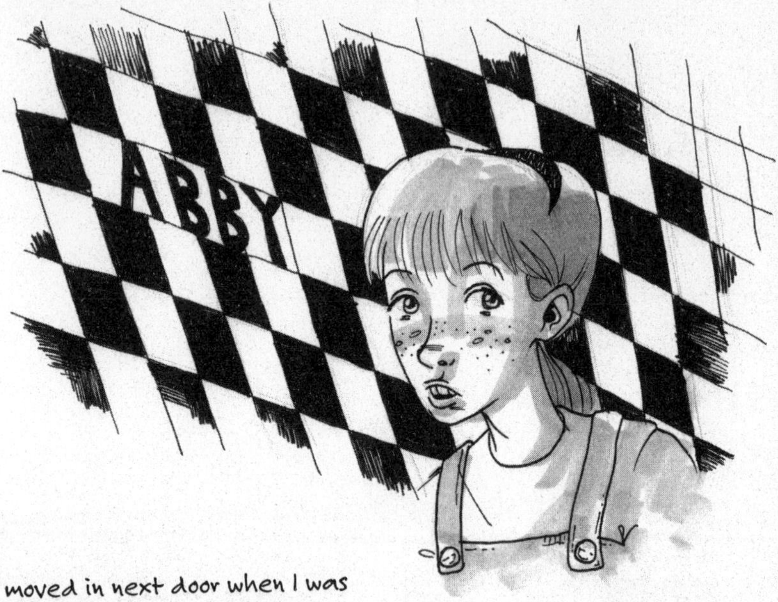
ABBY

Abby moved in next door when I was seven or eight years old. One of my earlier memories is an image of her the day she moved in, glancing back at me timidly and holding a teddy bear while I played alone in our little back-yard. At that age my days consisted of bothering Mom, bothering Ev, and chasing the cat around the house, wrapping it in blankets and making laundry basket jail cells for her.

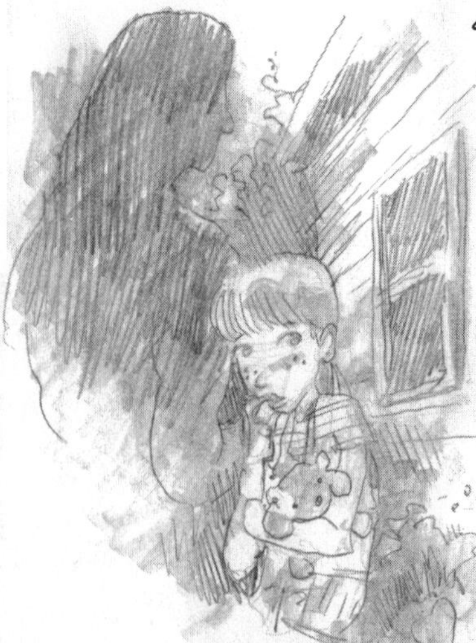

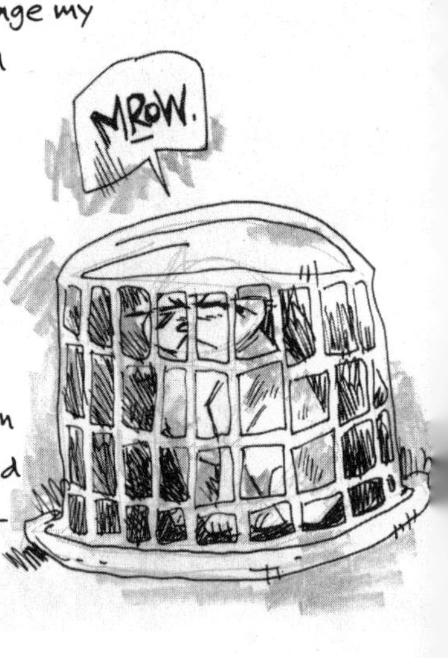
MROW.

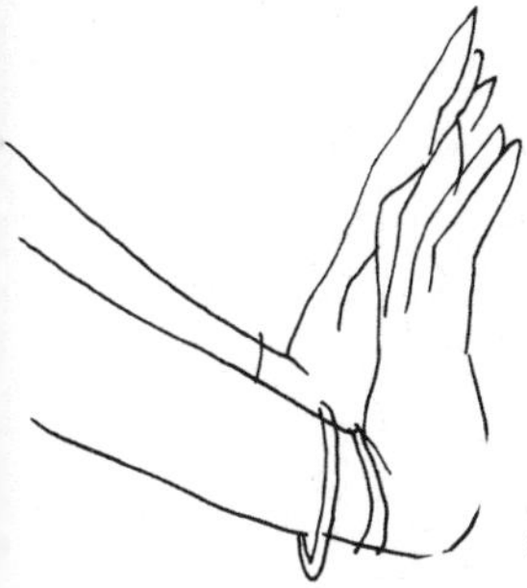

Mom pushed me to go talk to the new neighbor. Literally, she pushed me, right out the door. The first time I went next door I cried—tears of an unbearable shyness and a deep loneliness from leaving my family, crossing that long driveway to the next yard.

After that, Abby and I were inseparable. I would stop by her house after school every day and we'd make up board games, play doctor, and put on terrible awkward plays for the neighborhood. We would gather our parents together and knock on neighbors' doors and find anyone we could who was willing to come see us act out whatever Disney cartoon we'd recently watched. We'd get a dozen or so adults around, then freeze like deer in headlights, talking and walking stiffly, having no actual prepared scripts to work off of. Eventually we'd end up in giggles and the adults would quickly excuse themselves and return to whatever it was they were doing.

I never really had any romantic feelings toward Abby, but I assumed once we'd grown up they would develop. We'd be high school sweethearts and get married. You know, once the hormones kicked in and all.

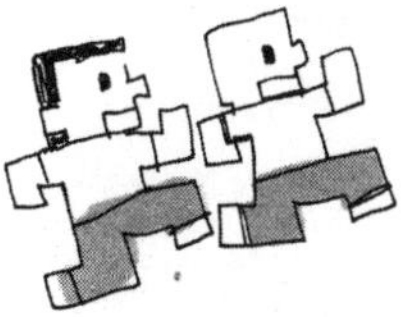

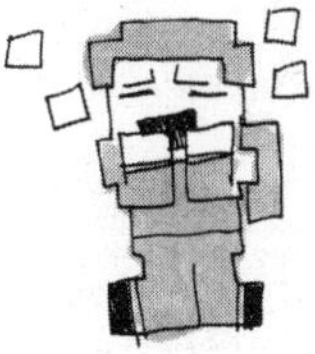

After a few years a new kid moved in across the street, Adam, who would also become my friend (ignited by a strong bond over comic books and video games). Adam was a part of the group but it wasn't long before Abby felt neglected, and Adam and I began to shun her and act like boys.

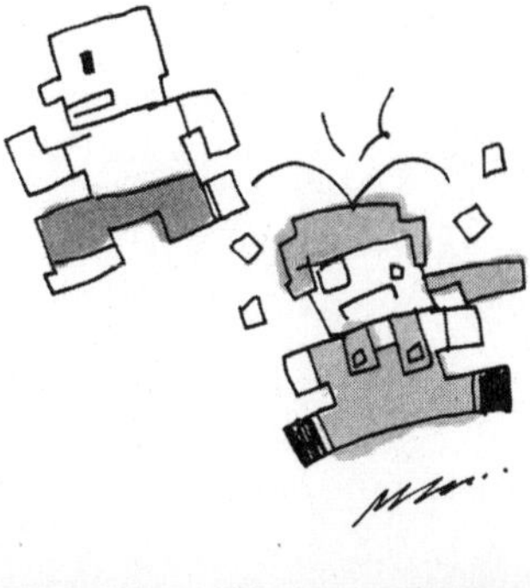

Eventually we stopped seeing her at all. I remember running around with our water pistols on a probably-too-cold-for-water-pistols spring evening when Abby came out and asked me why I wouldn't come over anymore. I guess I thought I was being cool, or that Adam would be impressed, when I drenched Abby with my water gun. We laughed as she slammed the door and her mom came out to yell at me.

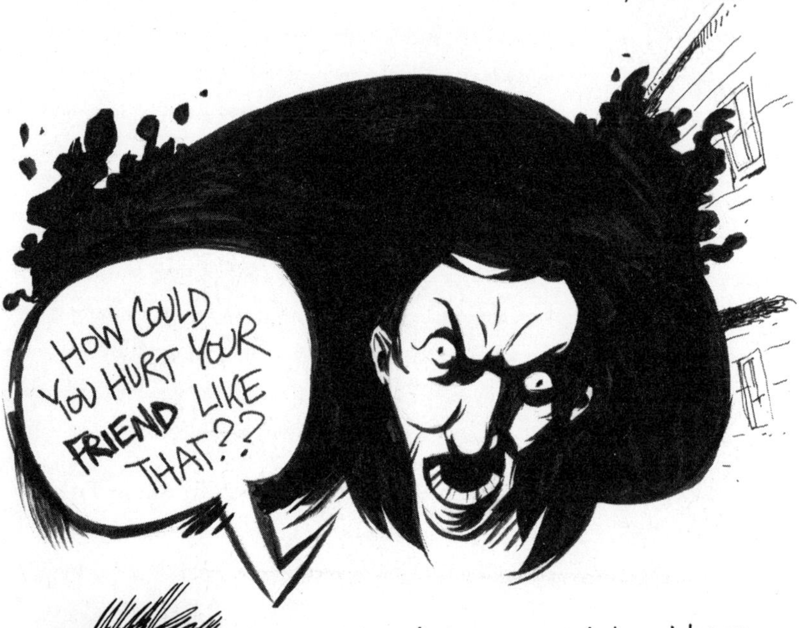
HOW COULD YOU HURT YOUR FRIEND LIKE THAT??

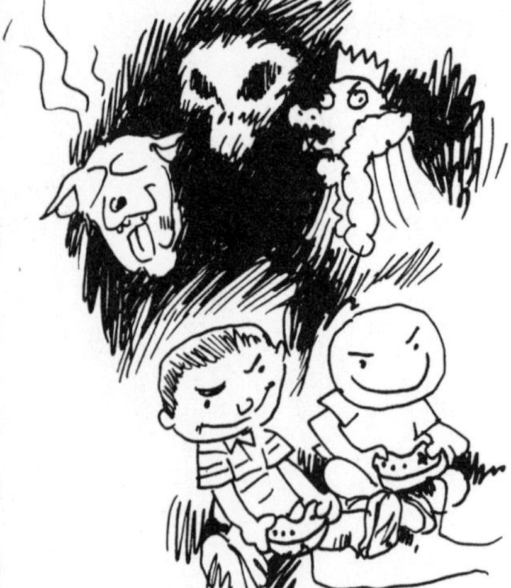

I bawled my eyes out; I went home and cried out a mix of emotions I couldn't grasp at all. Adam and I bonded further over our new enemy and spent the next months leaving gross concoctions of berries, flour, and mud in her mailbox and coming up with awful nicknames for her: Kibbles and Bits, Level Seven Boss Creature, Flabby, Labby, Saggy, Naggy, all the classics.

We eventually grew tired of it and kept to ourselves for the next year or so. On Halloween night, Adam and I were walking the block when we came across Abby and one of her friends.

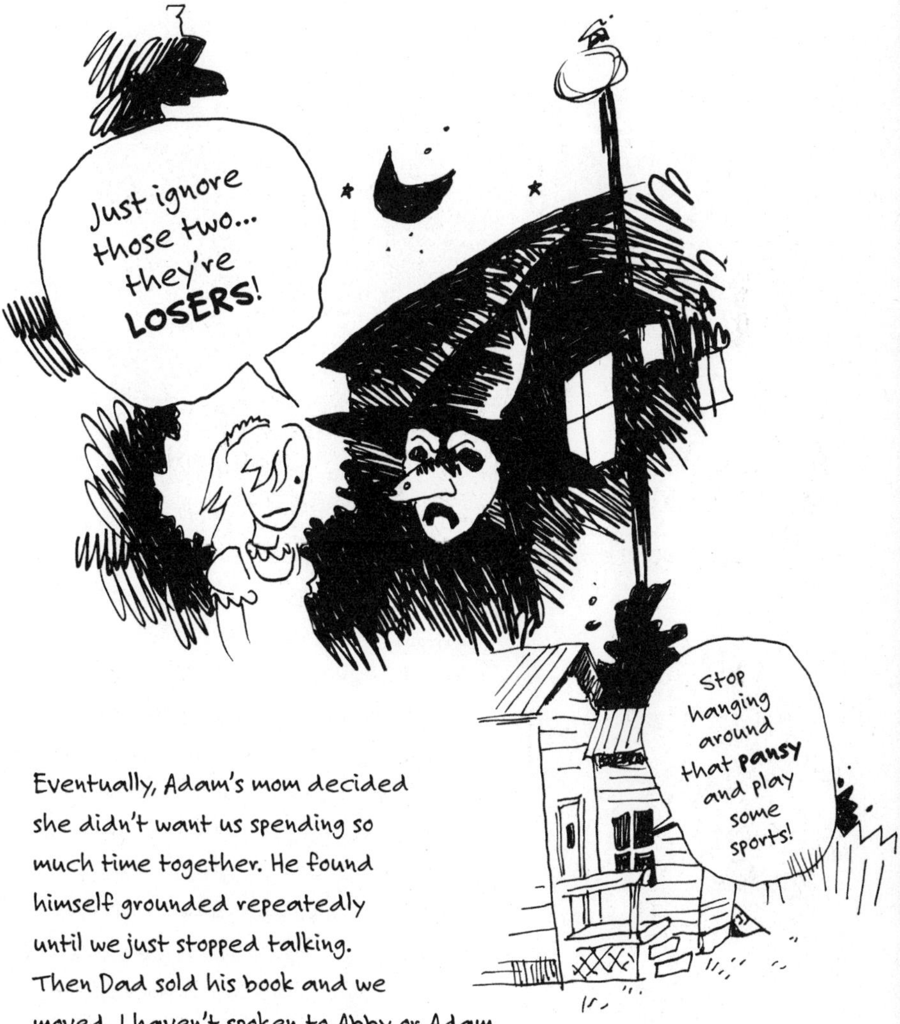
Just ignore those two... they're **LOSERS**!
Stop hanging around that **pansy** and play some sports!

Eventually, Adam's mom decided she didn't want us spending so much time together. He found himself grounded repeatedly until we just stopped talking. Then Dad sold his book and we moved. I haven't spoken to Abby or Adam since. I've only just recently even thought of them.

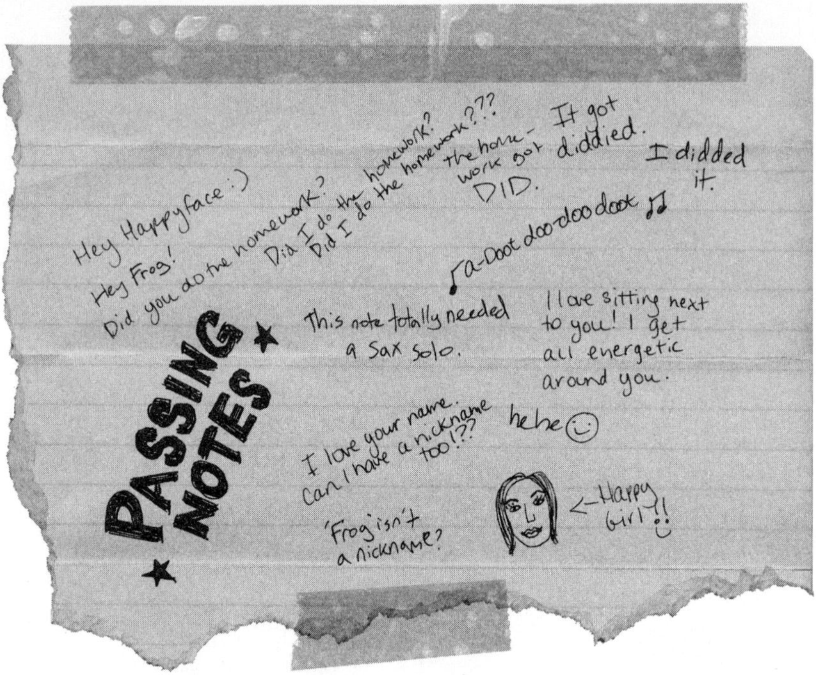
Hey Happyface :)
Hey Frog!
Did you do the homework?
Did I do the homework?
Did I do the homework???
the home- work got DID.
It got diddied.
I didded it.
a-Doot doo doo doo doot
PASSING NOTES
This note totally needed a Sax solo.
I love sitting next to you! I get all energetic around you.
I love your name. Can I have a nickname too!??
hehe
'Frog' isn't a nickname?
Happy Girl!!

10/6

I've been passing notes with Frog, the girl who sits near me in Molly's English class. She's so funny. She writes me these notes and laughs really hard in class when I talk, and she insists on following me to my next class every day. Maybe she thinks I am cool because I am friends with Gretchen or something? The weird part is that I don't even talk to her much in that class. Gretchen's a few seats away from me, and if I didn't know any better, I'd think maybe she was jealous that another girl is giving me attention!

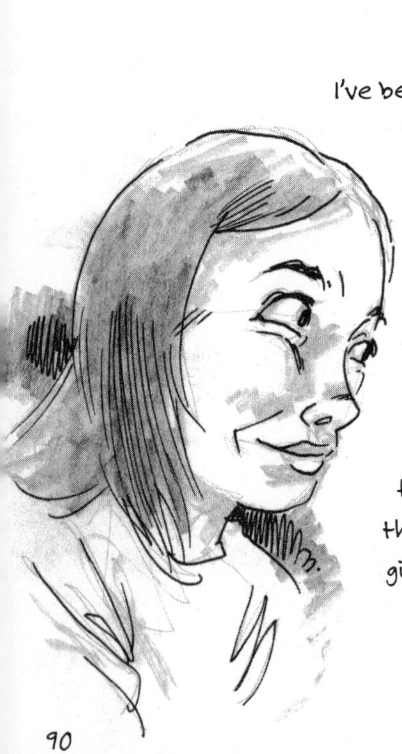

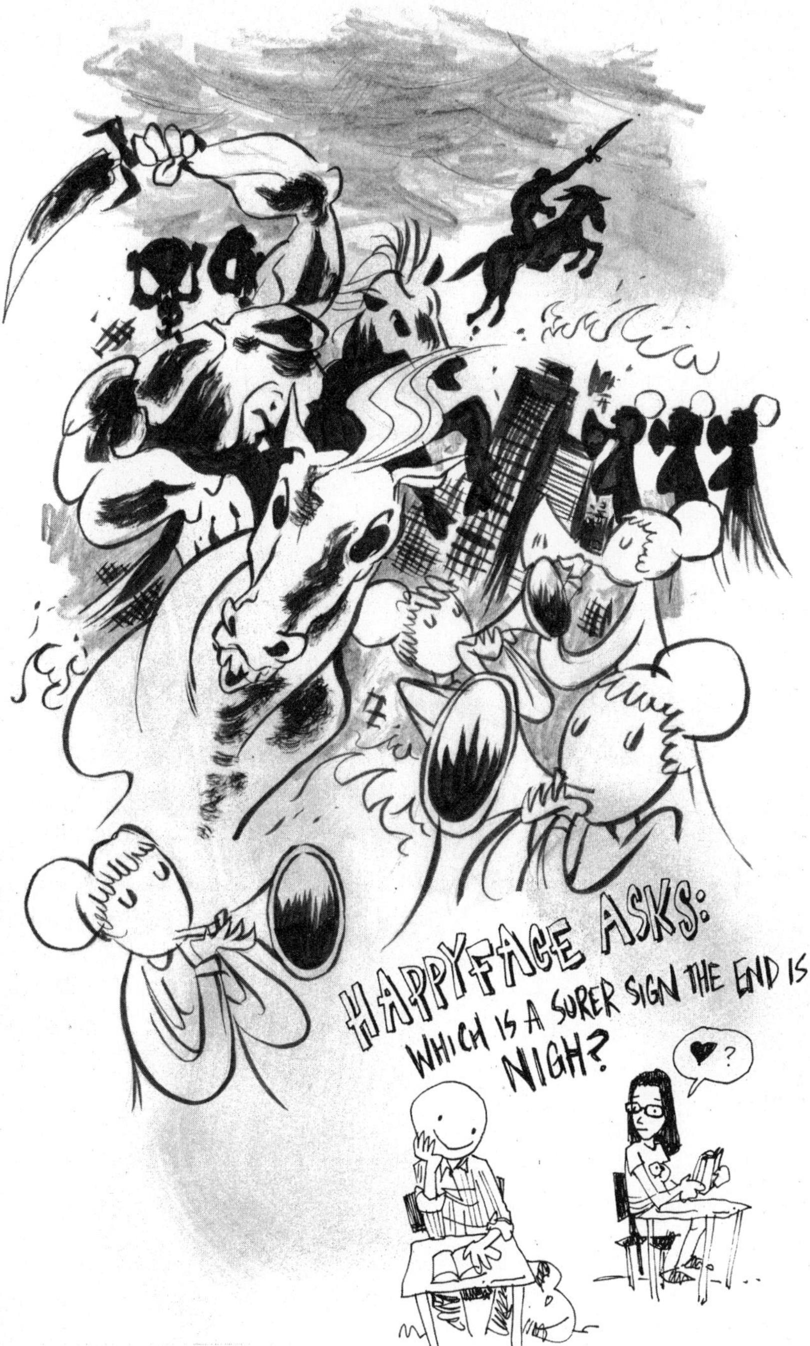
HAPPYFACE ASKS:
WHICH IS A SURER SIGN THE END IS NIGH?
♥ ?

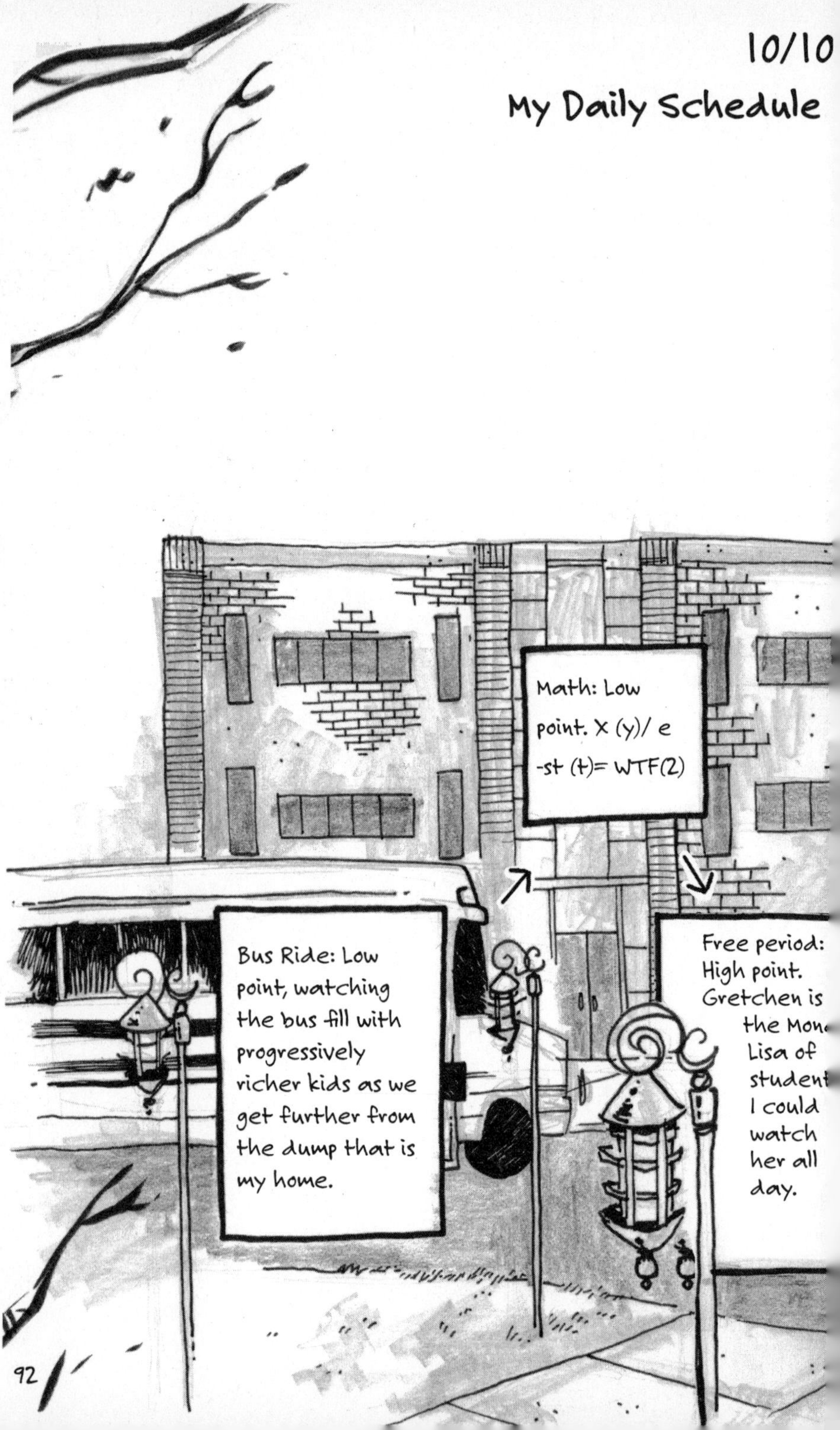
10/10
My Daily Schedule
Math: Low point. X (y)/ e -st (t)= WTF(2)
Bus Ride: Low point, watching the bus fill with progressively richer kids as we get further from the dump that is my home.
Free period: High point. Gretchen is the Mon Lisa of student I could watch her all day.

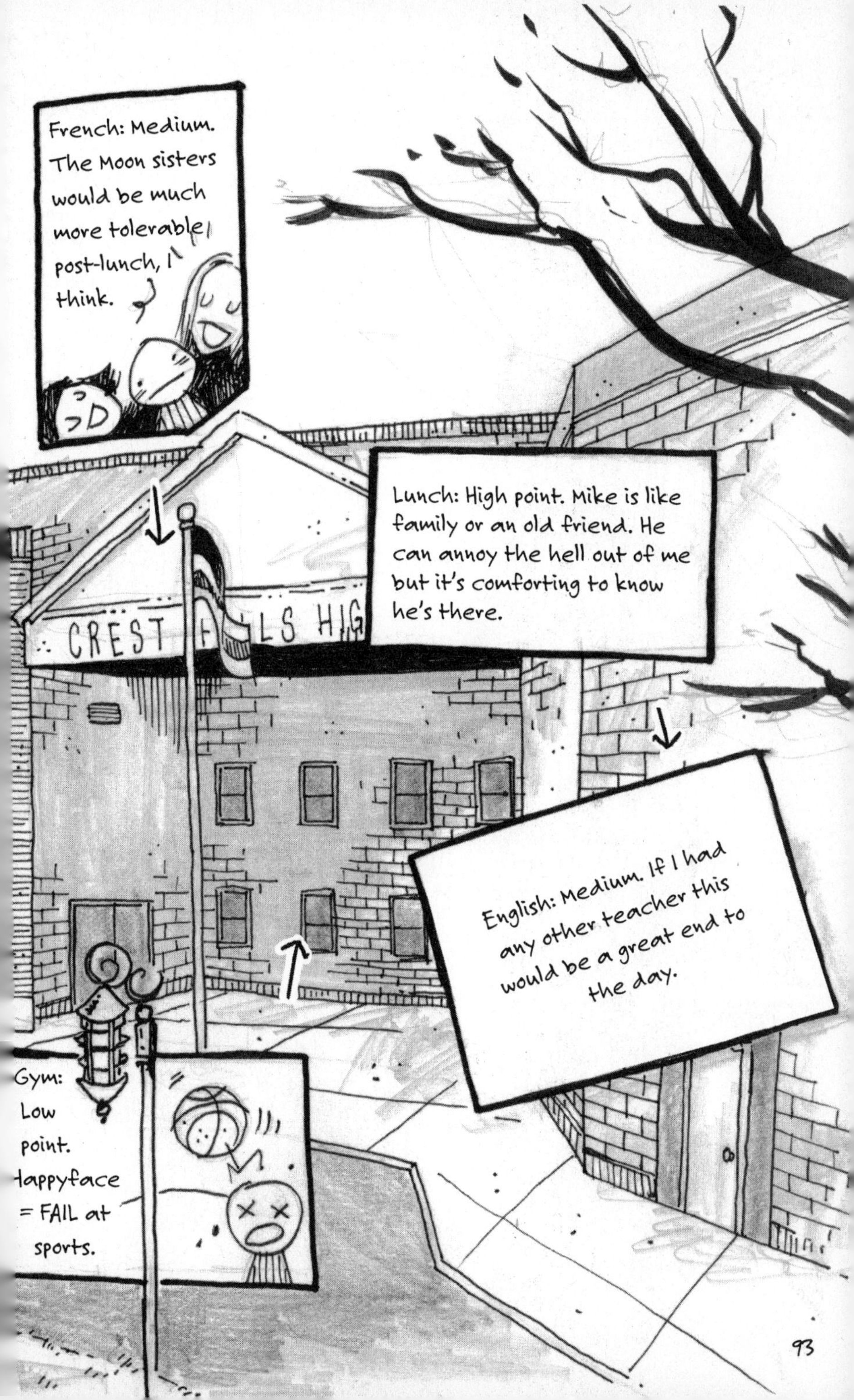
French: Medium. The Moon sisters would be much more tolerable post-lunch, I think.
Lunch: High point. Mike is like family or an old friend. He can annoy the hell out of me but it's comforting to know he's there.
CREST
LS HIG
English: Medium. If I had any other teacher this would be a great end to the day.
Gym: Low point. Happyface = FAIL at sports.

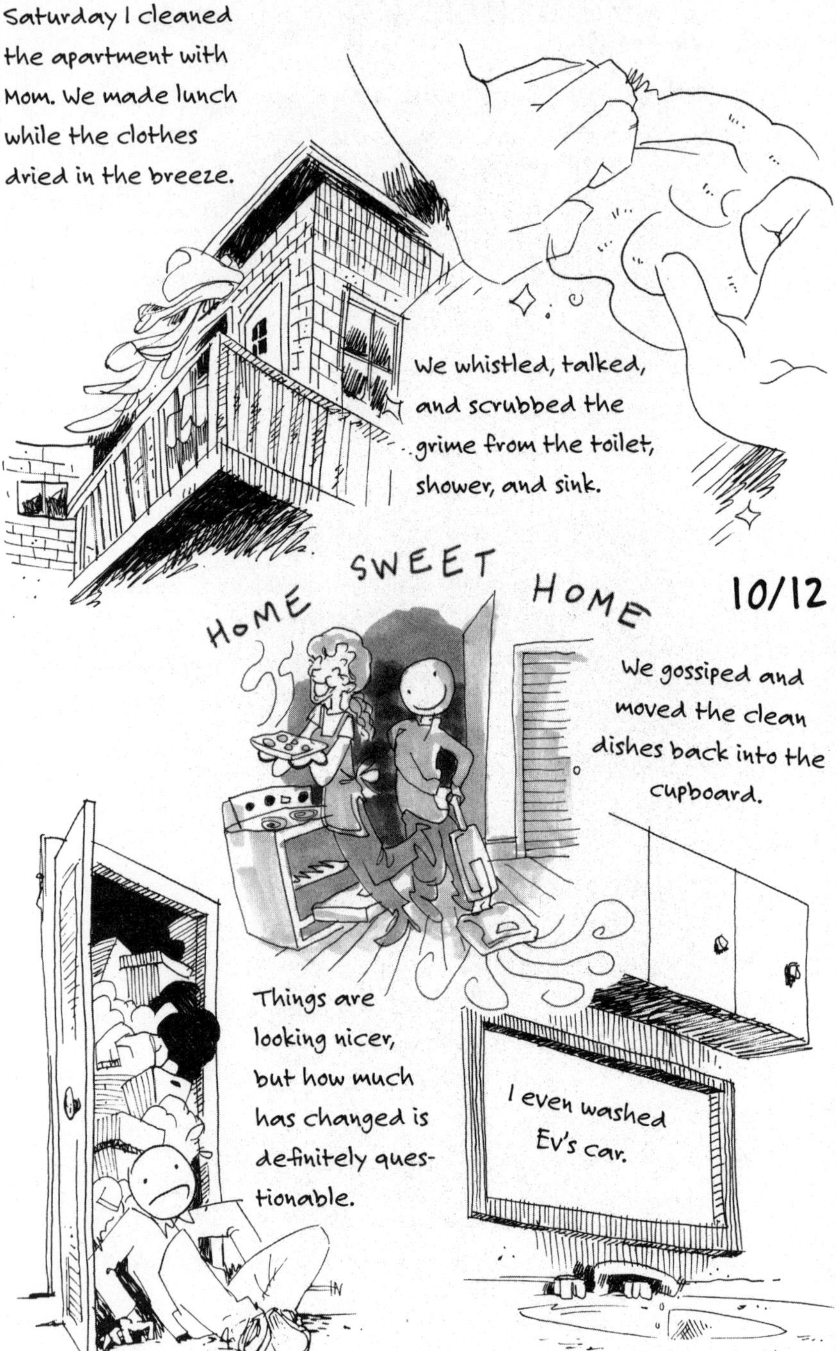
Saturday I cleaned the apartment with Mom. We made lunch while the clothes dried in the breeze.
We whistled, talked, and scrubbed the grime from the toilet, shower, and sink.
HOME SWEET HOME
10/12
We gossiped and moved the clean dishes back into the cupboard.
Things are looking nicer, but how much has changed is definitely questionable.
I even washed Ev's car.

"HAUNTED"

OR: IS A CRAZED MADMAN RELATIVELY SANE?

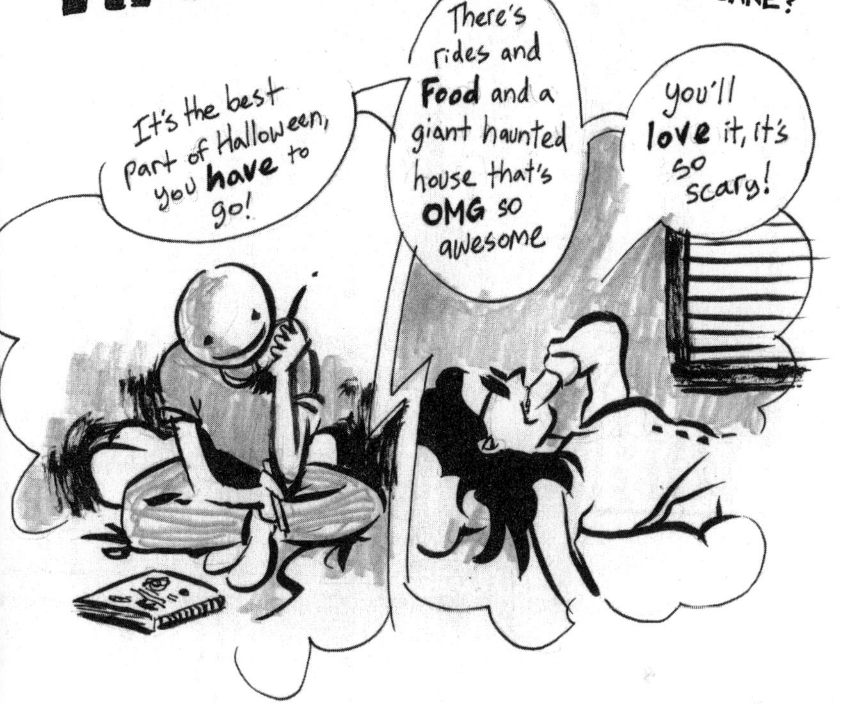
It's the best part of Halloween, you **have** to go!
There's rides and **Food** and a giant haunted house that's **OMG** so awesome
you'll **love** it, it's so scary!

The carnival was like what you see on TV, lights at night and hokey music, lots of teens and cotton candy. We went around six on a school night so it wasn't too busy, but it was cool enough. I was there with Gretchen and the Moons and Trevor and a girl named Jen. Gretchen was in rare form as she dragged us around excitedly like she had an agenda to fill. I thought for sure she'd turn into a pumpkin by midnight.

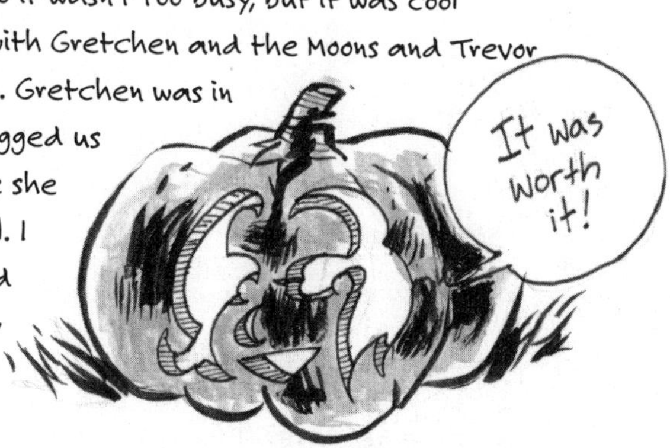
It was worth it!

Gretchen begged for me to go on the Tilt-a-Whirl with her but I just couldn't do it. I tried it once when I was a kid and threw up just as the ride was ending. It went everywhere in a traumatic incident that I think affected who I am to my very core. I sat out with Misty, who has a similar aversion to nausea-inducing rides. Trevor was happy to take my spot, though, and we watched them spin from the grass. When the ride ended, Trevor, Gretchen, and Karma were leaning all over each other and falling over. It was pretty funny. Once they'd gotten that ride out of their systems, everyone was ready to eat.

We got food at one of the stands and the girls had a contest to tie knots in cherry stems with their tongues. I'd never seen anything like it.

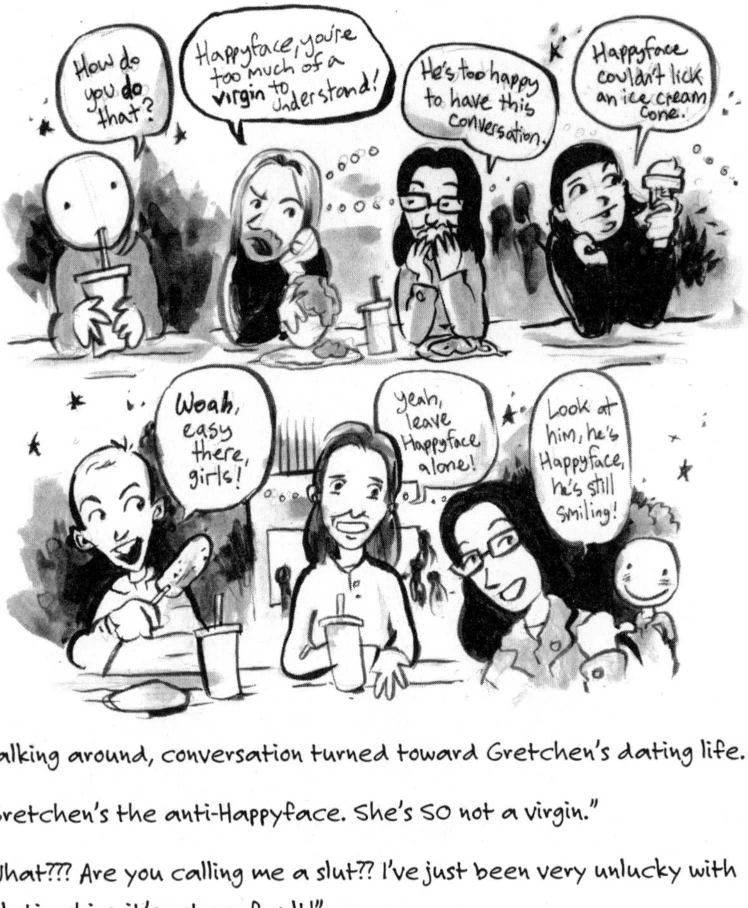
How do you do that?
Happyface, you're too much of a virgin to understand!
He's too happy to have this conversation.
Happyface couldn't lick an ice cream cone.
Woah, easy there, girls!
Yeah, leave Happyface alone!
Look at him, he's Happyface, he's still smiling!

Walking around, conversation turned toward Gretchen's dating life.

"Gretchen's the anti-Happyface. She's SO not a virgin."

"What??? Are you calling me a slut?? I've just been very unlucky with relationships, it's not my fault!"

Names were thrown around to knowing laughs: Tim, Jason, Jack, Dave . . .

Things got progressively uncomfortable as we rode the Ferris wheel. Gretchen sat next to me though she kind of cut the possible romance of it when she told Trevor, "Who else is he going to sit with?"

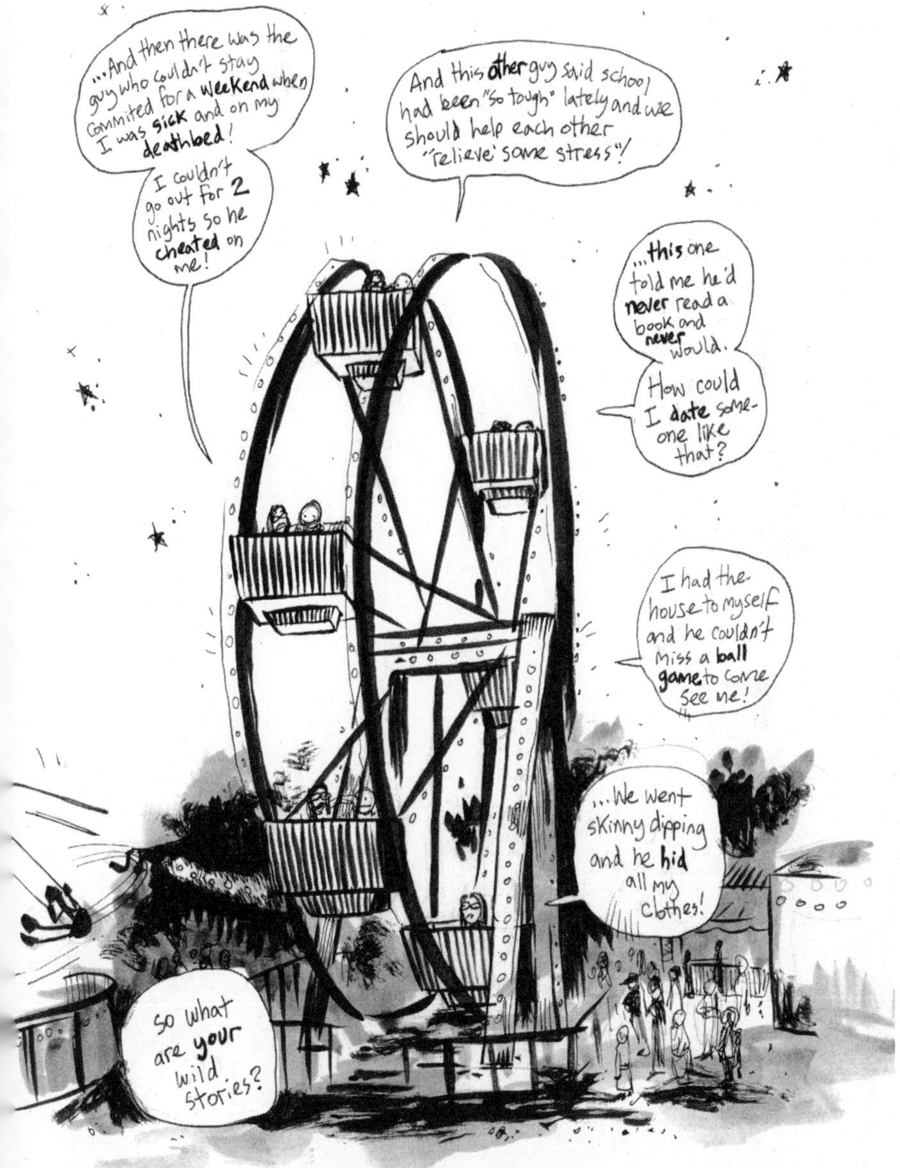

...And then there was the guy who couldn't stay commited for a weekend when I was sick and on my deathbed!
I couldn't go out for 2 nights so he cheated on me!
And this other guy said school had been "so tough" lately and we should help each other "relieve" some stress"!
...this one told me he'd never read a book and never would.
How could I date someone like that?
I had the house to myself and he couldn't miss a ball game to come see me!
...We went skinny dipping and he hid all my clothes!
So what are your wild stories?

Happyface never felt like such a virgin.

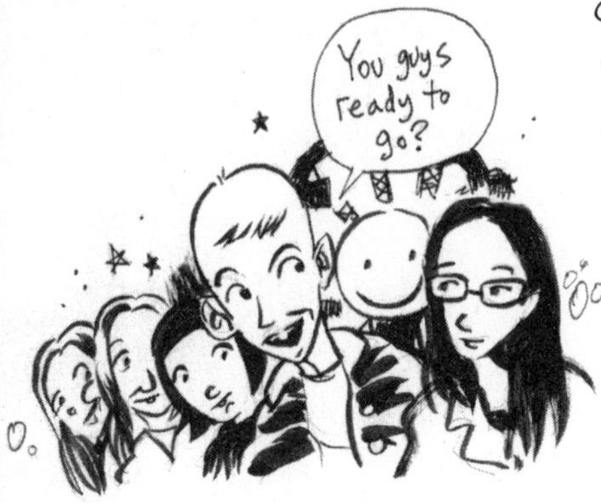
You guys ready to go?

Gretchen was getting more and more manic as the night went on. "I'm not going yet, you guys can go. I haven't even gone in the haunted house yet. That's why we came here!"

"Oh God, not that thing . . ." Trevor rolled his eyes.

"Well, YOU can be a chicken, then," Gretchen said.

"Chicken? It's made for third graders!"

"No way, it's dark and creepy and full of ghosts and crazed madmen and it's AWESOME and it's the best part of Halloween. You guys just go, I don't care."

Gretchen ran off into the haunted house as we stood around like a bomb had just gone off.

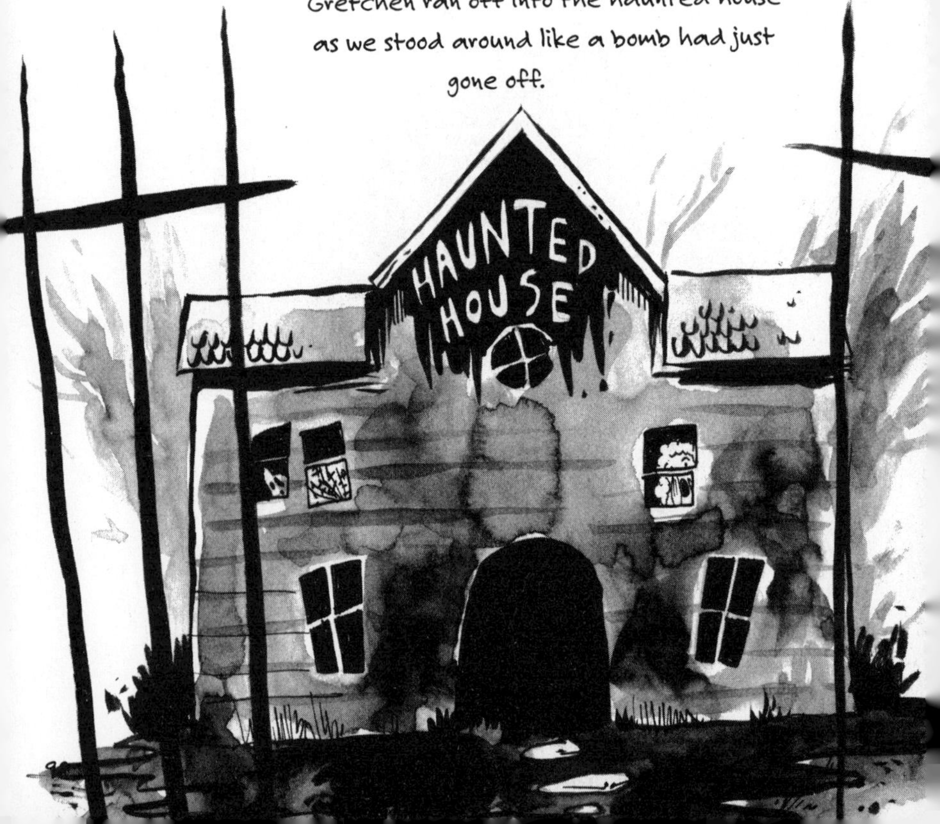
HAUNTED HOUSE

"I'm not going in that stupid thing," Trevor said. "It's principle at this point."

"Don't be a jerk!" Karma said.

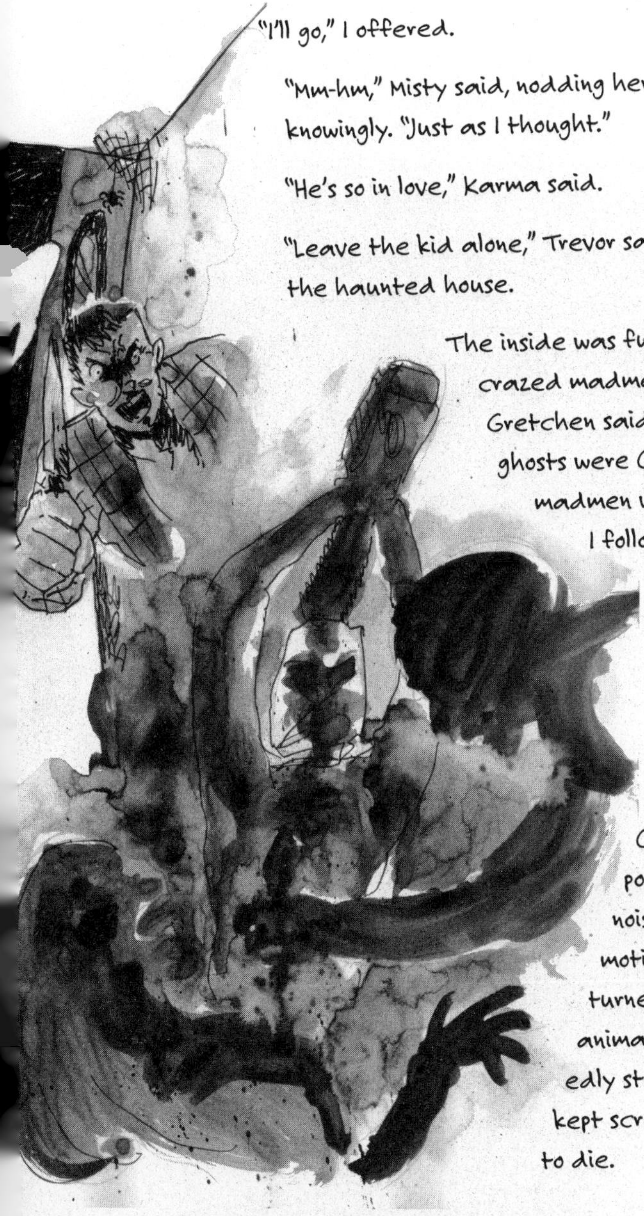

"I'll go," I offered.

"Mm-hm," Misty said, nodding her head knowingly. "Just as I thought."

"He's so in love," Karma said.

"Leave the kid alone," Trevor said as I went into the haunted house.

The inside was full of ghosts and crazed madmen, just like Gretchen said. Except the ghosts were Casper and the madmen were laughable. I followed the green lighting down one corridor to sounds of blowing wind, screams, and goofy cackling.

Chainsaw guy popped out at me, noisy but otherwise motionless. The halls turned red as an animatronic guy repeatedly stabbed a girl who kept screaming and refusing to die.

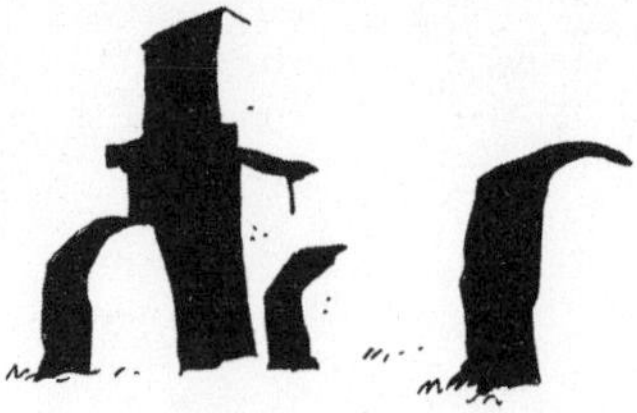

The next room was a graveyard and the lights turned blue. A hand reached out of the ground by one grave and someone was laughing maniacally, echoing through the room. At the end was a gentle sobbing. Gretchen was hiding behind a tombstone.

I sat by Gretchen as she cried. I glanced over at her a few times, but otherwise just looked down at my feet. A hand popped out of the ground and I kicked it. Gretchen laughed a little. I held her hand. It was definitely one of those times. When talking is overrated and it's better to just sit. And feel.

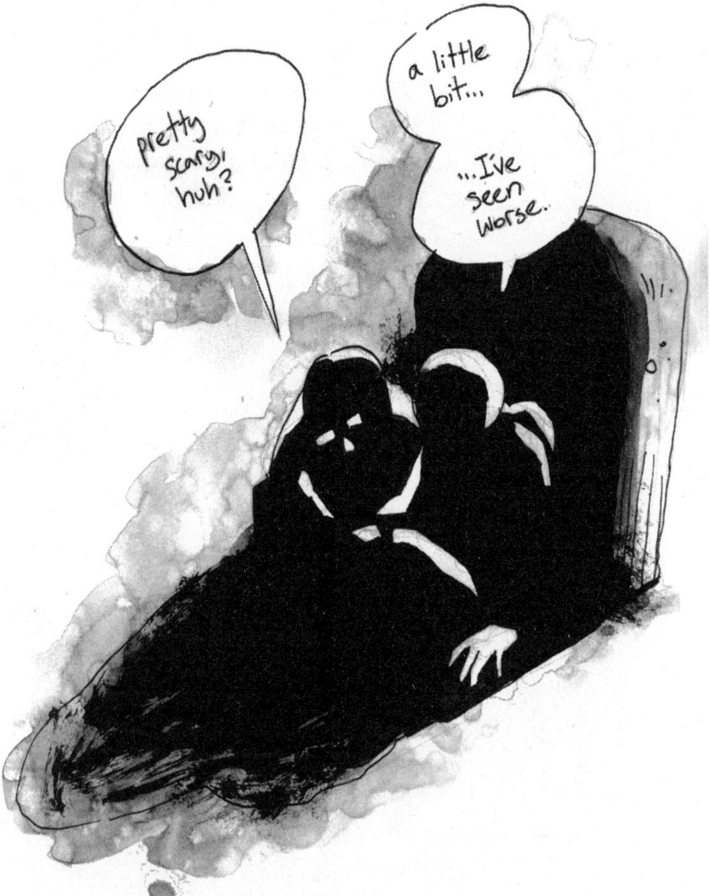
pretty scary, huh?
a little bit...
...I've seen worse.

BASEBALL! 10/22

Mike and I are what you would call "bad at sports." We are perceived as "not at all athletic." We are, as Coach Ford lovingly named us, "a couple o' nancys!" Or rather, we're simply more inclined to participate in the more cerebral arts: the games of the gifted and brilliant.

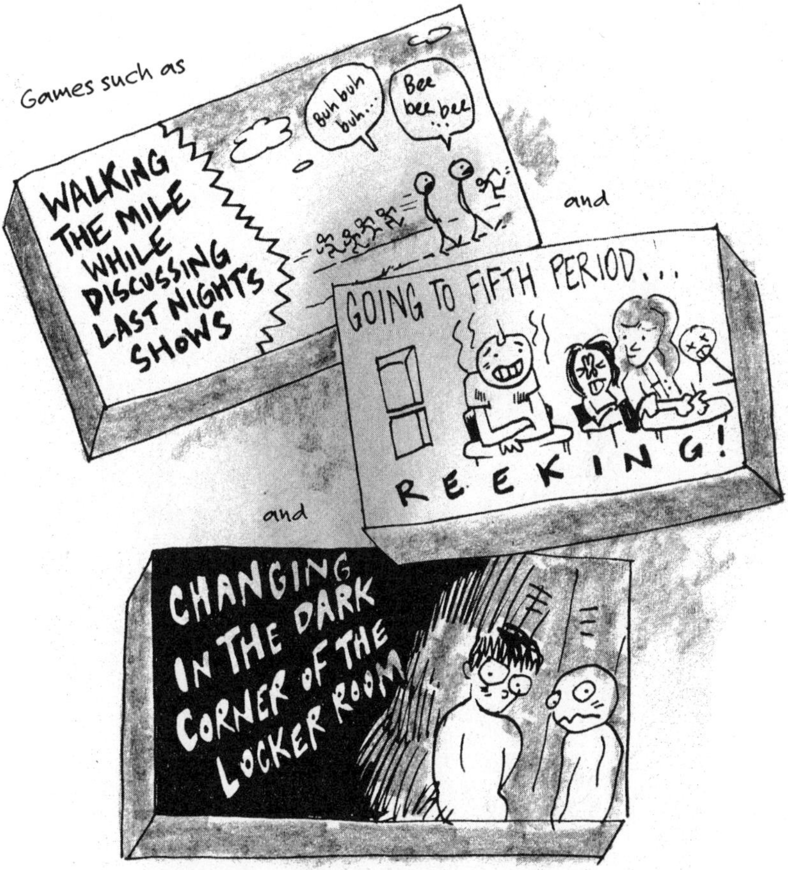

Games such as
WALKING THE MILE WHILE DISCUSSING LAST NIGHT'S SHOWS
Buh buh buh...
Bee bee bee
and
GOING TO FIFTH PERIOD... REEKING!
and
CHANGING IN THE DARK CORNER OF THE LOCKER ROOM

Trevor isn't exactly best buds with Mike and teases him pretty regularly. It kind of breaks my heart to watch.

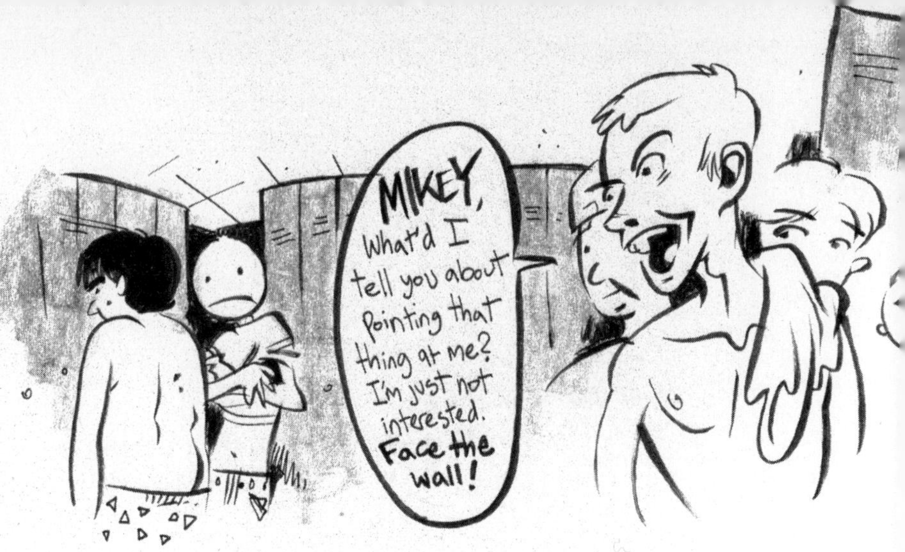
MIKEY, What'd I tell you about pointing that thing at me? I'm just not interested. Face the wall!

I felt bad for Mike. "Those guys are such losers. Why can't they just leave me alone?" he complained. Mike could probably stand to learn a lesson from me that sometimes it's best to just keep quiet:

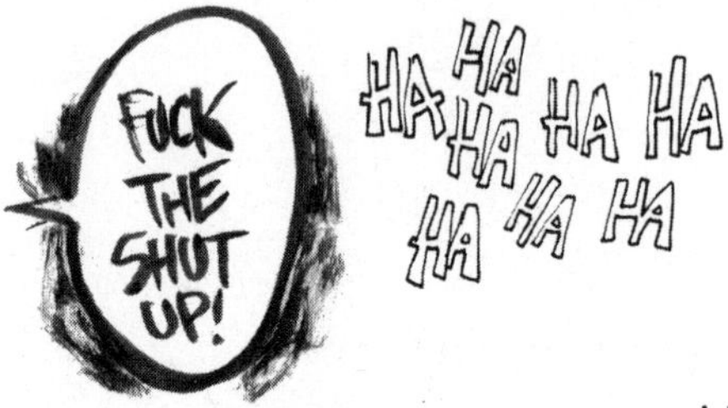
FUCK THE SHUT UP!
HA HA HA HA HA HA HA HA HA

Things were a little better out on the field. We were playing baseball. If I was the artist of the family, then Everett was the athlete. Sometimes I don't get how we came from the same genes. Standing on the field, holding that bat, though, I feel powerful. It would feel so good to hit that ball, God, I wish I could hit it. I wish I could swing and crack the bat in half and send that orb into orbit—here one second and gone the next. The other team would all suffer stiff necks from trying to find it, hovering up there in the sky.

But I always miss.

It hurts, too, swinging and missing. That energy, that stored up energy, it goes nowhere, it shoots down my arms and through the bat and right back into me with a shock, my arms stinging, numb and sore, my muscles twist like a pretzel.

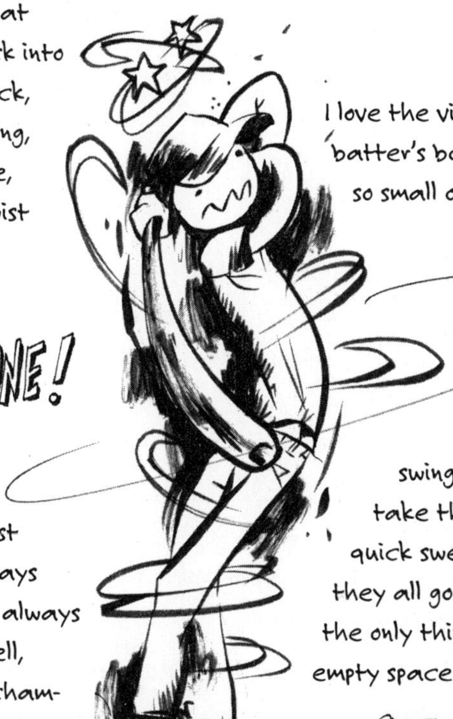

STRIKE ONE!

That's the worst part—they always know I'll swing, I always swing. I swing well, though, like a champion fighter, like I'm beat and blind but I know if I could just connect, it'll be something, it'll really be something. But it's a miss, again.

STRIKE TWO!

I love the view from the batter's box. Everyone looks so small out there on the bases, out on the field. From where I'm standing, I could swing that bat and take them all out, one quick sweep, and away they all go! But I swing and the only thing I clobber is empty space and air.

STRIKE THREE, YOU'RE OUT!!

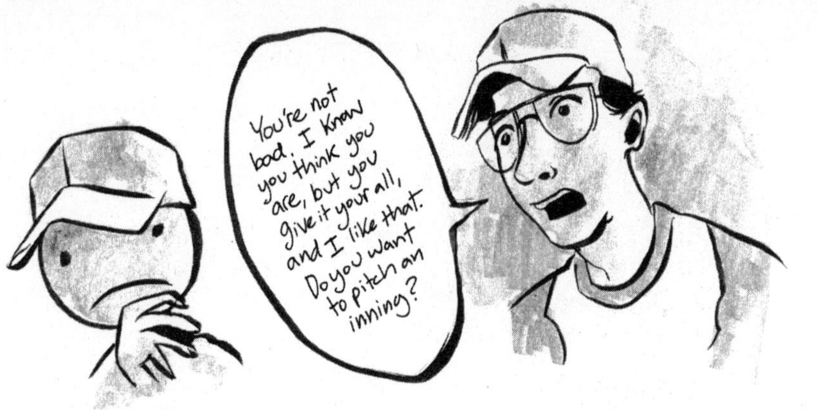
You're not bad. I know you think you are, but you give it your all, and I like that. Do you want to pitch an inning?

I didn't really, but these days I get the best reactions not being myself anyway.

I walked out into the middle of it all as the game started back up. It's a weird thing, being out there on the pitcher's mound. I've got my team behind me and the opposing team in front of me, and I'm in the center of everything. For a few seconds all eyes are on me. It's a little unsettling.

I wondered what Dad would think. I was never interested in sports like Everett was. Maybe he'd be proud for the ten seconds or so before I threw the ball like a girl. Maybe it's best that he's not around. Now there's no one to disappoint.

Mike was at bat first. I had to give him this hit. I pitched right to him, and he missed. And then he missed again. I tried once more and he hit the ball. That's about all you could say, was "he hit the ball," but that's something for Mike! It'd be something for me, too. The rest of the team had him out pretty quick.

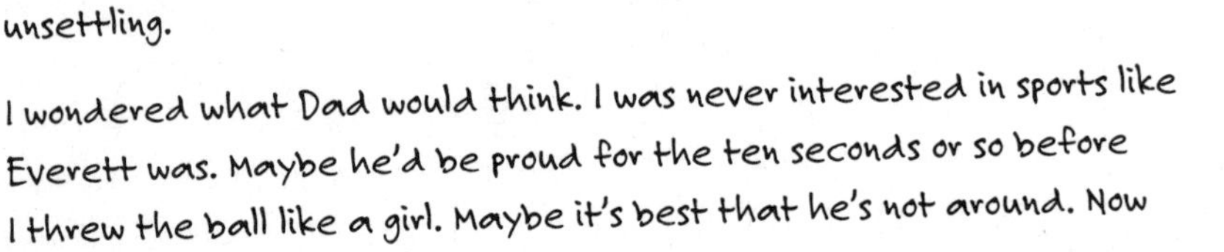
FORGOT TO DROP HIS BAT!

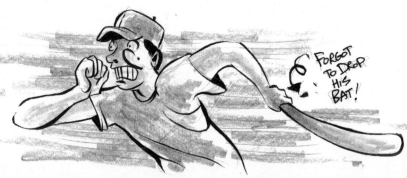

Now I was ready to get serious.

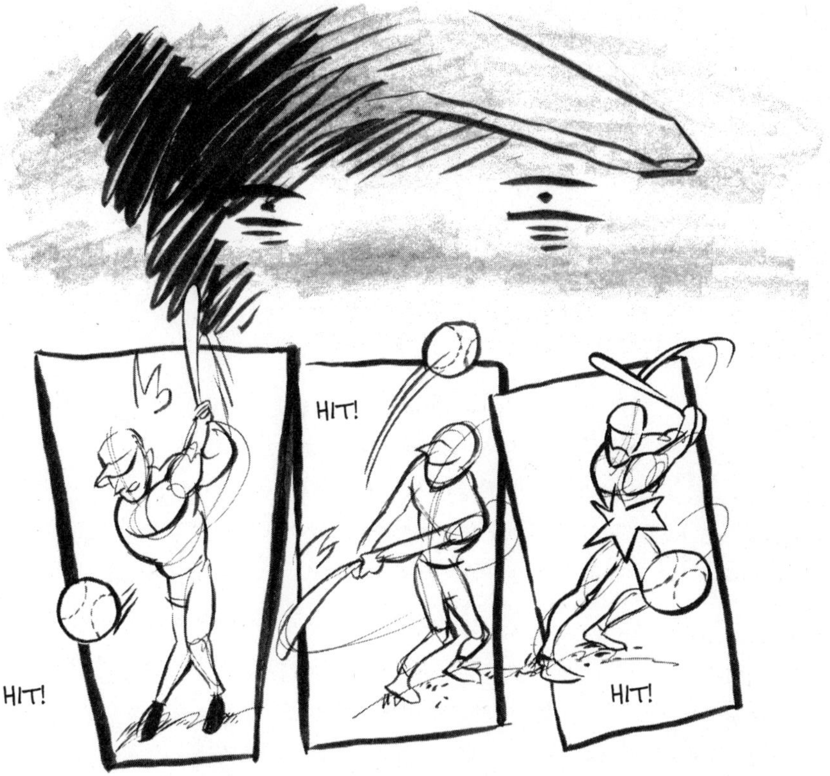
HIT!
HIT!
HIT!

I could say with no uncertainty that at least half the guys playing baseball that fourth period would vote me as permanent pitcher. If only they were on my team.

No, seriously, I sucked.

Trevor was up next and I threw a strike, the first I'd gotten since Mike was up!

"Whoa, I wasn't paying attention! Do over!" Everyone laughed.

But I was focused, I was intense. The energy wasn't going nowhere this time. I threw the ball again and it whizzed right past Trevor into the catcher's mitt. Strike two!

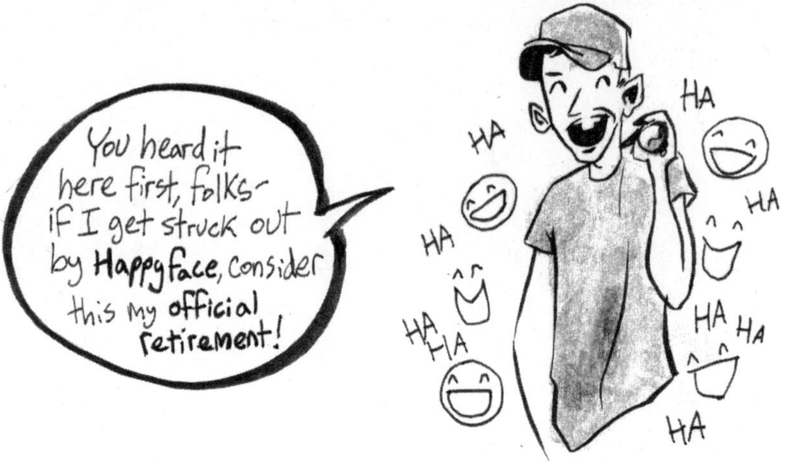
You heard it here first, folks- if I get struck out by Happyface, consider this my official retirement!
HA
HA
HA
HA
HA HA
HA HA
HA
HA

But he didn't retire and I didn't strike him out. He looked nervous and I was nervous and I looked him right in the eye. I was intimidating, I was good, real good. I was like a pro, real slow, winding up. I released the ball and let it fly, so fast and straight like a dart, it hovered over the grass, and it hit Trevor—it hit him right in the arm and he screamed.

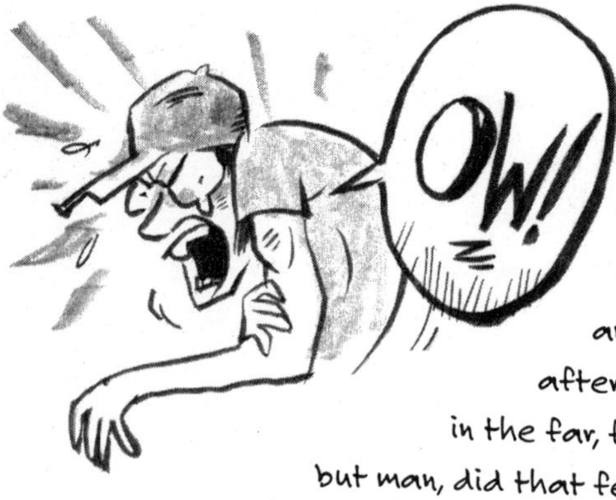
OW!

I thought he was going to pummel me, he turned so red. But he didn't because the bases were loaded and he just got a walk. I gave Team Opposition another point, and quite a few after that, as I secured my place in the far, far outfield. I really sucked, but man, did that feel great. Today I walked to lunch reeking of sweat with my head held high.

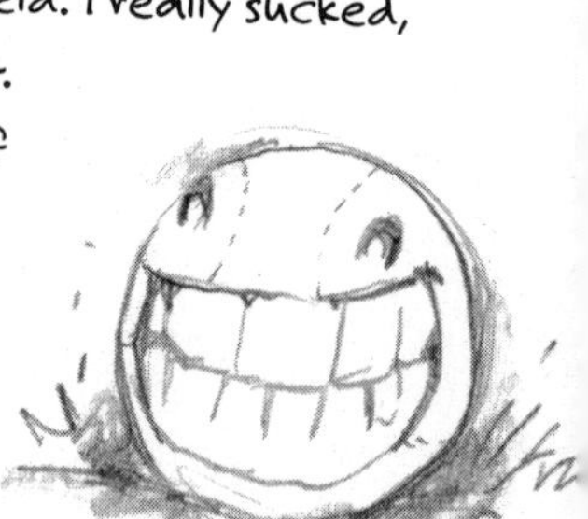

AT THE MOVIES

10/24

Two thumbs down. I was supposed to go to the movies with Gretchen tonight when you-know-who showed up again. It's starting to feel like Gretchen, Trevor, and I are a tricycle, and I'm the third wheel. I was looking forward to seeing Gretchen alone outside of school but today's excuse was some family argument, and Trevor had to get out of the house.

It's not that he's a horrible guy or anything. I mean, he can be funny at times, and he doesn't go out of his way to be mean to me, but he's not the kind of person I'd choose to be around. Gretchen, the Moons, those are people I wouldn't expect to hang out with because once upon a time I just wasn't accepted by girls like that. But Trevor is kind of a bully, and he's someone I wouldn't generally befriend myself.

He was the driver. Gretchen was in the passenger seat so he wasn't alone driving. I might as well be bound and gagged in the trunk. They have history, too. They talked about old friends, kids from middle school and what happened to them, old parties. Then they talked about his family, or hers, or even deeper stuff like religion, and I chipped in with "heh," "ha," or more often, "huh?" And I watched as he put his hand on her leg whenever he told her something. Very subtle.

We went to the movie tonight, and Trevor and Gretchen split the popcorn. I wasn't about to share popcorn with Trevor so they had that, which means they had to sit together. And because Gretchen likes to sit by the aisle, I ended up sitting between Trevor and some hippo who had the inability to realize not every movie is a comedy! The theater felt packed, but maybe it just wasn't big enough for the two of us.

OH HAI, ITZ HAPPYFACE: THE WEBCOMIC-IN-PRINT THIRD-WHEEL EDITION

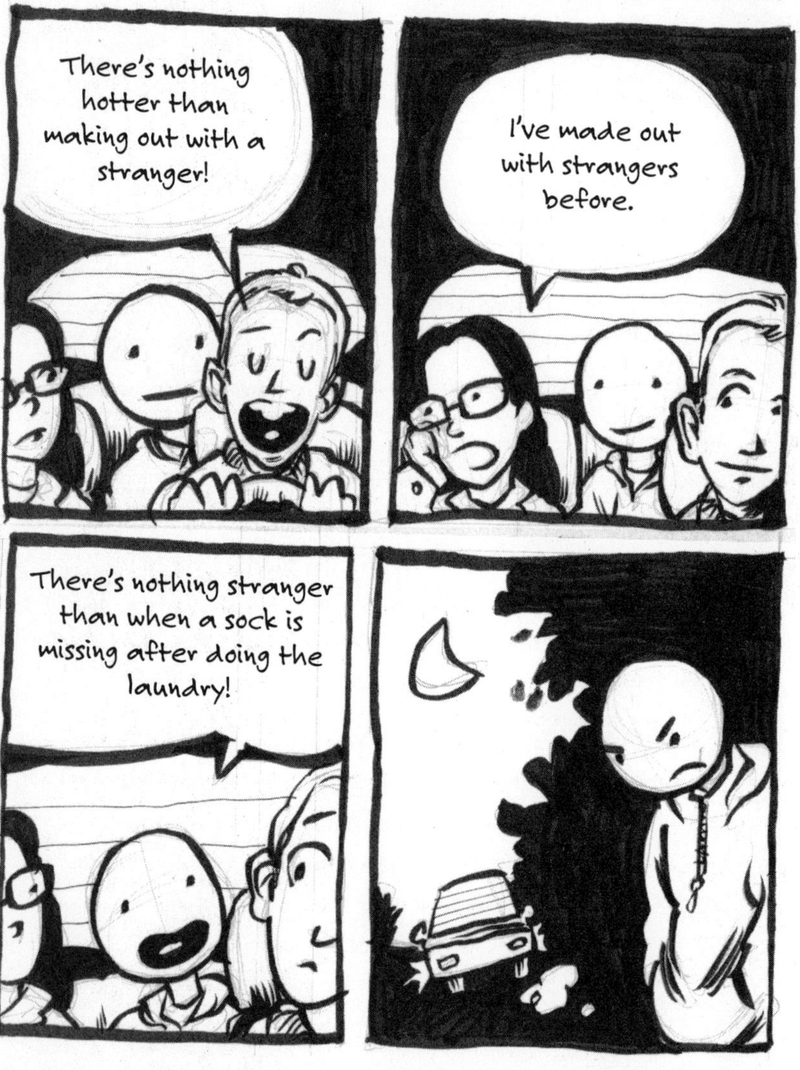
There's nothing hotter than making out with a stranger!
I've made out with strangers before.
There's nothing stranger than when a sock is missing after doing the laundry!

Idea for a movie: THIRD WHEEL

He's always been the third wheel—his friends are all coupled off, he's the youngest of three with two older brothers that were best friends. One day, it all changes when he meets the right girl. For once, he has someone's undivided attention. Until, that is, she tells him she's in a relationship. But she'd like to keep seeing him! Against his better judgment, he plays third wheel to her relationship.

When she meets his two buddies, sparks fly between her and his guy friend, and they begin to see each other.

Tired of it all, he runs to the wilderness, away from everyone. Away from civilization, away from society. Of course, he needs food and water foremost. Then he needs warmth and a place to sleep. In fact, he has to put his feelings a distant third.

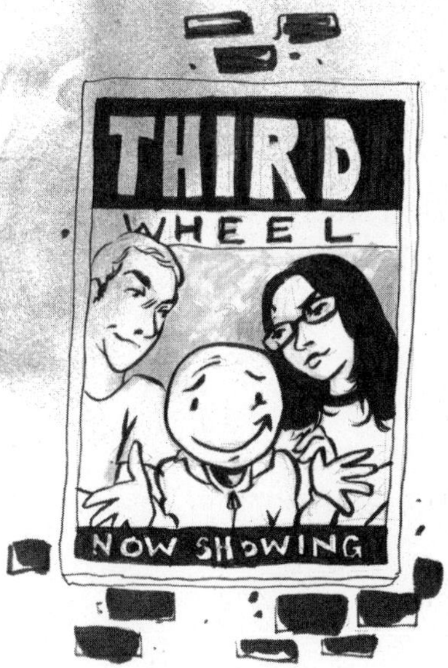
THIRD
WHEEL
NOW SHOWING

Weeks later, he goes back home. Here, life has fallen apart for all of his friends and the girl he loved. They need their third wheel to keep things going. Having no self-respect, he takes the girl back and they ride off into the sunset, on a two-wheeled bicycle.

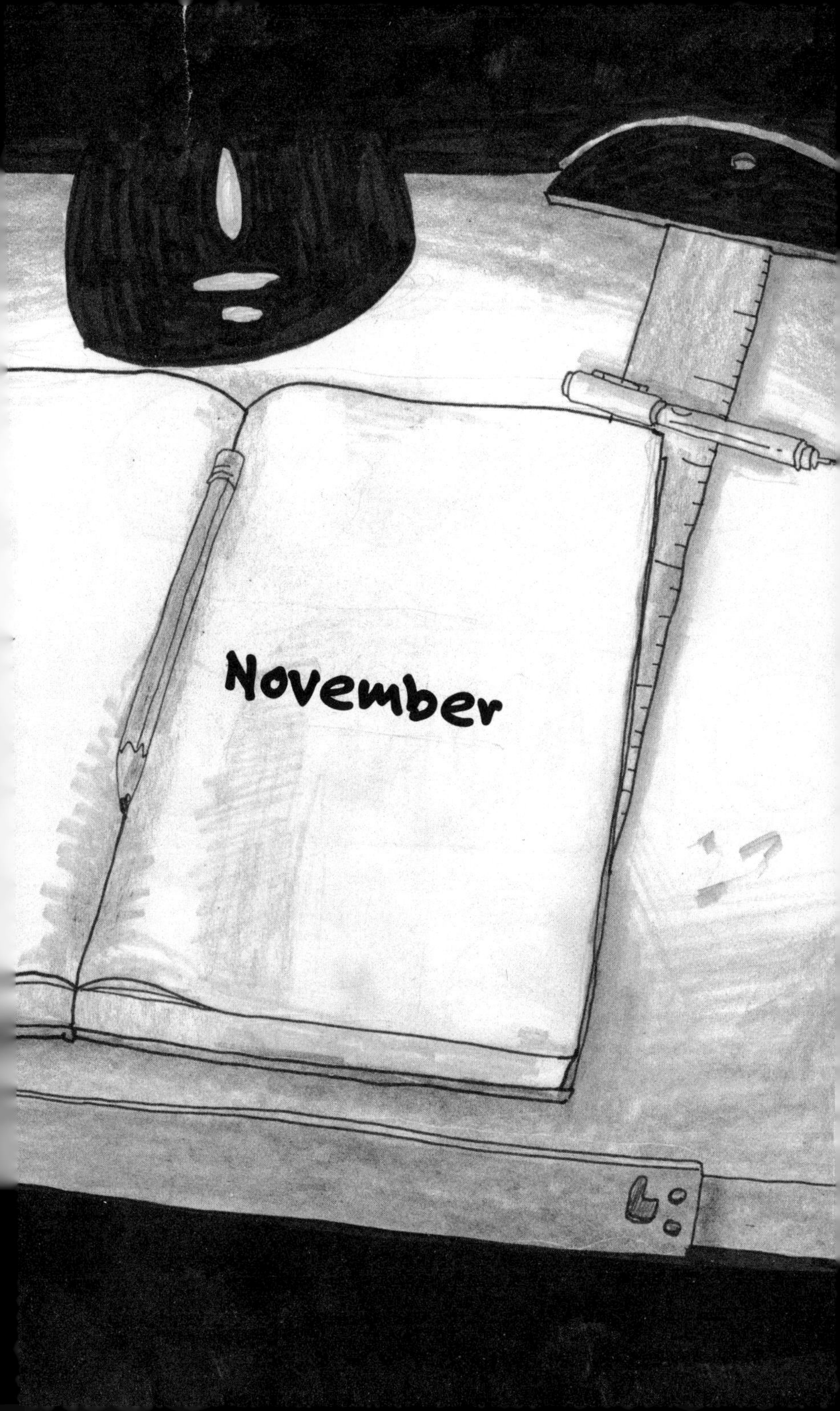
November

WHERE IN THE WORLD IS DAD?

It's been over two months now and I haven't even heard from Dad. I figured I'd get a call or visit or something, but I've left a ton of voicemails and he hasn't even responded to them. The phone doesn't even ring before going to some automated message. It's like he never existed at all. Like he got a call in the middle of the night and was told it's time to leave your cover family and resume your life as a secret agent.

I like to assume he's doing something interesting at least, even if he isn't a 007. Mom says, "He's home, he's living life, he's working, he'll call," but I find these circumstances more believable:

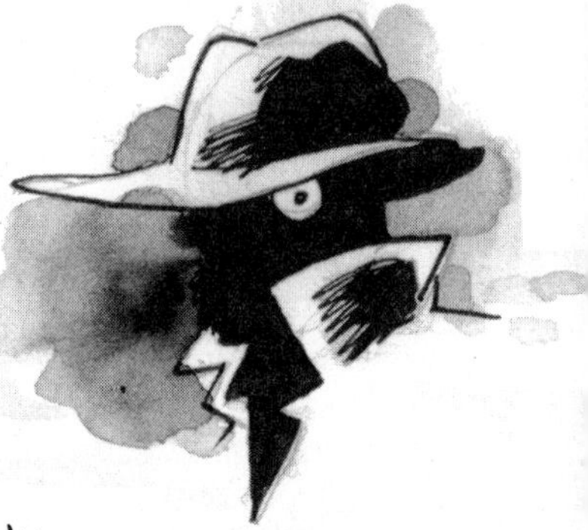

1. Witness Protection.

The whole separation or divorce or whatever they're doing is a diversion. Really, Dad witnessed some Mafioso stuff, some high-level official gets gunned down point-blank over seedy underground deals, putting Dad on the run. Of course crime guys that deep take note of details, so Dad has to change his number, get plastic surgery, and start anew in Mississippi for a few years. He can't keep in touch with us, and Mom can't tell me where he is because it could blow his cover and endanger us all.

2. The Great American Novel

Dad is using everything that happened as a chance to escape into the woods and write it all out, one of those epic tomes that delve into the human condition and never resurface, like he always wanted to write. Of course I'd be in it, and Mom and Everett, and the next time I see him will be on Oprah.

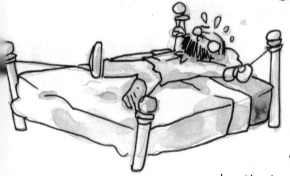

3. <u>Misery</u>

So maybe Dad started dating some young girl. Mom tells him, "You go be with her, then! We're leaving!" Mom doesn't want to talk to him ever again so she just tells me, "He's fine, he's home, he's working," but he'd still talk to me, so the "young girl" must have turned out to be some psycho fan of his books and she's kidnapped him and tied him up in some cabin somewhere. "Write me into your stories," she'd demand as she breaks his legs. Of course she'd take his phone and turn it off so she wouldn't be found out.

Or maybe he's just down south where it's warm now, finally rid of the wife and kids and enjoying life. It's still more interesting than Mom's version.

11/3

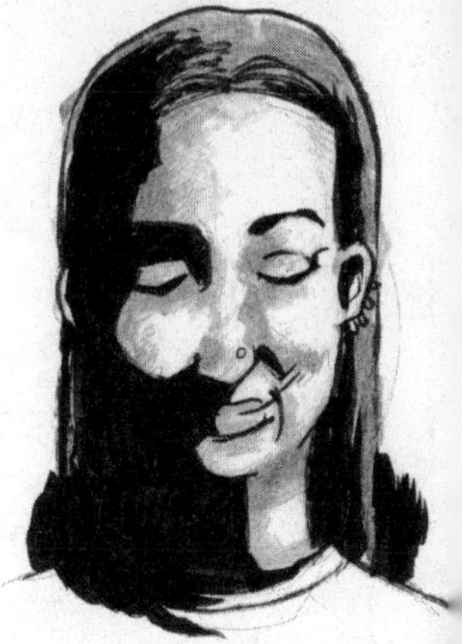

Today I became a deity as my popularity soared to never-before-seen heights. Yes, the legion of Happyface followers now contains two whole members! The following is transcribed as close to reality as memory allows, for the sheer awesomeness of Yours Truly:

MEETING ODDLY

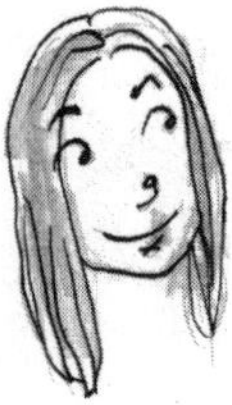

Frog: Happyface, this is my friend Oddly! She keeps asking me to introduce her to you.

Me: "Oddly"? Doesn't anyone have a normal name around here?

Frog: You've made nicknames cool.

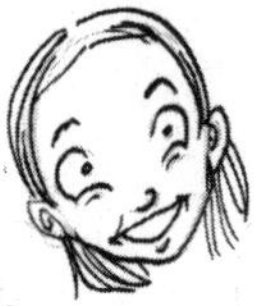

Oddly: It's Audrey. And Oddly was an insult, but it's one I kind of liked, thus, it stuck.

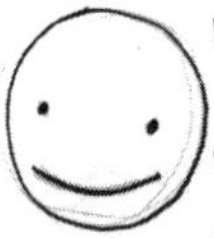

Me: And you wanted to meet me?

Oddly (giggling): Well, yeah, because Frog always talks about you and you seemed really cool and I think we have a lot in common, sooo—

Me: Cool, cool. *nodding my head slow, I've seen this on TV*

Oddly: So yeah, anyway, it's nice to meet you. . . .

Me: Yeah, definitely, very cool, I'm sure I'll see you around.

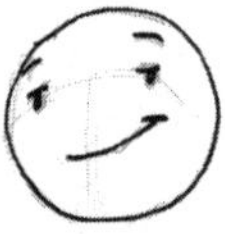

Yes, I was the cool guy. The big shot. The one girls geek out to. It was me. Happyface. Deity.

VENTING 11/4

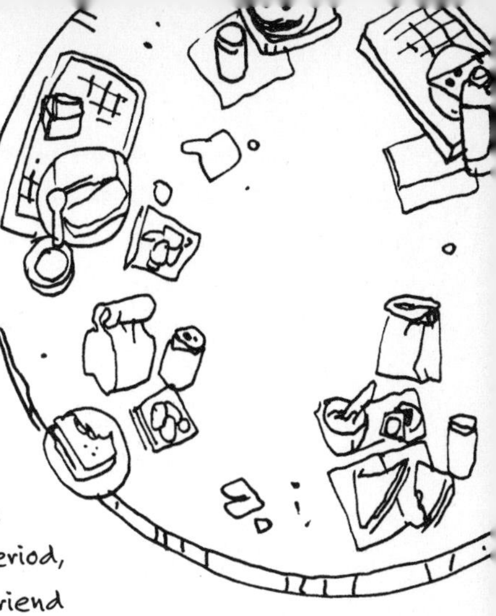

So this is the thing about Mike: He just doesn't realize what a loser he is. I mean, at least I realized that I was a loser before I became The Deity. He's so content with it that it drives me nuts.

I sit with Mike at lunch every day. Then the Moons found out I had lunch that period, and Karma and Misty joined us. Their friend Jessica joined as well, and then her friend Sharif. Mike and I started a loser table that has turned into the cool table. Mike's only there because he was in at the beginning. This table has quickly outgrown him. They talk about cool things, like parties and sex. They wear sunglasses indoors, mid-fall on cloudy days. They're the real deal.

I like Mike, I'm glad he's there, but he doesn't understand the situation at all. For instance:

THE TOP 3 STUPID THINGS MIKE HAS SAID THIS WEEK:

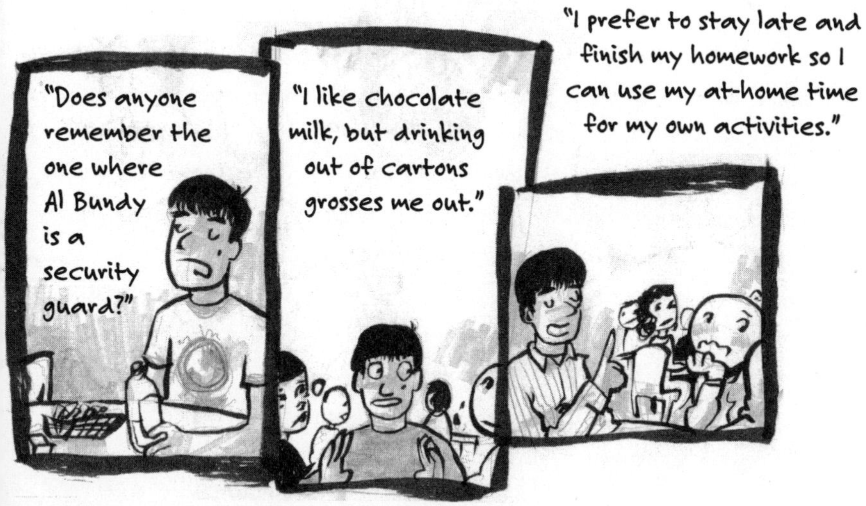
"Does anyone remember the one where Al Bundy is a security guard?"
"I like chocolate milk, but drinking out of cartons grosses me out."
"I prefer to stay late and finish my homework so I can use my at-home time for my own activities."

Sure they laugh and listen but they can't seriously be interested in that stuff. And that last one led to twenty minutes of masturbation jokes and Mike wouldn't even join in on those.

The frustrating part is that he doesn't get it. We sit with the cool kids now, he can be cool sitting here, he has an opportunity to include himself in their world and change his life around because certainly no one's coming over to his house to download obscure music with him. He can't be THAT content watching ABC Family and playing video games every night. People need more than that. He should need more than that.

I did my homework but the paper kept slipping out of my hands.

11/5 ALONE TIME

Gretchen and I were walking through the really tall grass behind school around nine this morning. We met in the hall after first period and started talking and Gretchen asked if I felt like skipping. For a minute I thought I had my proof that Gretchen saw me as a seven-year-old girl before I realized she meant skipping class. So there we were, en route to Gretchen's house when everyone else was heading to second period. I was nervous heading over there knowing no one else would be home. I could see it clearly, candlelight, soft music, me passed out on the floor because I forgot how to breathe. She likes to cut class sometimes; she says it's the only time she gets to be alone.

"My parents are so uptight," she said. "They don't even let me close my bedroom door." I probably wouldn't either, with what I've learned about Gretchen.

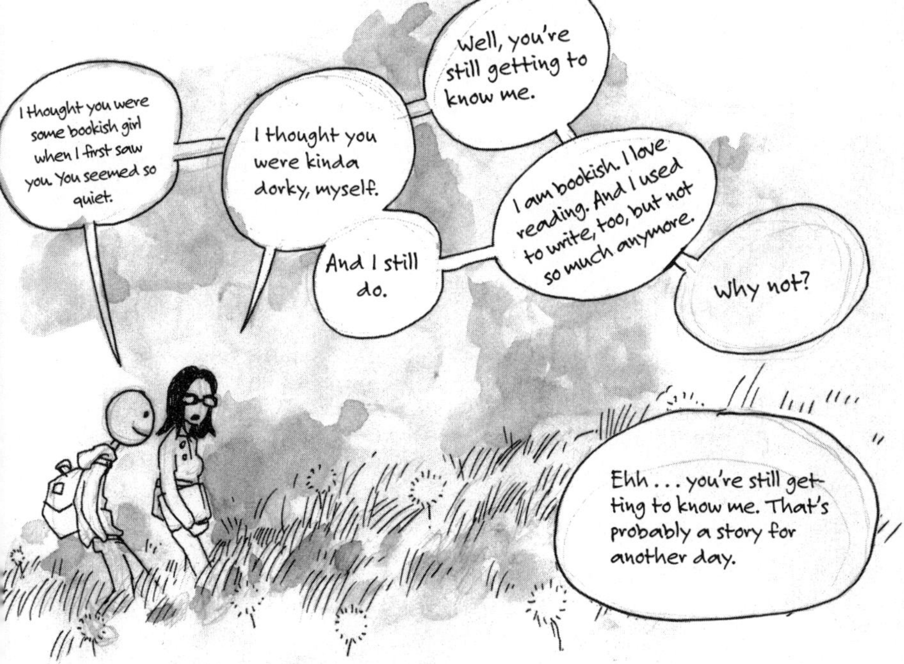
I thought you were some bookish girl when I first saw you. You seemed so quiet.
I thought you were kinda dorky, myself.
And I still do.
Well, you're still getting to know me.
I am bookish. I love reading. And I used to write, too, but not so much anymore.
Why not?
Ehh . . . you're still getting to know me. That's probably a story for another day.

Her house is pretty much down the street from the school. We crossed the road and headed up the hill that is her driveway and went inside. Everything was clean. Very clean. And not as quiet as I expected, as her two dogs were barking and three cats meowing. I can see why she never gets to be alone.

"Do you want a drink?" Gretchen offered.

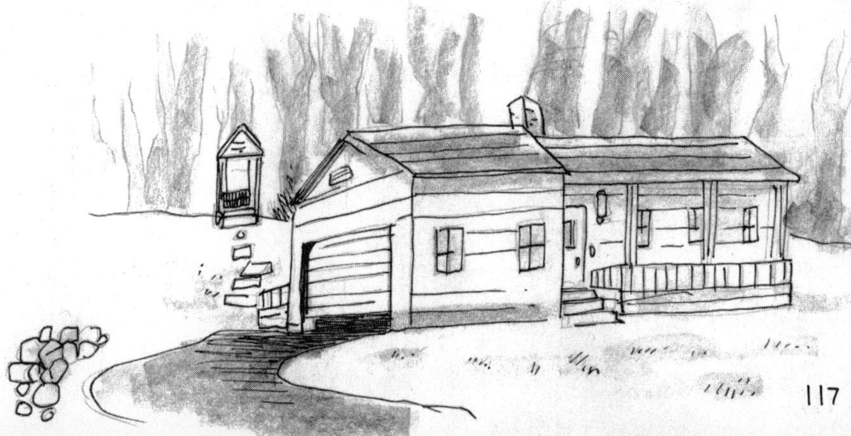

"Uh, jeez, not really, I'm all right." Secret: I thought she meant alcohol and I freaked out. I was actually very thirsty.

"Are you sure? We have some soda, Gatorade, water . . ."

"Oh, I'll have a Coke!" I could have made it less obvious, in retrospect. She didn't say anything.

HOORAY

Gretchen got on the computer and started looking at e-mail as I saw my entire guise slipping away. Look at me, nervous and probably red-faced over nothing, over being alone with a pretty girl. Stuttering, sweaty. Who am I fooling? Is this the best "Happyface" I could do?

I leaned against the bureau by the computer and pretended my arm did not slip on a magazine, causing additional embarrassment. "So what's going on, you don't have a boyfriend or anything?" I couldn't believe I said it. The five seconds it took her to stop reading her e-mail and answer me felt like an hour.

"Happyface, I invite you into my home, all alone, and now you're going to start putting the moves on me? I'm uncomfortable with this."

"Oh God, I'm so sorry, I didn't mean . . ."

Gretchen cracked up. "You never learn. You're such a sarcasm-sucker!" She kept laughing, such a cute laugh—she pronounces each "ha" separately. An actual "ha ha ha." I smiled and looked away.

"No, no boyfriends, boys are lame. I mean, I've had boyfriends, just not now. What about you? No girl from whatever mystery city you left behind?"

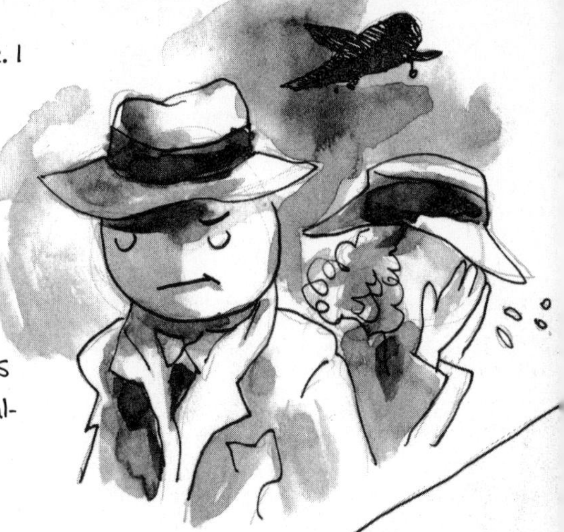

"Oh, the usual tragic romance ending, lovers parted and all that, broken hearts." Now THAT'S Happyface. That'll make her jealous for sure.

"Do you still talk to her?"

I shook my head. "Better to just let it die." I was like Humphrey Bogart.

Gretchen took me upstairs to show me something. Her room was small and girly and messy.

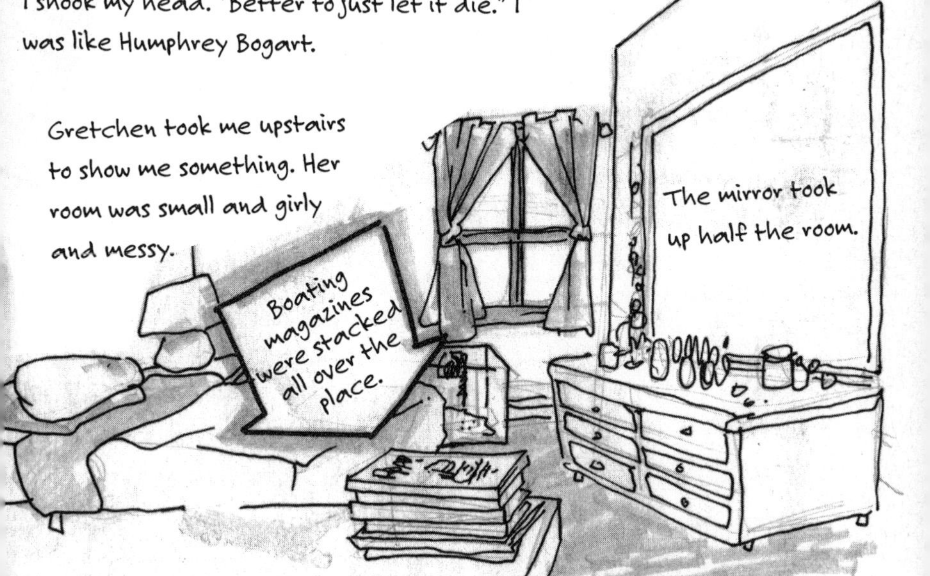
The mirror took up half the room.
Boating magazines were stacked all over the place.

Does Gretchen boat? She jumped on her bed and leaned over the side for a minute, and came out with a little friend in hand:

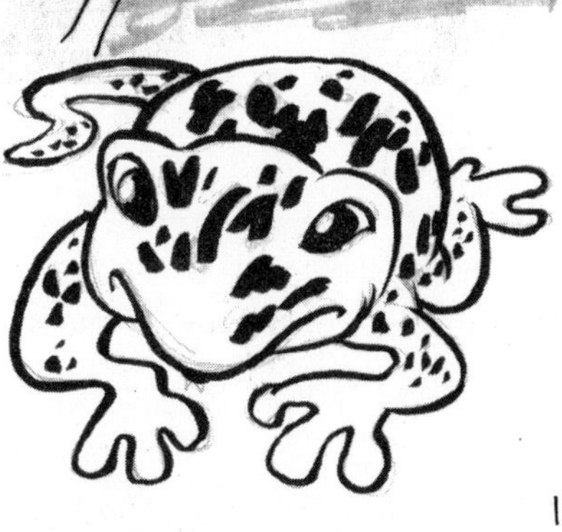

His name was Thompson and I wasn't about to touch him. I mean he's cute and all, but come on. He's so slippery and he was climbing all over her hand and arm. Frankly, he was a little creepy. Gretchen chased me around with him, trying to leave him on my shoulder.

"Gretchen, I'm going to feel really bad when that thing leaves your hands and ends up thrown against a wall!"

Gretchen faux-pouted.

We were looking at photo albums in the living room when she told me a story.

"So when I was in the fifth grade, everyone had to get tested for head lice with the nurse. There were these long lines of kids, and of course, my luck, the nurse finds something in my hair. I was so humiliated, and everyone in line backed away and I can hear them all going 'ewwww' and whatever. So the next day, my own boyfriend, my FIRST boyfriend, starts calling me Grossin' in front of his friends, like that's supposed to be funny or clever or something. It was like the worst experience of my entire life. So I dumped him and started dating this guy Robbie, who was way bigger and cooler than he was, so Robbie starts picking on him and he becomes like this total loser all of a sudden because I dumped him and Robbie was against him."

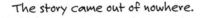

The story came out of nowhere.

"So then I ended up dumping Robbie like two weeks later, and he was all weepy and writing me letters all the time. He didn't date anyone else until high school. So yeah, guys are pretty lame."

I added what I could. "I wouldn't be any good at scaring ex-boyfriends off."

"No, but if I'm ever depressed, I know I can have ol' Happyface come visit."

"I'm there." It never really occurred to me that someone as cool and pretty as Gretchen would get depressed. I picture her busy with boys and friends and books and school. Everyone loves Gretchens. So why would the Gretchens ever be depressed?

We walked back through the grass around one because we had a test in Molly's class.

"I'm glad we got to spend the day together," Gretchen said. They were the few words we spoke on the way back. "But I can't say that I know you any better than I did before."

"Well, that's all part of the plan. Gives you reason to keep seeing me." See that? Charm.

"I knew you were putting the moves on me."

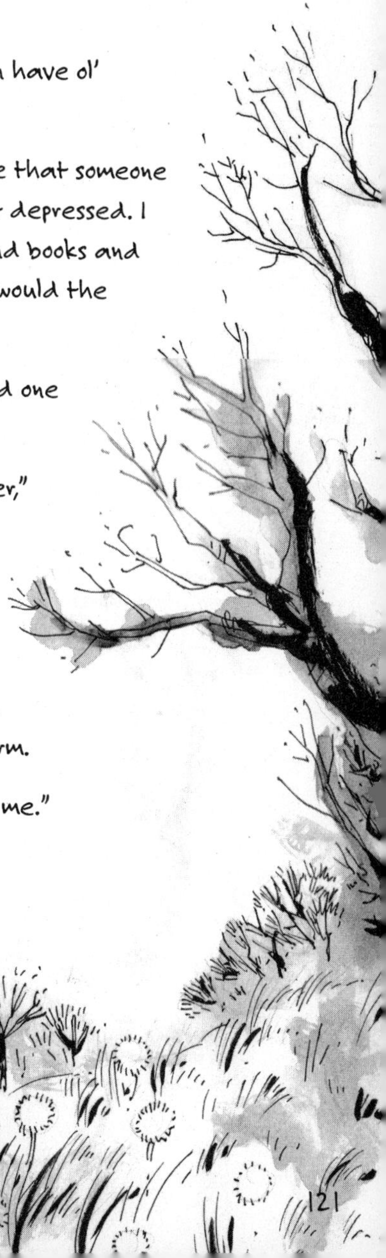

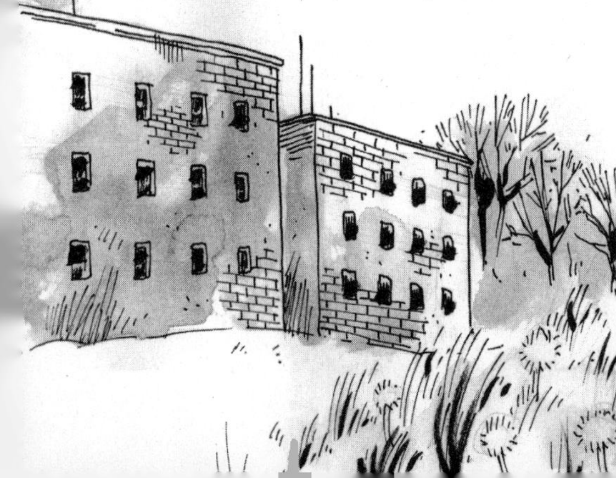

IM THE WALRUS!

Session Start (CartoonBoy:KarmaKameleon):
Wed November 5 21:20:25
[21:20] KarmaKameleon: FACE!
[21:21] CartoonBoy: Hey Karma
[21:21] KarmaKameleon: Face Dogg, what uuuuup!
[21:21] CartoonBoy: :)
[21:22] KarmaKameleon: I ASKED YOU WHAT UP.
[21:22] KarmaKameleon: Now answer me or I will hurt you.
[21:22] CartoonBoy: Wow!
[21:22] CartoonBoy: Just doing homework. Or not doing homework.
[21:22] CartoonBoy: I'm supposed to be doing homework. I'm supposed to be reading Keats poems.
[21:22] CartoonBoy: SO BORING!
[21:22] CartoonBoy: But it was either hop online or fall asleep in my book.
[21:23] KarmaKameleon: A real slacker, you are.
[21:23] KarmaKameleon: Are you and Gretchen like totally a couple now? Omg!
[21:23] CartoonBoy: Not that I know of! I'd have to say no.
[21:24] KarmaKameleon: Good, Gretchen would destroy you. She would leave you a shell of a puddle of a man.
[21:24] CartoonBoy: ??
[21:24] KarmaKameleon: I'm kidding, face. God you don't know me at all.
[21:24] CartoonBoy: :)
[21:25] KarmaKameleon: \^^/
[21:25] CartoonBoy: Is that a little smiley guy raising his arms?
[21:25] KarmaKameleon: No, it's a full-grown smiley guy raising his arms.
[21:26] KarmaKameleon: Gretchen is auctioning herself for a winter dance date at the Fall Festival aaaaaaand you should try and win her.
[21:26] CartoonBoy: Why's that?
[21:27] KarmaKameleon: So she doesn't get stuck with some creepo! Do you really want her out with some date rapist because of some stupid school festival suck-fest auction crap??
[21:28] CartoonBoy: I don't know
[21:28] CartoonBoy: no
[21:28] CartoonBoy: I suppose not
[21:29] KarmaKameleon: I wouldn't think so. You really have to learn to start thinking about other people, Face Dogg. You don't have to be like, married to someone to not want them getting kidnapped and tortured.
[21:29] CartoonBoy: How much do you think a thing like that goes for?
[21:29] KarmaKameleon: What would you pay?
[21:30] CartoonBoy: Jeez I don't know... what's average?
[21:30] KarmaKameleon: GOD, FACE, you're such an ass. Average??
[21:31] KarmaKameleon: Love is priceless; the answer is you'd lay down your life. You act like you don't love Gretchen at all.
[21:31] CartoonBoy: I think I have to go read some poems...
[21:32] KarmaKameleon: K BYE HAPPYFACE!

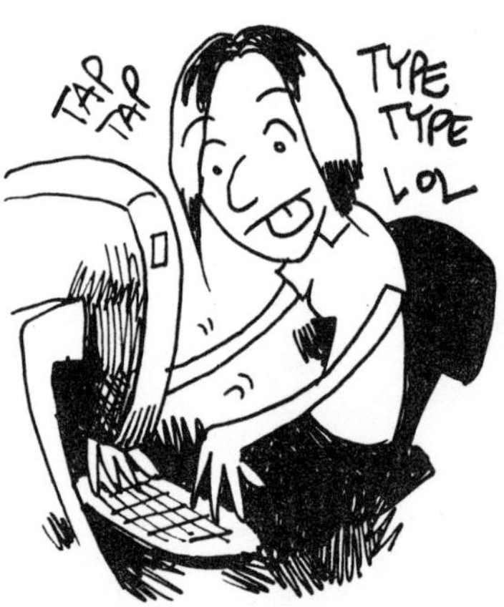
TAP TAP
TYPE TYPE LOL

Fall Fest

11/8

OR: IT'S AUTUMN AND WE NEED YOUR MONEY

Ahh, the smells of autumn, the drying of leaves as they hit the ground, the clean cool air, the smells of money fattening our school's pockets while we students are exploited for slave labor. Apparently it's yearly tradition at Crest Falls and never officially questioned. It goes like this: early November rolls around, and the students and teachers each do their part to put on the "Fall Fest," a kind of hokey northeastern fair. You buy your apple cider, go on the hayrides, play games, and look at the crafts. Some people make things, offer services or talents, and everyone shows up for the actual festival. And despite all the work they make us do, it's something the kids here actually look forward to.

I thought of offering my caricature-drawing capabilities but figured I'll play observer this year. I spent most of the day playing games.

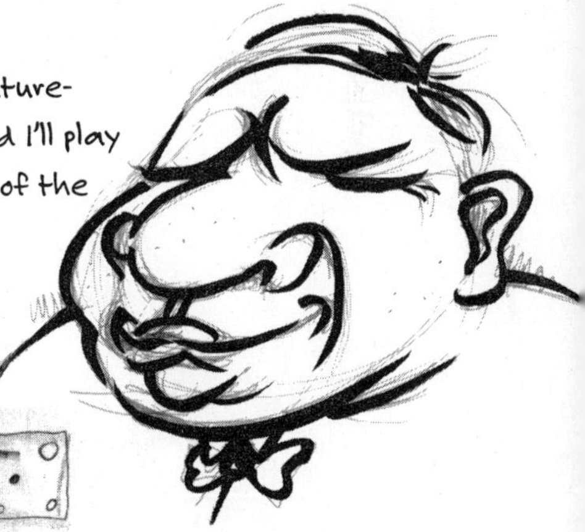

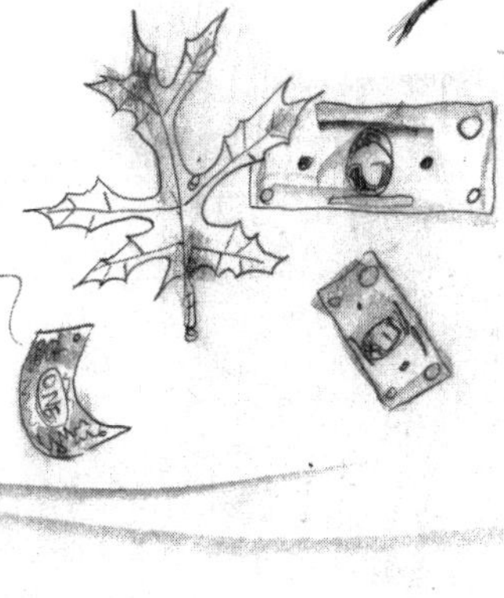

It started when I found Gretchen. Gretchen was at the basketball game. It was as simple as it sounds. You throw basketballs, and the more shots you make, the better prizes you can get. Gretchen was not so great.

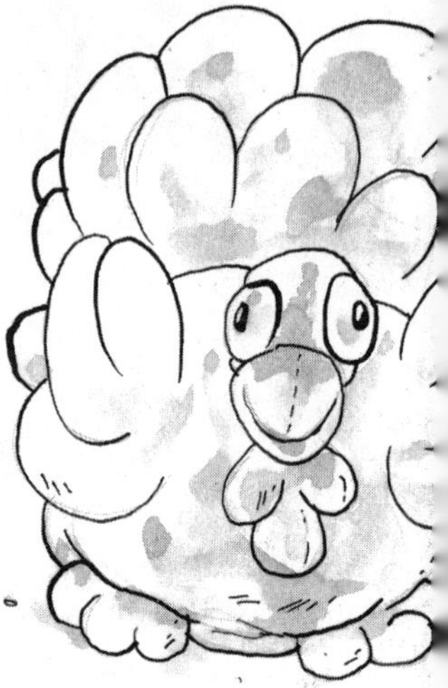

"I'm trying to win a turkey," she said, pouting. I figured I'd give it a shot. Surprisingly, I wasn't so bad—out of the five shots I paid for, I made three baskets.

"Did I get it?" I asked.

"Um, you kind of have to make more baskets," she said. "Like, a lot more. BUT, if you make all five shots, the next five are free. So it doesn't HAVE to be expensive."

I put in another dollar.

As I was shooting and Gretchen cheered me on, Trevor found his way over. He saw the commotion and joined in, doing his best cheerleader routine. As Gretchen explained what I was doing, he paid his own dollar and joined in.

We both kept making shots. I was losing more money but we were pretty equal, point-wise.

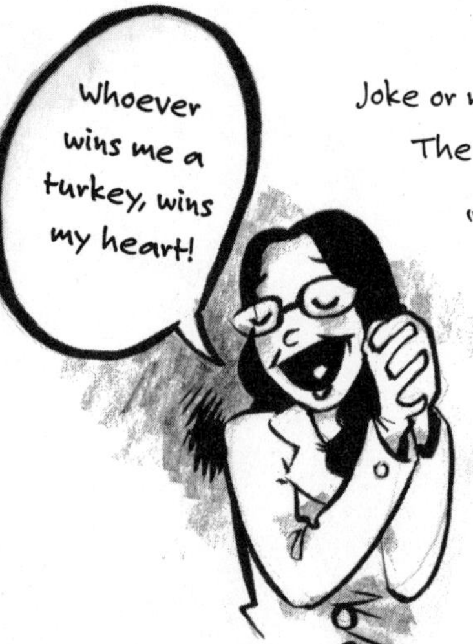
Whoever wins me a turkey, wins my heart!

Joke or not, we both wanted that heart. The game became competition.

"We'll get the turkey a lot faster if you just let me do it," Trevor said.

"Keep dreaming!"

"Hey, I'm helping you out. I don't want to see you go broke. My way is faster and cheaper."

"Sounds sloppy to me," I said as I sunk another one. I was there first and was determined to win that turkey.

I got faster and better as I went, but not quite good enough.

Trevor was nearing the sixty baskets he needed for the turkey, and I was desperate. I even bumped into Trevor, hoping it would buy me a little time. It didn't even faze him.

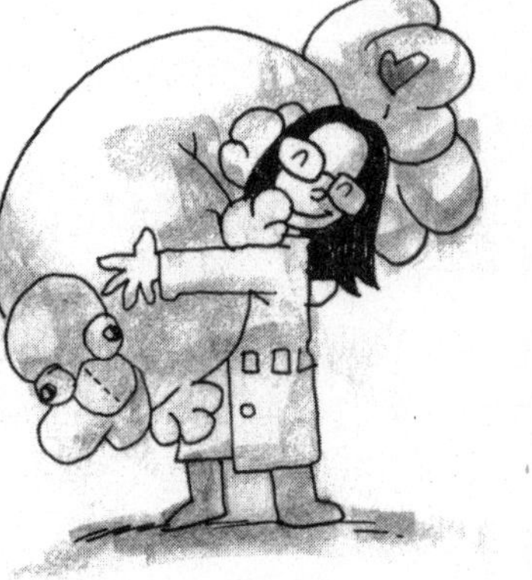

"Fighting dirty now, Face?" Trevor said. We were both getting sweaty.

"Lost my balance," I said.

Trevor made his sixtieth basket, I was still on forty-two. I kept shooting as Trevor gave Gretchen his giant stuffed turkey. (Which is not a metaphor, thank God.)

Not only did I not win the turkey, but I ran out of money trying, and somehow I still had to win Gretchen at the date auction.

"I've still got fifty bucks," Trevor reminded us as Gretchen complained about the potential bidders. I haven't had fifty bucks since my last birthday, and I certainly didn't have it now.

I had a taste for revenge after he stole my turkey, and I spent the afternoon devising ways to exact said revenge.

Plan A: Oh look, there's Trevor. "Hey, Trev, what's going on, how are—" WHAM!!! Sucker punch! Oh he's down, but he's not out! "I'm taking her to the dance, punk! Get used to it!"

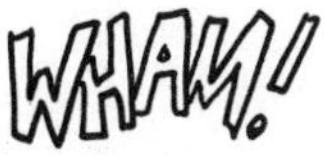
WHAM!

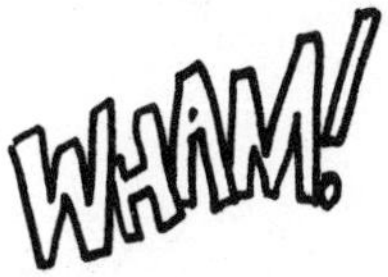
WHAM!

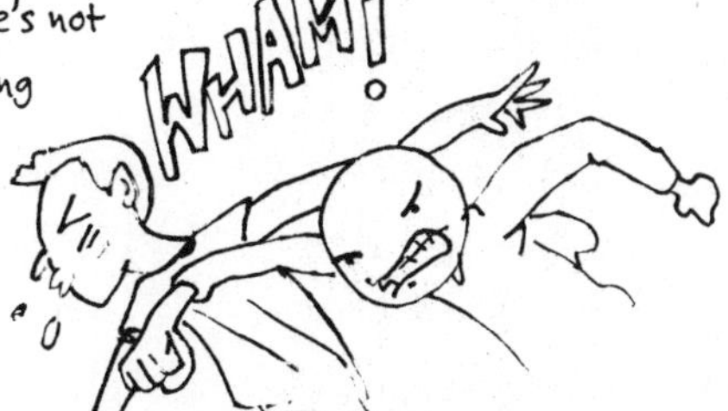
WHAM!

Plan B: I give up, Trevor wins the contest; he gets to take Gretchen to the dance. They slow dance, feel their bodies pressed against each other, Gretchen suddenly remembers why they dated in the first place, old feelings return. They kiss. Gretchen and Trevor are the class couple, he's funny and popular, she's cool and beautiful, everyone loves them, and everyone cheers them on. I grow older. Soon they marry; I attend the wedding because I've remained such a good friend. "Oh, Happyface, always so happy for everyone." I'm unable to love, to feel anything. I just smile. Eventually, we all die. This was a poor plan.

Plan C: Sit Trevor down, have a real heart-to-heart, Godfather style. "You beat me, fair and square. I admit this. So I'm going to ask you something, Trevor. I'm going to ask you to be fair and square with me. You know she doesn't love you. She never did. It wasn't meant to be. But there's something going on between her and me, and I want to explore that. And I'd like your blessing. Do the right thing, Trevor. Let me take her to the winter dance."

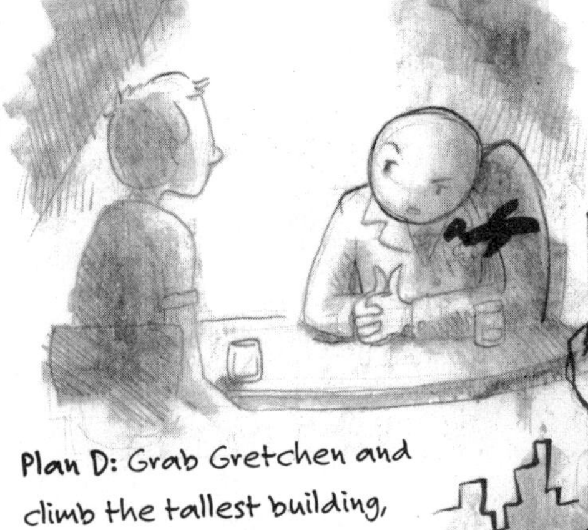

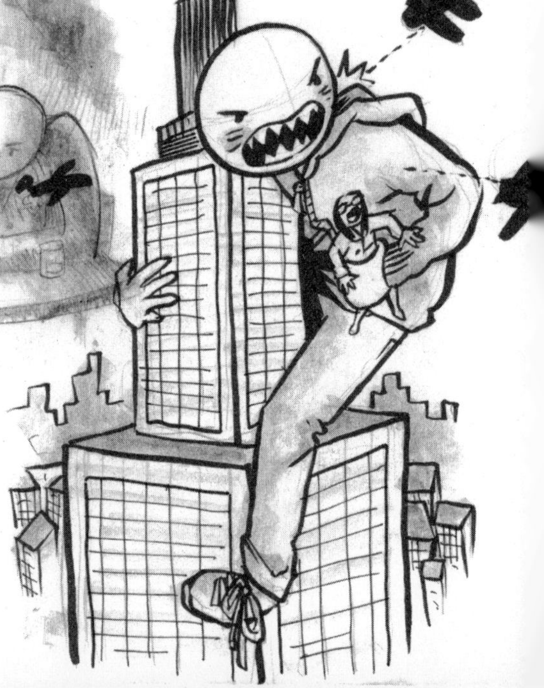

Plan D: Grab Gretchen and climb the tallest building, fight off airplanes and machine guns. Look her in the eye and let our love-struck gaze do the talking.

Luckily there was a Plan E. It started with Karma.

"I ran out of money at the fair. I can't bid for Gretchen," I confided to her.

"Face! You said!!!!"

"Look, if I can borrow like anything, ten dollars, twenty dollars, so I can at least make a bid, I will pay you back. If I don't win, you can have it right back."

"All right," she said, lending me a twenty. "But you give it back if you don't win. I'm going without nachos for this!"

She didn't know Trevor already had a fifty set aside for this. But if I could get twenty from Karma . . .

"I can lend you a ten, but that's all. You probably won't win," Misty said.

"That's all right, I just want her to at least see me bid."

I got another twenty from Mike, who simply takes joy out of seeing Trevor lose. Frog and Oddly parted with twenty for me as well. By the time the auction rolled around I was up to seventy dollars.

Most of the prettier girls from school were at the auction, most being won by complete dorks. I was excited to see this dance for that reason alone, although of course going with Gretchen would make it all the more sweet. Dates were sold for twenty dollars, thirty dollars, forty dollars. Christine Nicholson sold for eighty bucks!

When Gretchen came out, more people than expected were bidding. She's a party girl in her personal life, but at school she's always quiet and reserved, so I was surprised to see so many bids. Ten bucks became twenty, which turned to thirty dollars rapidly. People started dropping out. Trevor was smug as he kept bidding.

Then Frog bid forty dollars.

"What? She's a girl!" Trevor yelled out.

"So?" Frog asked as Oddly raised another ten.

"She's way hot," Oddly added.

"Quit being a homophobe!" someone else yelled out.

Trevor bid fifty-five dollars, more than he said he had. I finally joined in for sixty. Trevor raised another five. I made the final bid of seventy dollars and Trevor quit then. I tried to play it nonchalant like I could go all night, but that was every dollar I had. Now I owed money to the Moons, Mike, Frog, and Oddly. Money I did not actually have. It was worth it to watch Gretchen smile when I won the bid, though. The smiles didn't last long after.

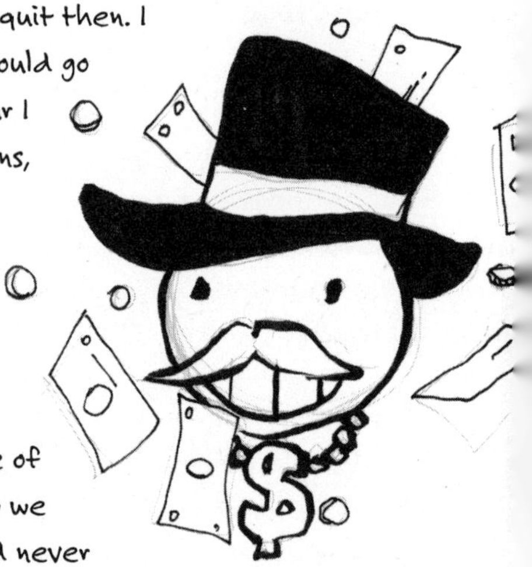

I met Gretchen in the hall outside of the auditorium. "Yay, you won! Now we can go to the dance together!" I'd never seen a girl so happy to go somewhere with me.

Trevor blew the good times. "You ripped me off! How the hell did you come up with seventy bucks?" Trevor fumed. I wasn't expecting him to be this angry.

"Through stupid games like everyone else," I quipped.

"No, you didn't, I've been watching you. Whose money was that?" Trevor asked.

"Well, it's the school's now," I said, quite honestly.

Gretchen interjected. "Leave him alone, Trevor. He won, you lost, big deal. It's just a dance, and we'll all be going, anyway."

"I don't care about the stupid dance. I just don't like getting ripped off by losers."

For a second I thought I was going to get into my first fight (i.e.: get beat up.)

"Get out of here, you ass!" Gretchen shoved him off. Trevor gave me a cold stare before walking away. "He's like that with every guy I'm friends with. He's always trying to show them he's better than everyone, but he's just a jealous jerk."

I watched Trevor walk away and looked back at Gretchen and savored the victory.

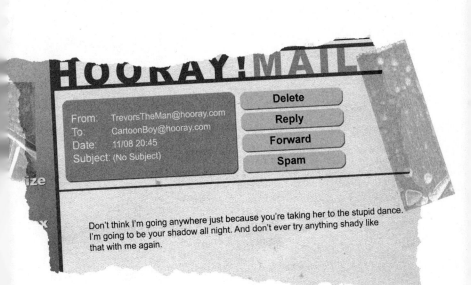

HOORAY!MAIL

From: TrevorsTheMan@hooray.com
To: CartoonBoy@hooray.com
Date: 11/08 20:45
Subject: (No Subject)

Delete
Reply
Forward
Spam

Don't think I'm going anywhere just because you're taking her to the stupid dance. I'm going to be your shadow all night. And don't ever try anything shady like that with me again.

Alone Time (Mom Remix)

This is the earliest I've been home on a Saturday night in a while, so I was surprised to find Mom acting mommish when I got in.

"I made dinner. It's cold now, but it's in the fridge if you're hungry," she said.

"It's nine o'clock. I ate. I'll have it tomorrow or whenever."

Then the interview began.

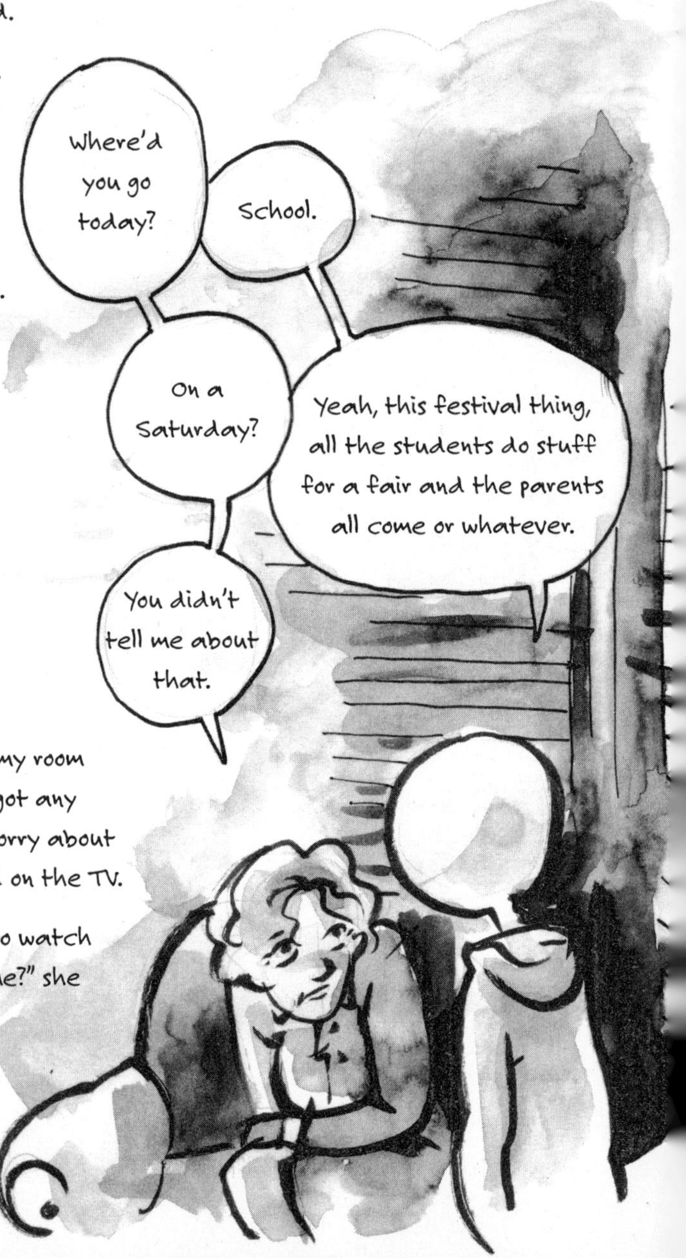
Where'd you go today?
School.
On a Saturday?
Yeah, this festival thing, all the students do stuff for a fair and the parents all come or whatever.
You didn't tell me about that.

I ducked into my room before things got any weirder. "Oh, sorry about that." I turned on the TV.

"Do you want to watch a movie with me?" she called out.

"No thanks, I'm just going to write."

I don't know, maybe I'm being a brat. My brat alarm is going off and I'm feeling guilty as I write this, but I have things to do, hot dates to plan. There's a lot to think about. People think being Happyface is all smiles and bad jokes, but this is serious work.

I haven't been spending much time around here or with Mom lately . . . not like I used to, at least. She did always like it when Ev or I would hang around the kitchen with her, talking about whatever. And I could probably convince her to make us some peanut butter cookies. . . .

All right, maybe I'll watch a movie. But I'm not paying attention.

OH HAI, ITZ HAPPYFACE: THE WEBCOMIC-IN-PRINT
Fall Edition

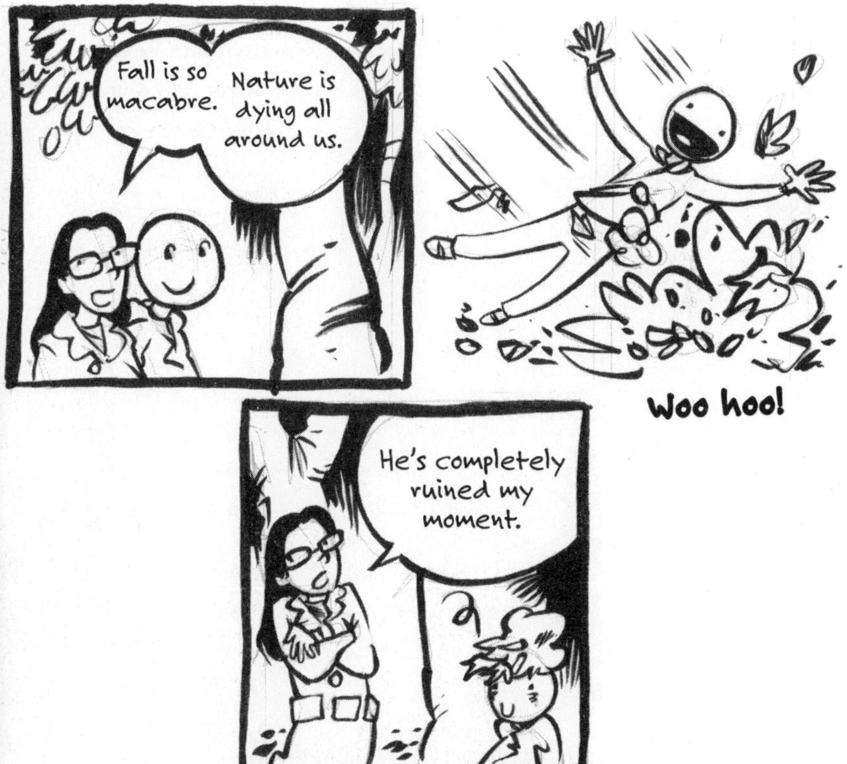

Fall is so macabre.
Nature is dying all around us.
Woo hoo!
He's completely ruined my moment.

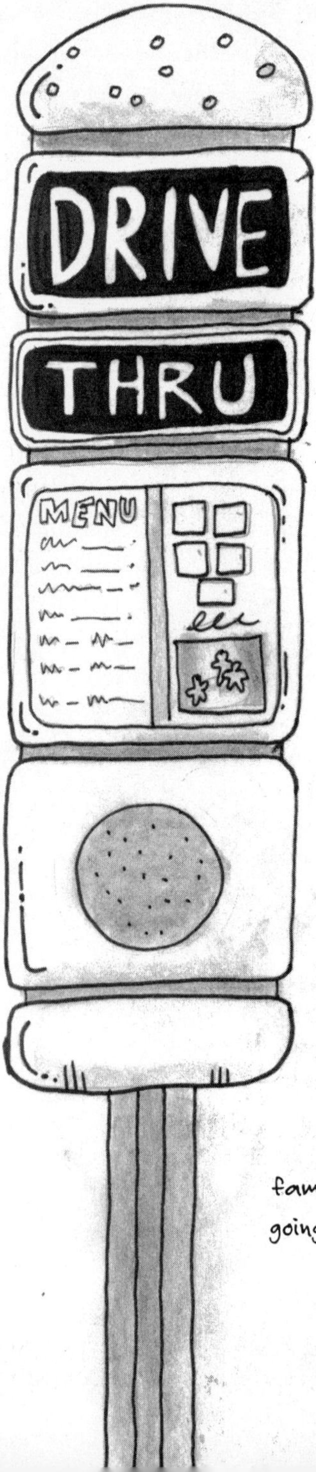
DRIVE
THRU
MENU

Mom and I were heading to McDonald's and I had my feet on the dashboard when I figured it was as good a time as any to bring it up.

"So Gretchen asked if I wanted to come over to her place for Thanksgiving this year. Is that okay?"

I don't see what the big deal is. I'll go to the drive-thru with Mom, and to a turkey dinner with Gretchen. Who says there isn't enough Happyface to go around?

Apparently Trevor usually went to Gretchen's on Thanksgiving since he hated spending any time with his family, but Gretchen didn't want him coming over this year after the date auction blow-up. She also didn't really want to spend the time with her family by herself, and to be frank, I'd rather spend the day with friends, too.

"What? Of course not," she said. "You can see your friends any day. Thanksgiving is for your family. Of course you can't do that."

I had to at least try. "But Mom, what family? It's just going to be you and me, and it's going to be depressing. What about Dad?"

"We're talking about you and me right now." She avoided my question, so I started avoiding her. "We'll make a dinner and it'll be good, we'll spend a little time together. We need that." She pulled up to the drive-thru. "What do you want?"

"Can I take your order?" the large sign asked.

"Just a second." She turned to me. "Come on, what are you going to have?"

"Nothing."

She gave me a violent look. "Nothing? We came here for you. You're the one who's so hungry. Come on."

"I was hungry then, now I'm not." I looked out the window, scrunched up in the seat, knees on the glove compartment.

"You're eating something. I'm not wasting my time." Back to the talking sign: "He'll have a Happy Meal, the hamburger." Back to me: "There. If you're going to act like a baby, you can eat like one."

"Mom, I'm not acting like a baby. If you'd think about it for a second instead of making judgments, you'd see it's not such a bad idea."

"I don't even KNOW this girl; you don't say two things about her! Why don't I get to meet her? You don't think I'd like to meet your first girlfriend?"

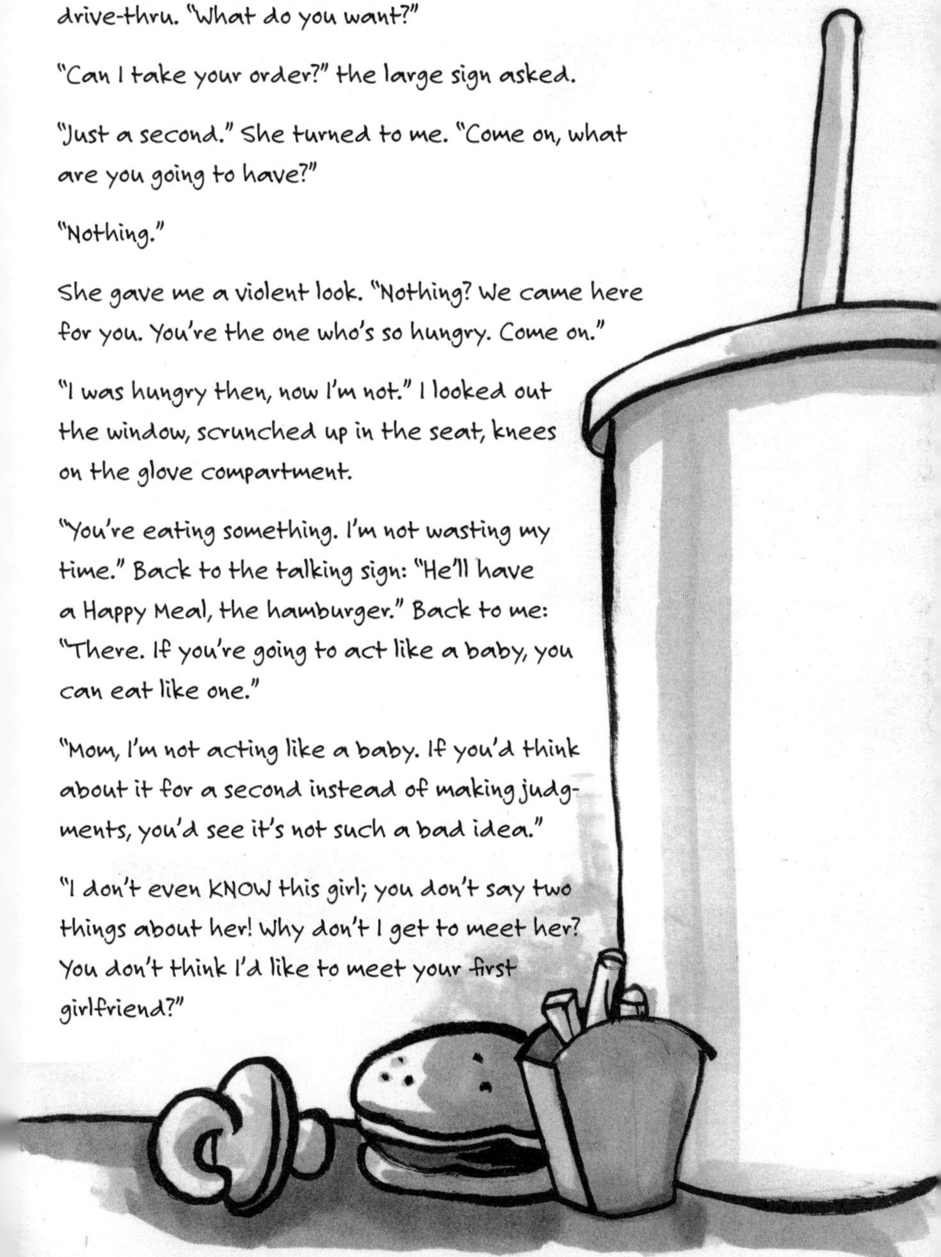

"She's not my girlfriend!" Now I was starting to feel like a baby. If Gretchen came over here, who knows how Mom would react. She's been unpredictable emotionally and there's just too much I'm not ready to tell Gretchen anyway, and there's no way Mom could resist blabbing her head off. It would be a disaster, plain as day, no two ways about it. She's crazy to think I'd bring Gretchen here. It'd ruin everything I'd accomplished the past two months. The end of Happyface!

"Then you don't need to spend Thanksgiving with her," she said. "You're behaving like a bad son."

She knows my buttons. "Well maybe you're a bad parent!"

"Maybe," she said, "but you're still my son so you do what I say."

"And how is THAT fair??"

"It doesn't have to be fair. You'll get it someday."

Yeah, right. I wanted to throw the burger out the window just to spite her, but it smelled good. Not to mention the plastic American Idol figurine. I made sure to face the window as I ate, though, furrowed brow on my face.

On Family

What's to say, really? My family is my family. If you watch any sitcoms on Nick at Nite, you've pretty much seen them all. Mom, Dad, two-point-five kids. That's me, my brother Everett, and my imaginary friend Skeeter, who I'm counting as the .5 even though he's character enough to count as 2!

My dad's the funny one. He has observations for just about everything. That's why he's a writer, as you know. I remember one time my brother and I were wrestling, and he said, "What are you, a couple of homos?" He always has a gem like that. My mom is the wacky one—she's always misplacing stuff so we never know where the remote is and my dad has to drive her to the gas station at one in the morning to see if she left her wallet there. Everything ends in smiles, though, and my family sure does like to laugh.

Everett's my hero. He gets the good grades, the good looks, and all the girls. With a brother that cool, you really don't have to try at all in life, what's the point? Hopefully I can take it easy and coast off his successes in the future.

And good ol' Skeeter, he's half Martian, you know. Half of my time is spent protecting him from the government. They're

135

out to cut him up and take a look at his insides, but no way, man, that's my family, and family means more to me than anything else. Friends and lovers come and go, I am told, but family is with you for the long haul.

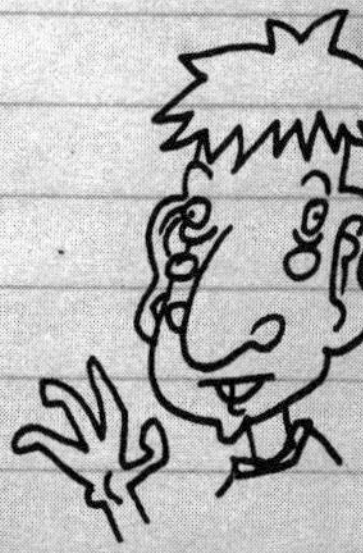

I'm sure you'll get an A in comedy writing, but for this class, let's try for a little more introspection.

11/21

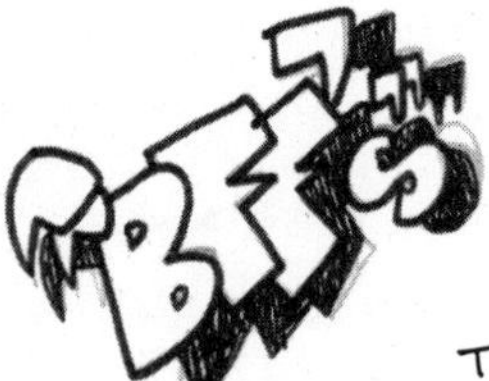
BFFs

After a second argument, Mom and I decided I could "do whatever I want" regarding Thanksgiving. Thus, I spent the day at Gretchen's.

The food smelled great and the house was warm, but I was too nervous to have much appetite. This was my third time at her house, but the first I'd met any of her family. I even successfully navigated Gretchen's uncle to the upstairs bathroom. Her parents were there, her aunt and uncle, silent cousin Aaron, and her grandmother, who was bound to a wheelchair. It was small enough that focus was frequently pointed at me.

"So do we just call you Happyface, or is there an actual name, too?" her mom asked me as Gretchen quickly abandoned me, left to the wolves.

"I don't even remember anymore," I replied, searching for Gretchen. "You can just call me Happyface, I kind of like it. You can shorten it to Happy if you want." Grandma laughed, and Mom smiled a plastic smile. She seemed intense. Both Gretchen's mom and dad were doctors. Various college degrees and certifications lined the walls along with family photos.

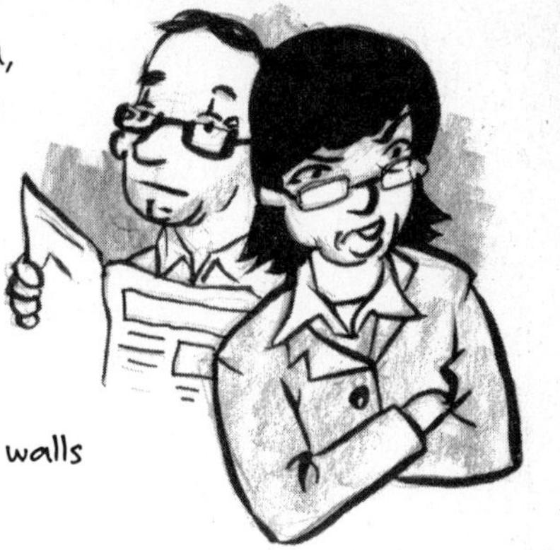

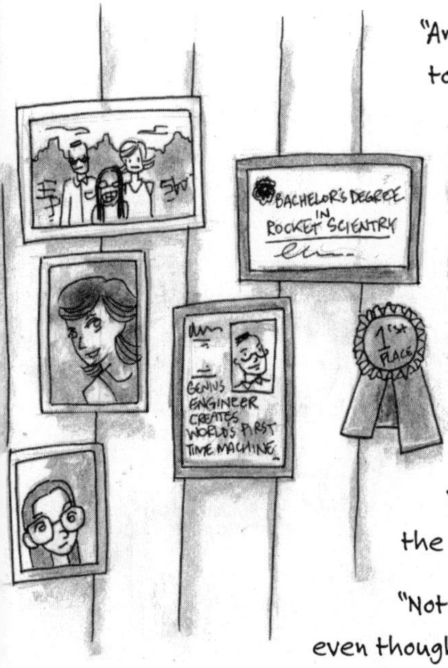
BACHELOR'S DEGREE IN ROCKET SCIENTRY
GENIUS ENGINEER CREATES WORLD'S FIRST TIME MACHINE
1st PLACE

"Are you a sophomore, too?" Gretchen's mom asked.

"Mm-hm."

She was setting the table while everyone else watched a Christmas movie in the living room. "Making plans for college?" I was trying to make my way to the living room. Gretchen was missing and must have gone to her room but I didn't feel comfortable roaming the house.

"Not yet, it's still early, I guess." I hadn't even thought about college yet. I hadn't even really thought about thinking about it.

"It's a big decision. You've got to start working toward it now. If you wait 'til you're a senior your options will diminish. There's nothing left." She has a way of talking to you that makes you feel like a five-year-old.

"Okay, I'll give it some thought. Does Gretchen know where she's going?" I asked.

"She has a list. Remind me after dinner. I have a number I can give you. One of Gretchen's other friends is going through the same thing. Maybe you can help each other out."

Was this lady crazy?

"Sure." I quickly made it to the living room.

I asked Gretchen's dad if he knew where she went.

"Upstairs, Trevor," he said, watching the TV with all the focus of a sniper.

"Oh." I sat down.

"You can go up."

"Okay."

Upstairs, Gretchen was playing a video game on her computer. "There you are."

"There I am? You ditched me!"

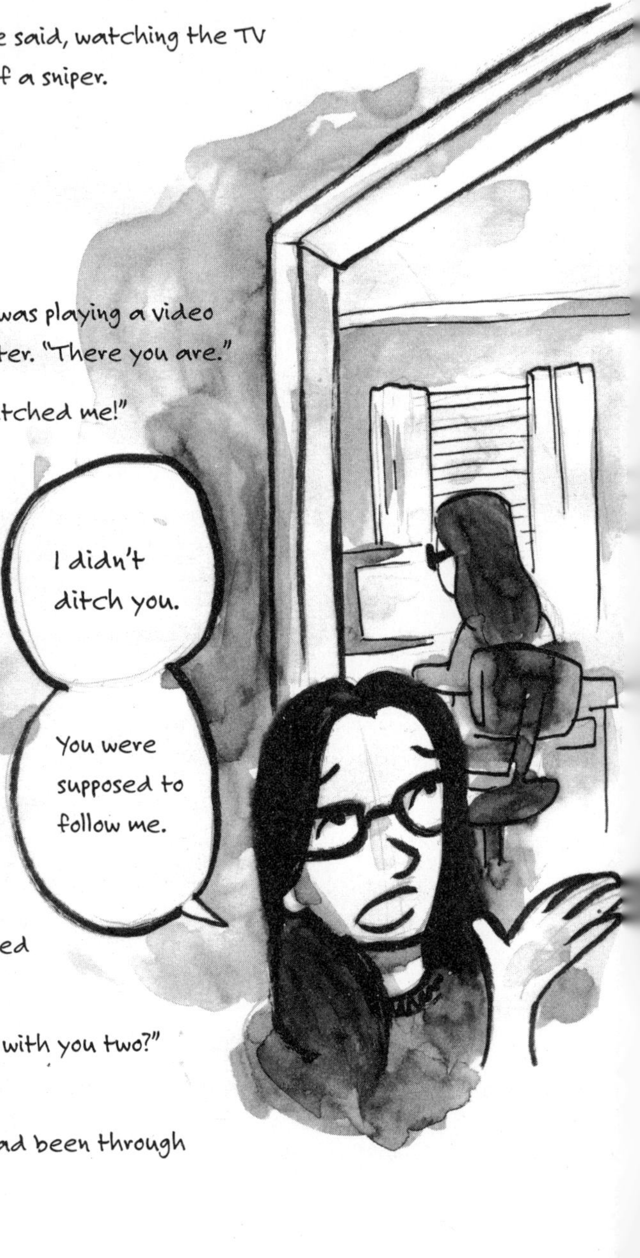

I didn't ditch you.
You were supposed to follow me.

"Oh."

The grilling continued later on at dinner.

"So what's going on with you two?" her mom asked.

"Mom!" Gretchen had been through this before.

Her mom took an angry tone, enough so that I knew not to mess with her. "What? It's just a question, I'm not implying anything."

"It's all right," I interjected. "We're just friends. I'm actually new to Crest Falls. I just moved here a couple months ago. Gretchen was the first friend I made here."

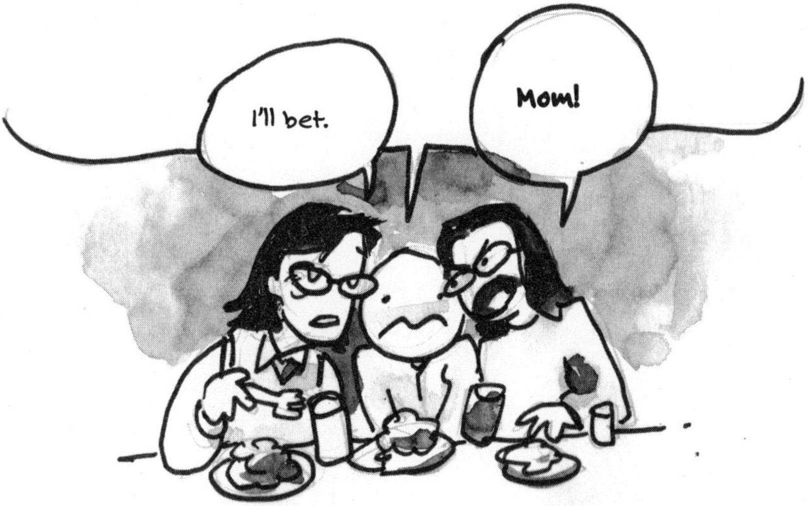
I'll bet.
Mom!

Mom glanced over at Gretchen and back to me. "So where'd you move from?"

"Just over on the shoreline."

"Any brothers or sisters?"

That journal I wrote for Molly was going to come in handy. "Yeah, two-point-five kids—my brother, me, and my imaginary friend." I smiled, waiting for a laugh that didn't come. Note to self: write that one out of the stand-up act.

"I didn't know you had a brother," Gretchen said. This was getting awkward.

"Uh, yeah, he's at college, though."

"What do your parents do?" Her mom wasn't even looking at me. She had this pre-scripted.

"My dad writes a little, my mom is a paralegal."

"Mom, you're getting a little personal, don't you think?" Gretchen said.

"You're right, I'm sorry."

Just as the conversation seemed to move on, her dad finally spoke up.

"So did I miss it, or did you say what the deal is between you two?" Inferring Gretchen and me.

"Dad!" protested Gretchen.

"We're just friends." I smiled, hoping to break the tension. No wonder Gretchen wanted company. The chandelier was beginning to feel like an interrogation light.

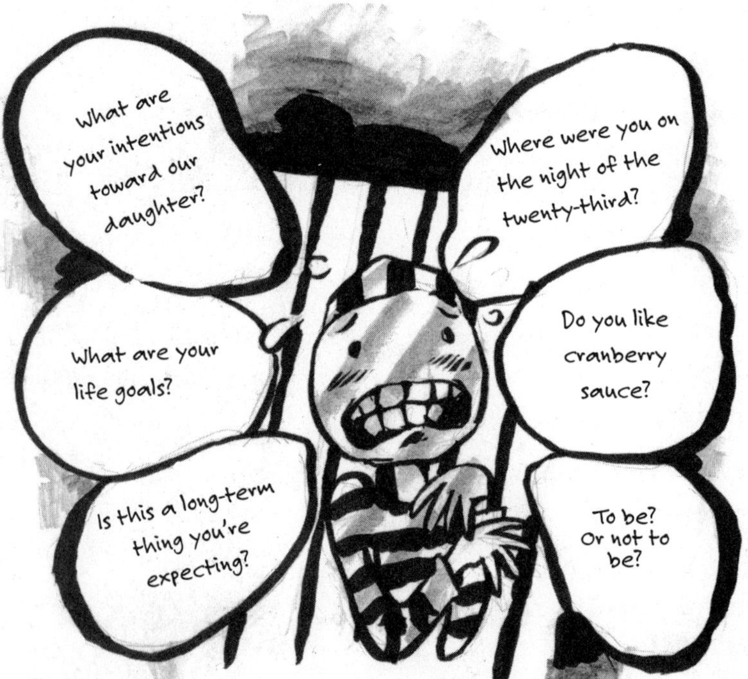

What are your intentions toward our daughter?
Where were you on the night of the twenty-third?
What are your life goals?
Do you like cranberry sauce?
Is this a long-term thing you're expecting?
To be? Or not to be?

After dinner, Gretchen and I sat outside on the porch. It was cold out but I was so hot from nerves that it felt good.

"So you made it through Thanksgiving dinner. That makes us official BFFs." Gretchen nodded her head as if looking back on a colossal achievement (which, for me, it was).

"Yes! Nice." I had to ask. "So did your parents think we're dating or something?"

"No, I have guys over all the time. They know it's no big deal. They've just really nosy."

"Why are they so nosy?"

She hesitated a minute. "You know all the boating magazines around the house? They used to be my <u>Seventeen</u> magazines, and <u>Cosmos</u> and all that stuff. My dad kinda caught me in a less-than-optimal position and canceled all my magazines and replaced them with those stupid boating magazines."

"And you keep them?"

"Yeah, I'm determined to learn boating now to spite him."

"So . . . I mean, no, it's none of my business." I couldn't ask her about the less-than-optimal position.

141

"They didn't catch me having sex or anything, if that's what you're thinking."

"Oh, no, I wasn't thinking anything."

"They caught me writing about it. For the record, diaries are stupid."

"Totally. I got rid of my sex diaries years ago." I could always get Gretchen to laugh.

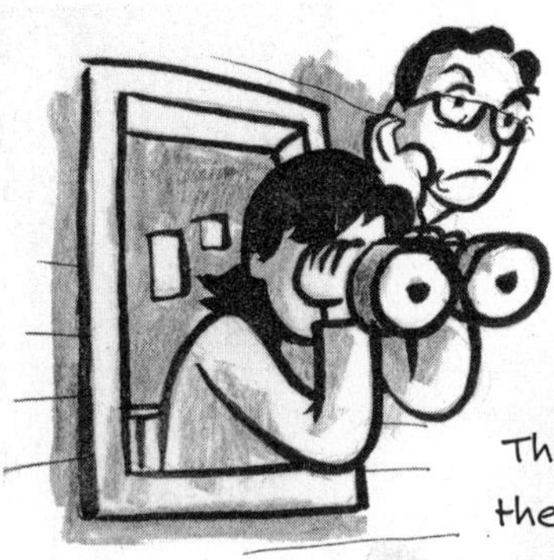

"They're constantly monitoring everything now, where I go, who I talk to. They definitely didn't think we were dating."

So that's why Gretchen's single, that's why she has so many "friends," and that's why I'm Gretchen's BFF, and not her BF.

There goes poor Happyface, riding his bike in the cold, walking across the lawn into his apartment on a bitter November night. New friends, fans even, a cute and popular BFF, everything he's never had. Still, he wants more.

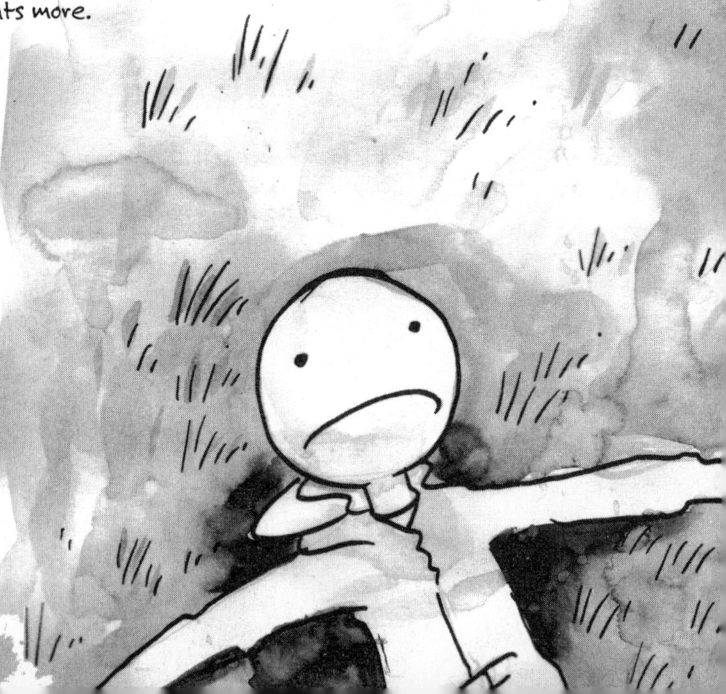

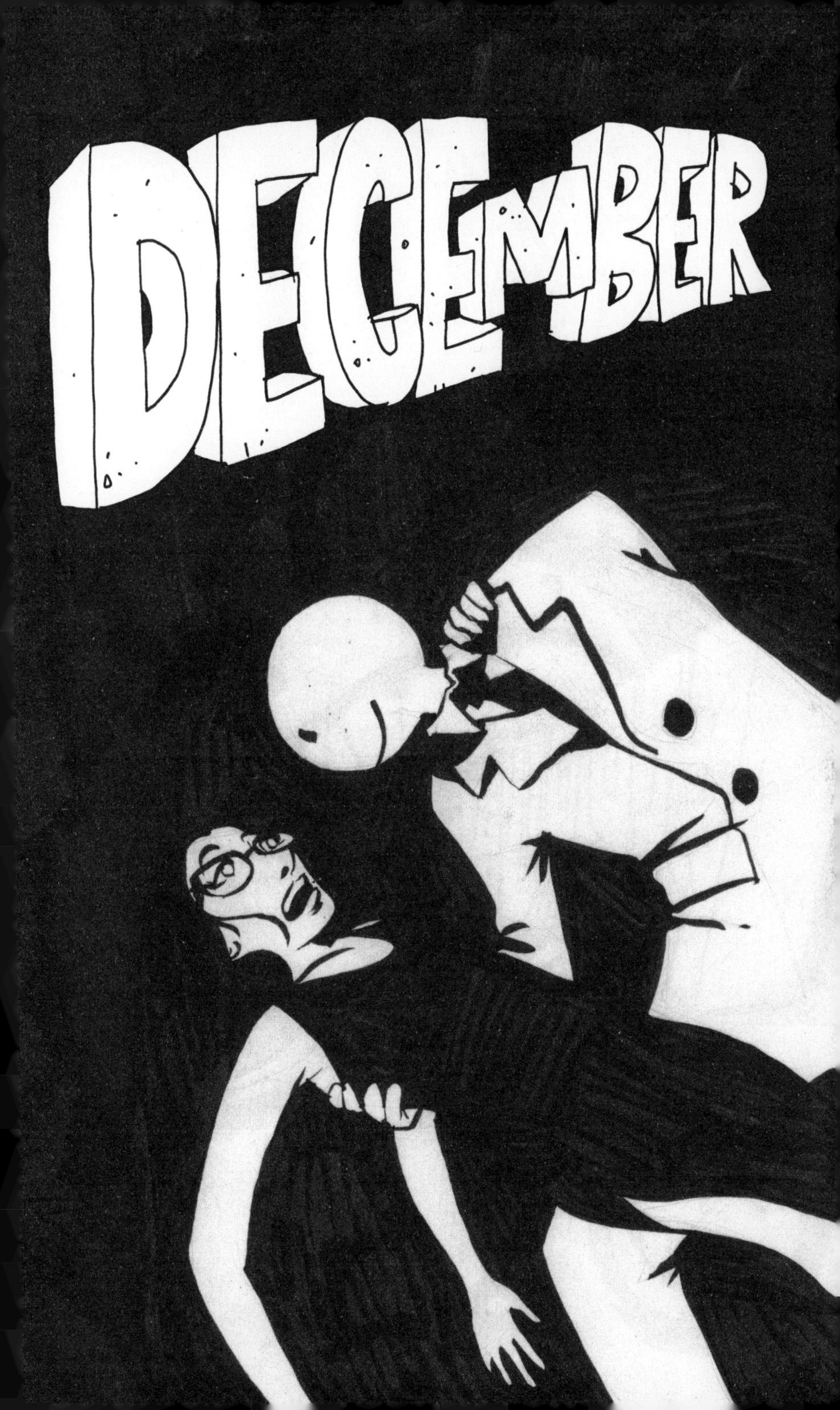
DECEMBER

I.M. what I.M.

Session Start (CartoonBoy:KarmaKameleon):
Tues December 2 19:30:10

[19:30] KarmaKameleon: H to the Fizzie.

[19:31] CartoonBoy: Hey Karm.

[19:31] KarmaKameleon: Soooo.... About that $30 Misty and I lent ya...

[19:31] KarmaKameleon: *whistles a tune*

[19:31] CartoonBoy: Augh, I'm sorry, I'll pay you back soon, I promise.

[19:32] KarmaKameleon: Okay. You must have really wanted to win that date, huh?

[19:33] CartoonBoy: Did you not want me to win?

[19:33] KarmaKameleon: No, I'm glad, better you than Trevor. They were bad news as a couple.

[19:34] KarmaKameleon: You should bring some of your old friends around sometime.

[19:35] CartoonBoy: That's alright, I prefer to just start fresh here.

[19:35] KarmaKameleon: Really? So there's no one at all?

[19:39] KarmaKameleon: Faaaaaaace.... Come out and plaaaaaay....

[19:40] CartoonBoy: Sorry Karm, busy with homework. See you tomorrow!

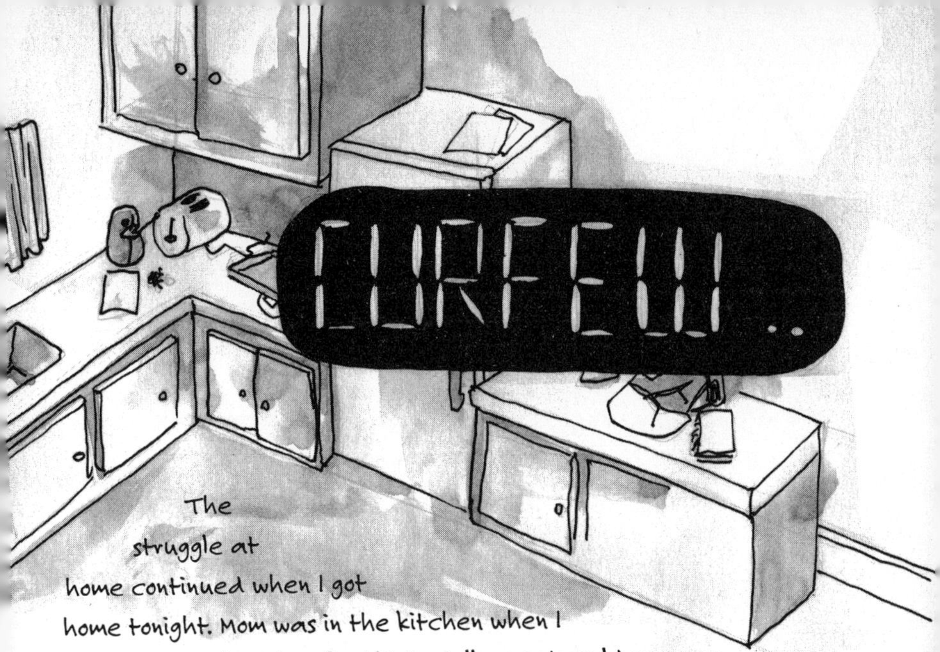
CURFEW..

The struggle at home continued when I got home tonight. Mom was in the kitchen when I got in and I asked her for thirty dollars so I could pay back the Moons at least.

"No," was her quick reply. "In fact"—I debated tuning out—"In fact, you should get a job if you're going to be going out all the time, so you can help pay for stuff. You're too old for an allowance, and you don't do anything around here to earn one anyway." I think she'd been saving that one up, and I could tell it felt good by the way it snowballed.

"You're going to have a curfew, too. We never had to establish one before because you weren't running around like this all the time, but now we have to set some rules. Everett had one when he was your age. He was home by eleven."

"No, he wasn't!"

"Well, he was supposed to be, that was his curfew."

Golden Boy came home whenever he felt like it and never got in trouble, and he was out actually doing bad things. I'm just watching TV, talking with friends, twiddling my thumbs, and staring at Gretchen.

"Mom, I'll get home when I get home. I don't do anything bad—"

"Listen to how you talk to me! You're like this all the time now, I feel like I don't even know you anymore."

"That's because you DON'T know me anymore! Not since we moved into this crappy little apartment, you don't!"

"This is what we could afford," Mom snapped back at me.

"We wouldn't even be here if you hadn't cheated on Dad! We'd still be in our home!"

"Go to your room. I don't want to talk to you," Mom said coldly as she looked away.

She didn't deny it. I wished I hadn't said anything. Mom went to her room and I felt bad again. When she's being strong, when she's acting like herself, we clash, but I still prefer it to Melodramatic Mom. Things are different for her and for me, too, and I think we're heading in two different directions.

She went back, and I moved forward.

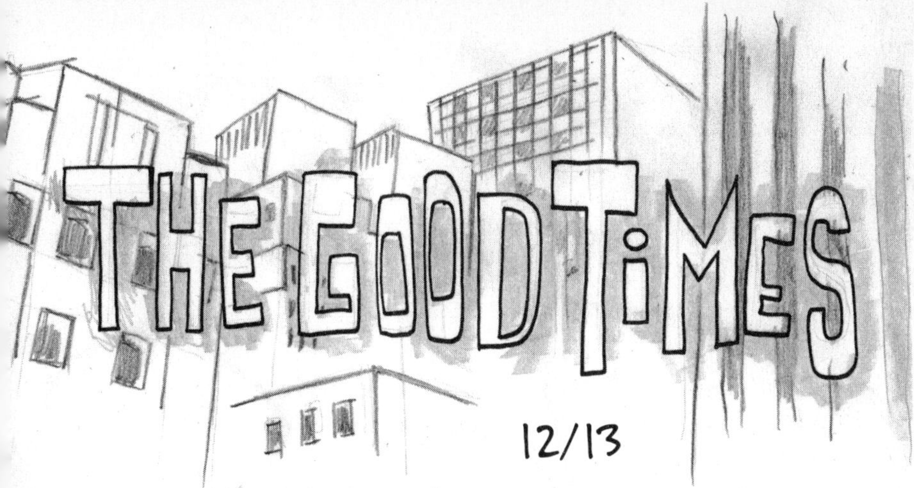

THE GOOD TIMES

12/13

If, when my life flashes back before me, there is a good-times montage like you see in the movies, today would be featured prominently.

Gretchen and I took the train into the city and we both lied to the parentals of our whereabouts for the day. I don't think Mom would extend my leash quite that far any more than Gretchen's ever-watchful parents would. Gretchen drove us to the train station and got cash out of the ATM so we could find her a dress for the dance and do some Christmas shopping. I was broke (i.e., in debt [i.e., screwed]) but went along anyway. I was able to scrape together enough change to eat but otherwise I had to pretend nothing I saw fit my impeccable tastes.

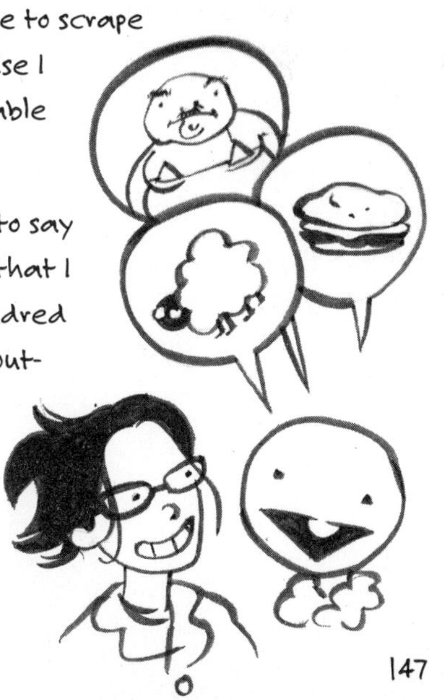

As I sit here writing this, beat, tired, I have to say that today could be the turning point and that I am completely crazy for Gretchen. One-hundred percent straitjacket-wearing joker-busting-out-of-Gotham-Asylum crazy. Everything was just right, from when she fell asleep on my shoulder on the train ride there and the flirty banter in the city, to the way she smiles every time I say something silly, stupid, or puzzled look-inducing.

I'd never been to the city without my parents before, but Gretchen sneaks away for a day every few months and knows her way around pretty well. Dad came here often for his book dealings and sometimes took me with him, but I was too young then to remember much. I would have looked like the dorky tourist left on my own, maps unfolding out of my fanny pack, camera slung around my neck. "What do your parents think of you coming here?" I asked.

"You think I tell them? Seriously, Happyface?"

"I thought you said they watched you like hawks."

"They do," she said, "but that doesn't mean they know anything."

And the mystery of Gretchen opens anew.

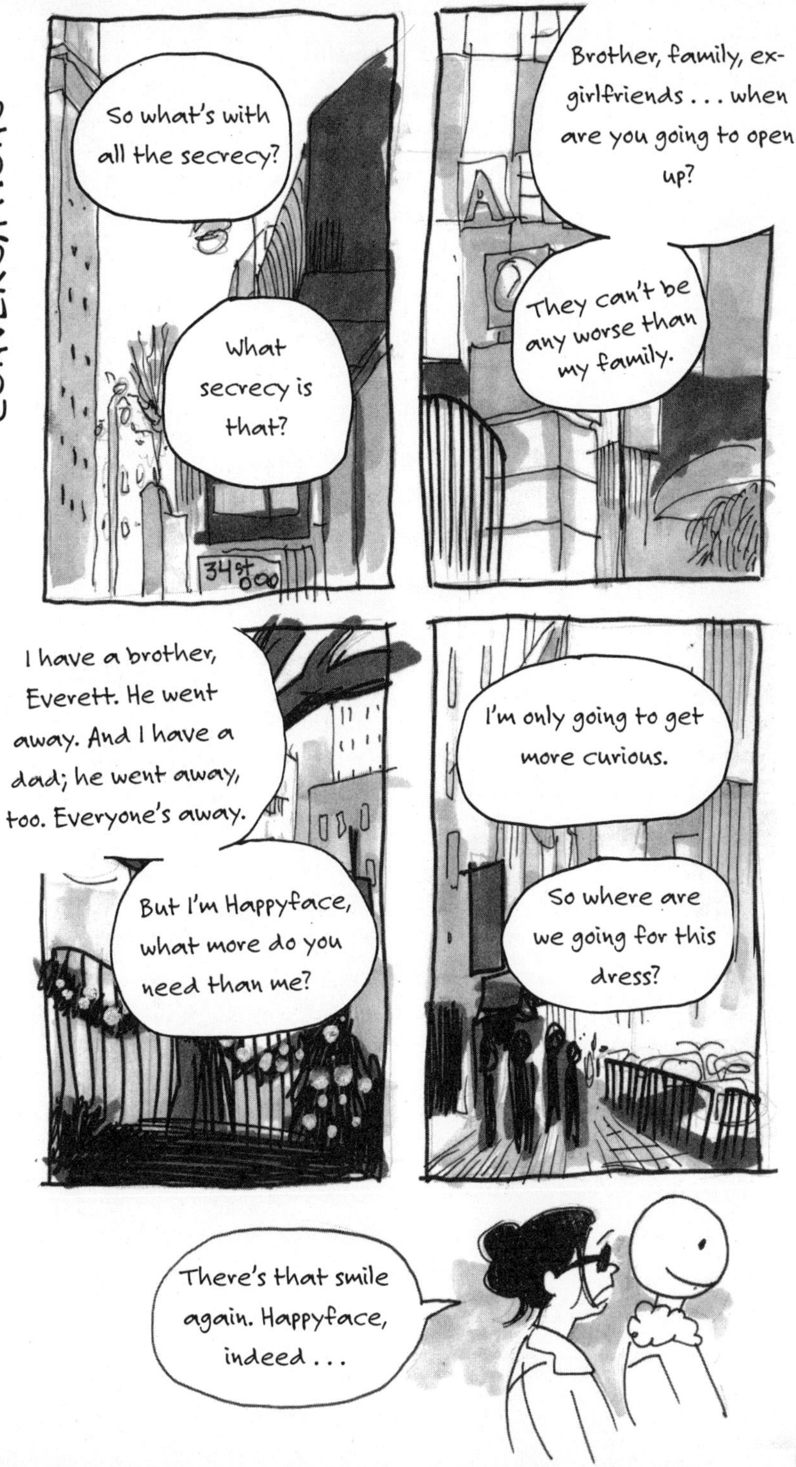
So what's with all the secrecy?
What secrecy is that?
Brother, family, ex-girlfriends . . . when are you going to open up?
They can't be any worse than my family.
I have a brother, Everett. He went away. And I have a dad; he went away, too. Everyone's away.
But I'm Happyface, what more do you need than me?
I'm only going to get more curious.
So where are we going for this dress?
There's that smile again. Happyface, indeed . . .

Part of me wanted to pour my every thought out to her, tell her every insignificant moment I've lived through so she can know me inside and out, but that would land me in pitiful Friendsville faster than you can say "Chloe." I want Gretchen to look at me and see funny, confident, and nice. Not "tragic lost cause."

Gretchen wanted to go ice skating before hitting the department stores. "I skate here EVERY year. It's tradition!"

I was reluctant, to say the least. I'd never skated before and can't even ride a bike. I have trouble walking most days. I tried escaping with "Maybe later?" But she knew as well as I did—

"No, we'll be too tired later. We have to do it now." She was dragging me toward the outdoor skating rink. "This is going to be the best moment of your entire life." It was a hard sell. I resisted a little more until she said "Come on, cool, confident guy like you, you'll get the hang of it in no time."

After renting the skates, we made it onto the ice. I quickly fell to the floor. The place was mobbed with people, and kids and adults alike were crashing into me as Gretchen struggled to pull me up. It was certainly a memorable moment, if not the best. Gretchen finally got me on my feet and held my hands as I leaned into her. And that was the snapshot— that was the best moment. I didn't want to move. She started skating backwards and pulled me slowly with her. I can't say I really learned to skate, but at an abysmally slow pace I did learn how to not fall.

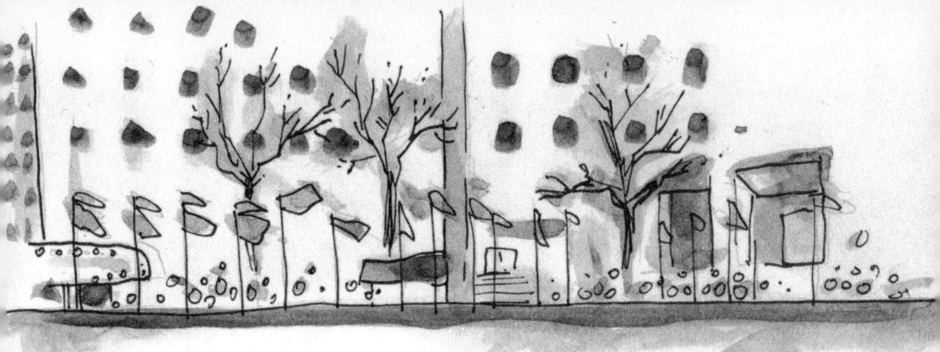

"I used to come here with my parents and my cousins, every year," she confided. "When I was little I used to want to be a figure skater."

"No way," I flirted, "I used to want to marry a figure skater. That's such a coincidence."

Gretchen opened her mouth in faux-shock.

"You're good," I said to cover the lingering awkwardness of my flirtation. It was at least a step up from "Not as pretty as you," back on the boat. I saved my good lines for Gretchen. "You're even better than me, and that's saying something. Very impressive."

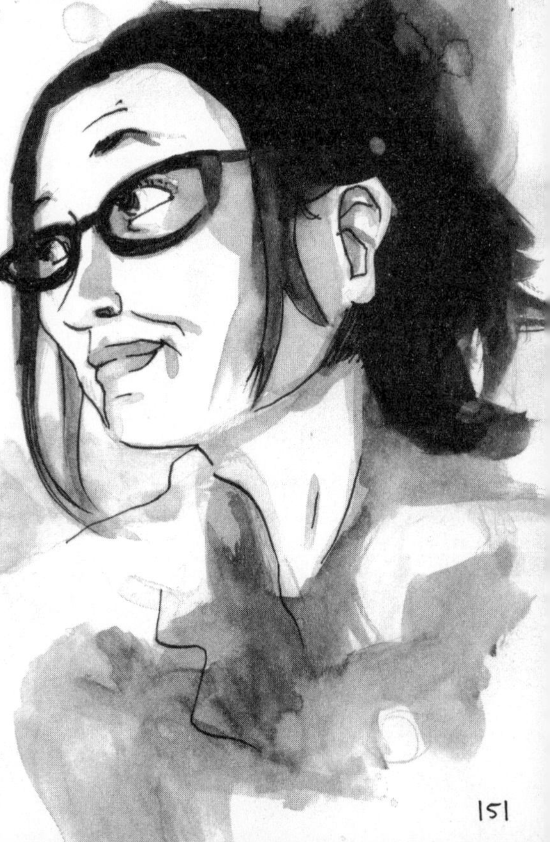

Christmas classics played over the speakers as families and boyfriends and girlfriends and children skated around. It really was something I'll always remember. When I looked at Gretchen smiling and laughing, skating, really in her element and knowing I was there with her, I wanted it to be like that all the time.

I couldn't say anything though. I can't say anything. If she doesn't feel the same way I do, it could ruin it all. It'd be just me and the Frog Force. And Mike. And Lol@Failure. And besides that, if Gretchen and I were to get together, she'd find out eventually, she'd see all the things I don't want her to see. She'd see the mountain of lies I've told. The pile of crap I crawled out from under. I wouldn't be her Happyface anymore.

Gretchen's the best thing to happen to me since Chloe. And I don't want to live through that again. We'd still be friends if I hadn't put so much on her. I'd been a burden.

I tried to picture what Dad would say. Maybe he'd give me some speech like he did on the boat.

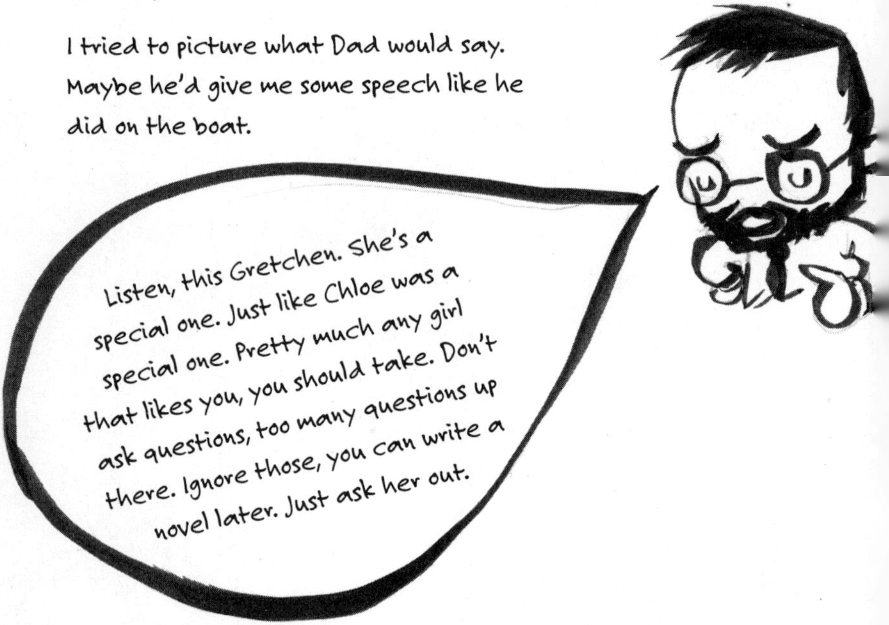
Listen, this Gretchen. She's a special one. Just like Chloe was a special one. Pretty much any girl that likes you, you should take. Don't ask questions, too many questions up there. Ignore those, you can write a novel later. Just ask her out.

I thought of what Everett would say before remembering he's the last person I'd listen to.

Gretchen led me around a line of department stores after skating and lunch. We explored the men's sections first, and I pretended to have more money than I did. Gretchen kept finding clothes for me, but I had to dislike them or tell her I'd seen them cheaper elsewhere. She'll probably never want to go shopping with me again.

"Come on," I said, "let's go find your dress before it's too late."

Gretchen knew just the store she wanted to go to. She looked drop-dead beautiful in everything she tried on. And I was no help in picking a dress.

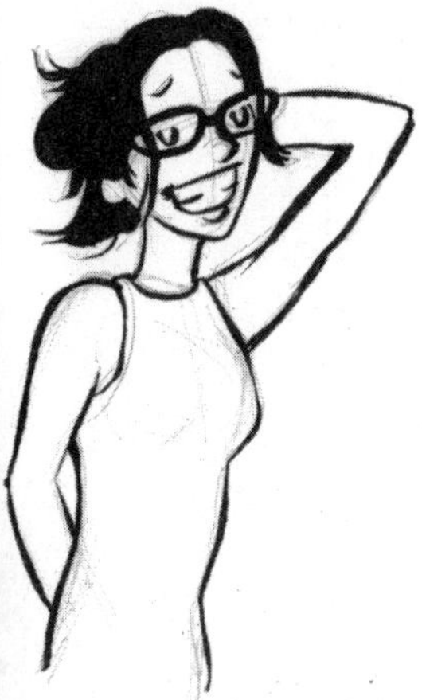

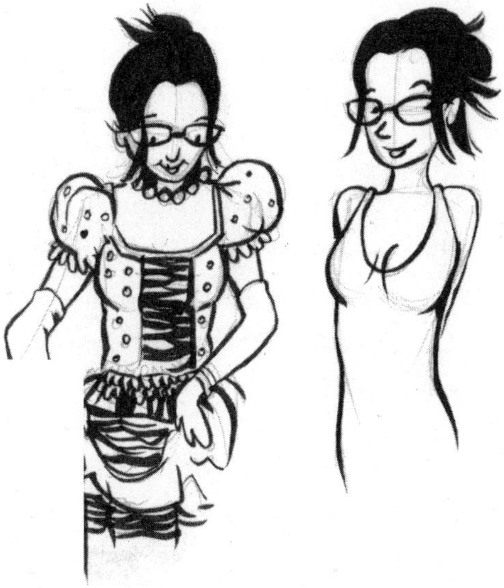

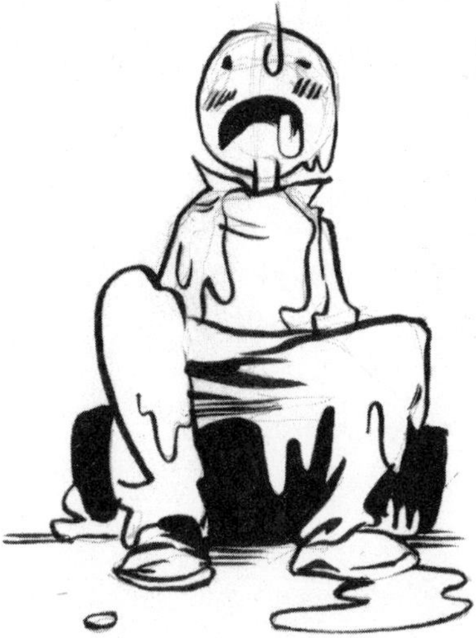

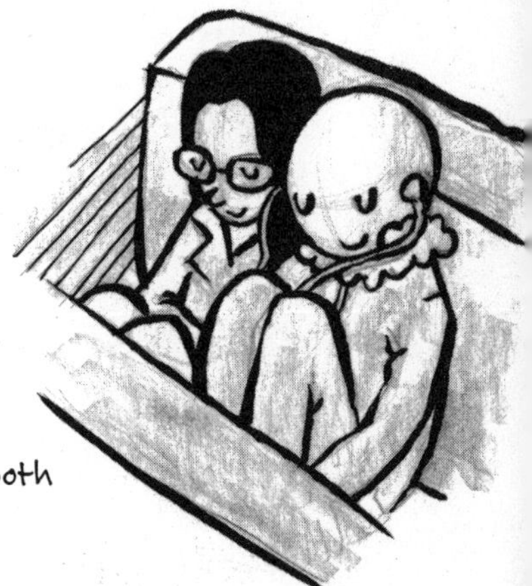

We talked a little more on the ride home. Gretchen said I was more fun to shop with than the Moons (is that good or bad?). She said Trevor's been a pain lately. Then we both dozed off listening to her iPod.

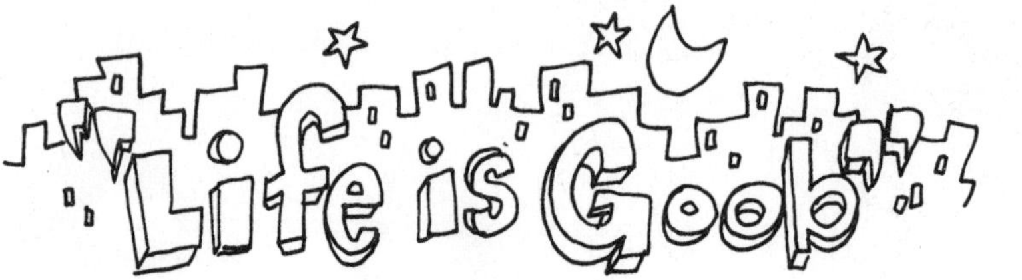
Life is Goob

Idea for a sitcom: Life Is Goob, about Goober, late twenties, failed **con-artist** in a small northeastern town. His career in the crapper and every cop in town knowing his name, **Goober** figures his aspirations to be a great con-man (like his DECEASED FATHER ALWAYS WANTED) are going nowhere. He runs from his failures to the BIG CITY, where he'll blend right in and con-jobs are like rats and garbage bags: everywhere you look! But once he meets . . . **Twixie**, a fellow small-town good girl who takes a shine to ol' Goob, his con-career might be kaputs. Can he put his past behind him for the love of a girl? This fall, see why crime and love don't mix in **Life Is Goob!**

KARMA PUTS ON THE RED LIGHT

I skipped my math class first period today to help out Karma. She wanted me to keep her company in the darkroom as she developed her photography project. "Please, it's so boring in there!" she pleaded. I didn't mind tagging along.

Karma and Misty are always a little weird and they get a kick out of making me uncomfortable, which is fine since it lets me really put an effort into NOT being uncomfortable. They keep me on my toes. But being alone with Karma in a tiny darkened room today took the cake for discomfort.

I was off my game right from the start. Nutty as she is, Karma *is* pretty, and today she had this little hat on, and she looked really cute. My mind wandered a little, being alone with her in that closet. She even smelled nice. I usually don't think of Karma that way. It didn't take long, though, before I remembered who I was dealing with.

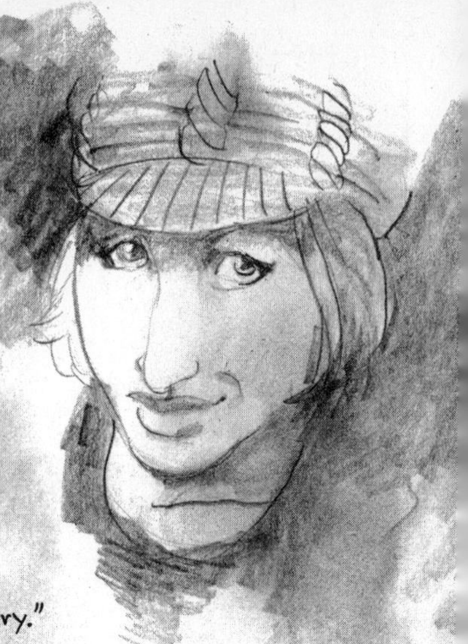

I was helping her out with her photos. "'Kay, dip it in that tray. Now shake that one off," she ordered. "There you go. Those hands really know what they're doing, don't they?" Ha ha, I get it. Let's make Happyface feel awkward. There wasn't even a payoff with the red light, since she couldn't see my face turn any other shades. I let the comment slide.

Then she bumped into me. Twice. "Oh, sorry." Karma let the bumps linger, though, so it was more of a brushing. I knew I was being made fun of and I could feel my embarrassment, but I didn't mind. It was kind of fun.

The flirtation continued: "It's so dark in here. I can't even tell if you're smiling today." She touched my cheek as I tried to back away. "Yep. You're smiling." At this point I was starting to believe. Maybe she really was hitting on me. I'd never seen either of the Moon sisters in any kind of open or affectionate way. Everything with them has always been sarcasm and general strangeness. Was she really trying to tell me something? And even if she was hitting on me, even if she was someone I'd consider dating, things were going so well with Gretchen, how could I not at least finish exploring that? And why was I enjoying this flirtation so much?

"You know, it's so weird having someone in here. It's usually so boring, me just working alone. And no one EVER comes in." She wanted me. I could feel my heart beating. "Oh, that picture should be done; can you take it out for me?"

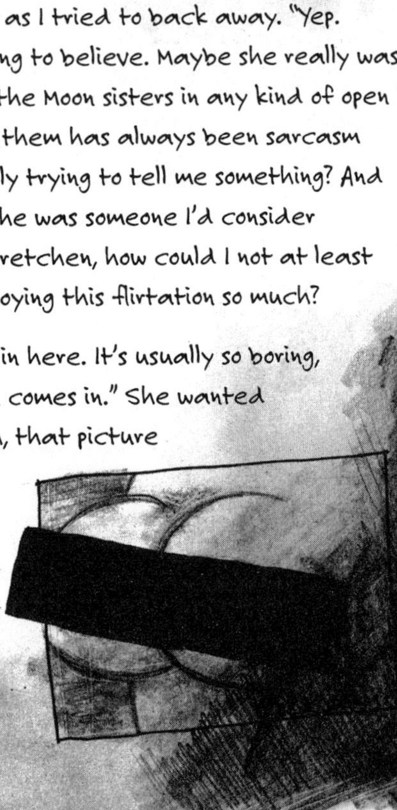

I lifted the picture, wet and glossy, and stopped in my tracks. It was boobs. The picture I'd been developing. It was boobs.

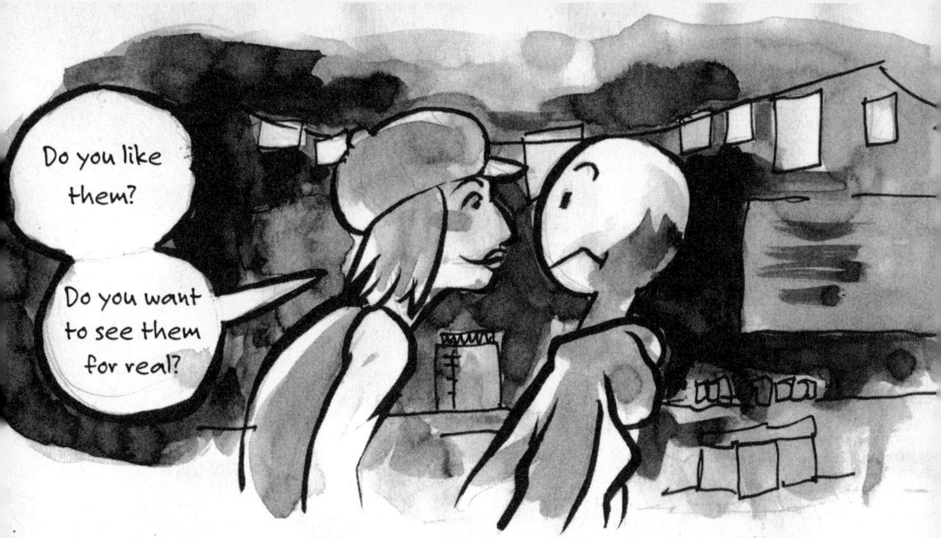
Do you like them?
Do you want to see them for real?

"Karma! What—I can't—what's—?" She didn't need to see my red face to know I was flustered. "I should go. I have some homework I have to finish." I backed into the magician-style rotating door.

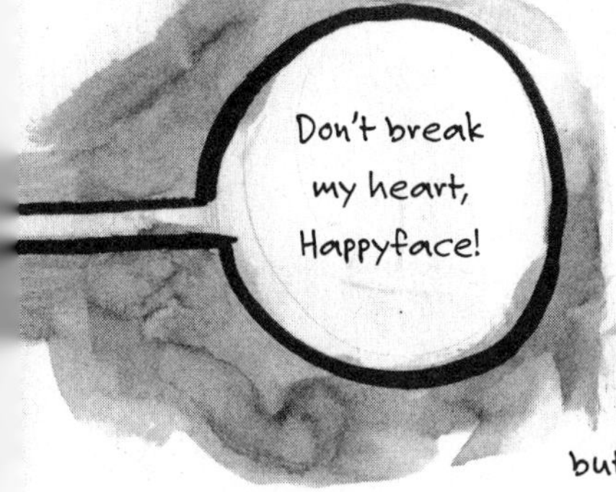
Don't break my heart, Happyface!

I spent the next period wondering what to do. Gretchen sat across from me reading through our free period. She's my perfect girl still, sure, but Karma was aggressive! She was really putting it on the table! What an option. Visions of Karma's breasts danced in my head.

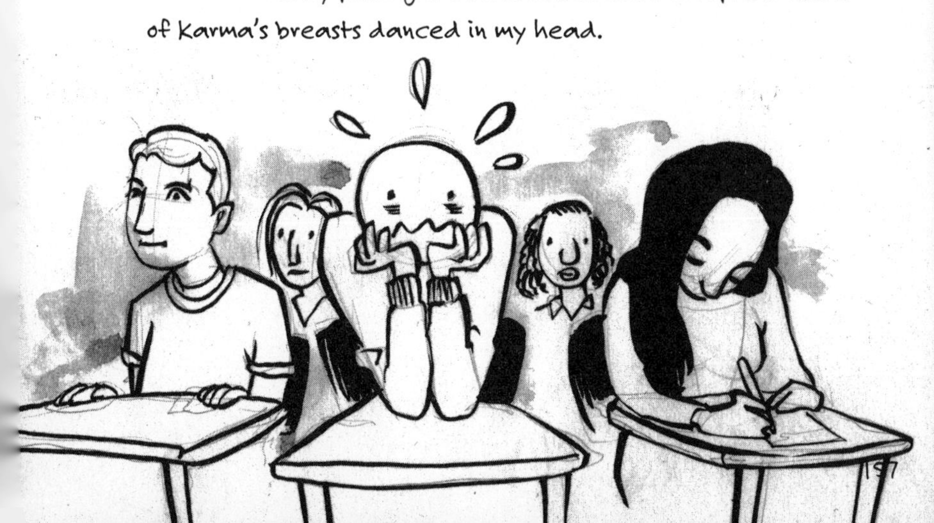

After third period, Karma and Misty found me in the hall.

"There you are!" Karma said. She wasn't embarrassed or angry, which was a relief. And Misty was grinning ear to ear. I wondered how much she knew.

"I have to get to class, so . . ."

"It was a joke, Happyface, relax." Karma seemed cool about it. I was less than convinced.

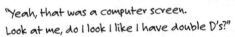

"A joke?"

"Okay, a test. I just wanted to see how serious about Gretchen you were. And you passed, turning all THIS down." She waved her hands along her body.

"Gretchen? But . . . what about the picture?"

"Yeah, that was a computer screen. Look at me, do I look I like I have double D's?"

She didn't.

"Such a virgin, Face. Such a virgin. But now I know you're not a perv, and the picture's a little clearer."

"And that makes me good enough for Gretchen?"

"Well, I didn't say that."

One thing's for sure, I'll have trouble looking at Karma the same way again.

TRUTH OR DARE

12/20

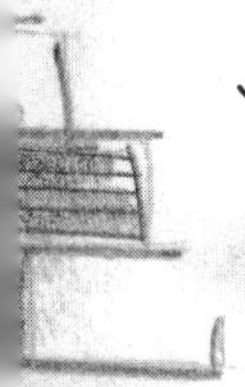

Yesterday was the Winter Dance, and as the day got underway, all I could think was, I can't escape Trevor. He'd managed to include himself in our plans, so we were now taking pictures with him before the dance and driving with him, and I was pretty sure he'd be more Gretchen's date than I would. That, on top of my regular nerves I get any time I have to do something out of the ordinary (which is more often than not), had me sick most of the day. I even contemplated canceling and letting Trevor take Gretchen. I've done more stuff in the past few months than I have in the rest of my life combined, but I still get nervous with every event, every party, heck, during most conversations. I think the butterflies in my stomach have set up permanent residence.

Gretchen looked beautiful when I arrived at her place. Trevor was already there, and he was the driver. We picked up Karma and Misty who, along with Trevor, were going by themselves.

We went out for dinner at a small restaurant by the ocean. After we took a few pictures, we went in to eat.

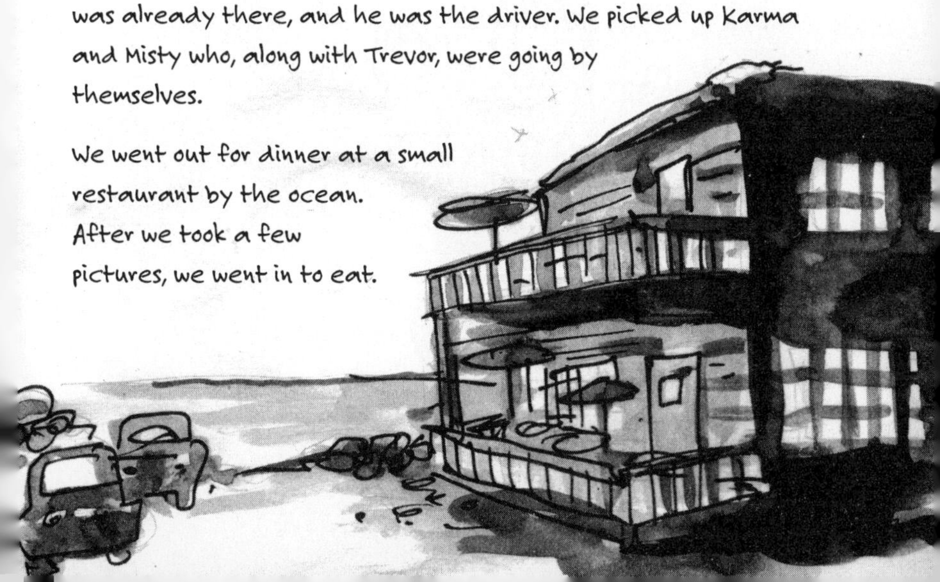

The evening really began then, with an epic game of Truth or Dare. Gretchen started the game, asking Trevor, "Truth or dare?" Trevor picked a dare. It was fitting as Trevor craves attention, and I can't think of much he wouldn't do.

"Okay," Gretchen said. "I dare you to order two dinners for yourself, and to eat it all. PLUS one thing from each of our plates."

"That's it? I could eat three dinners!" Trevor bragged.

"We'll see when you start dancing tonight." Gretchen and the girls laughed. He did order his two dinners, and he did eat it all.

Trevor targeted me next. Might as well get it over with, I figured. "Truth."

"Who gave you the money for the date auction?"

"Trevor!" Gretchen said, surprised. He was unfazed, though.

"Everyone," I said.

"Will you drop it?" Gretchen said.

"All right," I said, and let a still-pissed Trevor off the hook. It was my turn. "Misty. Truth or dare?"

Misty took the dare. It took me a minute to think of something. "All right. I dare you to flag down that waiter, ask for a refill on your drink, and slip him your number." Everyone seemed to think that was a good one.

"Excuse me . . ." Misty got the waiter's attention. "Could I have . . . a refill, please?" She handed him a paper that read "Call me . . . tonight."

After dinner, the game continued into the car on the way to the dance.

Truth: The last time Trevor thought of Gretchen while masturbating was that morning.

Dare: Karma flicked her tongue at a car in the passing lane.

Truth: Misty's dirtiest fantasy involves both tar and feathers.

The turning point of the evening came when it was Misty's turn. "Truth or dare . . . Happyface."

"Truth."

Misty turned in her chair to face me and asked, "Who is Chloe Hills?"

I looked at Misty for a second before observing everyone else's faces. Karma, Trevor, Gretchen. Who else knew about Chloe? What were they up to? No one said anything, they just looked back when I refused to respond. I just looked on, dumbfounded and wide-eyed. My mouth retracted to the slightest trace of a smile.

It was a complete invasion of privacy and it crossed a line. It's one thing to tease me, or whatever they're trying to do to manipulate my relationship with Gretchen, it's another for Karma to play with my feelings, but now they were actively digging for information, going behind my back, looking for dirt. My mind was on overload. What else do they know? Do they know about Everett? What do they know about Chloe? Where did they find out about her? Who were they talking to?

"Okay . . ." Karma took my silence to mean something. I still wasn't sure what to say.

"Is that the girl you were dating?" Gretchen asked. I didn't want to say yes. What if the Moons know I never actually dated Chloe? I still hadn't said anything.

"What do you know? Who's Chloe?" Gretchen asked Misty.

"I'm not going to say if Happyface doesn't want me to."

Trevor was curious now, too. "Happyface never had a girlfriend. What is she, your mom or something?"

"All right, I lose the game" was the last thing I said before arriving at the dance. Everyone was quiet after that.

"The Winter Dance"

12/20

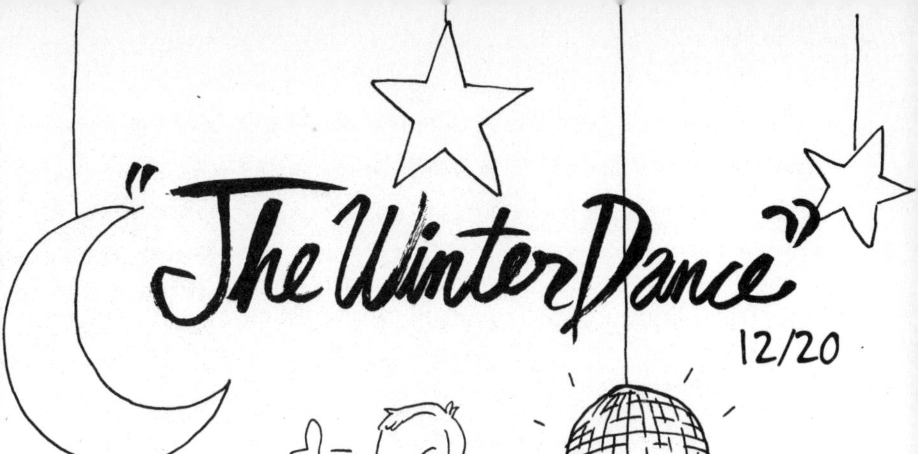

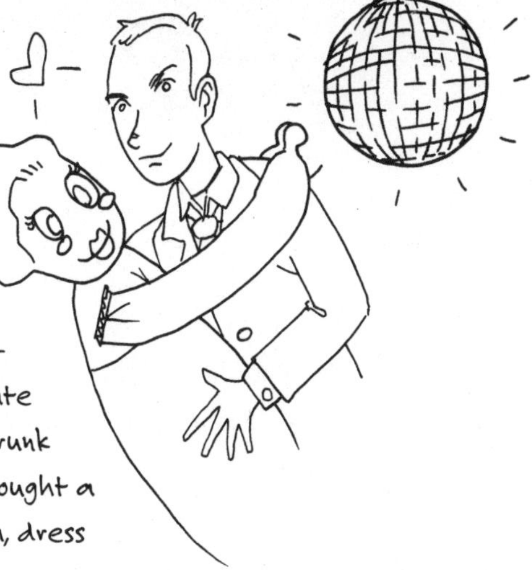

We all made it into the dance, Gretchen and I, the Moons, and Trevor and his date. I should mention Trevor had his date tucked away in the trunk the entire time. He brought a blow-up doll in with him, dress and all.

I wasn't having fun like I'd planned, even with Gretchen there. Neither of us mentioned Chloe, even though she was all I could think about now. I felt like I'd been run over and narrowly survived, and now I was expected to dance. I just wanted to go home. I didn't want to spend the night with the Moons, whom I'd lost all trust in, and I didn't want to spend any time with Trevor. And it was even weird hanging around Gretchen because I knew what she must be thinking. She probably trusted me less than I trusted Karma and Misty.

The tension wasn't just in my group. The gym was full of miserable couples, mostly nerds who paid to come here with girls who wouldn't talk to or dance with them. The gym was lit in cool colors, blues and greens, and cheap decorations plastered the walls. It was a desolate cocoon of heartbreak. The night couldn't go fast enough for me.

Gretchen and I sat at a table while the night plodded on, neither of us saying much.

"I'm sorry Misty asked about that," Gretchen apologized. "I know that's a sore spot, so I don't condone it or anything."

I gave her a smile. It wasn't her fault. "It's fine."

"It's not, though."

"No big deal." At least alone with Gretchen I can keep pretending Chloe was just some ex-girlfriend. "I should be over it anyway. It was just kind of a sucker punch, I guess."

Gretchen gave me a smile.

Once a slow song finally came on, I asked Gretchen if she wanted to dance. That was something I liked. I didn't have to try too hard, or pretend to have more fun than I was having, I could just hold Gretchen and sway gently. If it felt like the building was crumbling down around me, then Gretchen had a force field because for a brief moment I forgot about everything else. It ended quickly, though, and I soon found myself on the dance floor with an upbeat song playing. I still wasn't in the mood for it. The people around me formed a circle and were pushing people in. Gretchen twirled around before leaping back out, Trevor slid his doll between his legs and back and spun out, and some guy took his shirt off and threw it into the crowd. No, thanks.

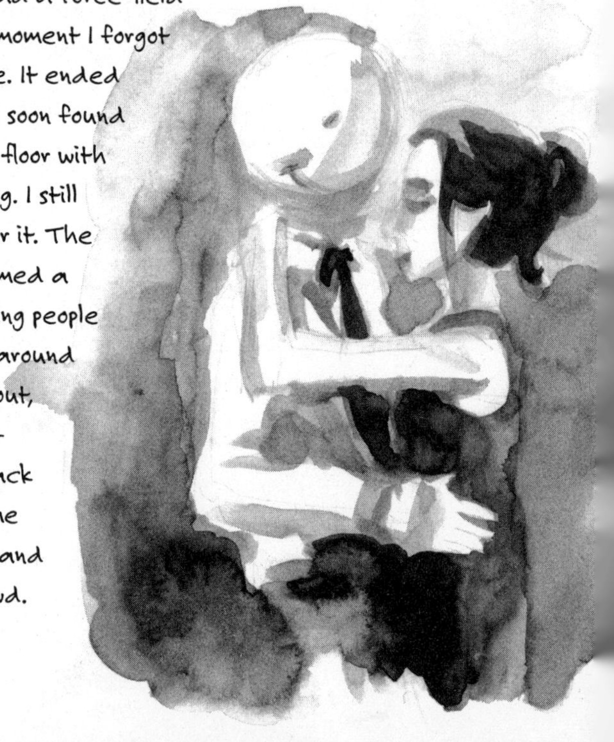

I got pushed in next, but I just wasn't feeling
   Happyface and quickly ducked back out. Gretchen spun me
around and pushed me back in. I did a little shuffle and
some jazz hands and escaped again. I made my way back to the
table so I could mope alone. I occasionally glanced back from the
now-empty table section and watched Gretchen having fun, the Moons
having fun, Trevor having fun. It was snowing outside. If the Chloe
incident was a snowball, then I was in a full-blown avalanche by this
point and I couldn't shake it.

I walked outside to cool off for a minute, and I felt a little better,
away from all the music and crowds and darkness and heat. It was
just me and my white breath floating against the black sky. The snow
silently falling had a calming effect.

I thought about Chloe more. About how I never even got to see her one
last time, no real goodbyes. She didn't "break up" with me to preserve
our friendship. She'd met someone else. She'd met Everett. I was
betrayed by two of the most important people in my life and I never
got to do anything about it, I never talked to either of them because
everything had already gone to hell when I found out. I was the
mockery of the world I'd left behind and now it was following me here.
The world that seemed so wide and open just hours ago was suddenly
crushingly claustrophobic.

The door opened behind me and I was surprised to see Trevor join me.

"Hey, Happyface," was all he said for a while. But there was more on his mind. "I know you like Gretchen, but . . . I like her, too. I don't think we ever got a real chance together." Honesty . . . very clever. "I just wanted you to know that I'm not giving up on her and I'm not trying to be an asshole to you or anything and I have nothing against you. I just can't stop thinking about her. I love her." This was getting awkward. I think I prefer it when he's a jerk.

"Trevor, she doesn't like you that way," I said. "It doesn't matter how you feel about her unless she feels the same."

"That's why I just want a chance to find out how she feels, like if she'd just really give it a shot."

"I think she likes me," I said.

He looked at me like he'd just been slapped. "Then why aren't you going out? If something was gonna happen, it would have happened by now. It's been months."

I could have sworn I saw my brother's face when I looked up at him. I took out the shovel and started digging my own grave. "How do you know nothing's happened?" He was listening. "We spent the day in the city together. She invited me over for Thanksgiving. Me, not you. We cut school and spent the day at her place."

"Please, you've never even kissed." He was trying not to show it, but I was getting to him.

"You don't know, and I'm not telling."

"Yeah, right, virgin." Trevor went back inside. Now I was ready to fight. I headed back in.

Trevor was talking to Gretchen at our table, which was still empty.

"There you are," said Gretchen.

"Want to go for a walk or something?" I asked.

"We're kind of hanging out," Trevor said.

"I understand, but if you'll remember, she's not actually your date and can make her own choices."

No one likes you, all right?

If you're hung up on Gretchen just ask her out already so she can turn you down and things can be normal again.

"And you're shady about everything. No one knows who the hell you are, let alone what you're doing here with us."

"Fine," I retaliated. I let it out. "What do you want to know? You want to know about Chloe? And my brother? They slept together.

My girlfriend cheated on me with my brother and yeah, I don't really like talking about it. I was hoping I could put it behind me." That's just the tip of the iceberg.

Trevor laughed and Gretchen got up to walk with me.

"Oh, come on, we're not done," Trevor said.

"Yeah," Gretchen said, "we are." She led me off to go find the Moons.

The night was pretty ruined, certainly for me, Gretchen, Trevor, and his blow-up doll. We gathered Karma and Misty, who were outside on the phone flirting with that waiter, and we all left early.

Trevor dropped us off at Gretchen's after a long, silent ride back. I got to talk to her for a bit before she went inside.

"I need to ease back with Trevor," Gretchen said. "He needs some time alone, I think."

"Gretchen, you don't have to do that."

"I do. He's had the wrong idea about me and him and maybe spending all this time together is a bad idea."

I nodded.

"I'm sorry tonight didn't go so well," she said. "You probably think you wasted your money at the auction. I should probably pay you back."

"Hey, at least we got that one dance. That was worth every penny and a million more."

"Are you putting the moves on me again?" Gretchen asked. I gave her a big hug. It was worth every penny.

OH HAI, ITZ HAPPYFACE: THE WEBCOMIC-IN-PRINT
Christmas Edition

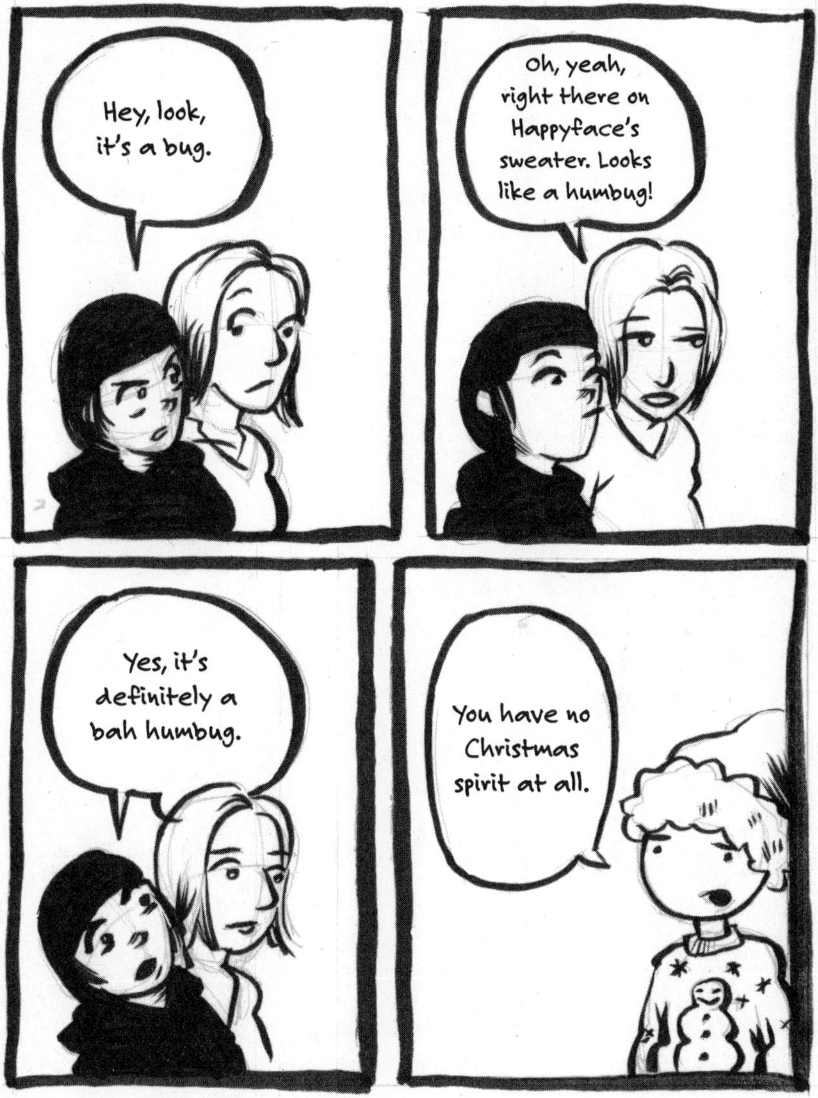

Hey, look, it's a bug.
Oh, yeah, right there on Happyface's sweater. Looks like a humbug!
Yes, it's definitely a bah humbug.
You have no Christmas spirit at all.

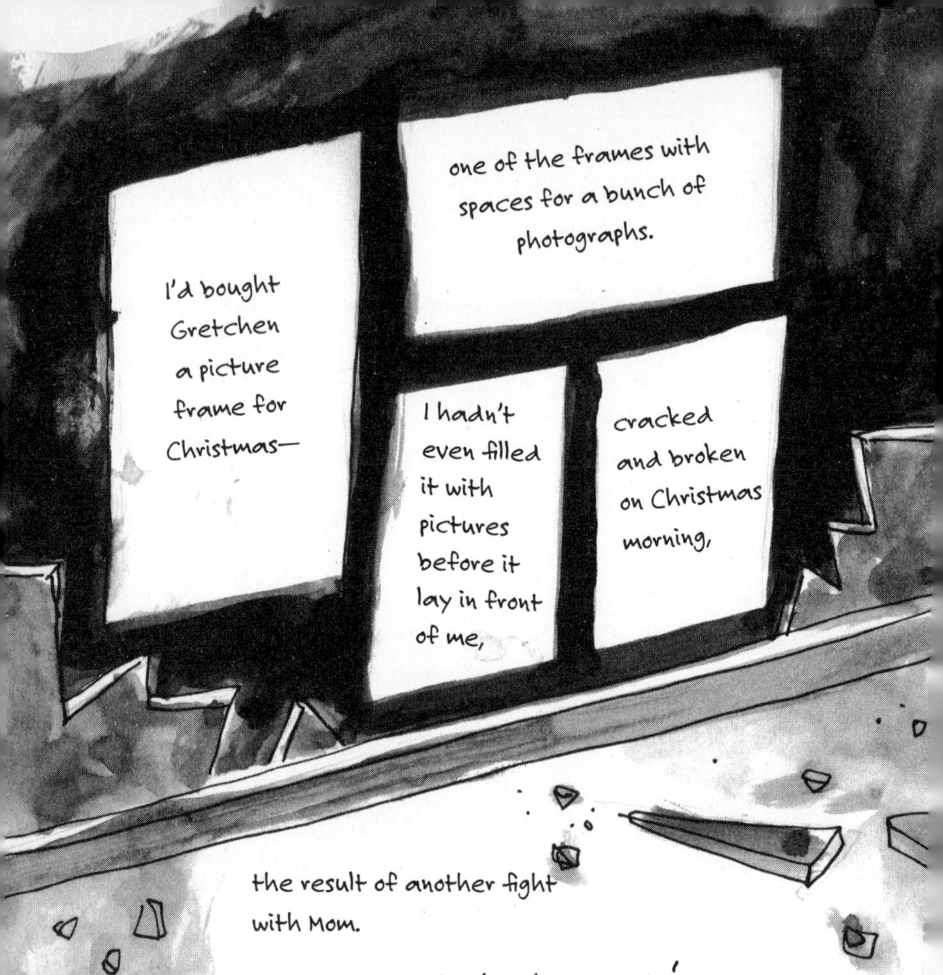
I'd bought Gretchen a picture frame for Christmas—
one of the frames with spaces for a bunch of photographs.
I hadn't even filled it with pictures before it lay in front of me,
cracked and broken on Christmas morning,
the result of another fight with Mom.

CHRISTMAS 12/25

I'd spent more money than I had (I still owe money to a few people) on it, but I wanted to do something thoughtful. Gretchen had given me more fond memories than I knew what to do with, and I wanted to pay tribute to them and let her know how important they were to me. Christmas morning, Mom informed me I couldn't go to Gretchen's to give her the gift.

"Again?" she asked. "Is this girl your family now? Is that where you're going every holiday? Doesn't she want to spend the day with her own family?"

"No," I said.

"Besides, the roads are covered in snow. It's too dangerous to take your bike out. She can come here if she wants, but you're staying home for Christmas."

The control issues, again!

"I'm going, whether you like it or not!"

"Can you do this one thing for me?" she asked. "We've had a rough year, and it's Christmas."

"Fine," I said, and threw the frame down the hall. It broke as it hit the floor. "I won't be needing this!"

"We don't own these walls," Mom said.

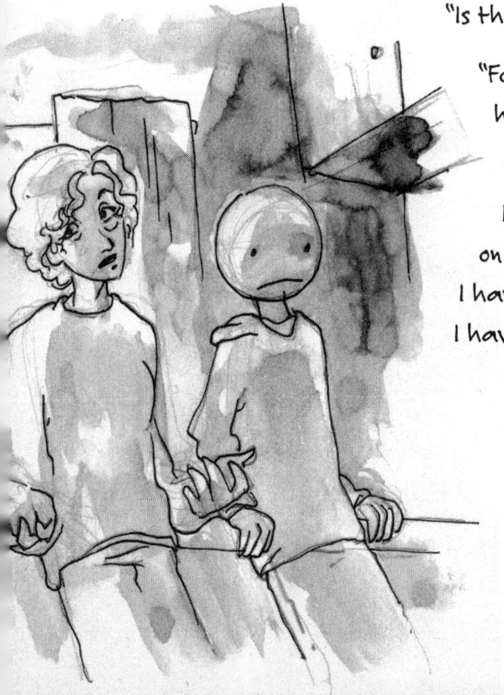

"Is that all you care about?"

"For crying out loud, give it to her tomorrow. Don't act like such a baby!"

I didn't want to ditch Mom on Christmas or anything, but I have more going on in my life, I have other people I need to see. Our horrible year is turning out to be the best thing to happen to me, but I had to somehow act like we're on common ground. Mom had been dwelling in the past, moping and being an emotional roller coaster, while I'd been using this all as a chance to create a new and better life. Things are only as bad as you make them, the way I see it. I just needed to avoid these tantrums and . . . and that's when I realized I'd just ruined Gretchen's present. I had no money to buy her another.

I still wanted to do something nice for Gretchen, so I drew a picture for her. It was just a picture of her, something I've gotten decent at. I don't want to be the art kid here, I don't want to be the "Kid in the Corner Who Might Be Drawing You," I want to be Happyface. And drawing pencil portraits may not be a very cool thing to do, but it's Christmas, I'd just thrown a picture frame at a wall, my mom was off sulking, and I was feeling incredibly emotional. I had images of Gretchen tearing up when she saw what I'd made, maybe looking me in the eye, and she'd grab me and hug me and kiss me on the lips.

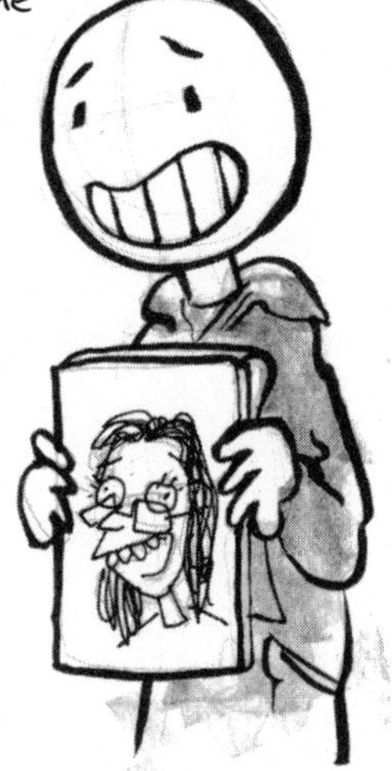

"It's all right, it's no big deal, it's just a picture," I'd say with great humility. "You know, a picture's worth a thousand words. But this one's just worth three. I love you."

Okay, that last part didn't even happen in my fantasy.

Mom cooked a big dinner. We ate in silence until Mom asked me how my grades were in school and I lied and said they were fine. Things have changed so much that it's kind of nice when I can just sit with Mom and talk. I didn't want to argue about grades. She asked about Gretchen so I told her a little about her and about the Moons and even Trevor and everyone else. She smiled in a way that made me blush, in that "my little boy, all grown up and making friends" kind of way.

After dinner, she said the roads were clear enough if I wanted to go see Gretchen. I just had to call home when I got there. We both apologized for earlier and hugged. I felt better about everything.

Gretchen was having dinner with her family but she said it was okay if I wanted to stop by and exchange gifts.

I went over around seven and said hi to everyone. Gretchen brought over a present for me. It was a necklace, a brown leather one with two rings on it.

"One is you and the other is me," she said. "I figure it's okay to wear since a girl gave it to you and all."

It was the coolest gift, way better than mine. Now I can keep a part of her around my neck all the time. I gave her the picture I drew of her.

"Oh, wow," she said. "I didn't know you could draw. Awesome!" She said she'd put it up on her wall. Her mom came over and took a look at it, too.

"Very nice," she said in a way that sounded kind of like "You're still not good enough for my daughter" to me.

Gretchen didn't cry or touch her heart but she did give me a kiss on the cheek. That's like half a base, and the farthest I've gone with a girl yet. I walked outside, red as a balloon and light as a feather and let the wind blow me home.

The Sordid Love Affairs of Happyface, Volume II: Megan

Gretchen isn't the first pretty out-of-my-league girl I've chased. In fact, neither was Chloe. Yes, the hero of our tale has lusted after many an unattainable female.

In the fifth grade, it was Megan Collins. Blond hair, perfect smile, big cheery cheeks that made her seem like someone you could just breathe in and she'd fix your every ailment. Of course, she hung out with the cool kids, and I hung out with comic books. Even the nerds she associated with were all really smart and sociable. I was a nobody.

I had a few brief brushes with her that set my fantasies ablaze. One time she wanted to borrow my game system in study hall. I told her sure, and she started playing and all the cool guys gathered around her to watch. She almost beat the game in a short thirty-five minutes, and what man's heart wouldn't skip a beat at that?

Now that I had established some amount of contact with Megan, I'd do anything I could do to be on her mind for even five seconds. I asked her every study hall if she wanted to borrow my games. I brought her sodas or chocolate each day. I'd ask if she needed help with homework. I was her subservient little toad, her pet, sitting at her feet, starving for any kind of attention. I'd have done anything for her.

It was in the same study hall. She asked me to draw her something on her textbook cover. This was something I was a little bit famous for, not to brag. Any kind of popularity or even tolerance from others I had always revolved around my art. One of the things I did was I drew pictures on blank book covers. I'd just make weird stuff up: inane conversations TV show stars would have with each other, comic book heroes fighting, comic strips involving other students. I did one for Megan that was a cartoon of her with a bunch of boys in chase. It was my way of saying, "Megan, you are beautiful. Enough so that I envision every boy here must love you."

She never commented on it. Just a smile and a thanks. Why won't a girl ever cry for my art?

Word got around about the book cover.

"Why don't you go out with Megan Collins?" guys would ask. The funny part for them was knowing a girl like Megan would never date a guy like me. I was lucky to be on her radar at all.

One day I was looking at her on the school bus. How could I not? The smile, those cheeks, her long neck . . . Then I heard,

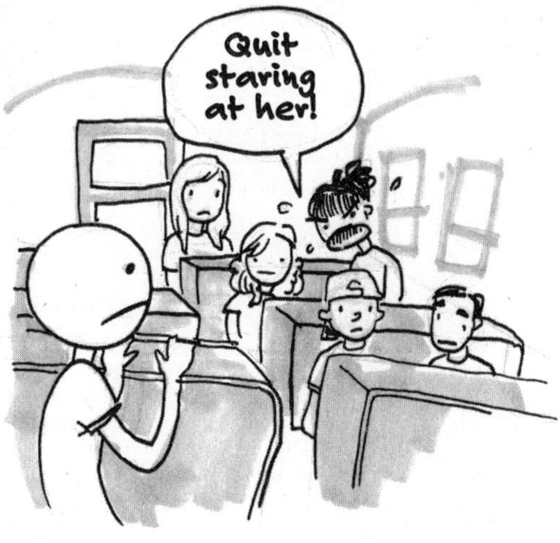
Quit staring at her!

One of her friends saw me. This started a backlash—I had gone through most of my days unnoticed, but when I finally was noticed, it was far worse.

Guys would pelt me with spitballs in class. They'd always pretend they were being nice. "I think Megan likes you; you should ask her out!"

They'd say, "We need to get you a girlfriend," before asking out every unpopular, fat, or mentally disabled girl in the lunchroom "on my behalf."

Each girl would turn me down as I was pointed out. This was all for my benefit, and of course it was always in front of Megan Collins.

With time, I could always disappear again, and the teasing would disappear with me. But I could never quit looking at the Megan Collinses of the world.

NEW YEAR'S EVE 12/31

Gretchen had been planning this New Year's Eve party for months, ever since she found out her parents were going to their friend's house on Long Island for the weekend. Sometimes I think she'd be much happier if, instead of her parents going away on holidays, it was the only time they came to visit. She really springs to life when she's got the place to herself.

I sat on the couch alone for most of the evening at the party. I sat and sulked and faced the TV, though I couldn't tell you what was on. My head was busy thinking about Chloe, thinking about home, thinking about Gretchen off in the corner talking to other guys. I was thinking about how we hadn't really talked in the past week since the cheek kiss. Maybe I'm just not interesting enough. Maybe girls can only like me until they get to know me. I shouldn't have drawn her that picture, now she probably sees me as some geeky art boy, sitting at home drawing all night. It's not inaccurate; it's just not how I wanted her to see me. I was thinking about the Moons, hanging out with their friends, telling all their in-jokes. Wondering why they had to go digging into me. Wondering what they found out. If they know.

I was joined on the couch by a chunky fellow, with dirty hair and a barely present moustache. A talker.

"Not feeling it, either, huh?" he said. I wasn't really in the talking mood, hence the sitting alone on the couch.

"Feeling what?"

"New Year's. I hear ya. It's all couples and kissing, and if you're someone like one of us, it's better to just stay home." He didn't look at me, at least. He just sighed and slouched farther into the couch.

I raised my eyebrows.

There was a burst of laughter in the dark corner where Gretchen was. Her group had grown by a few people. Gretchen was drinking.

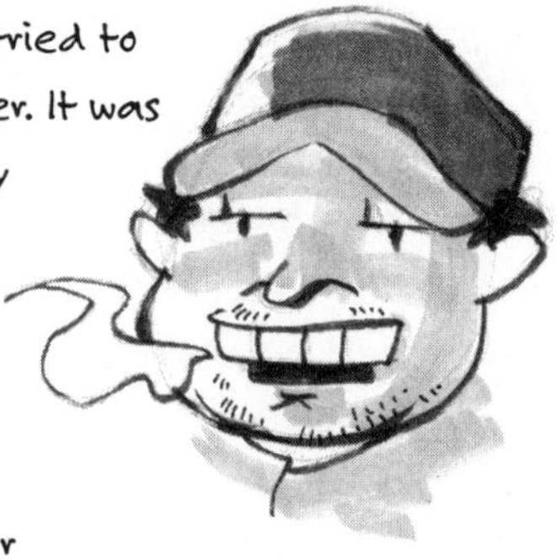

Creepy Guy burped under his breath. He tried to hide it, at least, but the smell carried over. It was sulfuric. This was punishment for sitting by myself, surely.

"Last year I had a girl," Creepy Guy continued. "I had Gretchen, actually. I don't remember seeing you here, but I guess you must know her since you're in her basement." The night was looking longer by the second. "She's different, man. She doesn't look at you the way everyone else does. She's got a way about her, she sees right down to your soul, you know? And she never judged."

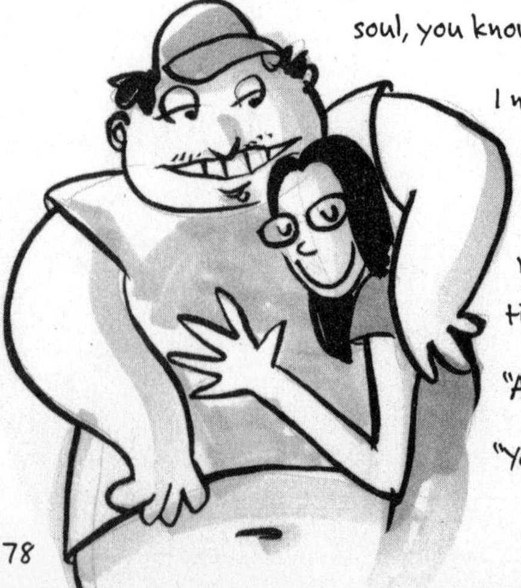

I nodded. Why would Gretchen date this smelly cretin?

"She was my one love. From December fifteenth to January fifth. Best time of my life."

"And then she dumped you?" I asked.

"Yeah, for now. My life here is over but

I'll be going to college in the fall and I'll just start over there, man. New start."

I could relate to that.

Someone put on a loud CD and I wondered if the night would ever end. I stared at the clock for a solid twenty minutes before it finally changed from ten fourteen to ten fifteen. Time had slowed to a crawl.

"You have a girlfriend?" he asked.

I lied. "Before I moved here."

"Oh, okay. So you know what it's like then. Everything's different; it's not so dark anymore. It's not so quiet all the time when you've got someone. It's like . . ."

He trailed off. "Sometimes I wake up in the morning and I'm not sure why I do it." I was considering dialing nine and one, just to be prepared. "So I just sit here and keep to myself, you know? 'Cause what's the point, man? You might as well, you know?"

He was making less sense, if possible. I don't even think he was drunk. Was this what I used to sound like?

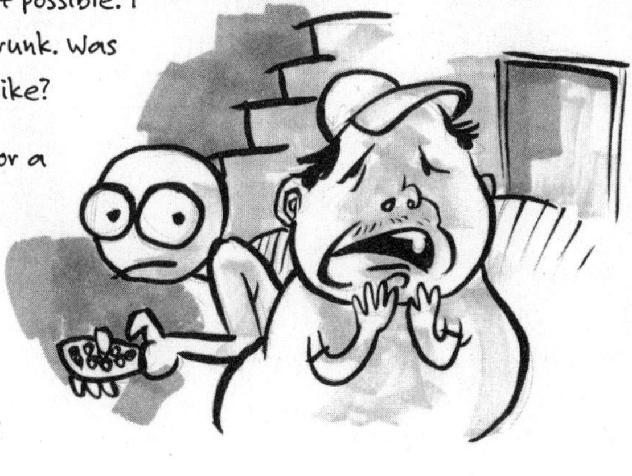

He watched TV with me for a while before Gretchen told everyone we were heading outside. At last. I got up quickly, but he followed suit. He gave me a hug and I hoped the smell didn't transfer.

"Hey, Happy New Year's, brother." I wished him the same. Better to be a friend than a potential victim.

Outside, we trekked down the street and into the woods. It was 11:30 or so, and every year they had some fireworks down at the lake.

I was thinking a little more positive on the way. If Gretchen could date someone like that, she could definitely date me. That gave me more confidence than ever to finally ask out Gretchen. I'd thought of writing a letter to her, but it would probably end up with the countless other letters I'd written to girls I liked and wisely never sent. It was almost January first, and my Happyface experiment almost crashed right in front of me. This was as good a time as any to renew my Oath. I don't want to turn into Creepy Guy, that's for sure.

When we got to the lake, I found Karma, hugging herself to keep warm. I gave her my jacket.

"Thanks!" she said.

"Happyface, there you are!" Gretchen was right near them. I talked with them as we sat in the sand and waited for midnight. My worries quickly melted away as I laughed and smiled with them. Even the Chloe thing was forgiven in my mind.

The fireworks started at twelve a.m. The sky lit up in light purples and blues but the fireworks were completely obstructed by the trees.

"Shoot, we need to get over there," Gretchen said, pointing to another clearing through some more trees. No one made any effort to leave, though. We were content where we were.

5th Grade

Hi Megan. I know we've never spoken or anything before, but that's why I'm writing this letter, I figure I can say awkward things more precisely in writing. Plus there's the problem of me being shy and unable to say anything in person.

Anyway, you seem like a really nice person and someone I would like to know better. Maybe we could go to a movie or something? I'm sure my mom could bring us there and back. We could do whatever else, too, I don't know if that's lame or whatever. So just tell me if this is creepy or whatever and we can pretend I never wrote anything. I'm pretty sure the paper is very flammable so we can just get rid of any evidence this ever happened, super easy.

I guess this is probably rambling now, so much for the benefits of pen and paper.

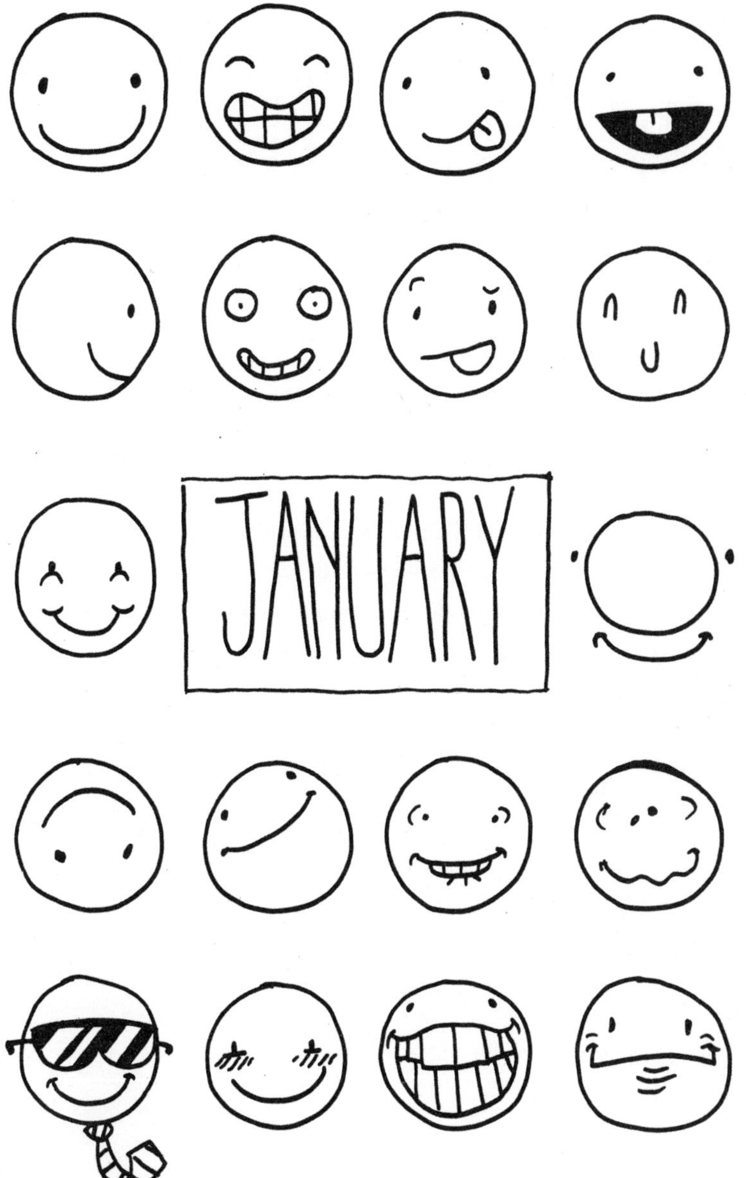
JANUARY

SUPERHEROES

I still have boxes of things I never bothered to unpack. I opened one of them tonight and found my comic book collection. I've always had an affinity for comic books, superheroes especially.

They're bigger than life. The secret identities, the cool costumes, the moral dilemmas, the villains; everything is always interesting. I always wanted to be a superhero. Maybe this is odd, considering how un-superheroic I am. I couldn't even beat imaginary enemies when Everett and I would play Batman when I was little. Somehow I'd always end up tied to chairs or locked in bathrooms for hours.

The things I'd do with the right powers . . . with super strength I'd have never been bullied. I could fly away in escape. Invisibility would be bad news, leading only to a life of perversion. If I could go back in time, I'd fix everything the past year messed up.

I guess the comic heroes are just what I wish I could be.

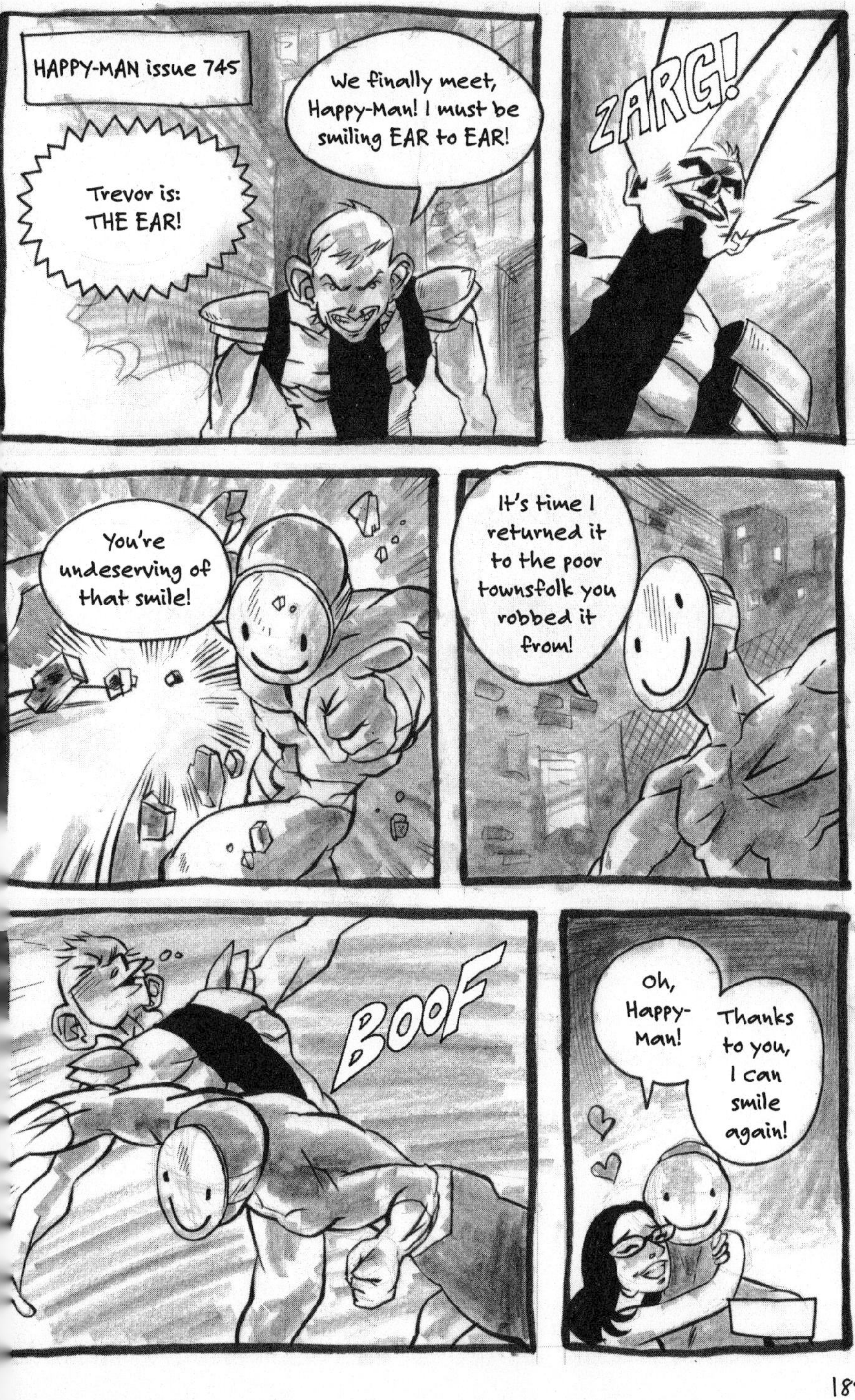
HAPPY-MAN issue 745
Trevor is: THE EAR!
We finally meet, Happy-Man! I must be smiling EAR to EAR!
ZARG!
You're undeserving of that smile!
It's time I returned it to the poor townsfolk you robbed it from!
BOOF
Oh, Happy-Man!
Thanks to you, I can smile again!

MY ROOM

I keep the TV on just so the apartment doesn't feel so empty. Money is tight, even in our little home, so Mom started working a second job. It's been really quiet. She works at the law firm all day and then she goes to this department store where she's the night shift manager. She leaves something for me to eat in the fridge with a little note usually, and other than that I only see her briefly before I go to bed.

It's odd how sitting in my room and writing and drawing with the TV on is basically how I spent most of my life, but knowing that Everett was next door reading comics, or that Dad was writing in his study or watching TV in the living room, or that Mom was reading or cooking things made such a difference. Even if I didn't see them.

Once Everett left for college, Mom started drinking more. Some nights I'd go out for a snack, and there she'd be, drunk with sharp knives around her, trying to cook stuff, the kitchen a mess. I didn't want to leave her, fearing she'd accidentally hurt herself, and in the early stages of drunk she'd be chatty. I actually liked sitting and talking to her then. Dad would come out and finish cooking with her, nodding his head toward my room and I'd head back in and shut the door.

I miss having Dad around to help with my homework and look through my drawings. He didn't rant and rave about them like some people did but he always had good advice, or at least something to say.

Where is he? Mom dodges the question every time I ask. Maybe he's just happy being a bachelor again and doesn't even think of me. I wish he was here. Even an apartment as small as ours is feels too big. I close my door and turn on the TV and all the lights and spread my stuff in front of me just to forget what's out there for a little while.

OH HAI, ITZ HAPPYFACE: THE WEBCOMIC-IN-PRINT HAPPYFACE edition!

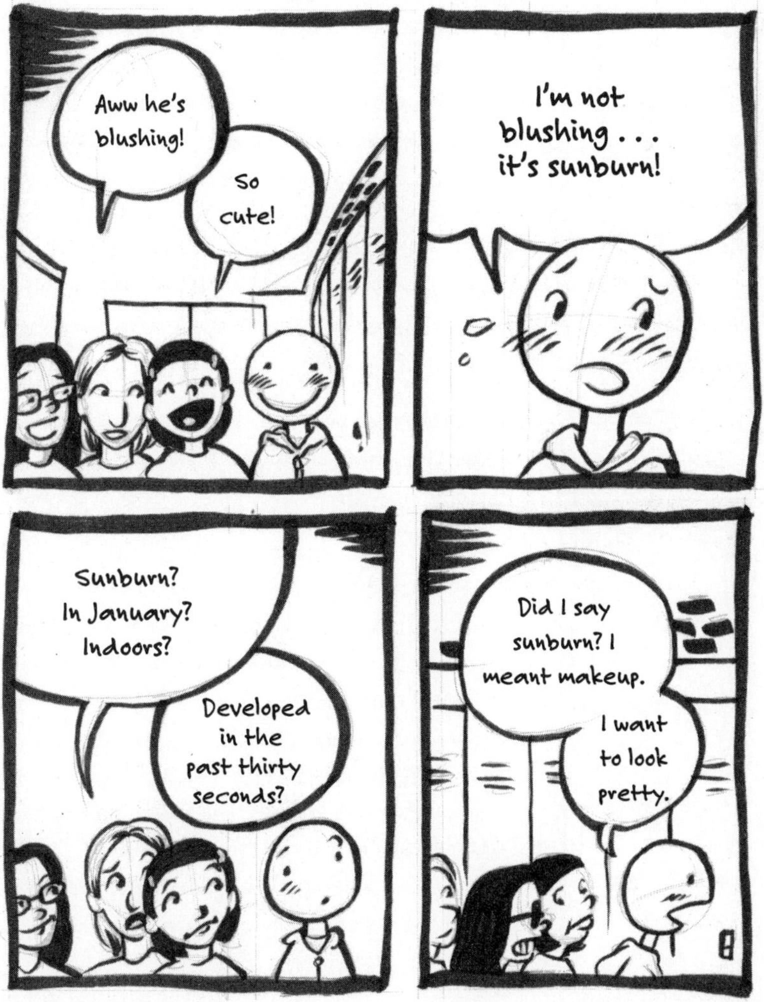

Aww he's blushing!
So cute!
I'm not blushing . . . it's sunburn!
Sunburn? In January? Indoors?
Developed in the past thirty seconds?
Did I say sunburn? I meant makeup.
I want to look pretty.

PROJECT HAPPYFACE

School life is going great as ever, which is number four for "Things I Never Expected to Say." I wish I knew how powerful attitude was earlier in my life, that a nobody can be somebody if he just wants it enough. It turns out when I'm not hiding, people honest-to-God like me, or at least do a good impression of people who honest-to-God like me. Mom's known me for sixteen years so there's only so much "Happyface" I can be at home, but at school I can be who I want and I'm rewarded for it. With the right laugh and smile almost anything can go my way, and everyone smiles and laughs with me. I don't even have to be actually funny. I don't even have to make sense. It's kind of easy when you think about it. The worst thing about it is my cheeks getting sore on occasion.

Just today, I'm talking to Gretchen one minute, and then Frog and Oddly pull me away the next. They had a bunch of pictures and clippings and stuff and they decorated my locker for me.

In Molly's class, I'm not even the new kid anymore. This kid Bryan Chamberlain is the new-new kid ("Bryan Chamberlain is... NNK", coming to Fox!). Bryan has these big giant glasses like no one wears anymore, but he seems nice enough. I inducted him into class. I told him that I was new here a few months ago and I had to stand on my chair and sing "The Star Spangled Banner" to gain acceptance. "It's like a gang initiation," I said. Even Molly chuckled at that.

Gym class has gotten better, too, since Trevor started leaving Mike and me alone. I still suck at sports, but at least I'm somewhat included in games. The small amounts of teasing I once shared with Mike are now wholly his responsibility.

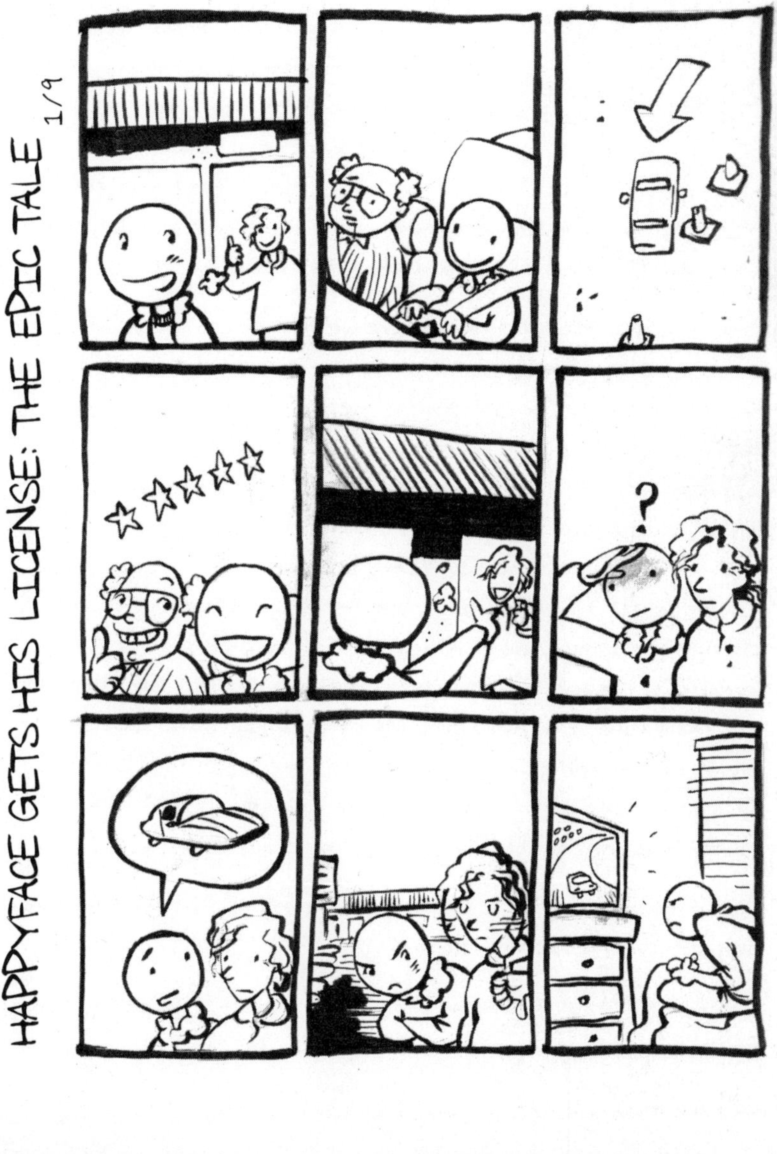

HAPPYFACE GETS HIS LICENSE: THE EPIC TALE
1/9
?

THE POEOKE
THAT ALMOST
WAS

So last night was to be the
night I asked out Gretchen.
Things kind of got there, though
with quite a few detours.

We were going to karaoke, for
starters, which made it a horrible night
to ask out a girl as I am completely tone-deaf and unable to sing.
That was the least of the awkwardness, though.

I took my bike to Gretchen's, where we all met up. The usual
bunch was heading there with a few extras. Gretchen, of course.
Myself, naturally. The Moons were there. Driving was the Trevor
replacement, Sharif, from lunch. Incredibly good-looking guy, and,
as I learned, another of Gretchen's exes. I was determined to not
use it as an excuse to dislike him, though, because she did date
that creepy guy at the New Year's Eve party, and Gretchen and I
have been getting along really well—some good-looking guy doesn't
change that. I needed to at least try. I couldn't be Happyface
twenty-four-seven and constantly be worried about Gretchen at
the same time. The two activities clashed like warm and cold
fronts and rained on my parade. (What a gem!) Even if Gretchen
said no, at least the tension would be gone and I could relax
finally, and that could only help my Happyface experiment.

"How about 'Poeoke'?" I asked on the ride there. "It's like karaoke,
but with poetry. You know, no singing."

"I don't think they do Poeoke here, Happyface." Gretchen looked
back at me. She was in front with Sharif.

190

I noticed that karaoke seemed to be located in awfully familiar territory. Then I noticed Gretchen whispering something to Karma and Misty. I wish I could have left it there, but Karma turned to face me.

"You're going to hate us," she told me in a gravely serious tone.

"What . . . ?" I was nervous enough about having to sing. This wasn't helping.

"Well, we made plans for karaoke night a while ago, and we kind of invited someone we maybe shouldn't have. And we tried to back out of it, but she really wanted to come. . . ."

"Oh, God." I realized where we were headed. We were nearing my old neighborhood. We were driving to Chloe's.

Karma and Misty apologized profusely. They didn't know things were so bad, they didn't know we "dated."

"What are you guys, best friends now?" I asked.

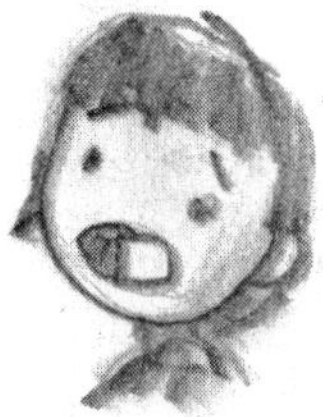

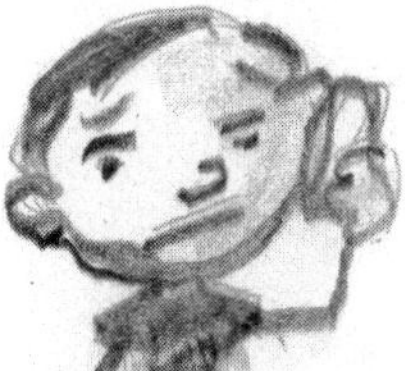

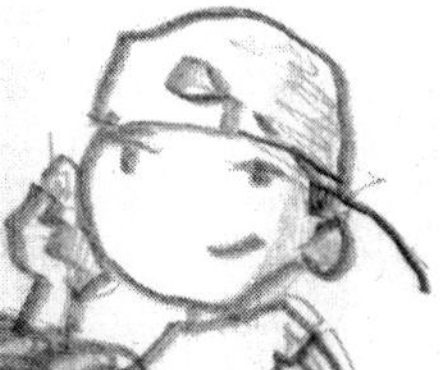

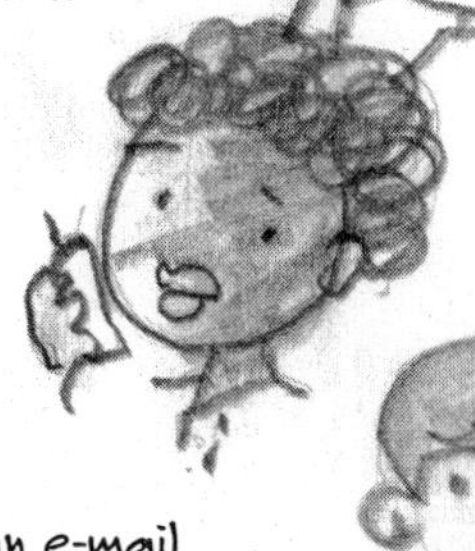

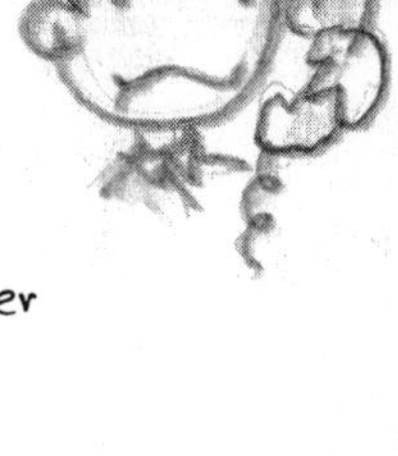

"No, of course not," Misty said. "I just asked my friend Bryan to call his friend Woody because he dates this girl Nya who went to the same school you did and she didn't know who you were, but she called her friend Chico, who said he heard of you but all he knew was that you hung out with this Chloe chick. So I found her on Facebook and sent her an e-mail and she seemed like REALLY interested in us all getting together and she seemed really nice so I didn't think it was a problem and karaoke is RIGHT by her house and I'm so sorry, I'm a horrible person!"

"Misty . . ."

"Face, I really didn't mean to. I added her on Facebook because I was curious, but I never even intended on writing her or anything."

"And?"

"And I made a post about karaoke and she wrote me and said it was right by where she lived and I might have mentioned you were going to be there. . . ."

This was definitely trouble. There's about a million things Chloe could say that would lead to everyone knowing everything and I could never be Happyface again.

"She wouldn't take no for an answer," Misty said.

We got to Chloe's. The floodlight went on. She ran out to the car, waved goodbye to her mom. This was feeling really heavy. She was wearing a hat; I'd never seen her wear a hat before. She opened the door and sat at the other end from me. She had a scar on her chin that made me feel queasy. I hoped no one would ask about it.

We were as squished as six people in a car can be.

"Sorry for the lack of space," offered Sharif. Stupid good-looking Sharif.

"It's okay." She looked over at me. She called me by my name to a startled car. This was not going well.

"He's Happyface around here," Karma interrupted.

"Our Happyface," Misty added.

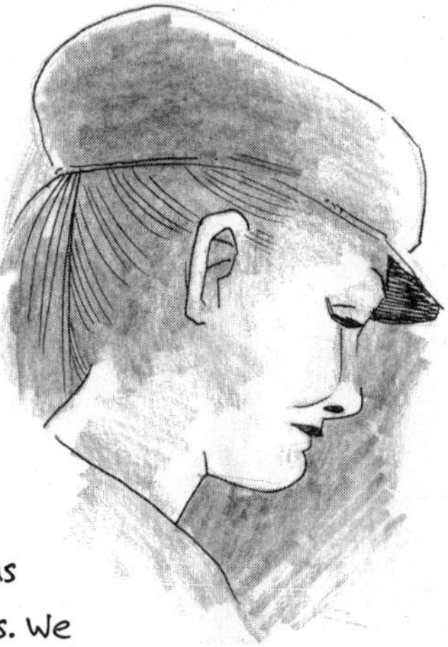

"Hi, Chloe," was all I could say. I felt my face flush while my knees jittered and I was trying my best to not be the insecure kid I was before coming to Crest Falls. Like Karma said, I'm Happyface now. Things were quiet and tense for the rest of the drive. Thank God it wasn't far.

We got to the restaurant where the karaoke was being held around nine, and the place was near empty. Old people were singing to old songs. We got a table and Chloe sat across from me. Somehow she was both incredibly beautiful and horribly ugly at the same time. I didn't know how to look at her anymore. It used to be like looking at the sun for me but now it was all toxic. She knew I didn't want to see her. She knew that when I never answered her e-mails or phone calls. Chloe is not part of "Happyface."

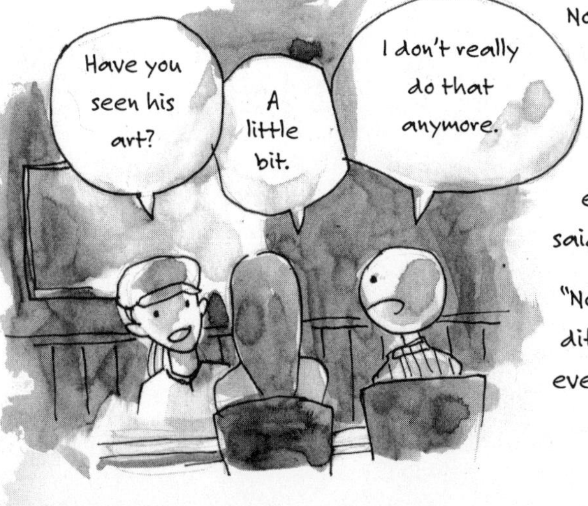
Have you seen his art?
A little bit.
I don't really do that anymore.

Not that I show anyone, anyway.

"But that was like your everything," Chloe said, concerned.

"Now I have different everythings," I said.

Another old couple got onstage and sang some old schmaltzy ballad. The music was depressing me.

"Have you been getting my e-mails?" Chloe asked.

"I still have Internet." I tried to be cryptic.

"Can we talk later, maybe?"

I watched the old couple singing and pretended not to hear her.

Gretchen had a songbook to look at. "Let's pick out songs!" she said, trying to help.

Sharif sang first. The jerk was a good singer, too. He sang some Neil Diamond song pretty flawlessly. He even kept the old people interested.

I was trying to stay fun while fighting the butterflies in my stomach. Giant butterflies. Poison ones, with razor wings. I smiled and joked about the song selection with Gretchen. I was hoping Chloe was jealous. These are my friends, cooler than yours. We have fun. We go to karaoke. You'd give anything to have friends like mine.

"So we're really doing this?" I asked. I was afraid more barf would come out than music.

"Uh, yeah! You're not backing out now, buster. We have to do something big and cheesy." Gretchen was looking at the eighties section.

"I'll do my best," I said. "I'm no Barry Manilow."

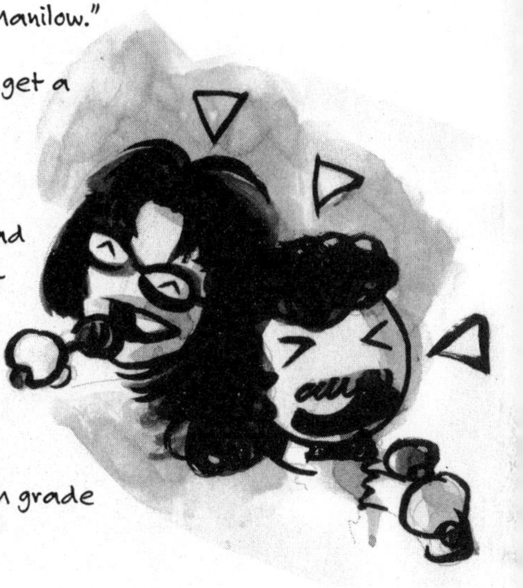

"Such a dork," Gretchen said. "Let's get a drink, that'll help. I need one, too."

I didn't think she was talking about Coke or Gatorade this time. Chloe had looked away, tapping the table like it was a typewriter. Drinks suddenly seemed like a really good idea.

"Do you have an ID?" I asked.

"Of course," Gretchen said. Silly fifth grade Happyface.

Gretchen went off to get us alcohol.

"This is weird, isn't it?" Chloe asked. "I shouldn't have come."

"Probably not," I said. "Whatever, let's just have fun. I'm really not about drama these days."

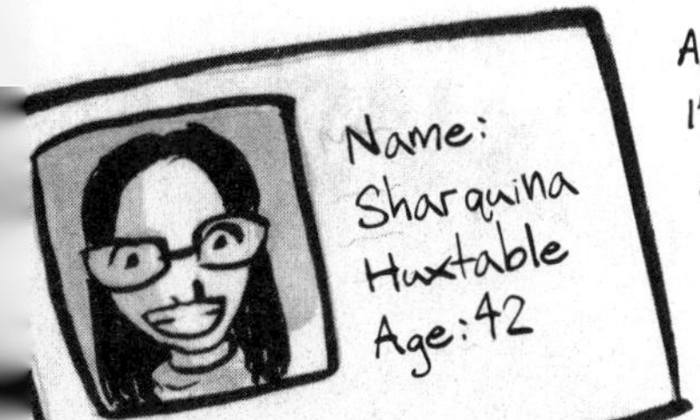
Name:
Sharquina
Huxtable
Age: 42

Against my every instinct, I smiled. I've gotten good at it. I can give an authentic smile without much work. "It's the past now."

To my amazement, Chloe smiled, too. Somehow I thought that she would be the one person to see past the smiles and know when I was lying. "I missed you," she said. I kept smiling, but I couldn't say it back.

Gretchen came back with some green drink. Alcohol had always scared me in the past because of what it would do to Mom and Dad. And Everett. Fights, ruined nights, lost jobs, and suspended licenses. Tonight was a different situation, though, and I knew it was just what I needed to get through this. An evil, sure, but a necessary one. I was sure it wouldn't taste like a lime Slushy, but I wasn't ready for it to taste disgusting, either. Gretchen laughed at the face I made, the one chip in my armor. Whoops.

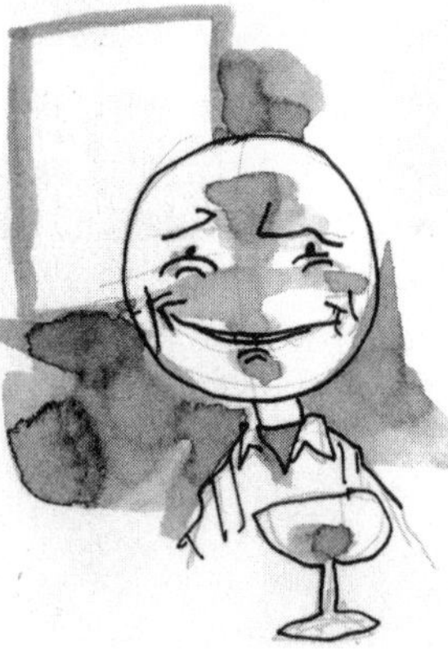

An hour later the drinks Gretchen and I were sharing had loosened me up.

Karma and Misty got up and did a rap song called "Baby Got Back" and were really funny. Sharif did a Nine Inch Nails song that had all the girls yelling for him and all the guys rolling their eyes. Gretchen and I did "Can't Fight This Feeling," though we both laughed through the verses. We cheesed up the chorus really well. I even got on my knees!

Chloe did some Beyoncé song. Sharif was yelling out for her and cheering and for a minute I wanted to punch him in his stupid handsome face. It's not like he even knew her. As we all had fun, I wished that Chloe and I could have been like this before. I didn't have any friends then, I was so antisocial. It all scared me. I always felt like any time I stepped out of my room I'd be shadowed by people with signs reading "inexperienced," "shy," and "weird."

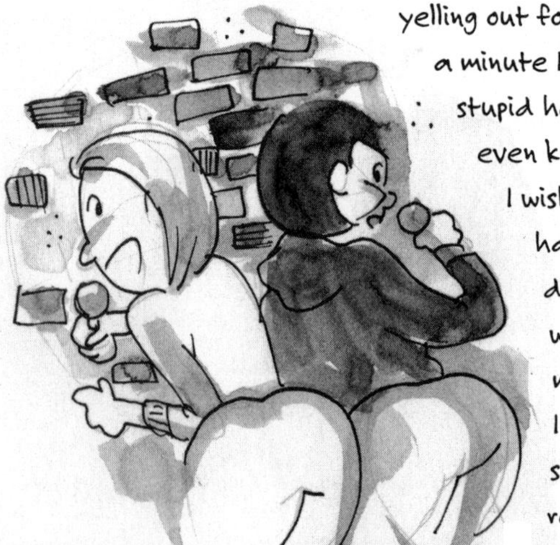

I gave Chloe a hug when she got down. "See, isn't this fun? I'm always having fun now," I said to her, probably in stupider words. I had to keep myself on some imagined pedestal. "It's too bad what you did, or we could have had more fun together."

I think Chloe was ready for it because she pulled me by my shirt and took me outside. Gretchen called after me but let it go.

"What? Did I say something?" I asked.

"No, you have every right, go ahead, say it, I've been waiting."

"I hate you," I said. Or maybe it was the drinks talking. "You ruined my life and I only hate you because I like you so much." In my head I wanted to shut up and just be cool but my mouth kept running on without me. If alcohol is a truth serum, then the truth is a sloppy incoherent mess.

"Why'd you have to do that to me, why would anyone do that, and now he's dead and I can't even say anything. I can't even fix things, he can't tell me what he was thinking 'cause he did something so goddamn stupid!"

I started crying and Chloe tried to hug me, but I pushed her back.

Chloe was looking hurt now, too. This wasn't doing anything, I decided. I wasn't feeling any better, just worse. I thought I'd made peace with this in my head. My brother was dead, he died in the accident with Chloe in the car, he died, Chloe lived, but they were both out of my life. I didn't need to deal with this now, because it had just become pointless and cruel.

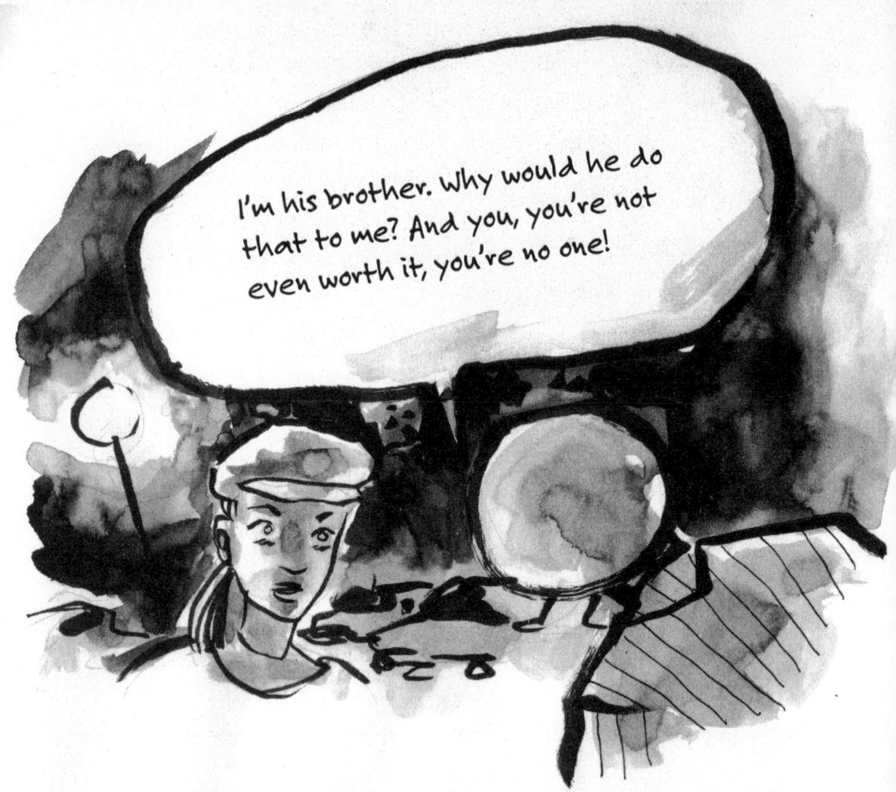
I'm his brother. Why would he do that to me? And you, you're not even worth it, you're no one!

I made my way back to the car and I leaned over and took some deep breaths. I wasn't crying hard or anything. I could recover still. I still had Gretchen. We could still be a couple. I emptied out my mind. Chloe stood back and watched.

"Whatever. I know I'm being insensitive. He was your boyfriend."

"You know he wasn't!"

"Is everything all right out there?" someone who worked at the restaurant asked. There were a few people standing around outside watching us.

I was calming myself down. Coming back to earth. I heard the bass thumping in the restaurant, felt the cold air. I was cold. It was warmer inside, so I headed back in.

Chloe and I came back inside and everyone was waiting for us. I felt dizzy and wanted to throw up. But seeing Gretchen turned in her chair in that purple and green lighting, waiting for me, out at some restaurant-turned-Tarantino set piece reminded me why I'd been smiling so much lately.

You okay?

"Yeah," I said as I got lost in the moment. "Thank you," I said as I leaned forward and kissed her, which at that second felt easier than asking her out. This is my life, Chloe. This is Gretchen. This is me and Gretchen.

She pulled away.

"No . . . ," was all Gretchen said. Chloe went back outside.

"I'm sorry. . . ."

"Can we go? Are you guys ready?" Gretchen said to the Moons and Sharif.

Gretchen apologized to them on the way out, and the Moons apologized back. I felt like an ass. I should have just kept my mouth shut. I was already embarrassed by the whole night.

"I'm sorry," I told Chloe as we dropped her off.

"You don't have to apologize for anything, ever," she said, before closing the door. "'Night, everyone. Happyface."

She must be so jealous, all the fun I have.

SOBERING UP

I wasn't myself quite yet when we got to Gretchen's house. The multiple moons in the sky were my first clue. Gretchen let me hang out for a while until I was okay to go home. She snuck me into her room from the basement so her parents wouldn't spot me and let us both have it. She turned on a soft lamp and shut the door.

"So, Chloe's pretty," she said. We both stretched out on her bed, watching the stars pasted on her ceiling.

"Yeah, but that's what I liked about her. She never acted like she knew it. She never acted pretty. She was very humble about it. That's what I like about you, too."

"Do you still talk to your brother?" she asked.

"He's dead," I wanted to say. But those were two words that would take me from party guy to pity party guy in an instant.

"Not so much," sufficed.

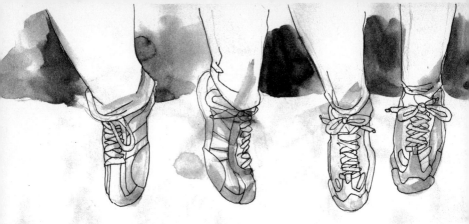

"That's too bad. I guess I'd still be mad, too," Gretchen said.

Was I mad? I was mad that he left without having to apologize, or face any consequences. Or that he couldn't at least tell me "You snooze, you lose," or some other stupid thing that would make me angry but maybe a little more proactive next time. I was mad that he stole Chloe when he knew how I felt, and almost killed her in the process. I was mad because he drove drunk with my best friend in the car with him and lost his life. I visited Chloe in the hospital and she told me she'd been seeing him for the past few weeks. And there she was, tubes sticking in and out of her and I had to pretend everything was okay. And I stopped talking to her right after that. I lost half my world.

But I couldn't tell Gretchen all that. Maybe she could read it in my face as it went through my mind, I don't know. Maybe she noticed my eyes well up.

"I'm not much of a drinker," was my one confession to Gretchen. She laughed. "I don't think I'll be drinking anymore."

Gretchen looked at me and didn't say anything and I could tell this was the kind of moment where a guy usually kisses a girl, except that I already tried that once with negative results. Now that I was more sober, I wasn't sure exactly how to kiss. Do I use tongue? Just lips? How long, if tongue is involved? Can I touch her? Is that forward? How much touching can I do?

Gretchen leaned over and kissed me and it all just happened. It was so natural and warm and incredible. I think I might even be a good kisser. Her lips touched mine and held them a second, pulled them toward her before letting go. Her eyes were locked on mine and that's all there was in the world: me, Gretchen, our eyes, lips. Her face moved toward mine and she kissed me again and our tongues touched. Gretchen held my hand, and pulled it to her leg, which I pet like a cat. She pulled my hand farther up, and I let it slide along her back. I was still afraid to be presumptuous. Gretchen's hand crept along my leg and inner thigh. I had an out-of-body experience as we sat there kissing at midnight in her room. She took off her glasses and I leaned over her and we continued to kiss. I stopped to catch my breath and my nose pressed against her cheek. I didn't know where it was supposed to go so I left it up to her.

"Are you sober now?" Gretchen asked.

I nodded my head yes and fell back into the bed, the stars on the ceiling reappearing. Gretchen snuck me back out and I went home.

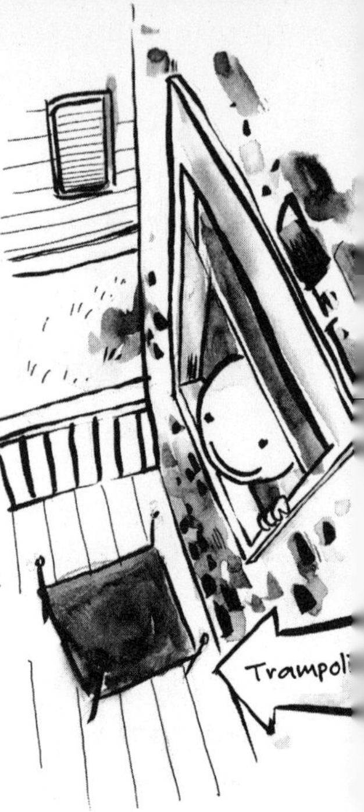
Trampoli

GROUNDED

My good mood would be short-lived. This was the second time my mom had ambushed me when getting home, and Gretchen's methods of sneaking in and out of her house were starting to look really smart. Unfortunately I'd have to grow a tree or something to reach my second floor bedroom without going through the front door.

"No more staying out so late," was the first thing she said. That was okay, we could work with that.

"You waited up to tell me that?" I asked, immediately regretting it. Smart aleck clashes badly with Mom.

"I got home from work an hour ago. It's not that late. I got a voicemail from your teacher Friday, he says you haven't been doing homework and you're failing in class." Ugh. Molly. "He says you tell jokes all class but you don't do any work. You want to explain that?"

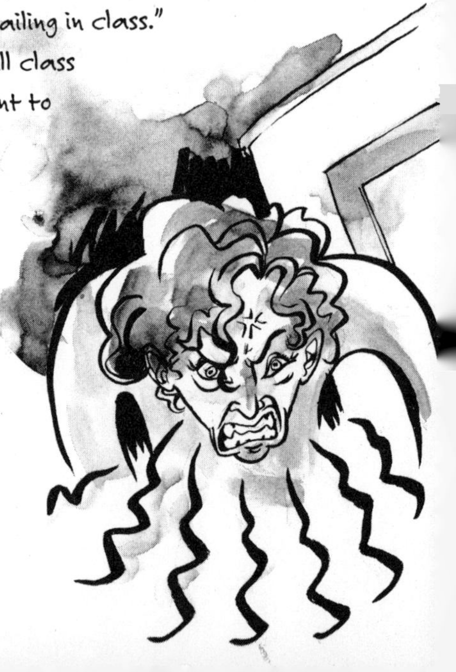

"You're just telling me this now?"

"When are you ever home?"

"Well, screw him," I said.

Mom got closer. "Screw him? That's your teacher. Great attitude!" She was too close, and I guess feeling sober wasn't the same as smelling sober. "Have you been drinking? Come here." She got close and smelled me as I closed my eyes and tensed.

She swung her hand back and slapped me right across the face.

"Mom!"

"How could you be so stupid? I can't believe this!" I was somehow crammed into the three inches between my mom and the wall.

"You know our family has problems with alcohol, you know what happened to your own brother, and your father, and me. What were you thinking? How could you do this to me? Say something!"

There was nothing I could say. Everett wrecked Mom's car when he was out drinking with Chloe. "Mom, it was just one time! I'm fine, okay?"

"No, you're NOT fine, you're not fine at all!" She had my shirt bunched up in her hand. "You can fool yourself and you can fool those friends you have, but I'm your mother, you can NOT fool me!"

She told me to go to my room, that she couldn't look at me and the next morning she told me I was grounded for two weeks and that I wasn't driving this year. Great timing. I finally get my license and I can't drive. I finally make out with Gretchen and now I can't even see her outside of school. I'll be the lame junior taking the big yellow limousine to school.

Two weeks. That's forever!

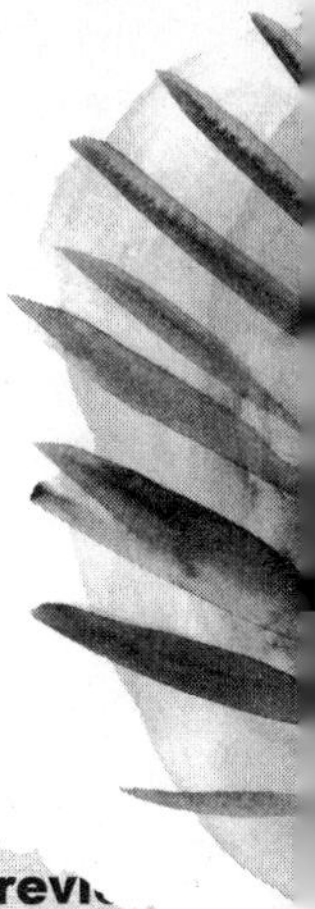

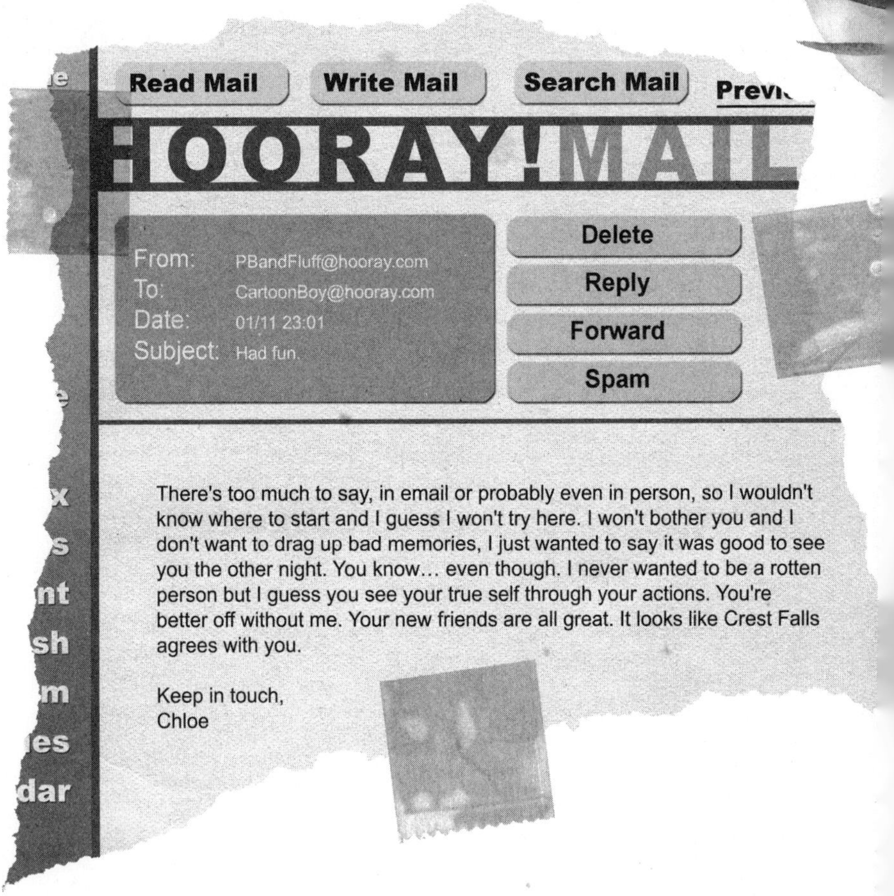

Read Mail | Write Mail | Search Mail | Previ

HOORAY!MAIL

From: PBandFluff@hooray.com
To: CartoonBoy@hooray.com
Date: 01/11 23:01
Subject: Had fun.

Delete
Reply
Forward
Spam

There's too much to say, in email or probably even in person, so I wouldn't know where to start and I guess I won't try here. I won't bother you and I don't want to drag up bad memories, I just wanted to say it was good to see you the other night. You know... even though. I never wanted to be a rotten person but I guess you see your true self through your actions. You're better off without me. Your new friends are all great. It looks like Crest Falls agrees with you.

Keep in touch,
Chloe

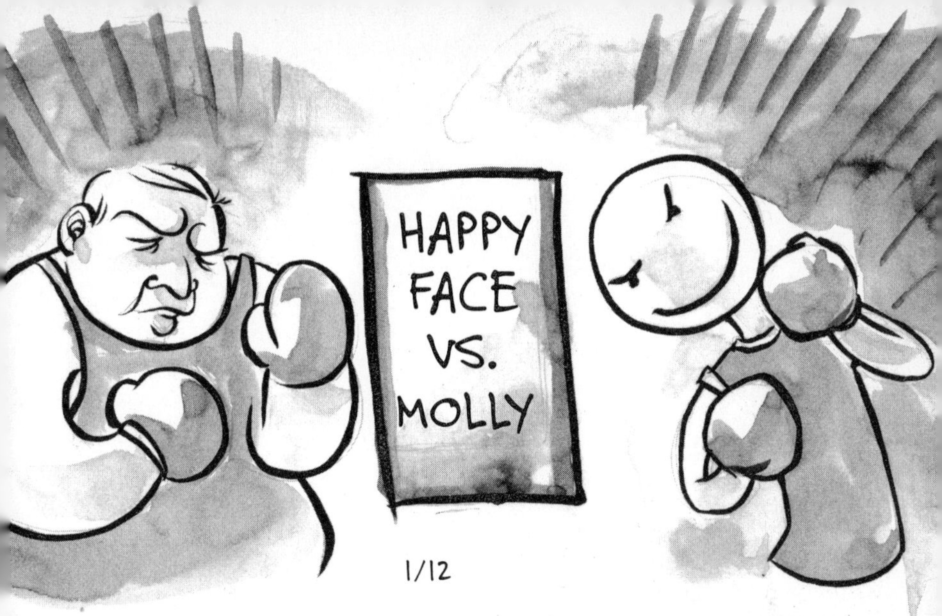
HAPPY FACE VS. MOLLY
1/12

Today was a drag as I didn't get any mention of our kiss from Gretchen. She smiled at me in a silly way during free period when I first saw her and that was as close to discussion of the event as we got. She probably regrets it already.

I was antsy through English, and I didn't let on how seething-with-rage I still was at Mr. Molly. I waited until everyone else left class before approaching him.

"Hey, Smiles," he said. I don't like Smiles. "How are you liking it here? We haven't gotten a chance to talk since you moved." He looked up at me like we were old friends.

I'm not really confrontational but I figure Happyface is. This could be an exercise. "Why'd you call my mom?" I asked. I was too timid to be much of a threat but I could at least talk it out.

"Well," he started, as if he had to give it thought. "Your grades have not been good. You haven't been taking class very seriously at all, which is fine. I'm all for fun in class, but even your journal entries are dripping with sarcasm. You changed a bit, from what I remember."

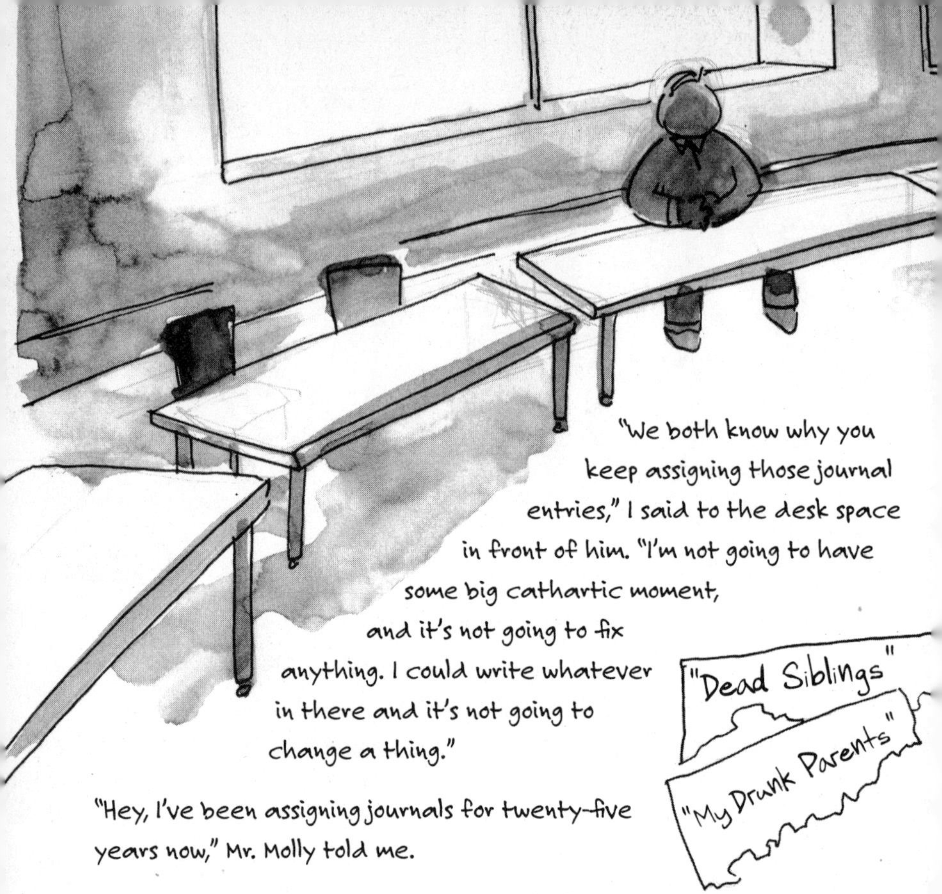

"We both know why you keep assigning those journal entries," I said to the desk space in front of him. "I'm not going to have some big cathartic moment, and it's not going to fix anything. I could write whatever in there and it's not going to change a thing."

"Dead Siblings"
"My Drunk Parents"

"Hey, I've been assigning journals for twenty-five years now," Mr. Molly told me.

I changed the subject, to not lose steam. "Why call my mom, why not just talk to me?"

"Okay, fair enough. So let's talk." He clasped his hands and smiled. That was MY move.

Molly had everything covered. I decided to leave before losing the battle completely. "If I talk to anyone it's not going to be the guy who flunks me out of class," I said before walking away.

Mr. Molly was the one who looked defeated now. "I didn't want to push . . . ," he started to say. Like I'd snap and lose it, go all crazy and attack the school. I'm just a dumb kid like every other tenth-grade failure. I lost some stuff, just like everyone else. It's really not so uncommon to lose a brother or a father or a best friend.

My family has history with Molly.
This certainly isn't the first time he's called my
mother. Everett had a class with Mr. Molly his senior year
of high school, and it became an ordeal that dragged its
way back home and affected pretty much everyone in the house.

At the time, Everett was drinking and smoking, he was out all
the time, and no one at home ever really said anything about it.
He was doing well with sports and generally pleasant around the
house, so the family just pretended it was no big deal. His only real
trouble was in class with Molly. Everett would complain to me and
say he was just a bitter old man who kept flunking him in class
because he was dating a cheerleader and Molly was creepy and
jealous. Ev would say that Molly's class was the only one he had
any trouble with, although that wasn't really true. Molly was just
the only teacher who bothered to call home and make it an issue.
When Everett couldn't get a decent grade in class, he stopped
trying altogether and ended the year with an F. He had to retake
the class in summer school in order to graduate.

I hated seeing Everett always leaving and doing who knows what
all night. Just a year earlier he was a different person, he was
actually kind of a nerd in a way. He was a lot more into computer
stuff and good grades. He was actually home more. I thought his
teacher must have seen him the way I did, and wanted him to
stay home more and do his homework and that probably Everett
really wasn't trying.

Looking back, though, Everett was right. Molly's an asshole. We
really could have bonded.

Yet Another of the Sordid Love Affairs of Happyface...

Miss Carland

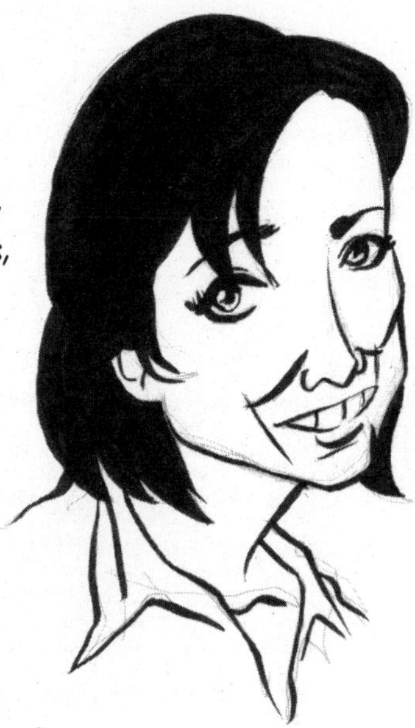

Gretchen is admittedly aiming high for me, considering my lack of experience with girls, and Megan was certainly aiming through the roof considering I was less than a nobody at the time. I was downright hated. But none take the cake quite as much as Miss Carland in the eighth grade. To be fair, it was cruel of the faculty to stick such a bombshell with a bunch of horny middle school boys. Miss Carland was outstanding. She was young, not middle school young, but younger than most of the buzzards lording over us.

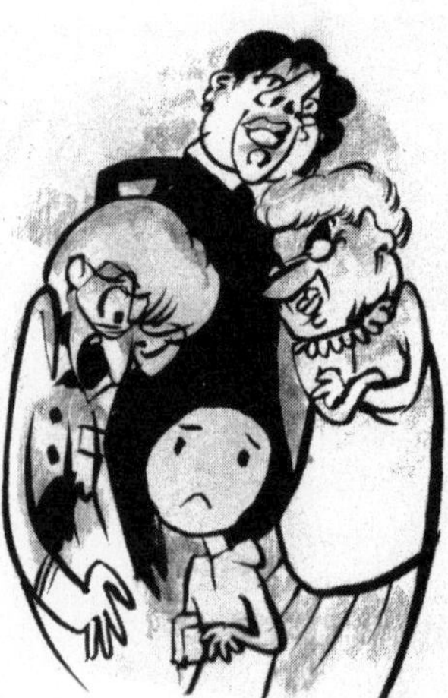

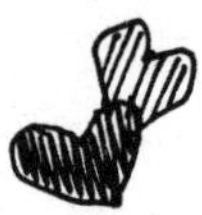

I was smitten with Miss Carland and found myself paying attention in class like I never had before. Miss Carland was the Ritalin for me. I lingered on her every word, and for the semester she was with us student teaching, I knew what it must feel like to be one of the smart kids. My grades jumped from C's to A's as I read and reread our English assignments, just to have something to talk about and raise my hand for in class. I asked questions, incited

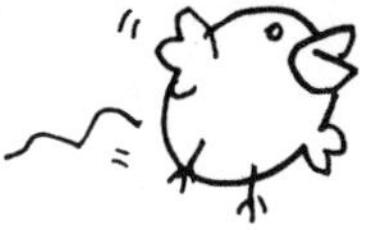

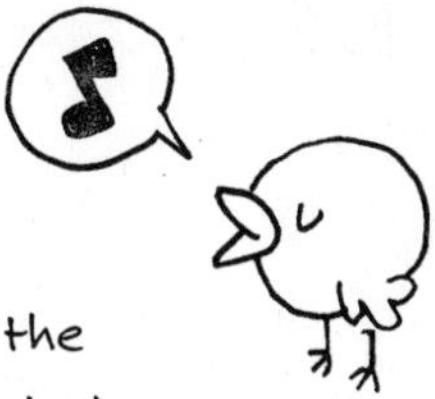

discussions. I read aloud when no one else would. I waited around after class because I had so many more questions I couldn't slow the class down with. I wanted to talk to her alone. I wanted to know things the other kids didn't; I wanted to know her personally. The Carland Era was probably the first time I really felt like I was in love. It wasn't just some cute girl I'd never talk to, or someone who would make me feel bad about myself. With Miss Carland, she'd talk to me and show an interest in me, and she was friendly. Sure, part of it was because it was her job, but on some level she had to have actually liked me. I was excited to go to school, I'd wake up early and try to look nice, and I was doing better with homework, so I actually looked forward to class. I drew cartoons for her every few days and she was always flattered. Soon it was spring, and the birds were singing and temperatures warmed and the sun shone bright.

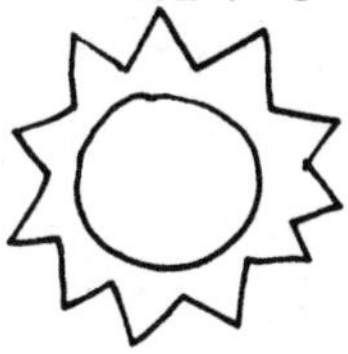

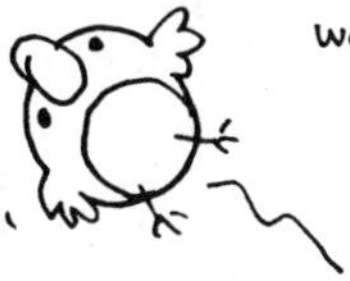

Then one day she wasn't Miss Carland anymore. Mrs. Sullivan was our teacher. Mind you, she looked like Miss Carland and talked like Miss Carland and even smiled like Miss Carland did, but this Mrs. Sullivan had a husband. I was devastated. I could be smart and sweet and outgoing and I could draw her lots of pictures but I was still just a kid, just another student like the rest of the class.

"Miss Carland?" I would ask at least once a class, before she'd remind me it's "Mrs. Sullivan now, please." Mrs. Sullivan. It sounded like a teacher name. It didn't sound like springtime and sundresses and pretty, shiny black hair. It sounded like the buzzards.

"Miss Carland, I had trouble with the reading assignment last night,"
I'd said after class one day, and she closed the door behind her.

"You know my name is Mrs. Sullivan now. I'm married. You're calling me
that on purpose. It's disrespectful and it's inappropriate." She was
scolding me. She looked down on me like the other buzzards. I didn't
know who this fellow was that she changed her whole name for, but
he'd taken away my Miss Carland.

"Terri?" I'd asked the next day, hand raised. It was her first name.
At least I hadn't called her Miss Carland again. The class laughed
uncomfortably as Miss Car . . . sorry, Mrs. Sullivan, blushed. That was
the day the rumors started. All of the staying after class, following
her like a lost puppy, led to whisperings in the halls.

Mrs. Sullivan called my parents and let them know what I'd done.

Class was miserable after that. My A's turned back to C's as I tried
to deal with my broken heart.

It was my fault. I was needy and insecure, and there was no one
smart enough or charming enough for Miss Carland. I was a kid. But I
couldn't help it. I was in love.

1/16

Mom had a whole dinner prepared when I got home from school. She had the night off from work, and she usually makes something to eat, but never like a formal sit-down dinner. Especially in the apartment here. We have one small table we can eat at and it's covered in papers and books. We took our dinner into the living room, which at least is wider.

"What's the occasion?" I asked as I put my stuff away.

"Well," she said, "we sold the old house."

It didn't sound like celebratory news . . . it sounded like closure. We really weren't going back.

"So . . ."

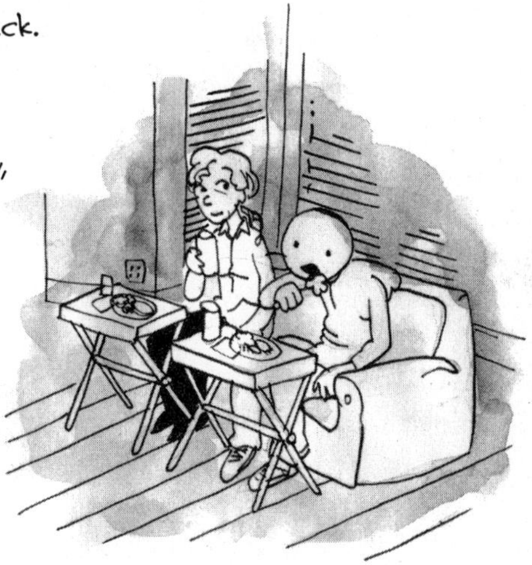

"Well, it's money. Not a lot of money, but things will be a little more comfortable."

"Can we get a car for me?" I asked.

"Nice try."

"Well, can we move out of here?"

"No, we're going to stay here awhile." I think she saw my shoulders droop. "Hon, you're going to be going to college, which is where we're putting that money. It's not that far away."

"Oh."

"Sorry, kiddo. You're stuck with me."

It was nice to see Mom in a good mood. I wondered again what Dad was doing, if he was keeping any of the house money. I guess it doesn't matter. I'll probably never know.

Mom and Dad

I always thought Mom and Dad were a good couple in that weird way, like they may not match, but somehow complement each other, like fuzzy mittens and getting punched in the face. Everett never thought they were good together, but I did.

Dad was an only child and always had hobbies. He was always into something. Even as an adult, he always had some kind of obsession; his photography, video cameras, his DVD collection, books, art. He could play lots of instruments at a base level. He was okay with drums, he was an okay guitar player, and I think he just never stuck with any of them long enough to get really good. Mom said in high school he was never very popular, even though she met him in college. She said he'd barely dated at all before her. In college he was considered really smart and became more socially outgoing there. He had one college sweetheart who left him after a couple years.

Mom on the other hand grew up with two sisters, who got better grades, were favored, and were better looking. This is all according to Mom at least. She became competitive as she reached high school, and I think she dated a lot of guys to get noticed by her sisters and her own mom and dad. Her dad (grandpa) was really strict and her mom was kind of a space cadet.

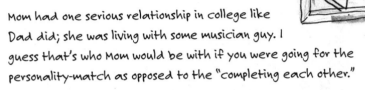

Mom had one serious relationship in college like Dad did; she was living with some musician guy. I guess that's who Mom would be with if you were going for the personality-match as opposed to the "completing each other."

Dad was the head of some kind of literary club that Mom was a part of, and that's where they met. I think Mom was drawn to his smarts and ambitions or maybe she just really liked his beard. Either way, she left the musician guy for him and Mom was really instrumental in Dad finishing his book and in getting him to actually submit it and find an agent.

They told me one creepy story that came off as a fond memory. Apparently when they first started dating, there was one time they were in a pool hall, and some guy had an issue with Mom. Dad threw a punch at him, and this became his one and only fight. Mom was really impressed by that. This led to a whole barroom brawl. Mom insisted she actually broke a bottle over someone's head. I don't know if that story is romantic or weird or scary or completely made up, but it sure changed the way I thought of them as Mom and Dad!

1/24

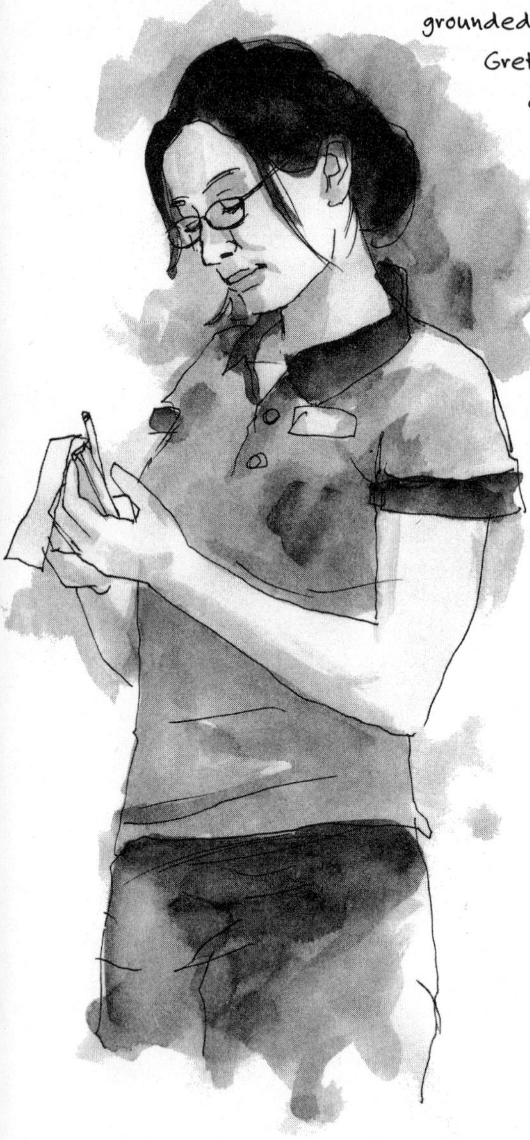

Two weeks is a long time when you're grounded. During those two weeks, Gretchen got a job working two evenings and a Saturday every week at Friendly's. I even asked Mom if I could work there since she'd brought up me getting a job so many times, but she said I had to fix my grade situation first. I wish she'd see it my way—I get over sixty percent of the questions right without even doing the homework! I thought she'd be excited I was motivated to work considering she works all day and night as it is, and maybe the extra income could help, but really, I was just going stir crazy. The first week was the worst because I hadn't seen Gretchen outside of class in a while and at school she was always preoccupied with school work. I just wanted answers but I don't want to push or make things weird between us.

I had images of the world moving on without me. My room used to be a sanctuary but when I'm stuck there it feels much more like a prison. Then Gretchen got her job and I felt a little better until I realized I probably wouldn't be seeing her as much at all with her working half the week and keeping up with school work. She always got good grades so I assume she spends her time at home actually doing her homework.

I had to get out of the apartment today since my punishment ended, and I was dying to see Gretchen. I took Mom's car for a planned five-minute excursion that went a little long. Like, replace "minutes" with "hours" long. I went to visit Gretchen at work to see what it was like. And maybe outside of class she'd be more open, maybe we were just keeping it on the down low. Maybe in private she'd tell me she'd been thinking of that night, too.

It was around eight or so and midwinter, so there weren't many people there. Gretchen was organizing the silverware when I came in. She asked if she could take a break but a customer came in and she had to help him. My only thoughts were about kissing... and if I'd ever get to do it with Gretchen again. And how exactly does one bring that up?

Gretchen was bored and, thus, happy to see me. I helped her out with organizing silverware while she told me about the creepy older guy who was hitting on her. We went outside in the cold for her break, and she told me all about the people there and how stressful it is and how lucky I was I needed to work on my grades instead of working. After break, she made me a free milk shake for my troubles. It was an off-the-menu shake she made up on the spot, something with chocolate and berries.

You must be TRYING to get my attention.

She called it the "Happyface: Guaranteed to put a smile on your face!"

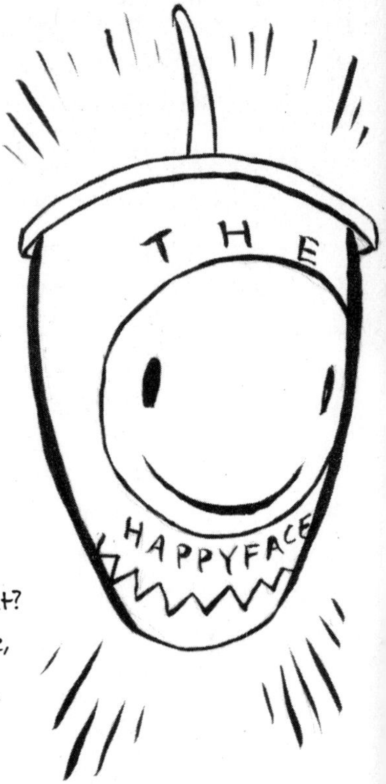
THE
HAPPYFACE

When I got home, Mom was less than pleased. She called out of work because she didn't have the car to get there.

"You steal my car when I tell you you're not even driving anymore, you don't even call to tell me where you are or answer your phone when I call you!" She took the keys from me and put on her coat while she lectured. "You are already grounded. I don't know what else to do with you!"

I didn't say anything, what was the point? I just stared, breathing through my nose, fists clenched by my side.

"Impossible," she called me.

"Mom, I need a car! I just got my license!"

"You're just not responsible. Besides, I need the car. You have the bus and your bike."

"I could use the Corvette," I told her.

"That's not your car," she said as she went out the door. "And we're selling it anyway."

"It's been half a year," I said to the now-closed door. "It's not going anywhere."

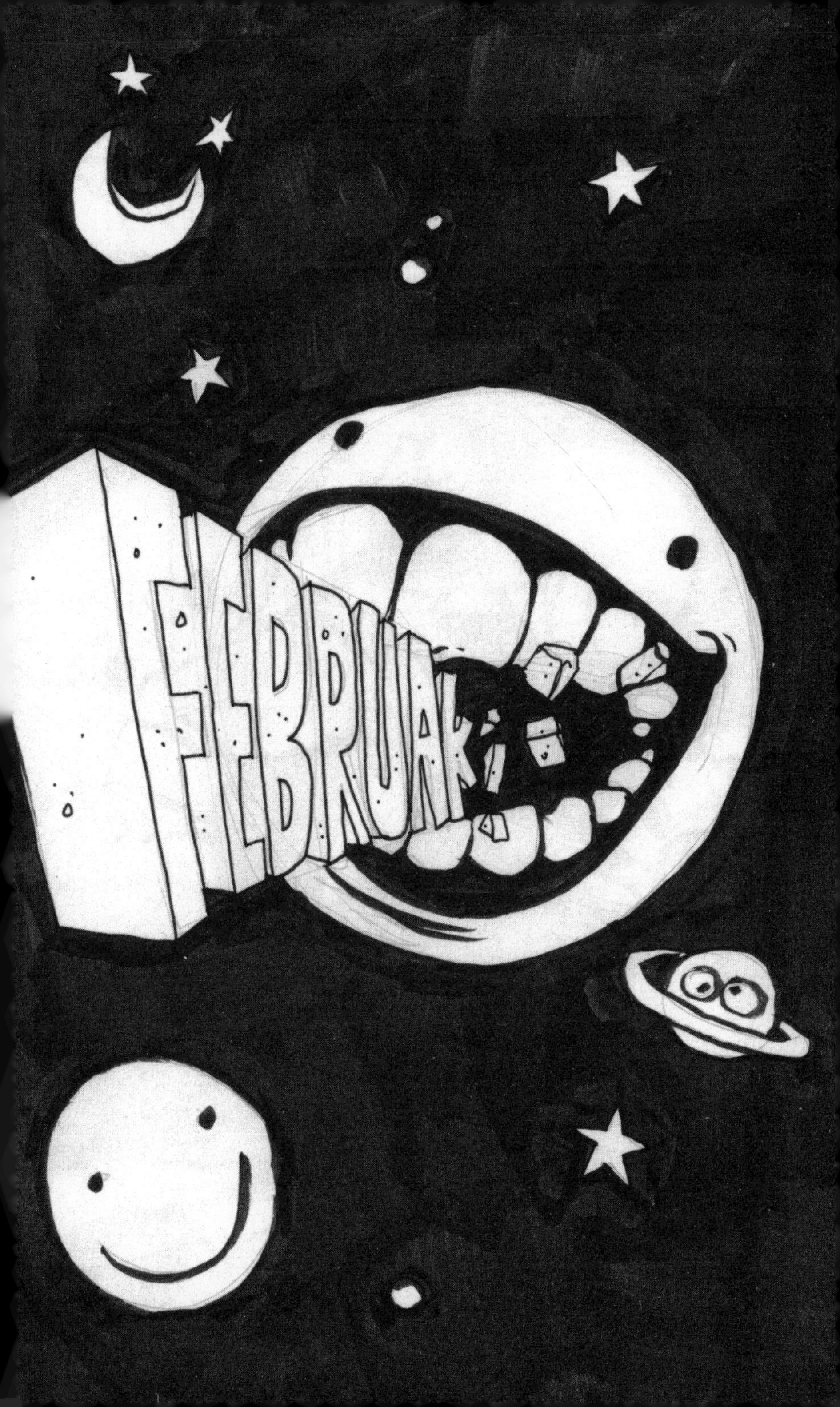

I decided to give Mr. Molly a break and attempt one of these journals without the sarcasm. If I was a teacher, though, I'd welcome the occasional laugh.

On Friends

I have more friends today than I did a year ago. I attribute a lot of it to moving, and to starting over. I live in a new town now, and there's none of the baggage of the old one here with me. It's freeing, it opens possibilities, and it makes me less afraid.

I have guy friends, and girl friends (though no girlfriend quite yet). It's a new world that I'm still uncertain in but it's exciting. My friends seem to be genuinely interested in me and see me the way I'd like to be seen, as someone fun and interesting and funny. Once upon a time I was seen as quiet, nerdy, and awkward.

There's things I haven't figured out yet: when I'm overbearing, when I'm ignoring someone, exactly what it is that's expected of me. I don't know quite how to balance friends and family and still have time for school but it's something I'm learning as I go. They make life interesting for me; they give me something to think about besides myself. Without them, I'd be in yet another world, and it would certainly be more claustrophobic. The uncertainties would just be larger.

Friends are A-OK, and knowing is half the battle.

FRiENDS

Having my freedom back put me in a really good mood the past week, and in dire need to escape Mom. I decided to spend some one-on-one time with all the friends I'd made in Crest Falls and found after-school activities to be my new favorite pastime. That's number three for "Top Things I Never Expected to Say."

MIKE

I'd noticed Mike hadn't been at the lunch table with us for a few days so I set off to find him on Tuesday. I checked the library first, and he wasn't there. I wandered the halls a bit, and didn't find him there, either. I never really saw him hanging out with anyone else so I wasn't even sure who I could ask that might know where to find him. Finally he turned up when I went outside by the cafeteria, sitting at one of the few benches out in the cold, alone. I was surprised to see he was smoking.

"You smoke?" I asked logically, to me at least.

He was still reading whatever textbook he was reading. "Yeah, sometimes," he finally replied.

"Why?" I asked.

He looked at me as if it was a really strange question. "Why does anyone smoke?"

"I don't know," I said, flustered, "I guess you just didn't seem like the type."

He looked back at his book. "You don't seem like the type to go to parties every week, but I guess appearances can be deceiving." He put his book down, maybe he thought that was a mean jab. It was accurate, though. "I only do it when I'm stressed. My sister smokes so I just steal them from her."

I sat down beside him. "So what are you so stressed about?"

"Well, we can't all be happyfaces." I let the joke pass, hoping he might open up again. "School work, grades. Social stuff. You know, the usual."

Mike and social stuff didn't seem to go along together any more than myself and social stuff a year ago. Maybe that was his point.

"There's a lot expected of me, you know. I'm Mike," he joked in his dry, sarcastic way.

"I could only imagine," I offered.

"Well, it turns out it's cold outside, so I'm going to finish reading this in the library," he said, closing his book. "Seeing as it's due in about twenty-five minutes and all."

"Yeah, I have some homework to finish, too," I said, following him inside. "I'll come with you."

MISTY

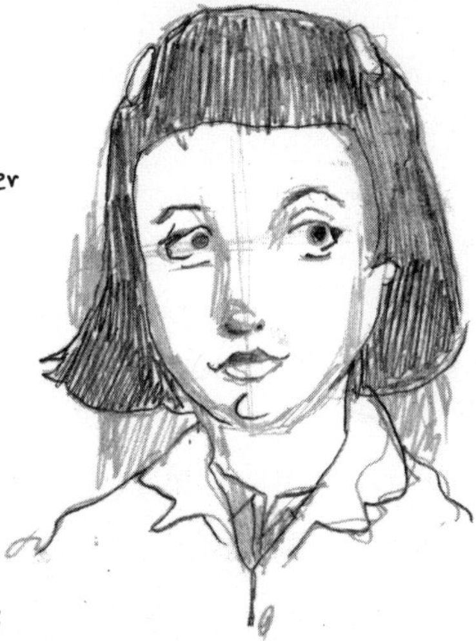

I helped out Misty on Tuesday after school by helping her recite lines for the school play. Misty is playing Domina in the school's production of A Funny Thing Happened on the Way to the Forum.

Misty had been ranting for days now. "I'll never learn my lines; so many choices, inflection, timing, it's too much!" It was rare to see Misty as anything but cool and sarcastic. This is par for the course, apparently, with any of her public performances. She was excited when I told her I'd go over her lines with her.

We found an empty room so she wouldn't feel self-conscious and could let it all out. I'd try out myself some time if my shaky voice and red face wouldn't ruin the show for everyone. Still, I was pretty good!

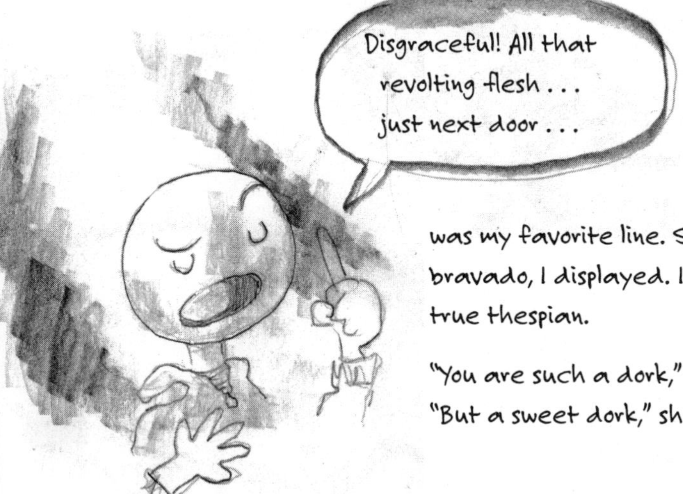
Disgraceful! All that revolting flesh . . . just next door . . .

was my favorite line. Such bravado, I displayed. I was a true thespian.

"You are such a dork," Misty said. "But a sweet dork," she clarified.

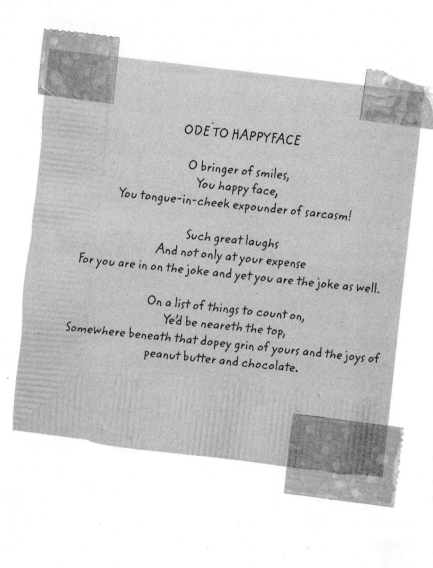

ODE TO HAPPYFACE

O bringer of smiles,
You happy face,
You tongue-in-cheek expounder of sarcasm!

Such great laughs
And not only at your expense
For you are in on the joke and yet you are the joke as well.

On a list of things to count on,
Ye'd be neareth the top,
Somewhere beneath that dopey grin of yours and the joys of
peanut butter and chocolate.

224

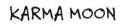

KARMA MOON

Karma had her own issues. I stayed after on Wednesday to hang out with Gretchen, Karma, and Sharif. Karma stayed after for Misty's rehearsals, and Gretchen, Sharif, and I . . . well, what else were we going to do?

Karma is going out with this guy Jake Freeman now. I've been here for a few months and even I know that's a bad idea. Jake is the odd fellow who is somehow a player and really dorky and weird at the same time. He isn't at all attractive, and he has an obnoxious personality, but he's outspoken enough that people are still somehow drawn to him. Actually, he's a lot like Trevor.

Karm doesn't seem to realize this and has been floating around like she's got some great catch, and no one in our crew is supportive of it. So Wednesday after school, we were all sitting out in the hall debating this, when Sharif and I decided to show Karma the error of her ways.

"Excuse me," Sharif said to a cute girl walking past us. She stopped and turned to us. "Have you ever talked to Jake Freeman?"

Her eyes lit up immediately. "Yeah, he actually asked me out once. I don't even really know him, though!"

225

The next girl who came walking by, Sharif asked, "Hey, Jen." She walked over to us. "You know Jake Freeman, right?"

Yeah, he's kind of a creep. He asked out me AND my sister.

He actually tried to grab my ass in French class. I slammed my book right on his hands.

He stood in front of my car and wouldn't move until I said I'd go out with him!

Jake is one of those guys who can take a swing at every ball and manage to hit one every now and again. There wasn't a girl we talked to who didn't have a Jake Freeman story.

"He actually kind of asked me out, too, Karm. Last year," Gretchen added sheepishly.

We managed to crush Karma, which I feel a little guilty about, but it's for her own good. Someday she'll thank us.

OH HAI, ITZ HAPPYFACE: THE WEBCOMIC-IN-PRINT
KARMA edition

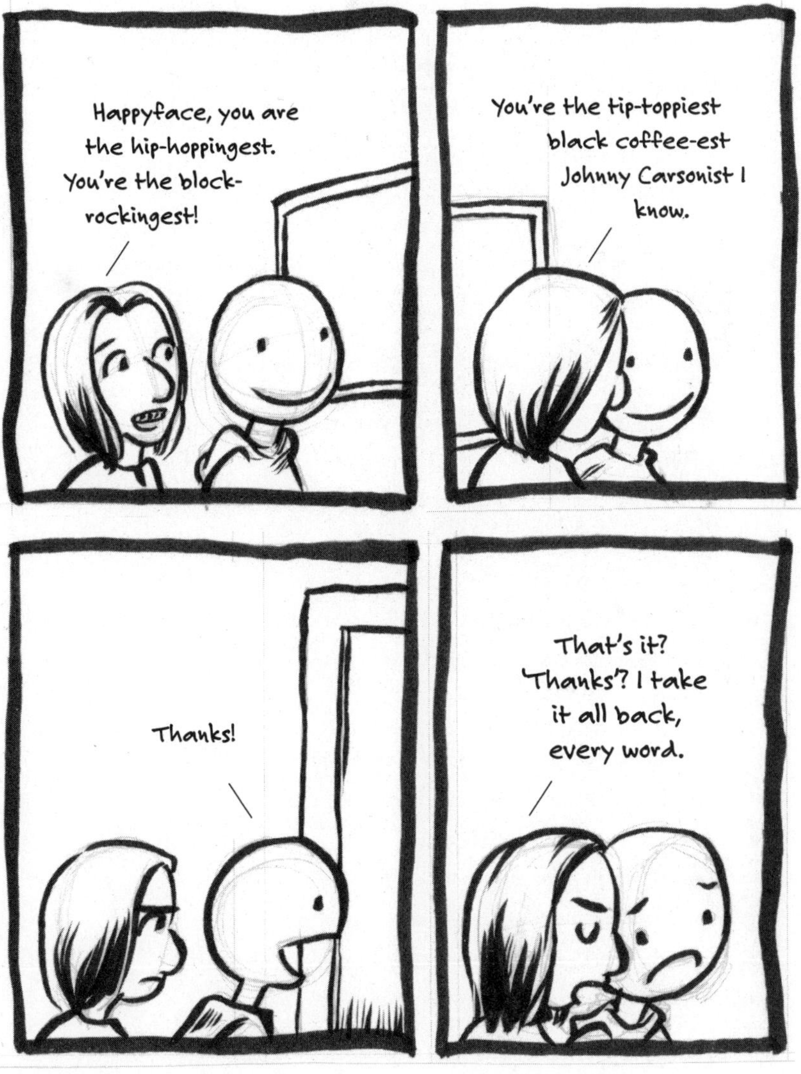
Happyface, you are the hip-hoppingest. You're the block-rockingest!
You're the tip-toppiest black coffee-est Johnny Carsonist I know.
Thanks!
That's it? 'Thanks'? I take it all back, every word.

ODDLY JENKINS

I even spent some time with Oddly Jenkins, who managed to swing the mood pendulum back to crummy. It started off fine when I walked with her to her next class.

She started laughing for no reason. "I'm sorry, I get nervous around you," she said, leaning against me. She blushed more than I did.

"Why?" I asked, puzzled but smiling.

"I don't know," she said, looking down and smiling. I'd never gotten a reaction like this from anyone. "I just think you're funny, and smart."

"I'm failing most of my classes," I reminded her.

"I know, see, funny," she said. "Plus you're a badass, which is attractive."

This one needed some definite clarification.

"Well, you're always joking in class and annoying the teacher and stuff, so that's kinda badass." Her face was far too close for comfort. "And your father's like some famous writer, right?"

This was not public knowledge in Crest Falls. Now I was the one who was red, stopped in my tracks. Is everyone visiting the Happyface website or something? First the Moons finding out about Chloe, and now somehow Oddly has researched my dad. Maybe she can figure out where he went.

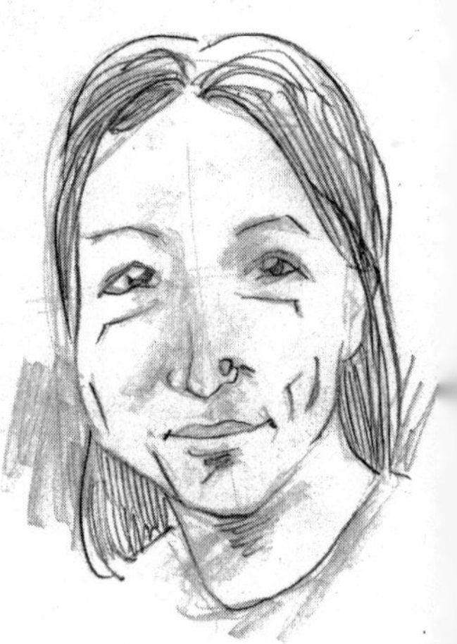

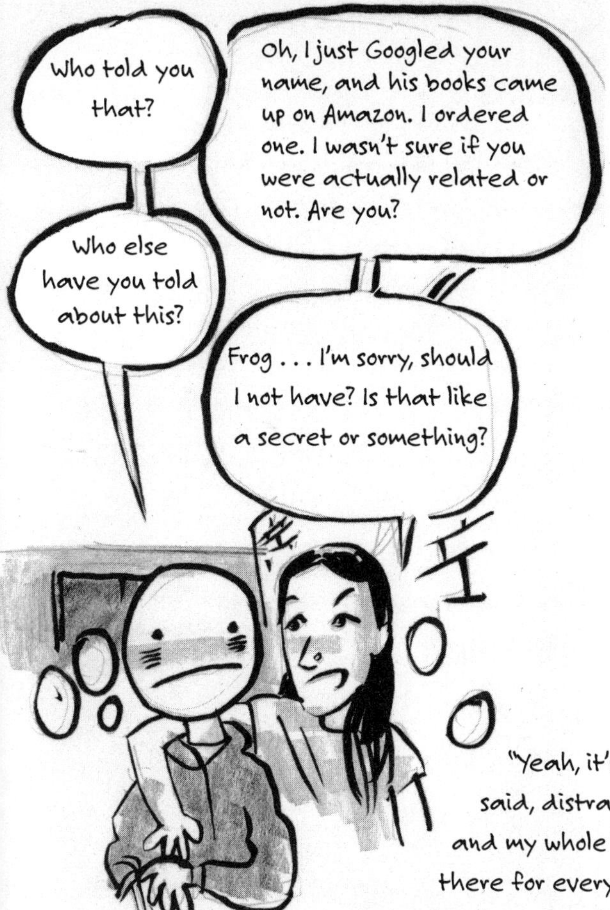
Who told you that?
Oh, I just Googled your name, and his books came up on Amazon. I ordered one. I wasn't sure if you were actually related or not. Are you?
Who else have you told about this?
Frog . . . I'm sorry, should I not have? Is that like a secret or something?

"Yeah, it's kind of a secret," I said, distracted. Another Google and my whole life could be out there for everyone to see. "Could you just not tell anyone else?"

"Yeah, sure," Oddly said. "Is there a reason you don't want anyone to know? I think it's cool."

Now I was looking suspicious. I didn't want to give her any inkling to press further. "No, it's no big deal, it's just, who wants to be known as the writer's kid, right? It's bad enough I'm failing English."

"Okay, yeah. No problem."

At least she was nice about it. I still felt the need to rush to the bathroom and vomit.

ABANDONED 2/7

Despite the possibly fatal embarrassment I narrowly avoided through Oddly and Frog's Googling, things managed to get worse on Saturday when I went out with Gretchen. Aside from seeing her after school mid-week, she's been pretty invisible lately. She's quiet in classes and she has that stupid job now so I don't even hear from her much at all. She's one of the few people I can actually get to on my bike, too. When she asked me to come on a trip with her this weekend for her photography project, I was glad to go and was ready to finally bring up the kiss myself, because let's face it, she wasn't about to, and it was driving me nuts.

Then, as Gretchen drove us to our first stop, she dropped this on me:

"I've been hanging out with Trevor again. What do you think, bad move?" she asked me. SHE asked ME! Of course it's a bad move, I can barely stand the guy and he probably wants to punch my teeth in! "He's the new and improved Trevor now, apparently, but I don't know if I buy it yet."

What was I supposed to say?

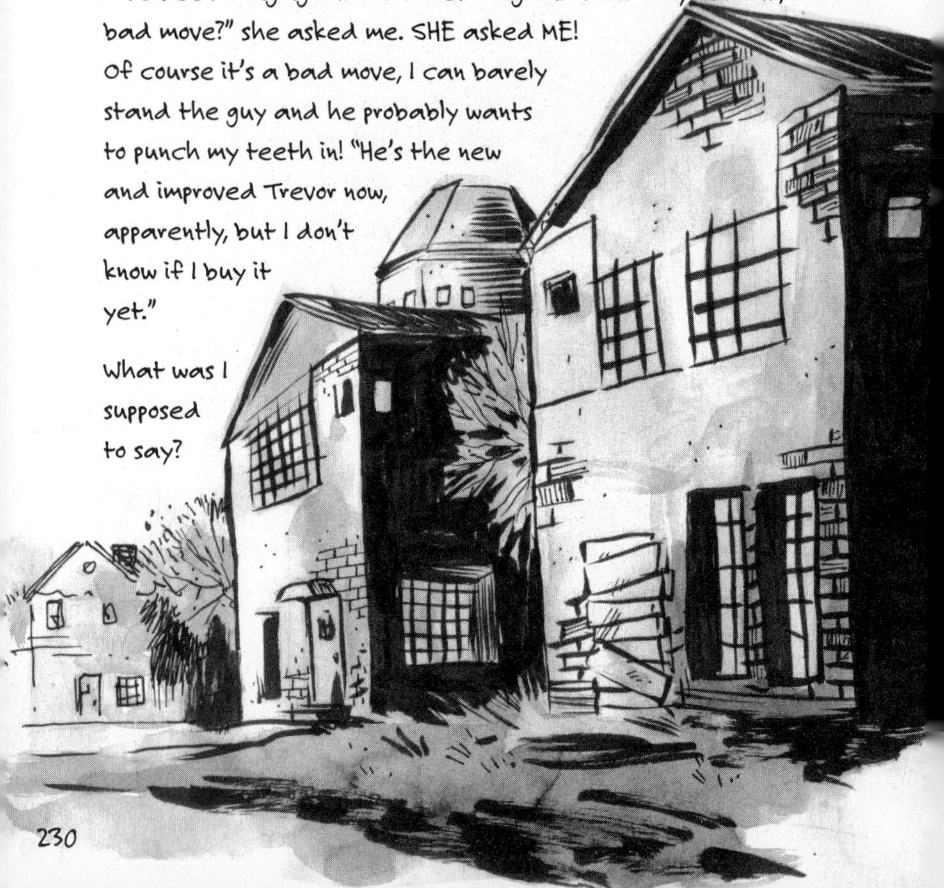

Was she dense? She finally has the bozo out of her life. She has ME! I'm shy and all, but we kissed. That was the hurdle, and we passed that. We kissed already! Why haven't we mentioned it since? Why are we bringing up TREVOR now, of all people? Why is she asking for MY advice on THAT?

"I guess you could just give it a shot and see if he acts weird or anything," I offered, though really I wanted to tell her he was a creep and she should never talk to him again. But then that might sound personal.

We went to some areas Gretchen had found online . . . various ghost towns and abandoned buildings. It was her theme for her photography class, and she wanted to take something for the art show next week.

"I want to find the places where manmade objects fail and nature takes over," is what she pitched setting out. We found an old series of buildings, an old psychiatric center, as it was labeled online. Spooky.

We parked down the street and walked to the campus where

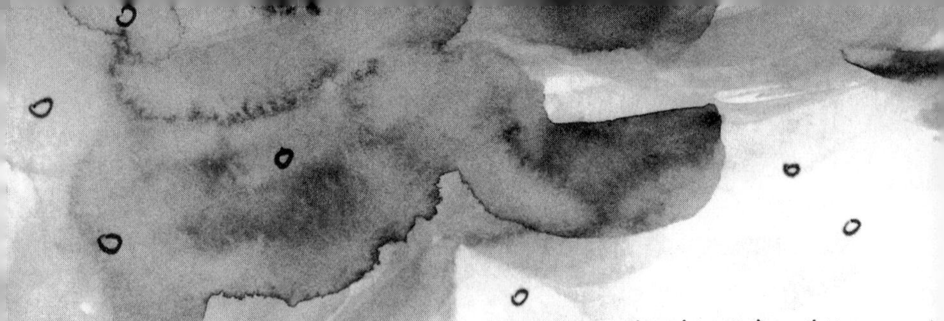

the old brick buildings were. It was quiet and calm out, exactly the opposite of how I was feeling. I was nervous going in, and after the Trevor thing I was angry, too. It started to snow and the clouds were dark, thick, and billowing. Some of the windows on the buildings were boarded up but some were still open, and the doors for the most part were unlocked. A few of them you probably couldn't tell were decomposing, from the outside. Inside was another story.

"Ew," Gretchen said, covering her mouth and nose with her scarf. I wondered if we'd die from asbestos as we walked into the dark. Gretchen started snapping pictures. The lighting was dramatic where the light shot through the windows and boards. The rooms were mostly empty aside from occasional tables or refrigerators, and one room had a bunch of paperwork lying around, too frail and soggy to bother touching, curious as Gretchen was.

"He wanted to see me alone, first," she continued, "because he wanted to apologize. He didn't try anything then, so I felt bad not talking to him."

"He didn't flirt or anything?" I asked.

"Well . . ." She thought about it. "Yeah, I guess he did. But that's just Trevor; I can't really picture him not flirting. He'll be at the party tonight anyway, so you can keep an eye on him and let me know if he acts weird."

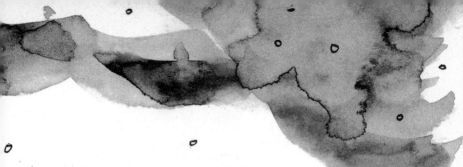

He's a scumbag; how am I supposed to isolate
one instance?

Gretchen dared me to open the refrigerator. What
were the chances of there NOT being a rat or some other
large creature in there, or maybe some kind of body parts some
murderer needed to hide? Was she trying to kill me now? I took
a deep breath of asbestos and pulled the handle quick while
running away. The fridge was empty, though the murderers and
rodents lived on in my head.

"Can we get out of here soon?" I asked. I
tried not to let on how I was feeling. If
she was going to play the kiss off as
no big deal, then I'd have to, too.

"I was thinking the same thing,"
Gretchen said, snapping a few
photographs of the snow falling
outside through the window.

Just then we heard a loud
crash from upstairs, fol-
lowed by what sounded
like ominous booming
thunder in the middle of a snow storm. We aren't wanted here, we
both thought as we ran through the building and out the door.

Gretchen held my hand tight as we bolted to the car.

After visiting a few more abandoned areas with Gretchen, I went home for a quiet dinner with Mom before heading back to Gretchen's for her picture party. She's been a little easier on me since I started doing my homework for Molly's class.

Gretchen tends to have people over anytime her parents aren't home, so Saturday night she had some of us over for a picture-taking party, more stuff for her class. I was dreading seeing Trevor hanging around Gretchen again and feeling like I had to compete for her attention. I wasn't backing down now, though. He wasn't changing, and Gretchen will see that and then things will be back to normal.

Only a few people were there when I came over, but Trevor was one of them. Josiah was playing Gretchen's guitar while Trevor sang in a reggae style and Sharif played bongos.

"Hey, Happyface!" Trevor exclaimed, and scooped me up in his arms, right off my feet. This set the tone for the evening: Trevor's glee and phoniness and my glumness. There I was, up in the air, with the nutty isn't-he-great-to-have-around Trevor, myself looking womanly and weak, not to mention stupid.

Gretchen was taking pictures all night, though Trevor needed to get in each one. Somehow this wasn't boorish or annoying, but cute and fun. I rolled my eyes to the point where I could see my brain.

When I posed for Gretchen's pictures, Trevor's hands or feet or face were in the background. When I took my picture with Gretchen, Trevor was between us. When I shut my eyes to blink, there was Trevor, somehow in front of my eyelids, grinning and waving.

What's he so happy about? I wondered, sitting there smiling through the aggression myself. I was the one who needed Gretchen. He'll live fine without her.

The party dragged on and I didn't stay out until three this time. I left early. I was frozen on my bike the whole way home and dove under the covers to go to bed.

OH HAI, ITZ HAPPYFACE: THE WEBCOMIC-IN-PRINT
Gretchen and HF Edition!
Hi, Gretchen.
I got run over by a car and mauled by a pack of rabid dogs.
Oh, no.
No one cares quite as much as you'd like them to.

VALENTINE'S DAY LAMESSACRE

2/14

I made out with a girl. It wasn't that long ago, just weeks. So why am I home alone on Valentine's Day? Why haven't Gretchen and I even discussed it? If a girl kisses you, that means she likes you, right? So what am I missing?

Gretchen had to work, but that's not why we aren't hanging out. She got called in last minute and we didn't have any plans before that unless she was going to call me last minute. That didn't seem likely though. I went to visit her.

I rode my bike the half hour to Friendly's so I could see Gretchen, because I wasn't doing anything myself. This is what was supposed to happen:

I go to Friendly's, there's Gretchen.

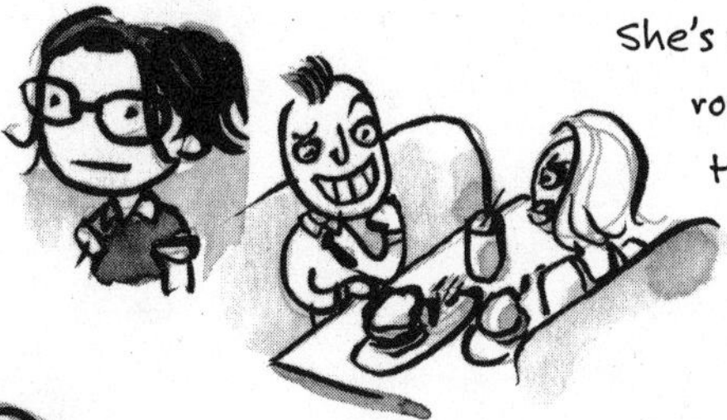

She's worn out from all the romantic couples going to Friendly's for their big romantic V-day dinners.

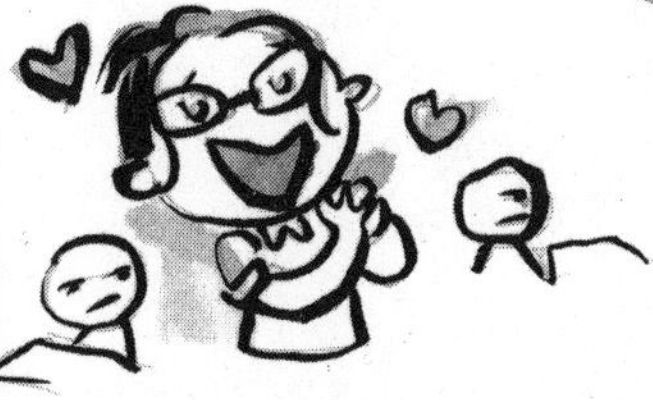

"Oh, Happyface, thank goodness!" she exclaims, though to other people it sounds like "Oh, hey, Happyface." She takes her break.

"Happy Valentine's Day," I tell her, as I give her a box of chocolates even though I wasn't really going to get chocolates anywhere. But for the fantasy, that's what I did.

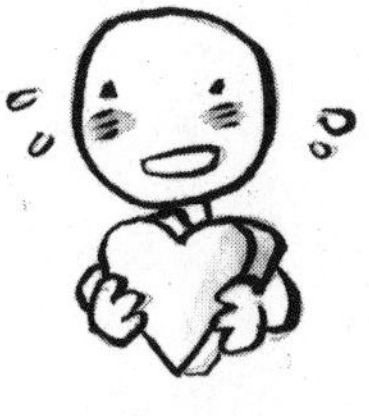

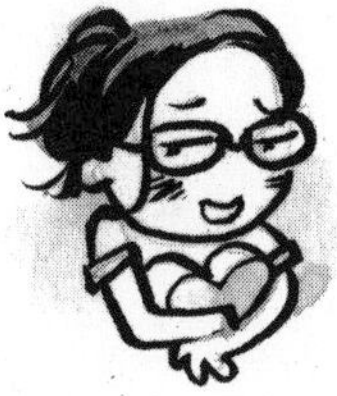

"Thank you," she says, unsure how to take it.

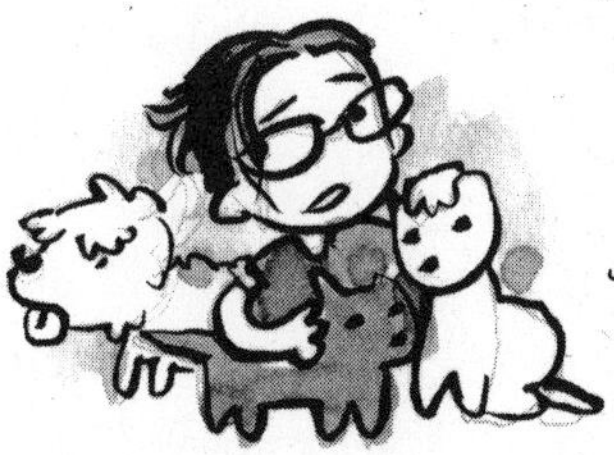

"Want to be my valentine?" I ask her. She jokes that she promised her cat she'd be his valentine, but she has so many pets, they can all take care of each other.

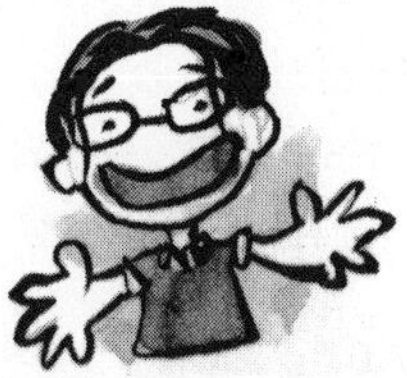

"Of course I'll be your valentine," she says, cheered up.

"So, I've been thinking . . . ," I start, unsure even in fantasy how to finish, but needless to say by the time I'm done talking I've told her how I think about her every minute and how comfortable I felt with her that night in her room and how I'd like for us to be more than friends. I tell her that without her, I'd be less than nothing again. She tells me she's been waiting for me to say those words, though she didn't expect quite so many of them, and in such a self-derogatory manner.

None of that happened, though, plausible as it all seems. Instead, I rode my bike to Friendly's sans chocolate, though really it was just the thought that made her happy in my fantasy. I got as far as the front door, when I saw through the glass that Trevor had beaten me to it. There they sat in a booth, sitting across from each other, each hunched toward the middle of the table. Gretchen was laughing, hysterically, like not even I can make her laugh. Trevor was all animated but his hand was touching hers. That said it all, she was his valentine. She was warm and happy and didn't need me. She had him, and I was alone in the dark and silent cold by myself, and that was my Valentine's Day, just like any other year.

Now I am home and writing this and it's eleven o'clock and Gretchen's been out for an hour at least and she hasn't answered any of my phone calls or texts. She's probably still out with Trevor.

It's my fault though, let's face it, I could have said something, any time the past month, I had plenty of chances but I kept waiting, like Gretchen was going to spill her guts to me, like she was going to ask me out. My fantasy never lines up with reality. She needs someone aggressive, like Trevor, who can tell her how he feels and doesn't have to go home and write about it in his journal. A journal he can't even show her, or anybody. Why can't I say something to her? Why can't I be aggressive? I've never been aggressive, I've never been "that guy," until Happyface, until this whole thing. So why can't Happyface ask her out?

Everything else has worked out pretty well this school year, thanks to the Happyface experiment. Maybe this is the ultimate test.

Art Show

2/19

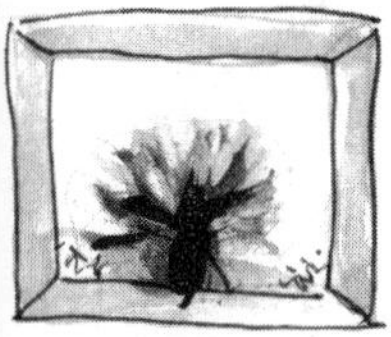

Gretchen never called me back and wasn't in school on Monday. By Tuesday it didn't feel worth bringing up anymore. Then there was the art show.

I went back to school around seven in the evening for the show, since Gretchen, Misty, and Karma all had work in it. Gretchen and Karma had both done a lot of photography I knew about and Misty had a set of paintings on display. Half of the school was turned into a gallery of sorts, with art lining the hallways and large stands in the wider halls for seniors with a lot of work to show. Usually I'd have my work up there, too, and an event like this is when I'd shine and people would actually notice me. I did miss that attention a bit, but I prefer the attention I get for just being me.

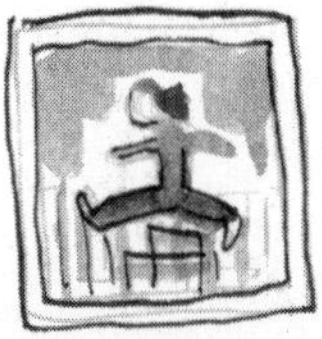

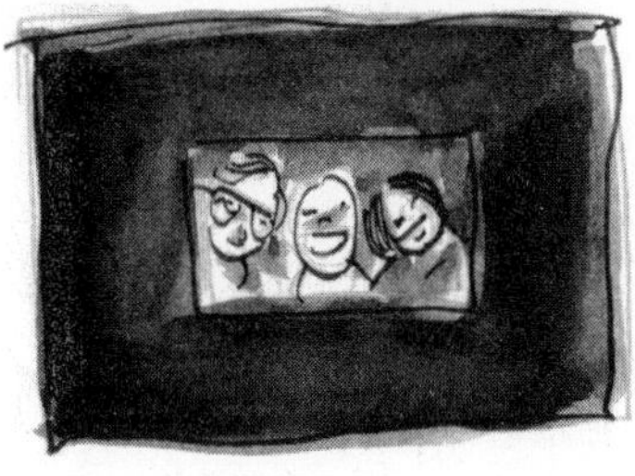

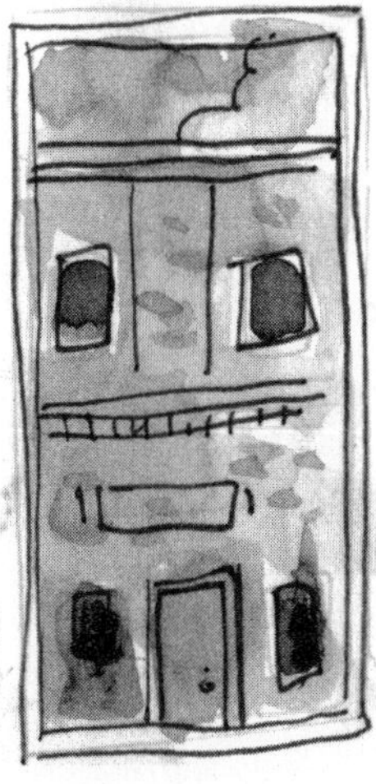

It was pretty quiet, even with the art show. I walked for a while until I found Gretchen's set in one of the smaller corridors. There was a blue ribbon beside one of her abandoned building pictures; I was there when she took it. It was the picture of the snow from inside the dark of the building. It came out amazing. She also had a series of Trevor pictures, most of them surprisingly serious. What does she see in that buffoon? He's mean to people, he's phony, and he's just trying to act however Gretchen wants so he can get back together with her. He's decent-looking, I guess. He's loud, assertive, and athletic. She would have loved Everett. Maybe she and Chloe can get together and chase after boring middle-of-the-line guys together, athletes and future lawyers. Cool kids. They could run around chasing boys and they don't even have to bother telling me. Why should I have to know? Maybe once Trevor's had some awful accident she can come out and tell me, "I loved him so, we'd been dating in secret!" How tragic. Maybe then she can be honest, when she's alone and feeling guilty.

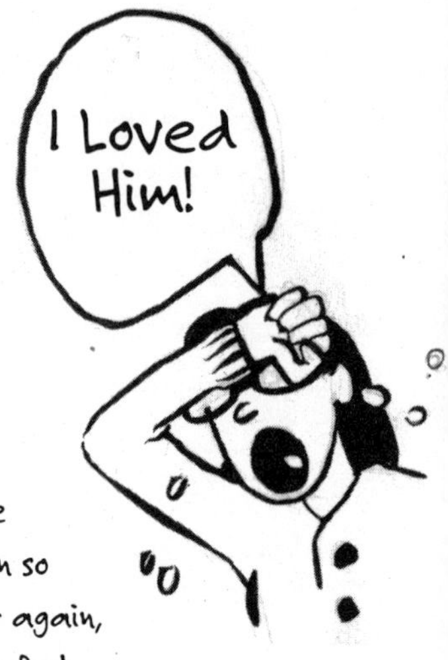
I Loved Him!

This was all running through my head as I set off to find her so I could congratulate her on the photo.

She was looking at paintings with Trevor, and I had all I needed to know they were back together. And that's why she'd been so distant. It was Chloe and Everett all over again, but this time I wasn't going to look like the fool.

"Gretchen!" I said, putting on my best excited face.

"Hey, you made it!" she said, giving me a hug.

"Can you walk with me?" I asked.

"Sure," she said before telling Trevor to come along.

"No, I wanted to talk to you alone if that's okay," I said. She seemed hesitant. I just wanted to get it all on the line now.

We started walking back toward her pictures. "What's going on with you and Trevor?" I asked.

"Nothing. He came here to see the art show, same as you. Why?"

"Well, ever since he started hanging around again, we haven't had like two minutes alone together," I said.

"Yeah, well, I have to work at a crummy diner, do homework, and I had this art show thing to prepare for," she said. "Sorry I wasn't available twenty-four seven."

"Well if you're not dating him, then why aren't you dating me?" I finally asked. "I thought we had something."

Gretchen took a deep breath. "Do we have to talk about this now?"

"Can we?"

We sat by the brick wall in the main hallway as students and teachers walked by, admiring the art.

"My parents are assholes," Gretchen began. "They've pretty much messed up any relationship I've had, since I've been old enough to have them. So I just gave up on it. They're just going to ruin everything anyway, so if I like a guy, then they just become good friends, because for whatever reason my parents are okay with that."

"So you're just going to be alone, or dating people you don't even like. . . ?"

"College is in a few years," Gretchen said.

"I don't believe it."

"You don't believe what?" she asked.

"Any of it. I don't think you just 'don't date.' I think you're dating Trevor, and for whatever reason you don't want me to know. Because you're trying to protect my feelings or something."

"You think I'm lying?" she asked.

One of Gretchen's teachers stopped by to congratulate her. "That's a beautiful picture, Gretchen. Where did you take it?"

Gretchen smiled, courteous and polite. She was a better faker than me. "It's an abandoned psych ward I read about online. We had to sneak in to take the picture but hopefully that's okay. . . ." She smiled that innocent smile, and the teacher laughed.

"Well, congratulations."

We sat quiet for a second. "You know, you're one to talk," she said. "I mean, if you want to talk about liars, welcome to 'friendship with Happyface.' We've been BFFs for months and I still don't know a thing about you. I have to hear things secondhand from Karma and Misty. I know you never dated that Chloe girl. You've never even invited me to your house! What do you do, live with a bunch of ax murderers or something?"

"Fine," I said, "you don't know anything about me, so let's just keep it that way."

"Whatever. And you don't know me, either!" Gretchen said before getting up and heading back to Trevor. If she wasn't dating him before, the doors were wide open now.

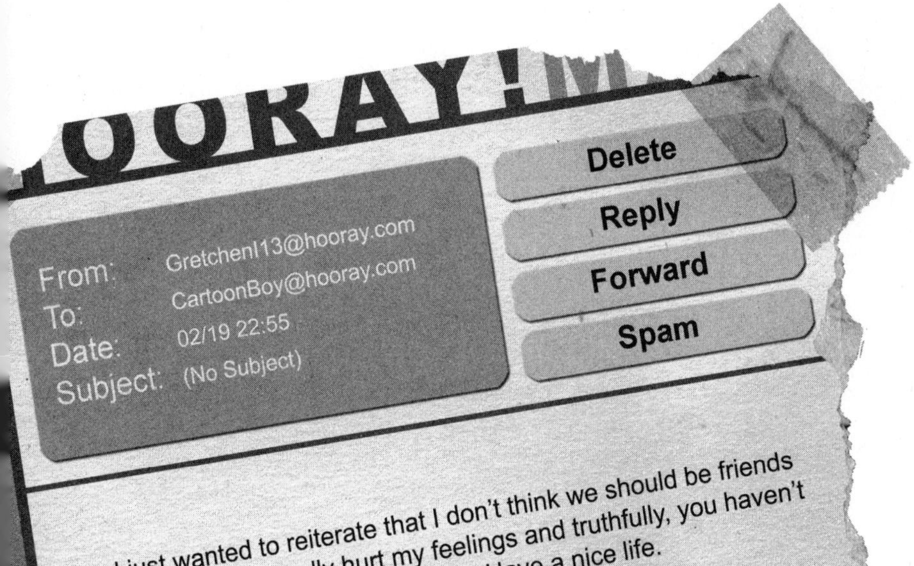

HOORAY!M

Delete
Reply
Forward
Spam

From: Gretchenl13@hooray.com
To: CartoonBoy@hooray.com
Date: 02/19 22:55
Subject: (No Subject)

I just wanted to reiterate that I don't think we should be friends anymore. You really hurt my feelings and truthfully, you haven't been a very good friend anyway. Have a nice life.

~Gretchen

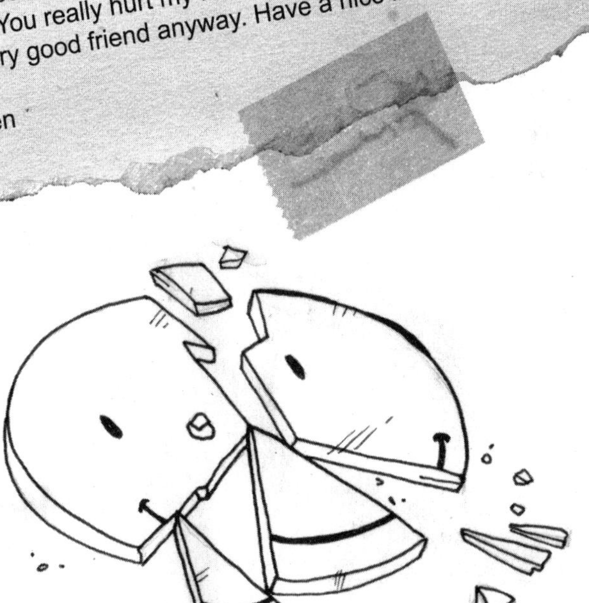

FROG FORCE 2/23

I've been having lunch with Frog and Oddly and their friends Rob and Danny, though I haven't actually been eating. There's too much on my mind, too much to think about and do, and I just forget or my stomach doesn't want it. I don't have Gretchen anymore, and because of that I've lost most of my friendships from this school year, but I still have my Happyface experiment and that hasn't failed me yet, and I still have Frog and company, who for whatever reason still find me cool, more so, even.

Maybe they're as much an experiment as the Happyface project. I'm really not sure I get them all but feel compelled to keep their company and see where this goes. I sit and smile as they play with their food and talk weirdly about things I don't understand.

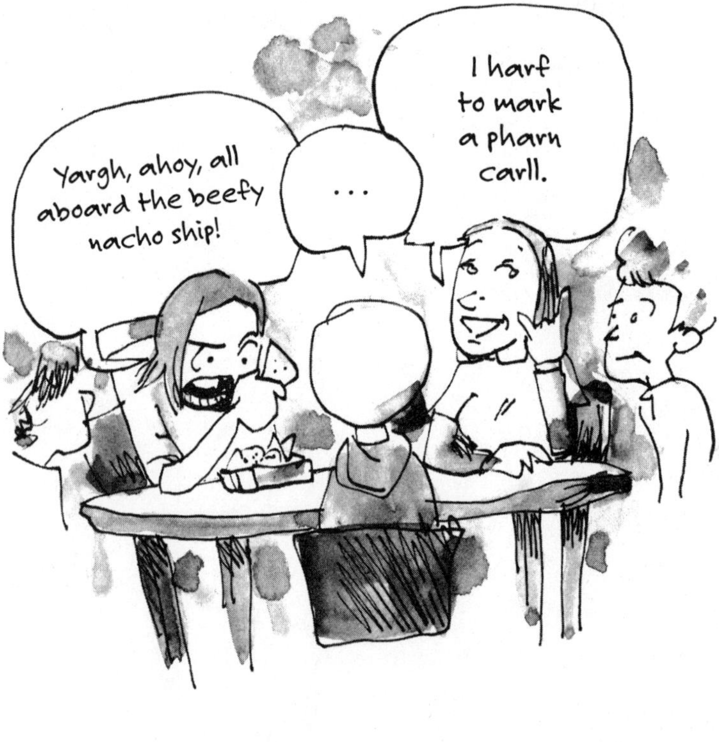
Yargh, ahoy, all aboard the beefy nacho ship!
...
I harf to mark a pharn carll.

"You're cooler anyway," Frog said as she poured milk on her pizza slice. "At least you have personality. Gretchen's boring. I think you're way better off without her."

"Yeah, and your dad's like a super mega-famous writer, even though we don't know that," Oddly added.

"She'll just have to fade back to obscurity," I chimed in. I have to smile and joke and be generally agreeable, even if it means turning my back on Gretchen. She turned her back on me first, so I don't feel any guilt. "Forget her."

I.M.

NOT 'FROGALICIOUS,' THANK GOD

Session Start (CartoonBoy:Frogaliscious): Mon Feb 23 19:20:20
[19:20] Frogalicious: Homeboy! Hehe.
[19:22] CartoonBoy: Hey Froggy.
[19:22] Frogalicious: ^_^
[19:22] Frogalicious: Guess what??
[19:23] CartoonBoy: ?
[19:24] Frogalicious: I ttly snubbed Gretchen today.
[19:24] Frogalicious: She was walking in the hall and I gave her the dirtiest look.
[19:25] Frogalicious: She won't mess with MY man. *giggle*
[19:28] CartoonBoy: Eh give her a break.
[19:28] CartoonBoy: She's suffering a broken heart, after all.
[19:28] Frogalicious: Yeah and she's mending it with Trevor.
[19:29] Frogalicious: Her loss, my gain!
[19:29] Frogalicious: You can date me 'n Odd to get back at her!
[19:30] CartoonBoy: Now we're talking!

FRUIT FLY 2/25

Mr. Molly's class has become a joke so I've started treating it like one. Molly is so obsessed with my home life, why should I bother working in his class? He can have Happyface in class or out of it, but not both. Let's see how long it takes before he's calling Mom again.

I've pretty much given up on it all. Gretchen's there every day ignoring me and the whole class is just one big awkward block of forty-five minutes that I need to either laugh or sleep my way through on a daily basis. It's only March, too; there's months to go.

Mr. Molly I think caught me with a distracted look on my face today, which is highly possible because I was indeed distracted. This fruit fly, this little gnat was floating around my head in class! I had this idea that it was the same one that's been bothering me at home because we live in a cheap little apartment now and that's what happens, you get bugs.

"I'm sorry, Molly, I was just looking at this fruit fly here"—this is how I actually said this aloud in class today—"and I think maybe it's the same one that bothers me all the time in my room back home. I feel like it's in love with me or something. I keep telling the dumb thing to go away, 'I hate you!' I yell at this bug, but the thing keeps floating around, looking at me like it's saying, in my head it's saying, 'nah, you're just tired, you don't mean it, let's talk in the morning.' But I totally mean it and I'd buy this stupid bug a bunch of bananas or a loaf of bread if it would just get the hell out of my room. Now the thing's following me to school, so I'm definitely distracted. Mr. Molly, you can see I've got a lot of problems going on here."

Everyone laughed except Molly; he just looked at me like I was a pain-in-the-butt kid and got back to class. I started drawing in my notebook. Another day down.

HOORAY!MAIL

From: PBandFluff@hooray.com
To: CartoonBoy@hooray.com
Date: 03/01 20:30
Subject: I miss you

Delete

Reply

Forward

Spam

Hi. I'm feeling really lousy. Can I see you again? Maybe just you? I feel like I'm
the lowest form of life right now and I don't even know what to do or say. I started
going to therapy for awhile but it isn't doing much. Have you thought of doing that?
Anyway it's all feeling really pointless lately. I still can't do the ballet stuff, my
grades are lower than they've ever been, it all feels pointless. I don't deserve
anything. I just keep thinking about you and I can't stop. I was thinking maybe if
I could see you it would help. Please? For me?
  ~Chloe

From: CartoonBoy@hooray.com
To: PBandFluff@hooray.com
Date: 03/03 03:10
Subject: Re: I miss you

Hi Chlo, sorry to hear things aren't going so well. I'll try to clear some time for you,
things have just been so busy for me, I've been spending so much time with all my
friends and Gretchen and I are really hitting it off so well. It's been hard to keep up
with much else! I will keep in touch though. Hope everything else is fine.
~Happyface

I still haven't had much appetite and I noticed last night I haven't been sleeping much either, but I'm coasting, flying, even. I'm a superhero! I feel good and I'm impervious to pain, which I learned today.

So I saw Gretchen and she won't even talk to me, just ignores me like I'm not even human, and after all we've been through, I mean I'm not even eating or sleeping much because of her, and she won't even say hi or anything to me. It's annoying, to be ignored, and I just wanted some kind of acknowledgement, I mean that's just common courtesy, even if she had to tell me to beat it or whatever, say something, right? So I followed her because we're in between classes, and let's face it, if we can't even say hi, if she just ignores me like I'm some loser, then I'm going to be upset all day. Even that kid from the New Year's party she kept in touch with, she doesn't have to love me or whatever, but we're supposed to at least be friends.

I was getting dirty looks from guys because every guy thinks if they knock down the creepy kid following the cute girl, then the cute girl will go out with them but that's stupid because Gretchen and I are really close, I'm not just some creepy kid, if she'd just stop for a second and say hi she'd see everything is fine, I don't even care about the art show or any of that anymore, I just want to be friends. It was so crowded in the hall, though, so it was hard to keep up. She turned toward the cafeteria and then through the double doors and up the stairs. Where was she going? She doesn't even go that way, she had math that period. It's offensive, right? Frog is right, she doesn't appreciate anything. She was lucky to have me as a friend, and here she's acting like it's a burden.

What's gotten into her that she's acting this way now? She said I was lying and all that, but how does she even know? Did Karma and Misty know more, does she know about my brother, or even my dad? Did Oddly say something to her? What am I lying about? All this is aggravating. Trevor is a

jealous idiot and I'll bet he's been saying things about me, telling her not to hang out with me so he can be with her. I never said anything bad about him to Gretchen, ever. She's always going

on about her parents, how she can't date anyone, she has to hide her relationships. I'll bet they know we kissed, they probably made her stop seeing me. They're so controlling, they probably have those nanny-cams set up, and maybe they saw that? That's when she started acting cold toward me; it all started changing around then.

I think I was saying some of this aloud as I followed her up the stairs. My stomach was turning over and the lights seemed to come and go and everything got really hot.

"What's your problem?" I remember asking her. "You need to grow up and think for yourself. You can be friends with whoever you want." Everything was spinning but she finally acknowledged me.

"You're embarrassing us both!" she yelled.

"No, THIS is embarrassing," I said as I fell backwards down the stairs, pratfall-style. I tumbled down a few stairs as a crowd gathered. They asked if I was okay, but not Gretchen. I could have cracked my head open and she wouldn't have lifted a finger to help me off the floor. She went to her next class.

"Have a nice trip, see you next fall," I said, laughing, as a football player lent me a hand. Like I needed that. I'm a superhero!

I was surprised to find Mr. Molly at my apartment when I got home.

"Your teacher's going to be joining us for dinner," Mom said as I ignored them and sped to my room.

"Not hungry," I said, claiming an easy defeat.

"I don't know what to do with him," I heard Mom say as I closed the door to my bedroom and dropped my book bag on the floor. I tried to tune out their conversation and clear my thoughts; there was just too much going on.

It's not like he's a bad kid.

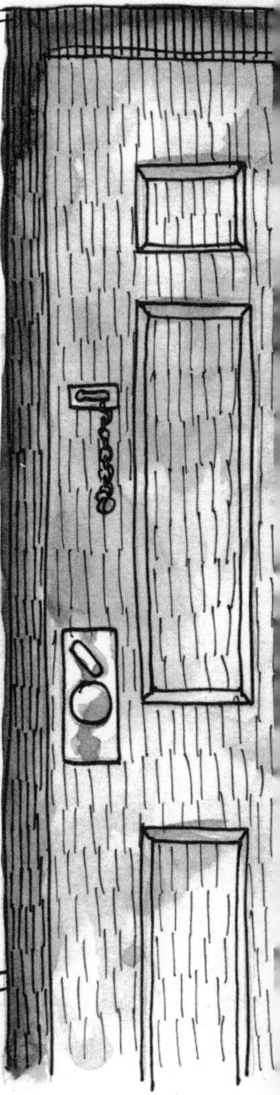

Was Mr. Molly supposed to be a father figure now or something?

Molly was getting to be old news anyway. I was more concerned with my friends and how to fix things there. Could I still be with Gretchen? I can't help but feel that if it wasn't for this recent mini-episode things were really on the right track. We saw each other every week; in classes, she laughed at all my jokes, and SHE befriended ME, really. We slow danced. She WANTED me to take her to that dance. We MADE OUT, for crying out loud! So it's not just friendship, that doesn't make sense. I can't figure out where the turning point came.

He's been really creative. I barely see him without his sketchbook. It's not like he's started smoking or cussing or getting into fights, although I caught him drinking once.

I'm the same guy, I can't see where I've faltered. I've been smiling. I haven't yelled or even complained much about anything aside from the Trevor thing. She knows what happened with my brother and Chloe, of course I'm going to be a little bit wary, and I should be forgiven for that. I haven't been negative at all. I haven't been reclusive at all, I've been outgoing, assertive. I've been everything a girl like Gretchen is used to. I've been the Trevor.

Molly started talking about my brother. I'd forgotten how when Everett had gotten into all that trouble a few years ago he used to stay after school with Molly. I'm not spending my afternoons with him, that's for sure. Is he in love with Mom or something? Why does he have to bother us? What did Dad think about all of this? What did they do after class? Is Molly some perv, is that why Ev got so angry? Is that why he had so many relationship issues?

I guess there's Mike, still. I can see what he's doing while I straighten things out with everyone else. If I just keep being myself and smiling and keeping it cool in class I'm sure things will turn around in no time.

"He's been making so many friends lately," Mom said. "I don't want to stop all the positive things he's been doing."

3/09

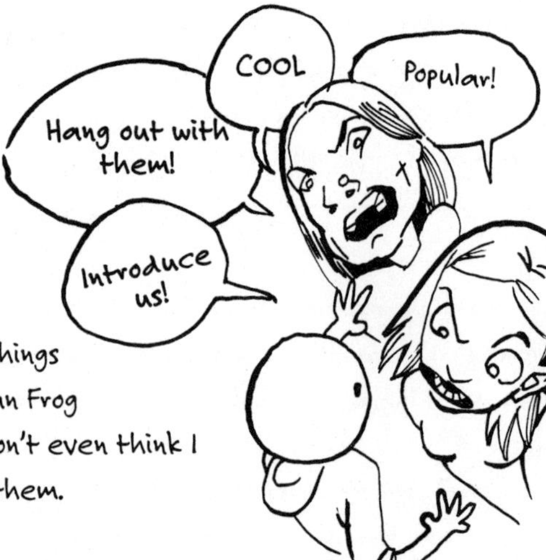
Hang out with them!
COOL
Popular!
Introduce us!

I've got bigger things on my mind than Frog and Oddly. I don't even think I like them.

"Are you okay?" Oddly asked me at lunch today when I spaced out for a while. "Gretchen and Trevor aren't even cool; you should hang out with, like, Bryce or Brigid, or Faye Dunmore. We should just start a whole new group; with just a few other people we could be way cooler than Gretchen and her lackeys."

"Who cares about them? You guys are so obsessed with that stuff." I was tired of hearing about how we could all be more popular, like that means anything. "I just want to be happy, who cares about popularity."

"Are you happy?" Oddly asked me in this obnoxious snarky tone.

"Yes," I answered, in my widest smile. "So why don't you just leave me and my deliriously happy self alone?"

"You should be nicer to me, you know," Oddly said. "Let's not forget that I do know things."

I kept smiling. Just a friendly chat.

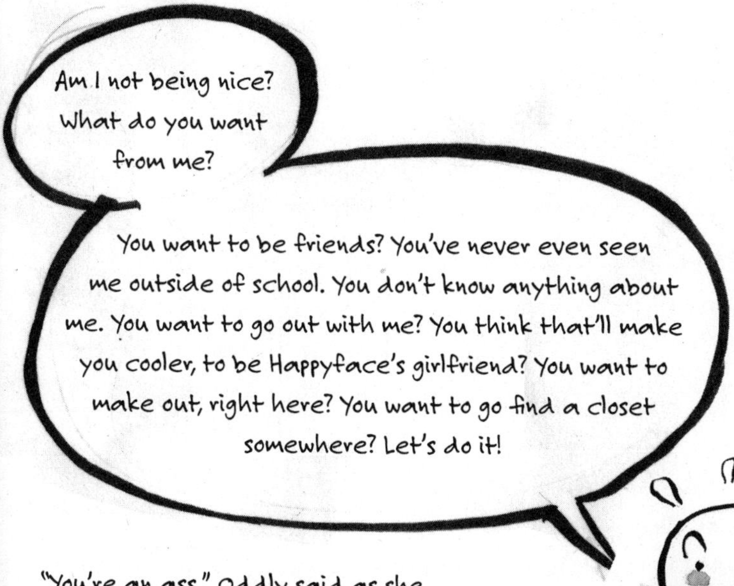
Am I not being nice? What do you want from me?
You want to be friends? You've never even seen me outside of school. You don't know anything about me. You want to go out with me? You think that'll make you cooler, to be Happyface's girlfriend? You want to make out, right here? You want to go find a closet somewhere? Let's do it!

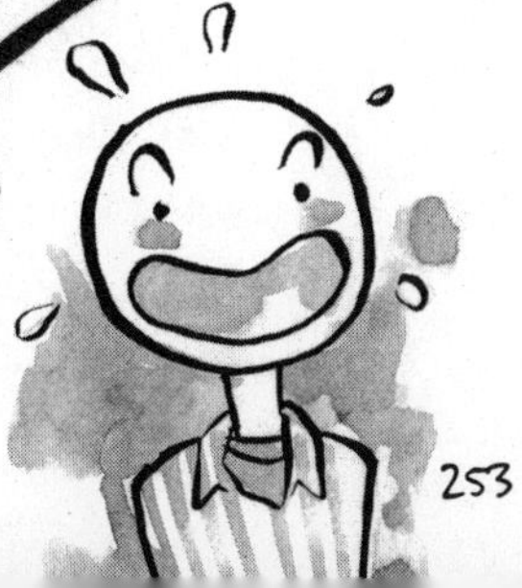

"You're an ass," Oddly said as she and her other lame friends got up to leave, rolling their eyes.

I don't need any cliques or friends and definitely not Frog and Oddly, I just need Gretchen. She's what made everything work; without her it all falls apart. She won't return my calls or talk to me in person, and now she thinks I'm some self-abusive paranoid freak, but if she'd just talk to me like normal then none of that stuff would even have happened.

I rode my bike over tonight, hoping I could just talk to her in person. At home, there's no work to be busy with or classes to go to or people to hide behind, so we can just hash this out and be friends again, I figured. I can't believe I even tried to go out with her; it was such a stupid idea. Last time I tried that I destroyed my friendship with Chloe; I probably drove her right to Everett. And here I had another chance, and I completely ruined it like an idiot. I'd give anything to go back a month and just have my best friend and I'd forget about all that other stuff. It was such a mistake, a complete miscalculation. So maybe the Chloes and Gretchens won't date me. At least they like me. Before I turn into a blubbering lovesick goon. It wasn't that I didn't put myself out there. It just wasn't me that they wanted.

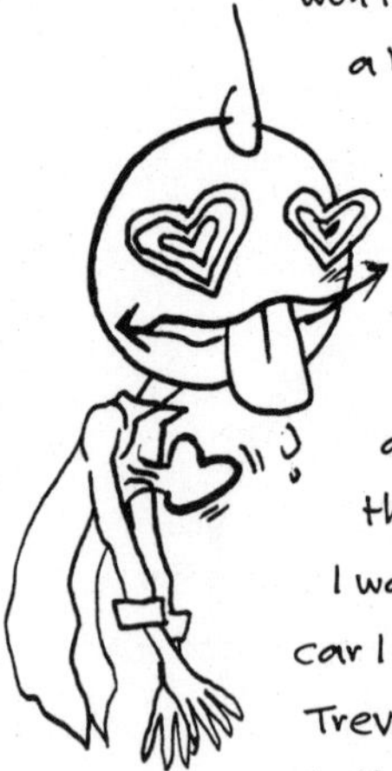

When I got to Gretchen's house, there was an extra car there, so I left my bike at the bottom of the hill, and when I walked up to the car I realized it was Trevor's. So they are dating, and that's why she won't talk to me. I don't even care anymore, though! I just won't date anyone, or I'll date someone else, it's fine, but I wish she would just be honest.

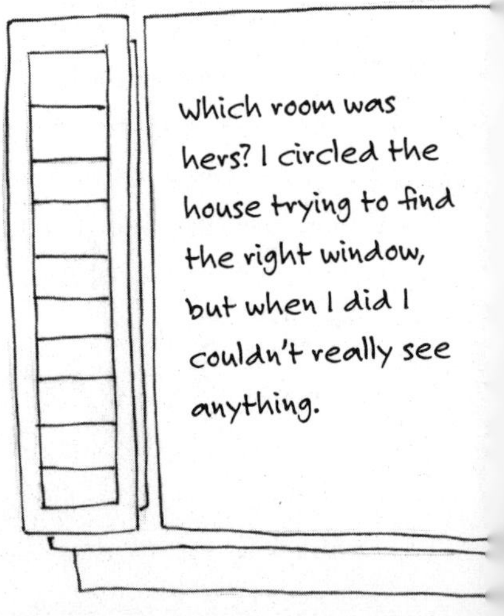

Which room was hers? I circled the house trying to find the right window, but when I did I couldn't really see anything.

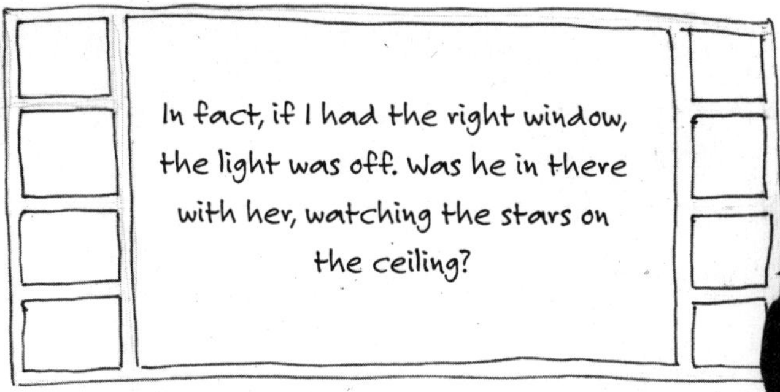
In fact, if I had the right window, the light was off. Was he in there with her, watching the stars on the ceiling?

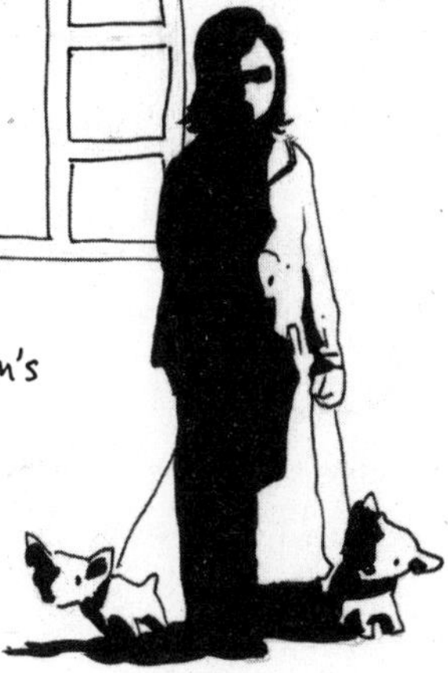

The back door opened and two of Gretchen's dogs came running around the corner. I walked back to the driveway, hoping it was Gretchen, but it was her mom. She stopped when she saw me in the floodlight, halfway up her driveway. She looked startled.

"Can I help you?" she asked, in a way that sounded more like "Should I be calling the police?"

"Is Gretchen home?" I asked timidly.

She took a second to tie the dog's leashes to the porch and walk to where I was standing.

"I understand you've become . . . quite fond of my daughter," she said in a way that made me horribly uncomfortable. I thought about running to my bike and peeling out, but I couldn't come back here if I did that. Better to just face this now. "Gretchen doesn't react kindly to bossiness, believe me, I know. You're not going to fix any bridges with the attitude you've had." I wondered what Gretchen said about me.

"I just want to be friends." I was trying not to let my eyes water.

"I'm sure you'll be friends again, with time . . . Happyface . . . ," she said, as if the nickname pained her to say. "But she's a sophomore in high school. There's going to be a lot of other friends, and a lot of other guys. That's something you're going to have to get used to."

I composed myself and gave her a calm, understanding smile. I didn't want to burn any bridges in case we do get together at some point. "Well, say hi to the family for me," I said as if I was an old family friend or an actor in a nineteen-forties movie. "Perhaps we'll meet again."

I walked my bike down the hill, occasionally glancing back as she watched me leave.

It didn't sound like they banned Gretchen from seeing me, though, and her mother didn't mention any hidden cameras or make-out sessions. Regardless, if Gretchen finds out I was there, she'll never talk to me again. A possibility that's all too real as it is.

I figured I would try to talk to the Moons, so I could figure out what I had to do next, because I don't want to lose everyone right now, so if there was something I could do . . .

I e-mailed Karma with no response last night, and Misty's tough to find online in the first place, so I had to interrupt her at the rehearsal for her play.

"Psst! Misty!" I called. I could tell she heard me when her eyes rolled but she didn't acknowledge me, so "Psst! Misty Moon!" I called again. She was onstage but she wasn't acting or talking or anything yet so I figured it was okay.

"We can take a small break," some guy with an obvious toupee said. Misty walked down the stairs at the side of the stage.

"What do you want?" she asked. "Do you know how embarrassing that was?"

"I'm sorry, Misty, I'll be really quick," I said. "Why won't Gretchen talk to me?"

"Because you're a psycho, will you beat it now?"

I gave her a look to let her know she was being silly. "Come on, you can tell me, is it Trevor?"

"Is what Trevor?"

I huddled in closer. "Do you think her parents won't let her see me anymore?"

"Seriously, what's wrong with you?"

"Well, at least tell me why you and Karma won't talk to me anymore."

"Because you stopped hanging out with us, because you're hanging out with those weird girls," Misty said, referring to Frog and Oddly, whom I don't even talk to anymore. "I don't have anything against you. We're still friends, okay?"

I gave her a big hug. Misty, my buddy, in her silly toga outfit. I was getting all emotional, and at the same time starting to realize how annoying I was being.

"Look," Misty added, "Gretchen is REALLY picky about who she hangs out with. It's not like her parents told her who she can and can't see, but . . ."

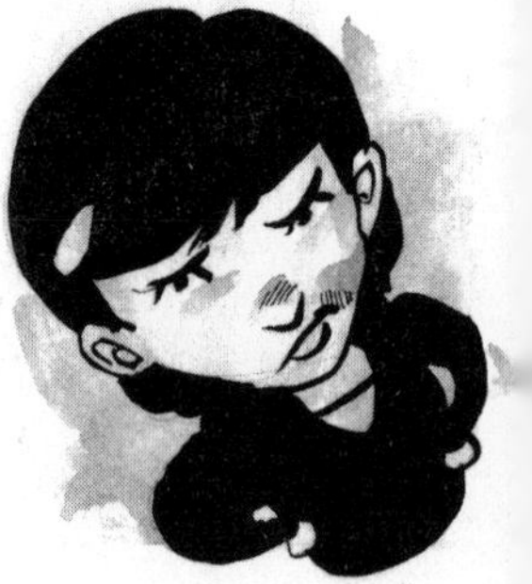

WHAT I LEARNED FROM MISTY

I am jealous. I am possessive.

I have not been acting like myself.

I "kinda creeped her out."

Dishonesty. This ties into owing people money, the competitiveness, the family stuff, the Chloe stuff.

I mean, not bad, right? That's what I thought. It could have been that I smell bad or I'm too ugly. She doesn't think I outright suck or anything. This stuff is all fixable!

Toupee signaled for her to come back. "Just chill out and be yourself!" she said. "It'll blow over. Are you sure you're all right?"

"Yes, ma'am." I saluted her. "Sorry for the interruption!" I shouted to the rest of the room.

This interaction put me in a good mood, and though Gretchen's mom told me it'll take time and Misty told me to chill out, I felt confident that we could bypass that time. After Molly's class, I followed Gretchen out.

I just had to tell her that I get it, that she doesn't like bossy guys and she's picky and I'll be laid back and cool and funny like I used to be, I'll smile and I won't be angsty or ask her out anymore or anything like that. Faulty wiring, that's all. I couldn't figure out how to word that at the right second though.

"Hi, Gretchen! It's me, Happyface."

She turned around, worn out.

"Hi," she said, eyebrows raised.

I sat there smiling, though my chest was caving in. "So are we still friends?" I asked.

"What is with you? Why'd you go all jealous ex-boyfriend on me?" she asked, walking to her locker. "It's like you and Trevor just switched roles all of a sudden."

"Why do you bring up Trevor every five seconds?" I asked her, regretting it instantly. "Are you guys going out again?"

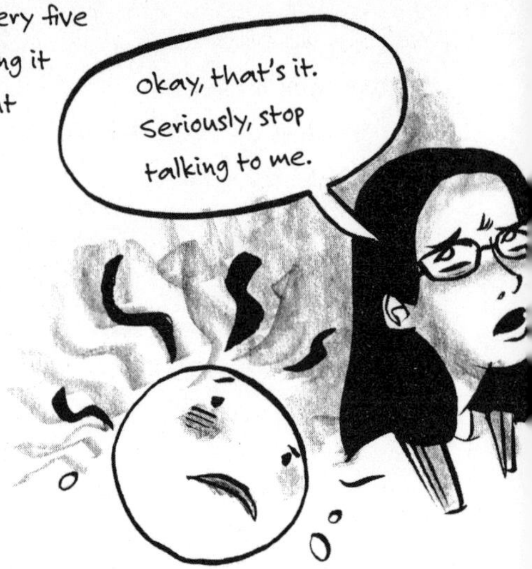
Okay, that's it. Seriously, stop talking to me.

"Gretchen, wait, I'm sorry," I begged. "I'm just . . . I'm failing a lot of classes and . . ." I was having trouble making words. If I lose Gretchen, I have no one. Happyface fails. I can't live like that, I can't face that life without Gretchen. "I'm just having some home problems, and I don't mean to take it out on you. I don't even know why I'm saying these things, they're just coming out. All I want is to talk."

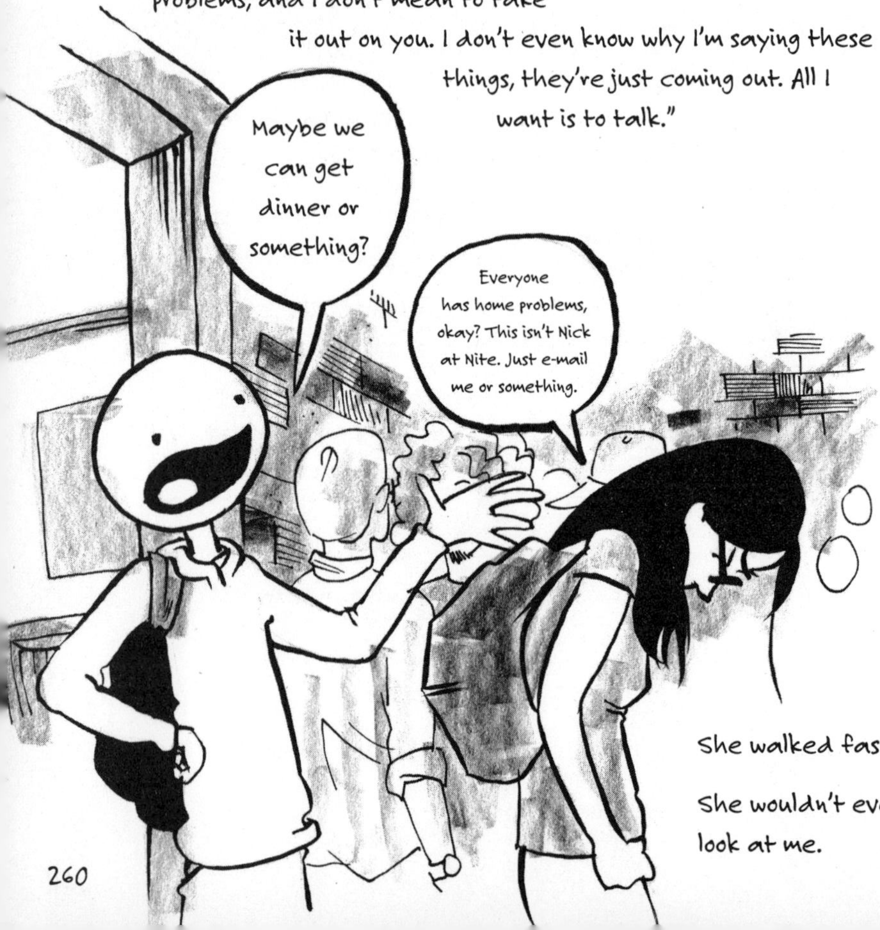
Maybe we can get dinner or something?
Everyone has home problems, okay? This isn't Nick at Nite. Just e-mail me or something.

She walked faster.

She wouldn't even look at me.

"We'll run away together or something," I suggested. "Like get married or whatever and just skip all of this, and the parents and the other people and teachers and everything. I'd like to do that, do you want to do that? It'd be a lot better with you."

She looked at me like I was insane. It was an awful feeling. My whole body felt like it was caving in on itself. I got dizzy but couldn't stop talking.

"We'll just pretend the last whatever, the last month didn't happen. We can go somewhere else and go skating like we did. We can get away from your parents and my parents. Yours are just as bad as mine, Gretchen, why are you so glued to them?"

People were starting to stare at me. This was not going as planned.

"That's not even slightly realistic," she said, back turned to me.

"But it would be," I told her. "Whatever we DO is REAL, it becomes real when we do it. You can do whatever you want, I know it." I'd done it all year.

"You've got to deal with all that stuff eventually," she said.

"But why?"

"Because you won't be happy until you do."

THE LAST DAY

I'd been waiting for today to happen. I guess it was only a matter of time.

When I got to school I could see almost instantly that everything had changed, and as the day moved on it became more and more pronounced. The stares and whispers were all very familiar by now, old hat even, and I was reminded of my last day at my old school back in September. Back then my father was a drunk but he hadn't left me yet. Back then I was the loser whose best friend screwed his brother, who wrecked his old car in a drunken stupor. Back then I was humiliated and crushed and I could barely hold myself together. This time I didn't have my head-phones on and I didn't keep my eyes on the floor. This time I had to meet their gazes and smile and walk with confidence. I'd been looked at like that before, but I had gotten used to being the watcher now, of being the one to observe and see how everyone ticks. I'd spent so much time thinking about other people, Gretchen, my family, Molly, that to have the tables turned and be the person on everyone's minds was foreign. Familiar, but foreign at the same time. I wasn't sure who found out or how, but the game had changed and I had to adapt.

Other students smiled at me like they were saying "Hey, tough breaks about your crazy family." They looked at me with pity like I was supposed to accept it. They looked surprised when I smiled like "Nothing's wrong here." See, that's the thing, they all want to be around you when you're Mr. Smiles and the life of the party; you're a magnet for people when life is good because they all want to be around the good life. But the thing is, every one of them is waiting for this morning. They're all waiting for the moment it all falls apart so they can be in on it. So they can watch you break and feel better about their own lives. The air was dense with pity. If people are drawn to happiness, they flock to pity.

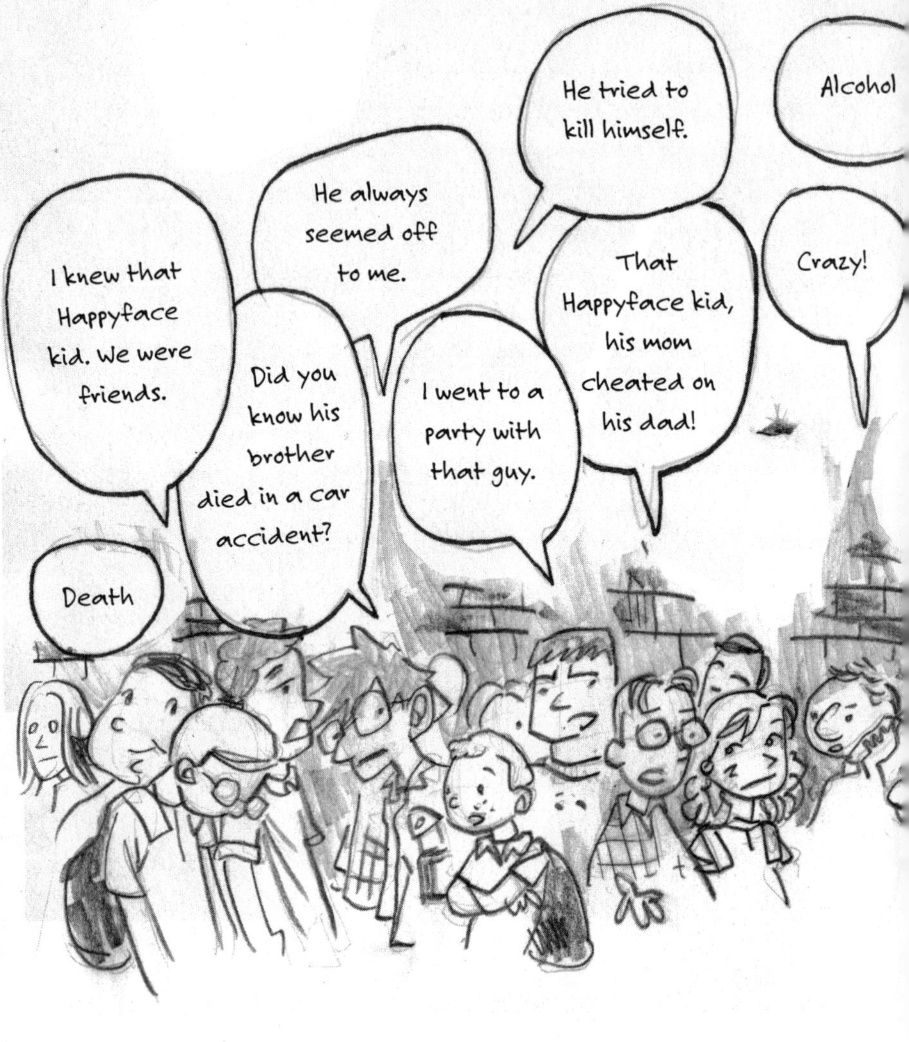
Death
I knew that Happyface kid. We were friends.
Did you know his brother died in a car accident?
He always seemed off to me.
I went to a party with that guy.
He tried to kill himself.
That Happyface kid, his mom cheated on his dad!
Alcohol
Crazy!

But if I keep smiling, there's nothing to gossip about. So I smiled all morning long, if anyone had anything to say to me, all they were getting was a grin and a "How's it going?" Because there's nothing wrong here, there's nothing to pity.

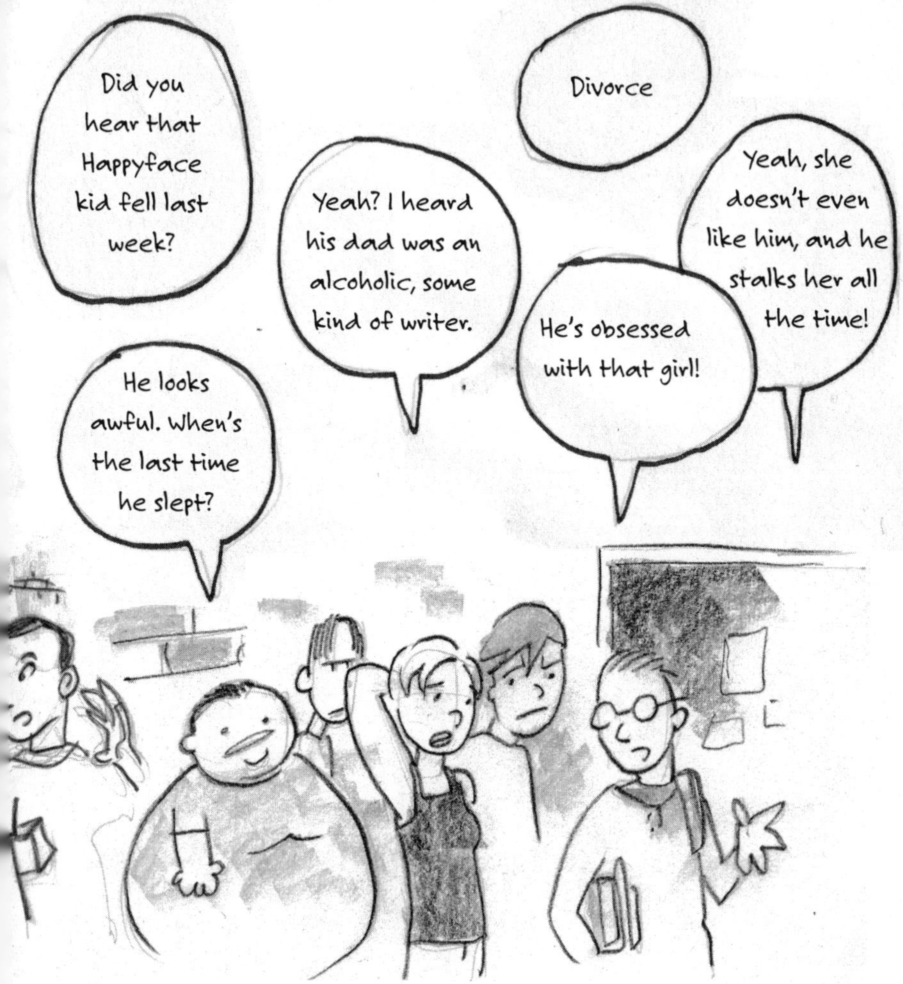
Did you hear that Happyface kid fell last week?
Yeah? I heard his dad was an alcoholic, some kind of writer.
Divorce
Yeah, she doesn't even like him, and he stalks her all the time!
He's obsessed with that girl!
He looks awful. When's the last time he slept?

If they wanted to talk about my mom, or my dad, or Everett, then I'd laugh and joke with them. They couldn't pity me if I did it first. And if I made it funny, all the better.

OH HAI, ITZ HAPPYFACE: THE WEBCOMIC-IN-PRINT
DARK HUMOR edition!

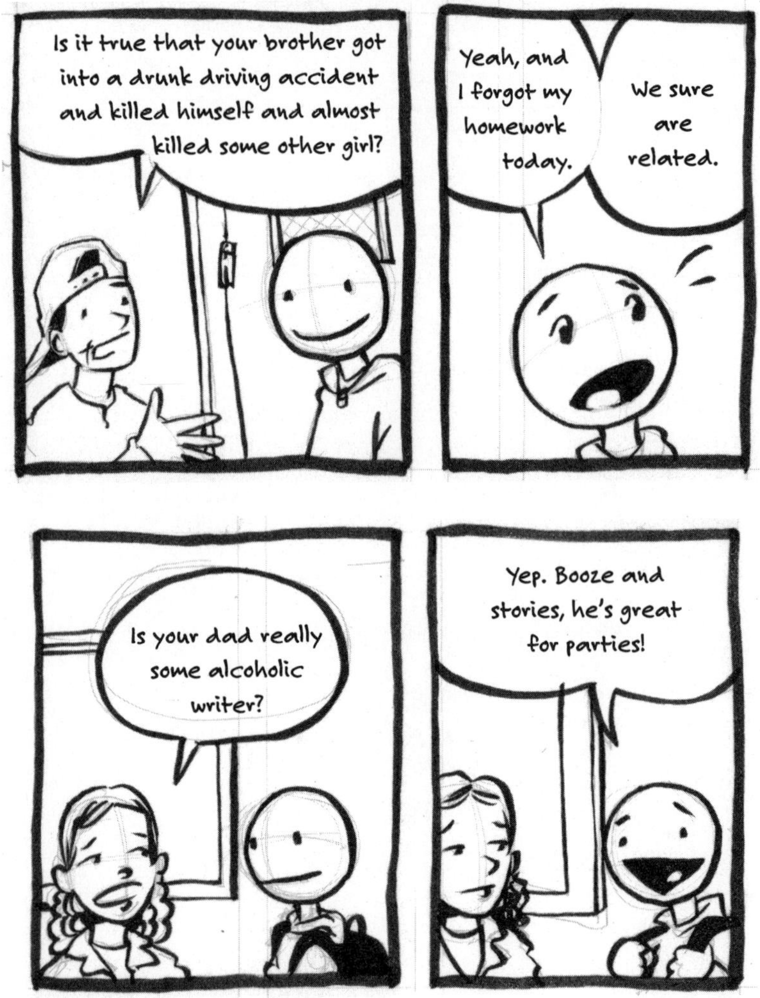
Is it true that your brother got into a drunk driving accident and killed himself and almost killed some other girl?
Yeah, and I forgot my homework today.
We sure are related.
Is your dad really some alcoholic writer?
Yep. Booze and stories, he's great for parties!

"Hey, I heard what happened," Trevor said in the hall before gym class. "Why didn't you tell anyone?"

"Because there's nothing to tell and it's nobody's business," I said.

"Well, I'm sorry, anyway," he said. I was thinking that he must be laughing on the inside. He has Gretchen, he must know she won't even talk to me anymore and probably knows I keep asking about him. He thinks he's winning.

"Don't be sorry for me, I'm fine. That was all months ago anyway. I feel sorry for you."

"Why's that?" Trevor asked.

"Because nobody likes you. They only pretend to because you're a bully. You're mean to people and you don't deserve Gretchen, even as a friend. You're just a lame, pathetic person."

I'm paraphrasing at this point because I don't really remember what I actually said. I just know it was mean and by the end of it Trevor didn't pity me anymore, I pitied him. Trevor had turned his back to walk away when I shoved him. I wasn't going to lose to Trevor. He lost his footing and almost fell over, but didn't. Instead he turned around.

And then I got punched in the face. I lost my front tooth in what I think is accurate to describe as "a bloody mess."

"Oh, shit," Trevor said with more remorse than he needed.

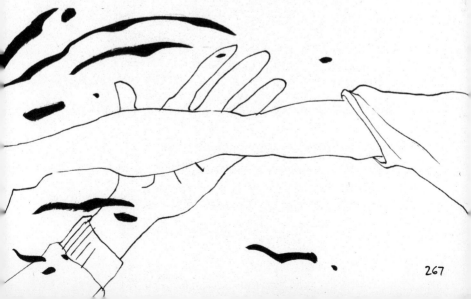

I was called to the main office a half hour later, and I left the nurse's room, ready to go hear more about counseling or grief or going home early for the day. My mouth was bloody and sore, and the ice pack I held to it did very little.

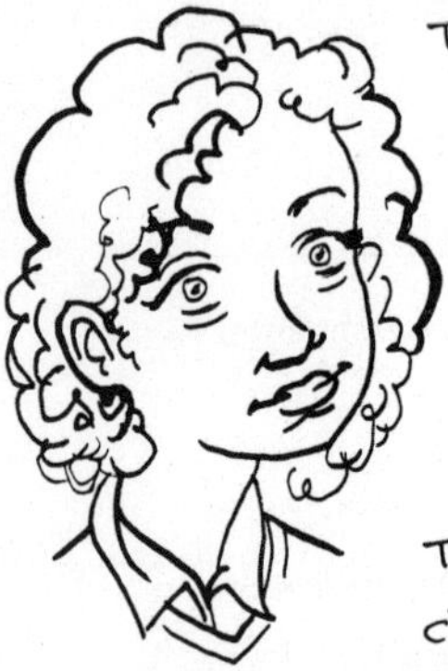

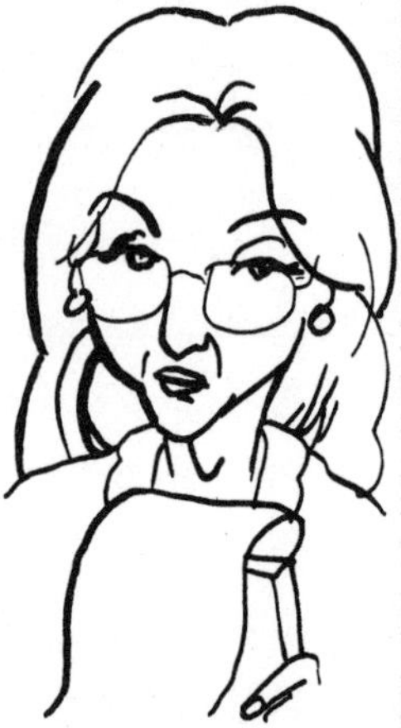

There was a guidance counselor there who had tried to talk to me a few times, but she was too young and pretty for me to open up to her about my personal life. The school psychiatrist was there, and even the principal. They were gathered in a semi-circle, and it felt like walking into an intervention. I was trying to figure out how to "Happyface" the situation when the principal, Mr. Crompton, started to speak. He was a very serious zombie-looking guy with a brow that made caves of his eyes. He always intimidated me.

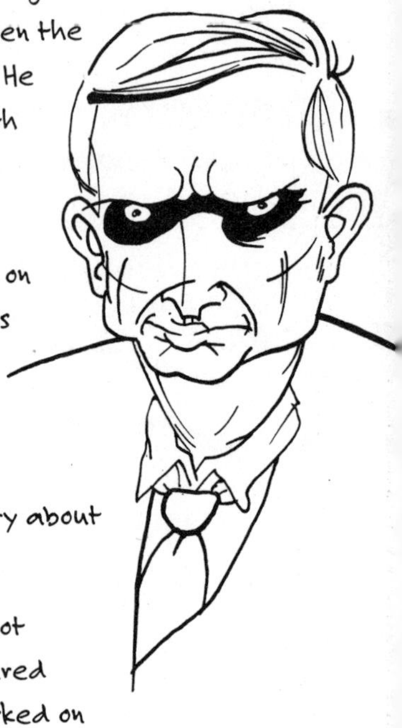

"First off, we want to offer condolences on your brother," he said, "and we know this information leaked out today and that you'd been trying to keep that to yourself, which is understandable."

Everyone chipped in with apologies. "Sorry about the tooth."

"Fighting on school grounds, however, is not acceptable," Mr. Crompton said. I wondered why it was so acceptable when I got picked on growing up. "You'll have to take a three-day suspension."

"I'm sorry," I said. I didn't want them calling Mom.

"Maybe this will be good for you," the guidance counselor added. "And if you need someone to talk to, I will give you my number here; you can reach me anytime."

"Do you have to call my mom . . . ?" I asked. They all nodded.

"Should give me time to grow a new tooth, at least," I said, backing toward the door. My family fell apart, I lost all my friends, and now my tooth, but according to Crest Falls High, I still need to be punished.

"The suspension is effective immediately, so just have a seat in the office while we arrange to have you picked up."

I tried as hard as I could to not cry as I waited for Mom to come take me home.

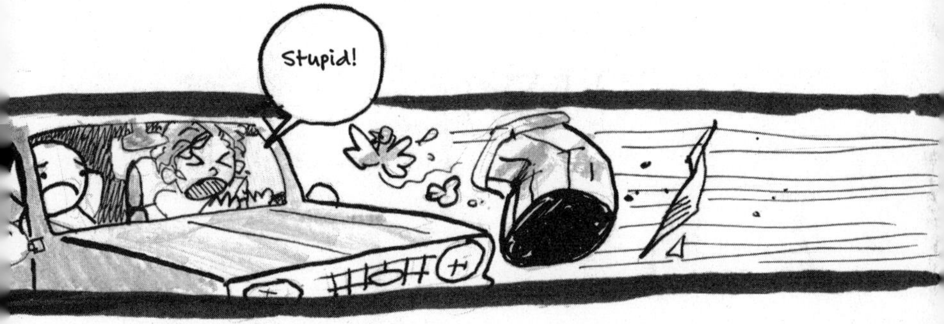
Stupid!

"Stupid!" was the first thing Mom said as she drove me home from school. I could tell there was more she wanted to say, but hey, I'm a kid and I lost my brother, so I had some amount of sympathy to play on. I mean, how mad could she get without looking like a tyrant?

"Failing grades, and now fights . . . ," she said, trailing off. "I blame your father."

"He didn't do anything," I said.

"No, he didn't. He should have, he should be around. You listen to him. I can't do anything. I'm just no good at this."

"Mom . . ." I was surprised to hear her say any of that. I didn't want to think it was true. And I certainly didn't want her to think that. "That's not true," I said. I gave her a sympathetic smile, closed-mouth per the new aesthetic.

"I don't know what's up with you and the constant smiling," she said. "It creeps me out."

I stopped smiling and looked out the window until we got back.

THE LAST HURRAH

3/13

I'm grounded, and suspended, but tonight was Misty's performance at the play. I left Mom a quick note—

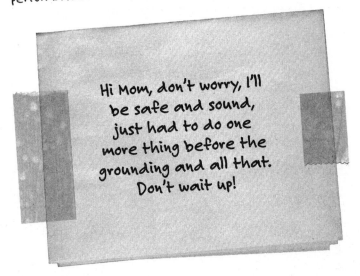

Hi Mom, don't worry, I'll be safe and sound, just had to do one more thing before the grounding and all that. Don't wait up!

I assumed it would add to my punishment in some form, but I had to go. Everyone would be there. Besides, I'd already told Mike to pick me up at seven.

The hard part would be not getting noticed. I'm pretty sure "immediate suspension" includes not going to the school play.

Mike was right on time. I gave him a closed-mouth new Happyface smile.

"Lost a tooth, huh? Heard about that," Mike said as I got into the passenger seat and fastened my safety belt.

"You should see the other guy," I said.

"Trevor? He looked fine when I saw him."

"Yeah, but he's hurting on the inside."

"Glad to see you haven't lost the Happyface wit," Mike said as he turned the radio on to a jazz station. It fit.

"So I don't think I'm supposed to actually be IN the school for a while," I told Mike.

"Yeah, I'd wondered about that. It should be all right, though, right?"

"I hope so, because I'm not going down without a fight."

I'm pretty sure Mike was ready to kick me out the door until I told him I was kidding. "So did you sneak out of the house?" Mike asked.

271

"No, I'm not grounded," I lied, figuring it was what he needed to hear to relax. "My mom doesn't really care what I do."

"Well, I hope you've learned something through all this."

Of all the arrogant . . . "Like what?" I asked.

"Well, all of this obsession with being cool, and hanging out with popular kids. Look where it got you."

Completely unrelated. If Gretchen would have gone out with me and Trevor didn't exist, everything would have worked out just fine. "It's not so bad," I said. Luckily we were a few minutes from the school and could just watch the play in silence.

"Maybe you didn't notice, but I've been having lunches by myself lately. I prefer it," Mike said. He would prefer it. "I stay out of trouble and I can use the time at lunch to get ahead on my homework."

"And who are you, my guidance counselor?" I asked.

"No," he said. "I just think you need to cool it down a bit, concentrate on your schoolwork, get a hobby. Otherwise you'll end up like my sister."

"What's wrong with your sister?" I asked.

"She's the black sheep of the family."

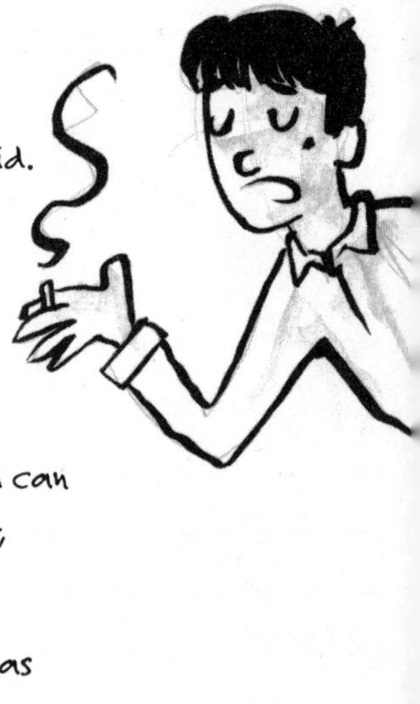

"You smoke. It's not like you're some angel," I said.

"I smoke RARELY, and only with due cause," he said. No wonder this kid has no friends. "You shouldn't even be arguing. Your missing tooth says it all."

"I'll have a full set of teeth as soon as my mom can get a day off," I told him. "We'll see who's right, then."

There was a good turnout at the play. Misty was awesome, and I was so proud to see her up onstage.

I couldn't find Gretchen or Karma or anyone, though I was looking for them through the whole show. It was almost over when I was visited by Mr. Crompton, the principal. His brow was furrowed and he scared the crap out of me as I turned and saw him two inches from my face. It's how I imagine death will be. One minute you're laughing and enjoying yourself, and the next, the Grim Reaper's looking you in the eye and sucking your soul right out. Mr. Crompton was a soul-sucker.

"I got a call from your mom," he said. "Go ahead, enjoy the rest of the show, I told her you'd be home right after the play. You shouldn't be here, but we'll let this slide since it may not have been fully clear."

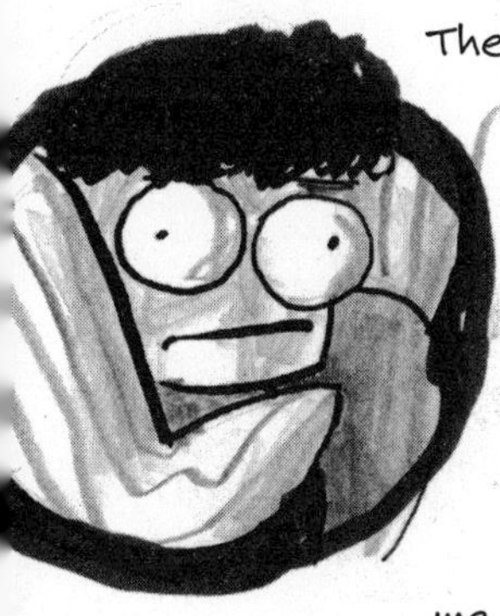

Then he flew backward, evaporating into the shadows. Mike looked like he was the accomplice to a murder.

"He didn't even know you came with me, you're fine," I said. He still looked uncomfortable.

After the show, I met Misty in the hall outside. That was when I saw Gretchen and Trevor and everyone else. I gave Misty a hug and told her she did great. Then I apologized to Trevor.

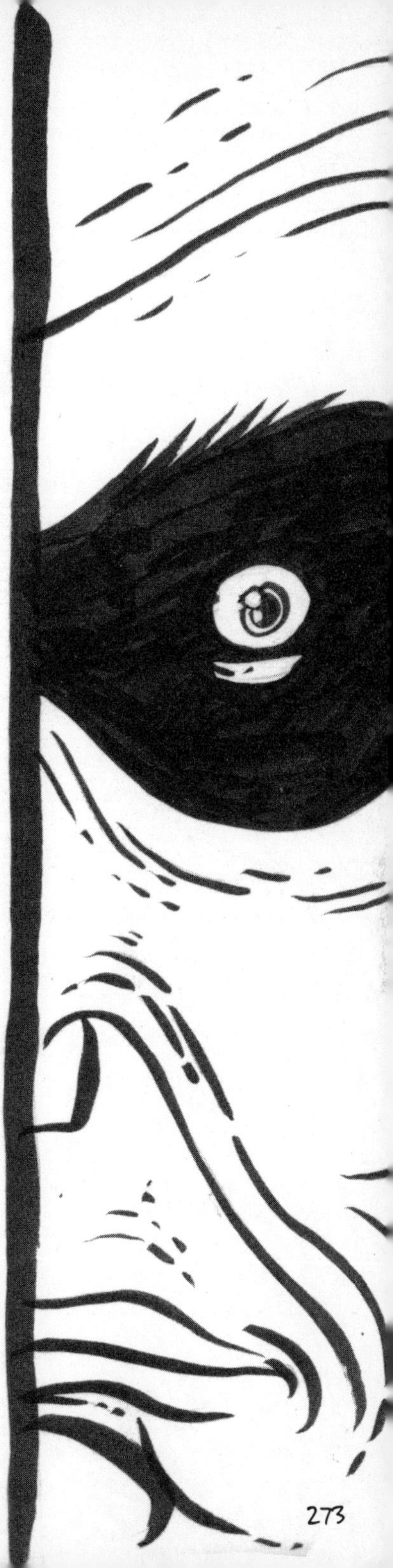

"I shouldn't have let it get to me," he said.

"Yeah, but I was a complete ass," I said.

"But look at your face, you're a mess," Trevor joked.

"I'll survive the messy face. If you can do it, so can I."

Gretchen and the Moons laughed at us, and I guess it did seem silly. A couple of guys fighting over a girl and laughing and shaking hands after a face was busted up. I must actually kinda like the guy on some level. Gretchen gave me a hug.

"I'm sorry about everything," she said, referring to my family. I smiled.

"Shouldn't we be leaving?" Mike said, interrupting the conversation. I really wanted to patch things up.

"Don't worry about it," I said.

"Oh, there's an after party at our house," Misty said. "Are you guys coming? It's mostly going to be cast and crew from the show, but you're welcome to join."

"Actually, we're supposed to go straight home," Mike said.

"Yeah, we can pop in for a few minutes, definitely!" I said as Mike's shoulders hit the floor.

"Great, I'm going to change but you can head on over," Misty said.

"You haven't learned a thing!" Mike said as we left the building. He crossed his arms in a huff, but we were heading to the after party.

"Can't you have any fun?" I asked Mike as he sulked the whole way to Misty's house.

"You're probably going to get grounded twice over now. How's that for fun?"

"Your problem is you just don't put yourself out there," I said. "You had an in with a bunch of great people at lunch and you choose to sit by yourself and do homework."

"We have differing views on life, then."

"You're not a bad guy, Mike. But you can have interesting views on things, and you can be clever or funny, but you know what? Nobody knows that! You don't exist!"

"I exist. I just don't need the approval of a bunch of people to know that."

"Fine," I said. "Live your life unpopular, with no respect, and hide and smoke cigarettes to get through it, then." We pulled up to the Moonses' house and parked down the street. There was already a bunch of people there. "Meanwhile, I'll be enjoying life."

"Let's at least make this quick," Mike said as I dragged him to the party. Mike needs a Happyface to pull him out of his shell as much as I did.

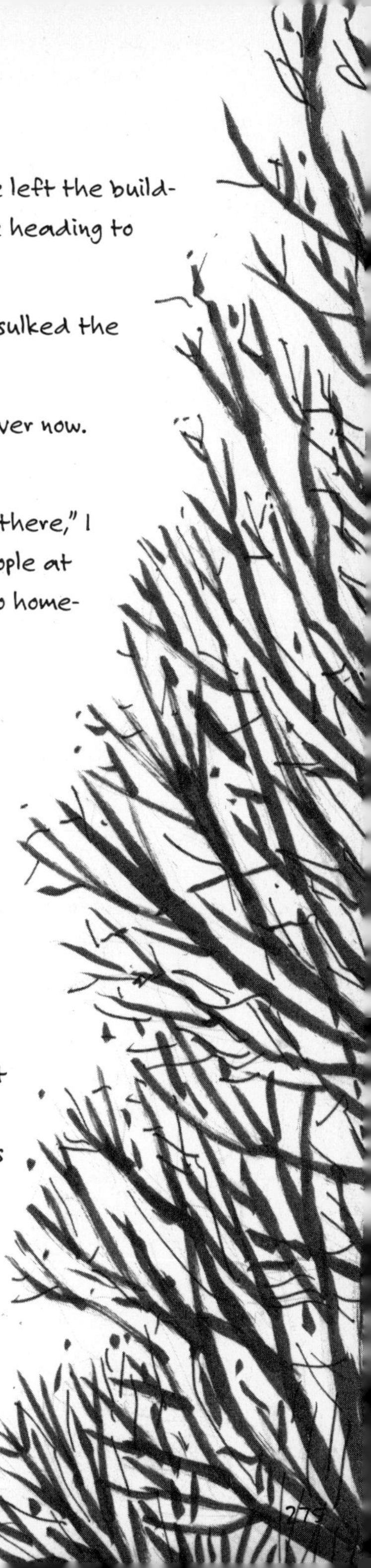

I tried to show Mike how much respect I had, all the people I'd met, so I said hi to everyone I'd known even through classes or just people I'd seen laughing at something I'd said, or, more often, people I knew vaguely through Gretchen and Misty and Karma. Most of them gave me a simple head nod or smile or an "isn't he that kid . . . ?" look. It was what I wanted to avoid, but I might as well use my newfound notoriety to my advantage, I figured.

I quickly ditched Mike, sink or swim, tough love, all that. I sat with the first people who talked to me coming in, and went ahead and let out the sob story, studying reaction so I could optimize it in future conversations. The right exaggerations really drew out the emotion. This night could be very productive.

THE SOB STORY OF HAPPYFACE:

"It all happened so quick, my life got flipped upside down. I was a normal kid, you know? Brilliant father, fun-loving mother, and my bro, he was the coolest. It was an awful tragedy. I lost my only brother. I feel like I flew through that windshield with him. My dad, he hit the sauce pretty heavy and started knocking me around, and Mom got us out of there. I left all my friends behind, my cheerleader girlfriend, our three-story house, and started from scratch. Now it's just me and Mom, leaning on each other, trying our best to make it, taking it day by day."

And for bonus points:

"I'm talking with a publisher about turning my story into a book, but I really don't want to exploit the situation. That's my family. I might have to change names."

276

Had to drag Dad through the mud a bit but it could have happened, I mean, it's not SO unbelievable, and it makes a great story detail at the least.

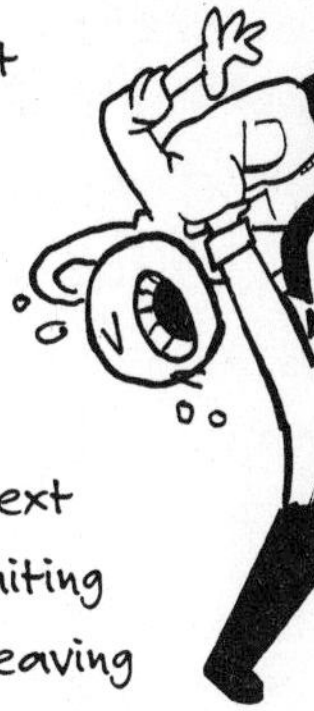

I was talking to a few theater kids at first, then some cute girls were there, and next thing you know, there was a whole crowd, waiting to hear my stories. And then they started leaving me. To play POOL. With Mike.

Mike was taking on anyone and beating them all, another of his odd talents. Playing pool. He was taking away from my attention and he wasn't even being interesting or funny, he was just shooting pool and being all bravado about it, like he's some big shot. He was supposed to be nervous and awkward, like me. I was supposed to show him that his reclusive lifestyle was damaging, but that lifestyle made him an expert at all these stupid little hobbies, and he was actually smart enough that he could talk about anything. It was annoying. He should falter somewhere.

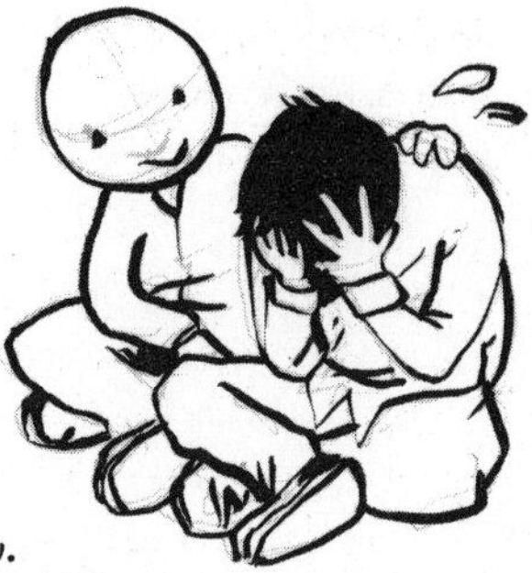

Misty showed up and became the belle of the ball, and people were all talking to her now. Gretchen was there too, but she was sitting at the top of the stairs all night talking to some guy. I asked Misty if there was any alcohol around, thinking it might take the edge off and help me relax.

"Sorry, I didn't know it was going to be a 'Happyface' party," she said. Funny.

Now the cute girls were playing pool with Mike. He had his camera out.

"I'll send you the pics, just give me your e-mail," he said. Flirting, now? Who was this guy?

Karma was with Jake still. She didn't heed any of our warnings. He was draped all over her as they made out on the couch. I should have gone out with Karma. Gretchen was never interested in me at all. Everything would have been different if I'd just chosen the right girl. Then I'd have a girlfriend. I'd be the one making out on the couch. I'd probably still be friends with Gretchen, too. I kept waiting for the guy on the stairs to make some kind of move on Gretchen. He should, before he gets stuck in the friend category like I did.

There wasn't even anyone to talk to anymore. Everyone was all grouped off. I just stood there like an idiot while Mike of all people had everyone in stitches. He's not even funny! He's no one! He just sits around his home all night baking cookies with his mom and memorizing TV shows. I have tragedy, I have comedy, I'm interesting. I got into a fight today! I got suspended! Look at my face. I'm missing a front tooth! Why isn't anyone talking to me?

"Come on, let's get out of here," I told Mike.

"Let me just finish this game," he said.

"No, we have to go now. My mouth is sore, and I want to go home."

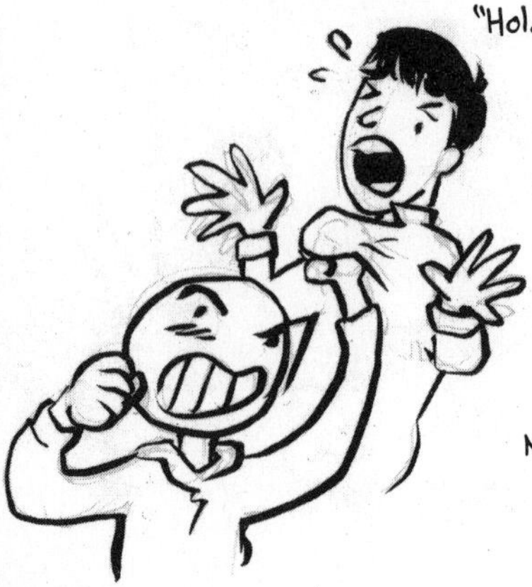

"Hold on, Happyface." He said Happyface like it's some kind of joke now. I should have hit him. I should have made his mouth look like mine. Who did he think he was, making fun of me? I make fun of Mike.

"Fine, I'll walk." I stormed out of Misty's house and was ready to walk home when Mike came outside.

"That was fun," he said after a moment's silence.

I turned on the radio as Mike drove. My whole body was tense. A tear forced itself out of my eye. I wasn't crying or anything, but that one escaped.

"You've got to put yourself first," Mike said. "It's more important than anything else."

It's so much easier to put them first. They're normal.

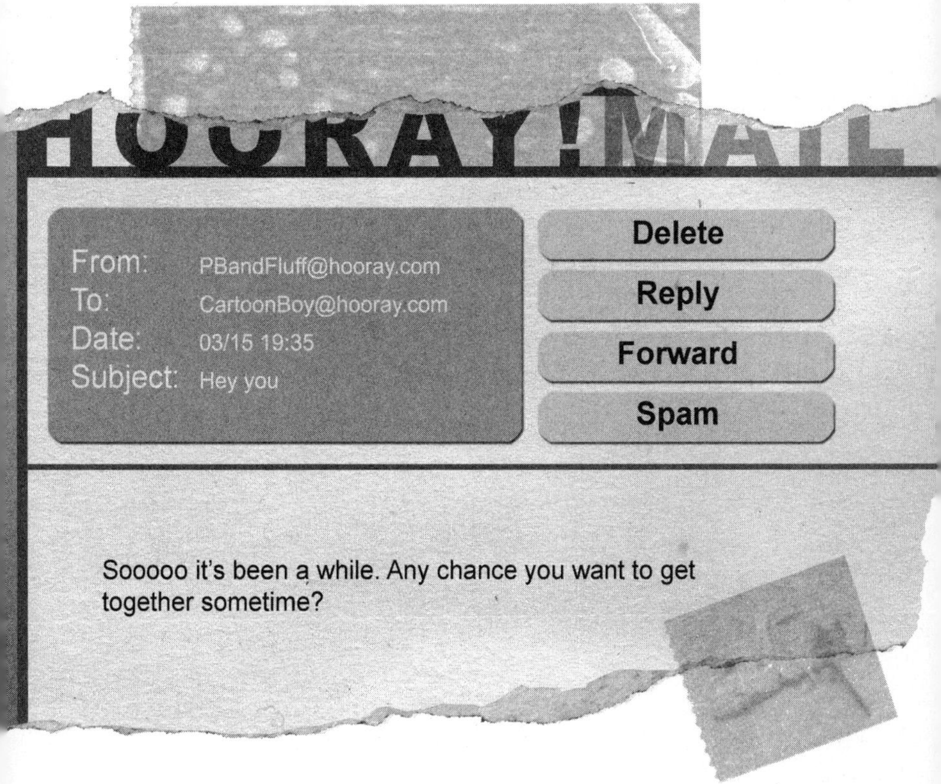

From: PBandFluff@hooray.com
To: CartoonBoy@hooray.com
Date: 03/15 19:35
Subject: Hey you

Delete

Reply

Forward

Spam

Sooooo it's been a while. Any chance you want to get together sometime?

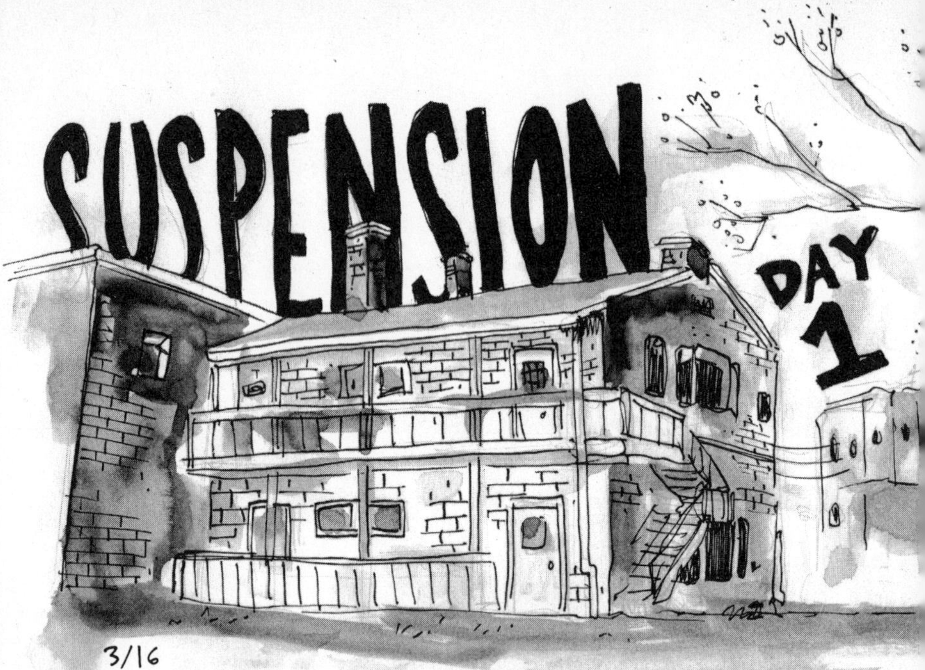
SUSPENSION
DAY 1

3/16

I had Chloe come visit me after school since I knew she'd come over and keep me company and I could only be grounded so much. I mean, Mom works two jobs, so who's watching me?

"Oh, my God!!" she exclaimed when she saw my mouth. The whole tooth-missing thing is really disturbing looking and I think gives me that badass edge Oddly was talking about. You don't really mess with guys with a missing front tooth. I might keep the look.

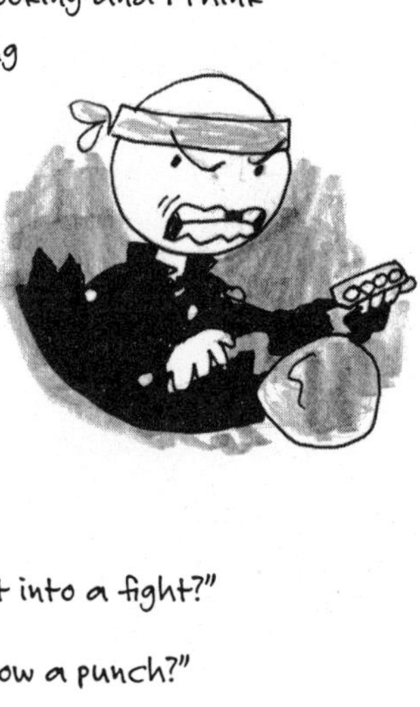

"Oh, this old thing?" I asked. "It's no big deal."

"What happened to you?" Chloe asked. What hadn't happened to me?

"I'm fine," I told her.

"Fine? You're missing a front tooth! Did you get into a fight?"

"Is it a fight if you don't get a chance to throw a punch?" I asked her.

"Stop, it's not funny."

"Not funny?" I asked. I pointed to my missing tooth. "It's hilarious!"

I asked her what I could do to show how fine I was but she wasn't playing along. I asked her if we could just go out for a ride.

I took her out to the Corvette and showed her the keys I'd found and snuck away from Mom. Who was she to say who could drive the car? It wasn't mine, but it wasn't hers either.

"I'm not going in there, come on . . . ," she said.

"Why?" I asked. "Girls love Corvettes, don't they? Oh, what, because it was Everett's car? He barely drove it."

Chloe was turning away.

"What? It's not even the car you guys crashed. That was my mom's car. This one's barely been driven!"

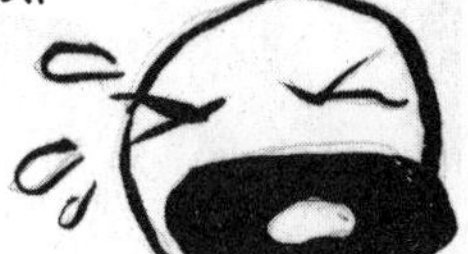

Chloe wasn't saying anything, just looking at me.

"What? What is with you people?" I asked. "What is so friggin' special about this car that NO ONE can drive it? It's just a car. It's a good, nice, clean car and it's STUPID not to drive it! It's sitting here, just waiting. If we don't drive it, someone will. It'll get stolen eventually. No one else is taking it out. Its only owner is DEAD, okay? Ev doesn't mind if we take it for a spin, no one minds! I'm sure he wants to see it used!"

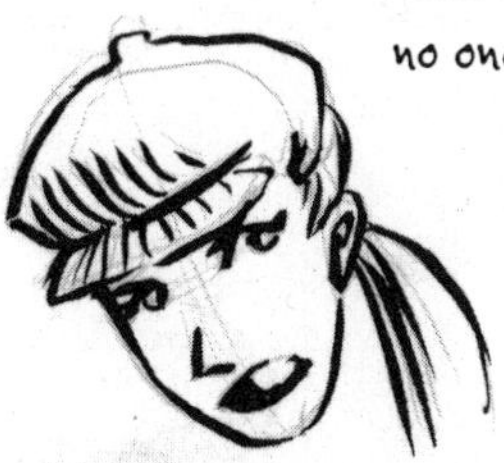

"I'm not getting in that car, okay? That's sick," Chloe said.

"Fine, no one will ever use this stupid car! We

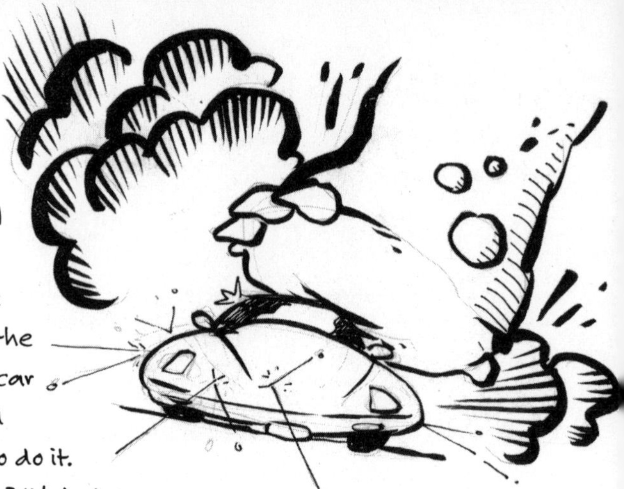

won't drive it and we won't sell it, it'll just sit here like some useless piece of junk!" I kicked the front side of the car as hard as I could and it felt good to do it. Who cares anyway? It's just metal and plastic with leather interiors at this point. I tried to kick the headlights.

"Stop it!" Chloe yelled. "When are you going to stop with this?"

I tried to elbow the side window. I threw every pound of my frame into it, over and over, but the car just sat there shining and red. I kicked and kicked and clawed at it but the damn thing wouldn't even scratch.

I started looking around. Anything, a weapon, a rock, a stick. I saw a cinder block by the building and walked after it.

"Stop it right now!" Chloe was screaming, and I saw people looking out their windows. I picked up the cinder block and it was heavy, but I was so angry, I couldn't think, I just lifted it right up and Chloe followed me and grabbed onto my arm.

"Let go!" I said.

She tried to grab the block out of my hands and was about to get hurt. I could have dropped it on her feet or something.

"Let go!" I said again.

"No, stop it, just . . . let's go inside! Please!"

"No!" I said, and shoved her off me. Chloe was crying, and the neighbor upstairs said she was going to call the police if we didn't knock it off. I dropped the block and sat on it and looked at the car. What was I going to do with that car?

I still had the keys so I unlocked the Corvette and sat inside. Everett's glove was in the back. His CDs were in the glove compartment. Some of them were still wrapped. Nobody will listen to them. It was still Ev's car, and it had never left August. I could still see Dad and Everett pounding away at this thing when it was dirty and rusty and the hood didn't cover the engine. I missed that. For a minute it was like sitting next to Everett, but he couldn't talk back. It was like sitting with my brother and not saying anything, because I didn't have to, and he didn't have to.

I looked out the window. . . . Chloe had gotten off the ground and was walking to the car where she joined me.

"I'm sorry," I said. I can't believe I pushed her. I didn't mean to. I'd never do that. I'd never in a million years. I couldn't remember how it happened at all at the time.

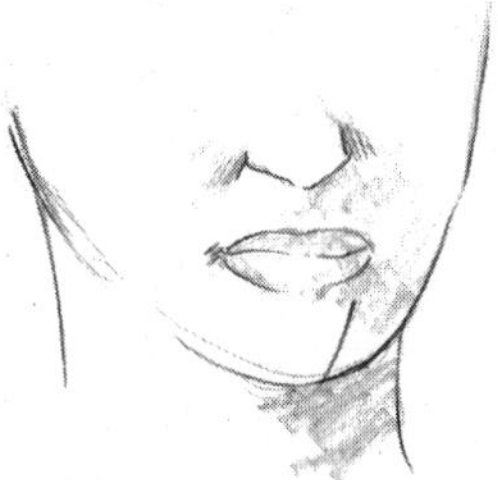

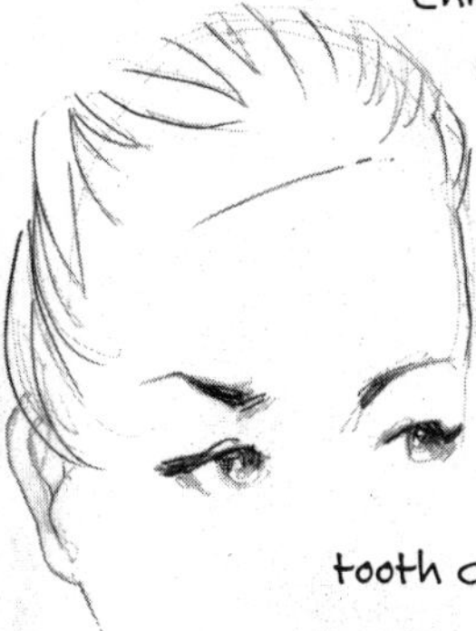

Chloe looked through the CDs. "I still can't get over that tooth," she said.

"You've got your scars."

"The chin?" she asked before lifting her hat to reveal a larger scar by her hairline. "I have this one, too." At least my tooth can be replaced.

"Oh," I said. It reminded me that she was actually there when he died. She saw it. She had the scars to prove it. I figured I'd change the subject before that got too heavy. There was one thing I wanted to know still.

"Did you ever really like me, like more than friends?" I asked, trying my best to not sound like a fifth grader. That's still about where I am when it comes to dating. "You know, before everything."

"Yeah," she said quietly. "Couldn't you tell?"

I smiled. Okay, it was a goofy grin that made me look stupid, I couldn't help it.

"Then, why . . . ?" I started, trailing off.

"You never asked me out."

"You knew how I felt."

"Maybe, but Everett said it aloud. And sooner."

I should have put myself out there. "You didn't think there was anything wrong or weird about dating Everett?" I asked.

"It doesn't change how things were with you and me, but . . ." she looked for the right words. "Your brother was cool. He was confident, older, in college. . . ."

"Yeah, and he dated high school girls, he smoked and drank, he was a jock," I said. "What's so great about him? So what if he's outgoing and assertive. He was still mean and obviously didn't care at all about his own brother."

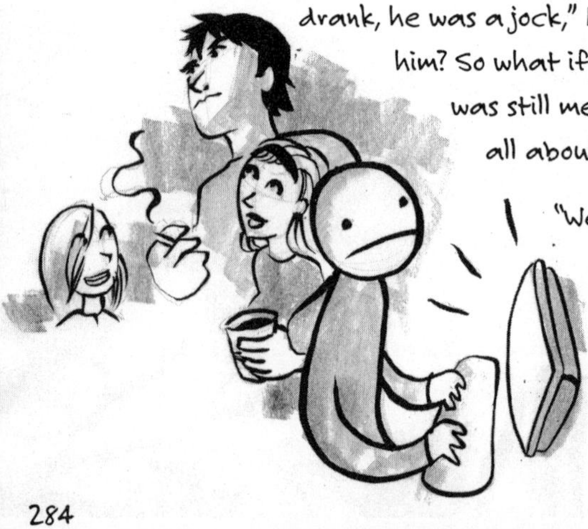

"We talked about YOU. He wanted . . ." She played with the bottom of her shirt before changing her line of thought.

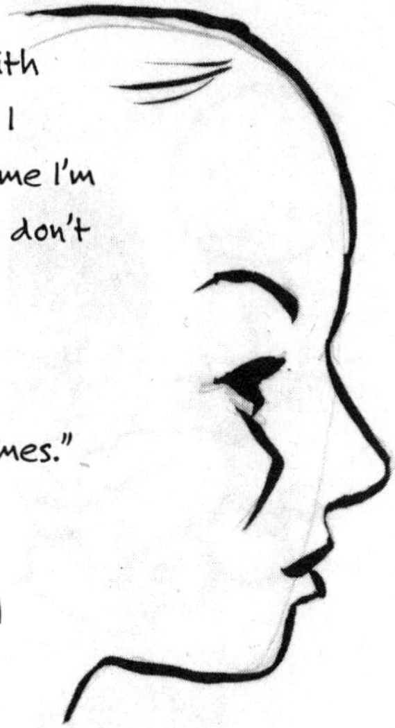

"I'm not exactly Miss Confidence. I busy myself with all kinds of activities and I do well in school and I try to look pretty but I still need someone to tell me I'm worthwhile. To show me attention. I don't like it. I don't like it at all. . . ."

"So it was Everett who came on to you?"

"It happened, and we went out drinking a few times."

"I didn't know you drank."

"I didn't. And I didn't want you to know about all that and neither did he."

"Did you like him?"

"We went out twice. How would I know?" she asked. "I liked you more."

"But I never said anything," I said, knowing the rest of the story.

"And I never had the guts," Chloe said.

I guess Dad was right when he told me we're all just people. Chloe isn't just some popular supermodel ballerina; she's a girl, with feelings just like mine.

I changed subjects and told her about all I'd been through since moving to Crest Falls. When condensed to a fifteen-minute talk, it was all actually kind of funny. And it was funny to think of Everett sitting in the backseat listening to that whole conversation, but I like to think he'd be okay with it. I think he wanted Chloe and me together anyway.

The Sordidest of Love Affairs Involving Happyface...

Chloe

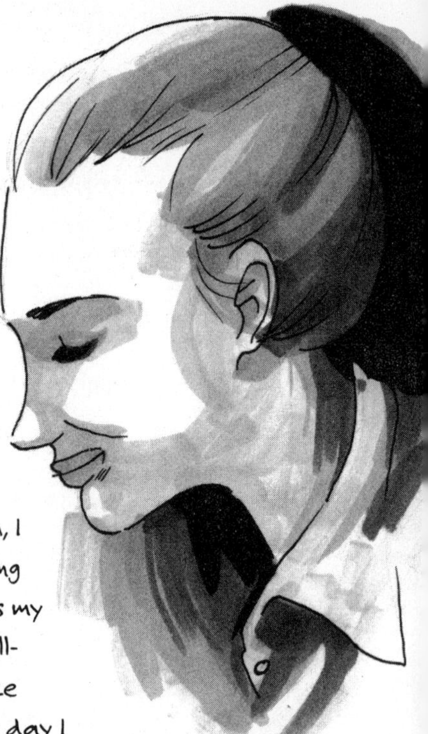

In case I haven't stressed it enough, I was never very popular. The one thing people seemed to like about me was my drawings. In fact, I'd have been well-received had I just drawn a life-size cutout I could stand behind. Every day I would draw at school, during free periods, before school, at lunch, I was always filling up my sketchbooks with all kinds of drawings. Inevitably people would stop by and see what I was working on. They'd ask me to draw skulls with wings, or cartoons of themselves, or cartoon characters from TV. These people never really had an interest in me, but for a few minutes each day it would create the illusion of popularity, or at least of a mild acceptance. Once they had their drawings, I'd be left to my lonesome once again.

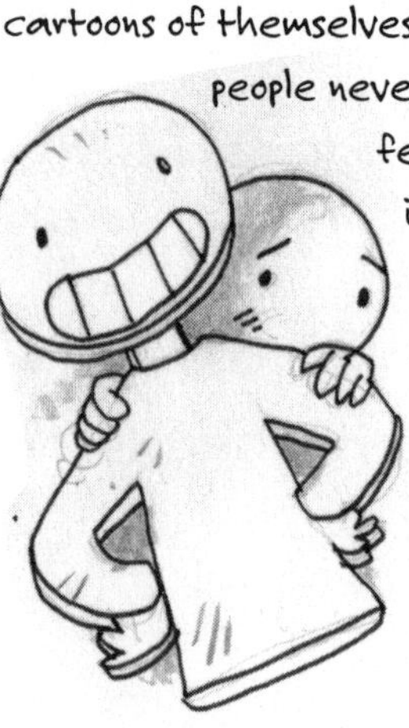

The two different middle schools merged once high school started, so there were a lot of new faces around.

The prettiest of those faces belonged to Chloe Hills. Once or twice there would be a popular girl who would want a drawing of Marvin the Martian or something, but Chloe was different from the beginning. I'd noticed her before but she had her own friends and I was too busy entertaining my doubt and fears to meet anyone new. It wasn't until late winter of freshman year that I really had any interaction with her. She saw me drawing one day and asked if she could look. She seemed more interested in me than most people who'd peek through my sketchbooks. She really got the stuff I did. Chloe would sit with me each day for at least a few minutes at first, and later she'd spend our full free period with me. She'd ask me questions about what I drew; she'd peruse my sketchbooks that I'd bring in for her. She knew some of the comic book characters, and she loved when I'd draw video game characters. She would even read my early comic-making attempts. It wasn't long until my books I kept at home became filled with pictures of Chloe.

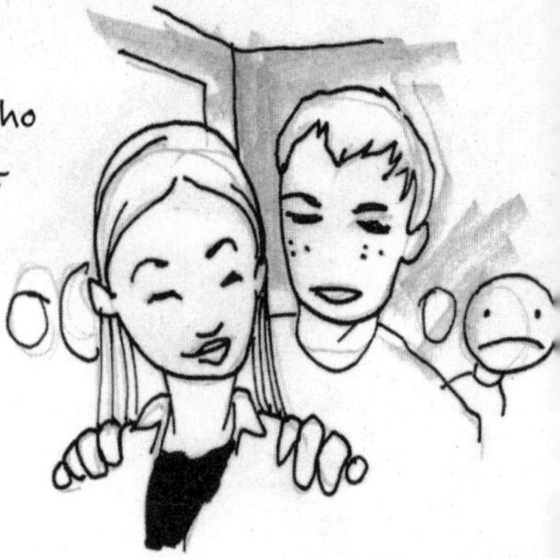

I was still shy. I had never found a girl who would really even like me as a friend let alone as a boyfriend, and I didn't think Chloe Hills would be the first. Over the few months that we were friends, she dated a couple guys for brief amounts of times, and they'd break up and I'd wonder how anyone could stand to lose Chloe. Every day was a rollercoaster. Would I ask her out? Stay best friends? Wait for her to open up to me? Wait for a clue that I can ask her out? All the same things I felt again with Gretchen.

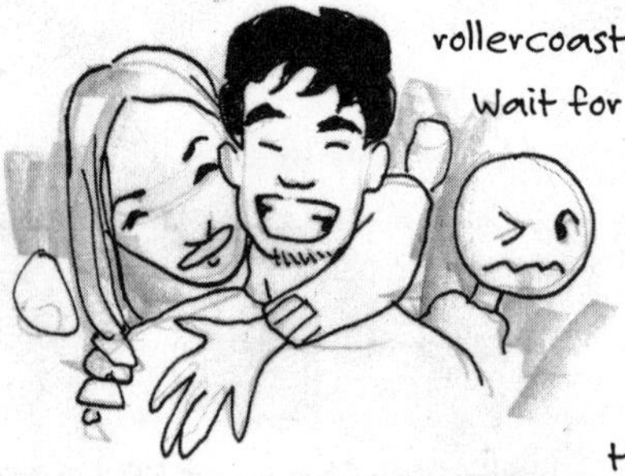

The thing with Chloe, though, was that I didn't have to be anyone else for her. I didn't have to act like I was tougher than I was, I didn't have to pretend I was smart, I didn't even have to draw things she wanted to see. I could just be myself.

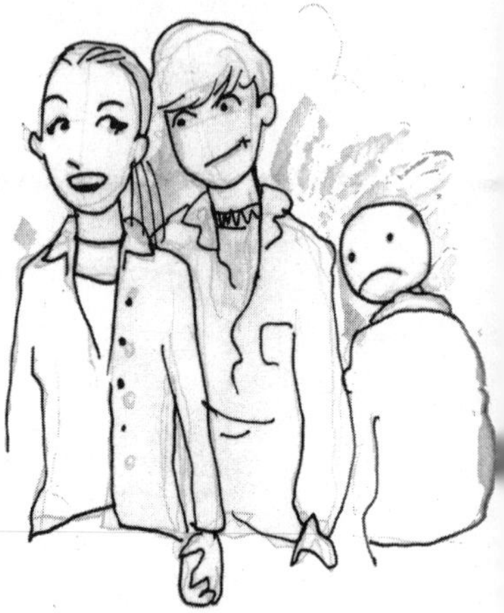

That all changed when I saw her in the hospital after the car crash and she told me she'd been seeing Everett. Her boyfriends were always everything I wasn't. They were cool, confident, compelling, though probably less alliterative people than me. And I thought maybe she wanted the A-type boyfriend.

But she just wanted someone who would ask her out.

SUSPENSION: DAY 2 3/17

Mom took today off so she could take me to the dentist, and then we went to the cemetery to bury Badass Happyface and visit Everett's grave. I hadn't been there since the funeral and found myself just as angry today as I was then. I was surprised.

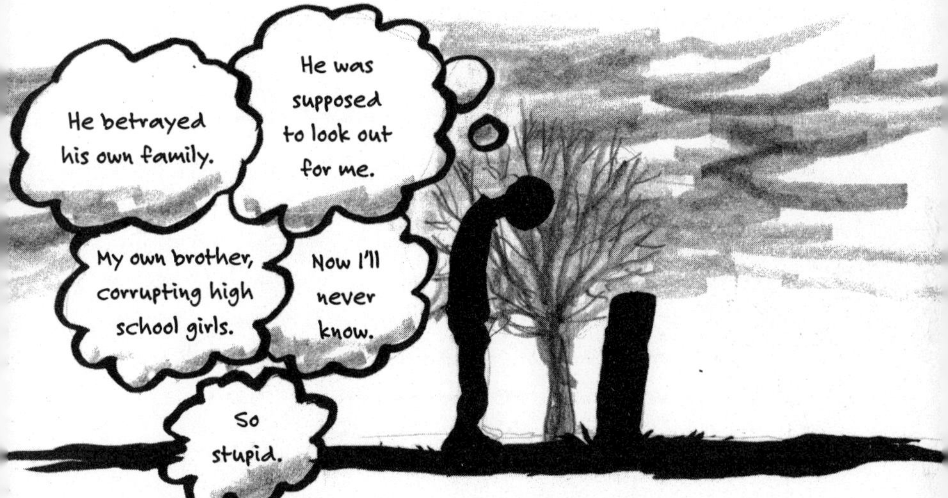

He betrayed his own family.
He was supposed to look out for me.
My own brother, corrupting high school girls.
Now I'll never know.
So stupid.

The truth is, I'll never know why he did what he did, and I'll just go nuts assuming. He always looked out for me, up until then, so I'll just have to remember the good things when I think of Everett.

We sat there by his grave while those good and bad thoughts ran through my head.

"Hey, Mom?" I asked.

"Yeah?" She seemed to be lost in her own series of running thoughts.

"I forgive you for your affair."

"Affair?" I thought she'd tell me I was crazy. I'd maybe even hoped she would. "And why is that?"

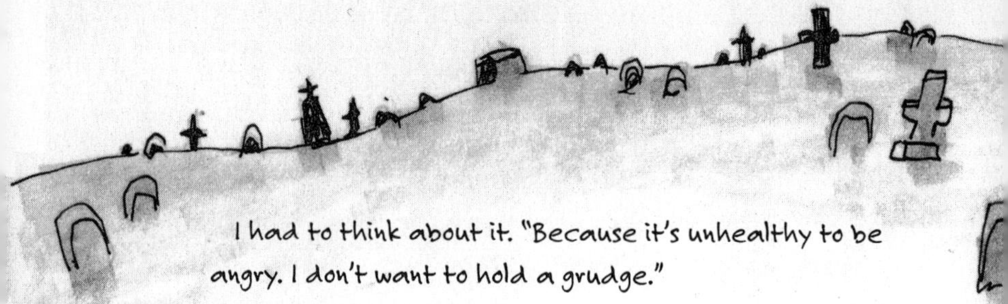

I had to think about it. "Because it's unhealthy to be angry. I don't want to hold a grudge."

"Just like that, huh?" She took a deep breath. "Well, we should probably at least talk about it."

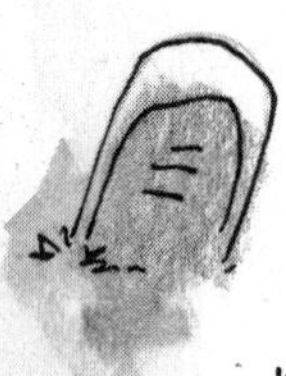

Talking seemed to help with Chloe, so bring it on, I thought. I had a lot of issues with Mom. All of them amplified while I was living in that apartment with her. It was my mom who took me and left Dad. She was the one who had cheated on him; she was a drinker just as much as he was. She was in no position mentally or financially to raise me alone, let alone after my brother, her son, died. A lot of what was going on, the struggles we were facing, were directly caused by her.

"I never intended to cheat on your father. It's inexcusable, and I don't want you to feel at all like I'm saying what I did was okay," she started.

"Was it some athlete guy? Or someone rich and successful? Was he cool and popular?" Maybe those aren't the kinds of questions you ask your mom but then usually you're not in the position to ask them. It was hard to ask, actually. I didn't really want to picture the guy but I've had images in my mind already. I was curious how they measured up.

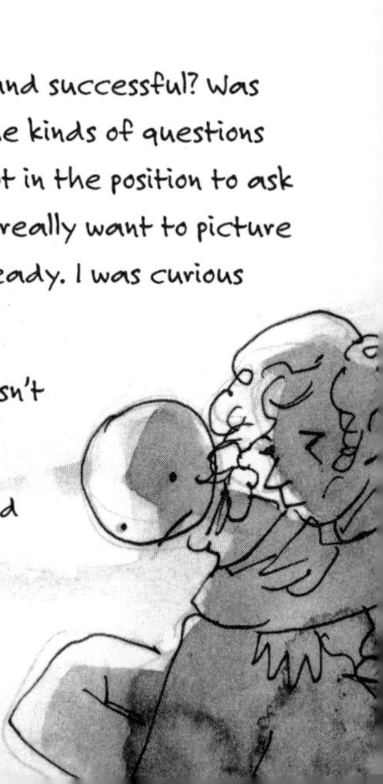

She shook her head. "No, it's not that. It wasn't about what the other person was. . . ."

"Is it because Dad was a writer and needed to be alone all the time?"

"No, I loved that your father wrote. He'd

write me into those books, you know. It was so romantic. Here were these entire worlds he'd create in his head, and I'd be a part of them, and that was always very special to me, that he brought me to those places no one else could go."

I never thought my mom gave his books much thought, and she certainly never complimented him like this before. I wondered what Gretchen would think if she knew about all the pictures I drew of her and all the things I've written about her. I wonder if she would find it romantic, surprising, or if she'd just be creeped out.

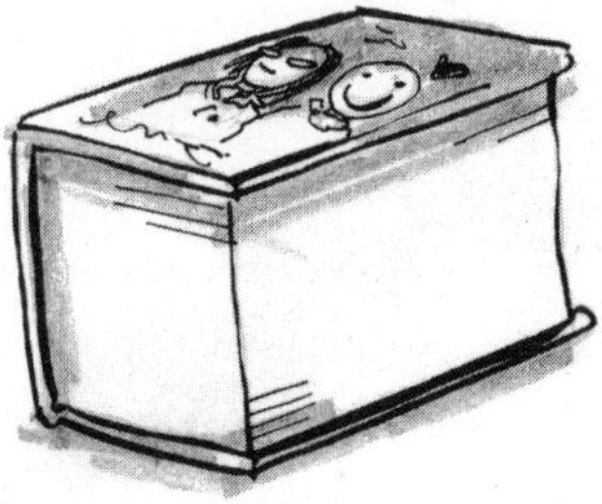

"We'd lay in bed reading together until the sun came up some nights. Those were always my favorite nights, each in our own little world but still somehow together."

I still didn't see why she had to break up their marriage. It sounded good to me.

"The problems were always outside of books. Sometimes when a guy spends so much time in his head he loses track of reality," she said. I'd have thought she was speaking about me if I hadn't known these things existed in my father first. "The jealousy, the drinking; he was an angry drunk . . . he'd get very sullen, dark, and paranoid."

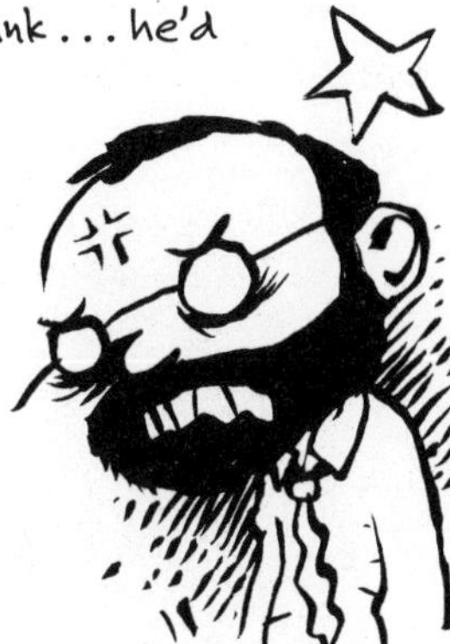

"So that's why you cheated on Dad?"

"No, I cheated on him because I was stupid. And eventually I figured that out."

"Then why aren't we living with him?" I asked. Maybe forgiveness wasn't so easy.

"Because it was time to move on. It was a culmination of a whole lot of things, hon. It's hard to even really say what it was."

We both sat and picked at the grass for a while in silence.

"That's not the whole truth," she finally said. "Your dad did ask me to leave and he asked me to take you with me."

"Why?"

"Oh, we were never a very solid foundation," she said, occasionally looking at me. "After your brother died we were all very upset, and Dad was drinking more than usual. Everything got worse. It was after one of our long fights, you weren't home, that he decided he needed to stop the drinking and make some changes. It's so hard, losing a son, and I think living in that house, all of us seeing each other every day . . . there's too much baggage."

It was depressing to think about.

"We could have stayed together but I think in the end it would have been for the worse. I don't think we could ever heal."

"I never thought it seemed that bad," I said in a whisper.

"You don't remember all the near-divorces? Your brother did," she said, touching his tombstone. "I don't think he ever forgave us."

No wonder Everett had so many commitment issues.

3/18

SUSPENSION DAY 3

This is the last day of my suspension before going back to school, so I'll probably put this book down for a while. I need to fix my grade situation and spend more time with Mom. I have a lot to fix, actually.

"Where is Dad?" I asked Mom this morning. She tried to avoid the question, so I kept repeating it. "Where is he? Why won't he call me? What did I do?"

I didn't think I even wanted to see him anymore. When Mom and Dad first separated I wanted to go with him, but then months went by without a word. No calls, no Christmas gift. No Dad. He didn't see all I've done with my art. He didn't see me make so many friends at school and have a real social life like Everett did. He missed it all. He can just have his books and his alcohol and TV, then.

"He just needs some time," Mom said. "Everyone handled Everett's death a little differently. Dad just needed some time and some space. So he could get better."

Get better?

Chloe came over after school and we went to see him. Mom insisted. She said I could drive Ev's Corvette there if I went, and that sealed the deal for me. Maybe if I drive it well it can be mine. I think Everett would like that. When I sat in the car the other day I felt at home in it. It made me feel close to Everett again.

I was glad Chloe came because I needed the encouragement, and Dad and I never really had a whole lot to talk about. If things felt awkward, then the more bodies the better.

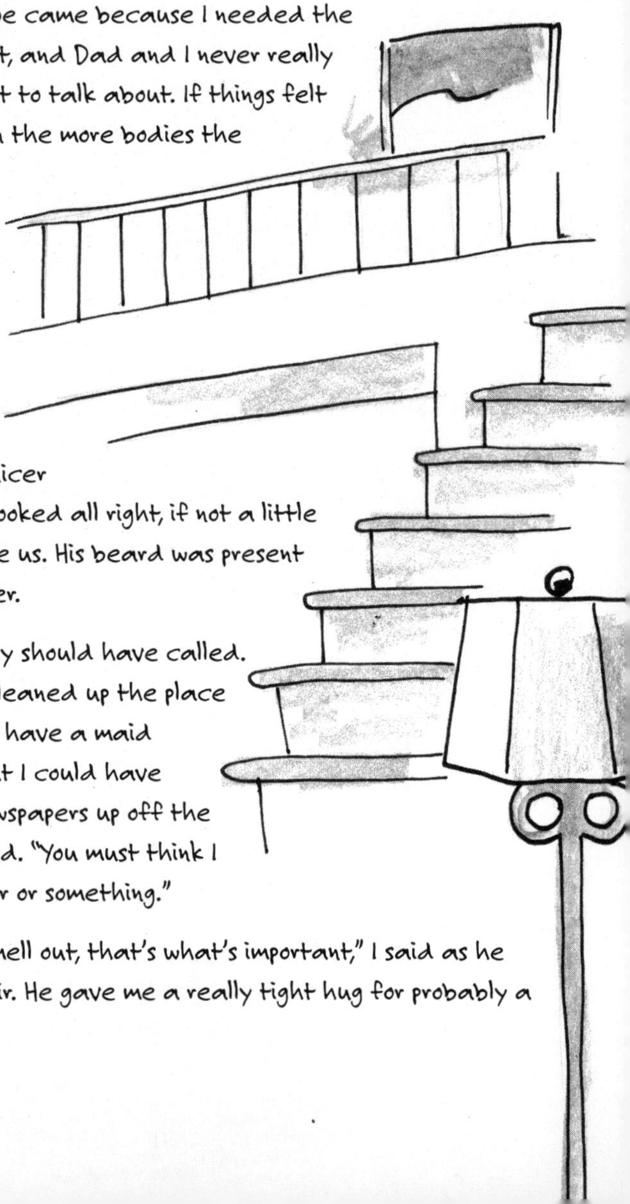

Dad moved out of the house and he was living by himself, but his place was still a lot nicer than ours. He looked all right, if not a little surprised to see us. His beard was present and full as ever.

"Jeez, you really should have called. I could have cleaned up the place a little. I don't have a maid or anything, but I could have picked the newspapers up off the ground," he said. "You must think I pee on the floor or something."

"You got the smell out, that's what's important," I said as he ruffled my hair. He gave me a really tight hug for probably a full minute.

"So glad to see you Chloe, I'm sorry about everything," he said as he gave Chloe a hug, abridged version. "I'm glad you're still friends. We always liked you." If he only knew what we'd really been through. Still, I was glad to have her there to cut some of the awkwardness down.

It was strange to be visiting my dad in a social way, like not just getting home and seeing him in the study or passed out on the couch while Ev and I did our homework. We were forced to actually interact.

"So . . ." I wasn't sure what to say next.

"I don't know what your mother told you, but, ah . . ." He looked uncomfortable. "I checked myself into a rehab for a little while."

"For drinking?" I asked.

"Yeah. Not just drinking. It was somewhere I needed to be."

Mom was right—dark stuff. I never thought of my dad as such a dark person, I just thought he was quiet and lived more for books than other stuff. Life stuff. I admired the "quiet smart guy" thing, I could feel that in me. Now I feel it all in me, the quiet, writing-at-home-alone stuff and the things Mom talked about. The jealousy, the paranoia. I used to think he was an eccentric and an intellectual, which he is, but I think he also had a hard time relating to people in general.

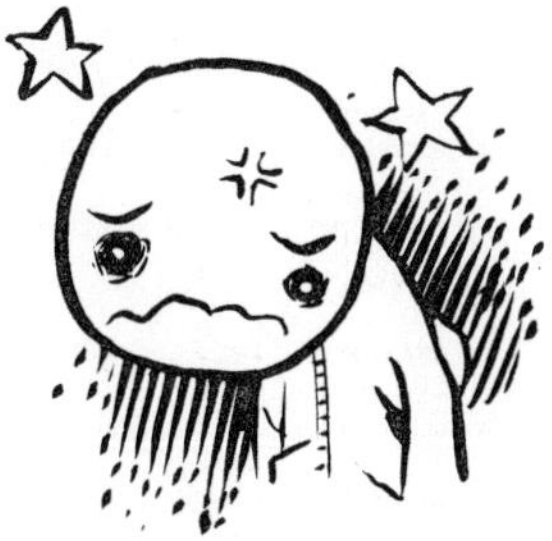

The place was kind of a mess. It made me worry for him.

"I didn't really want you to meet me here like this, but it's good to see you," he said. "Real good."

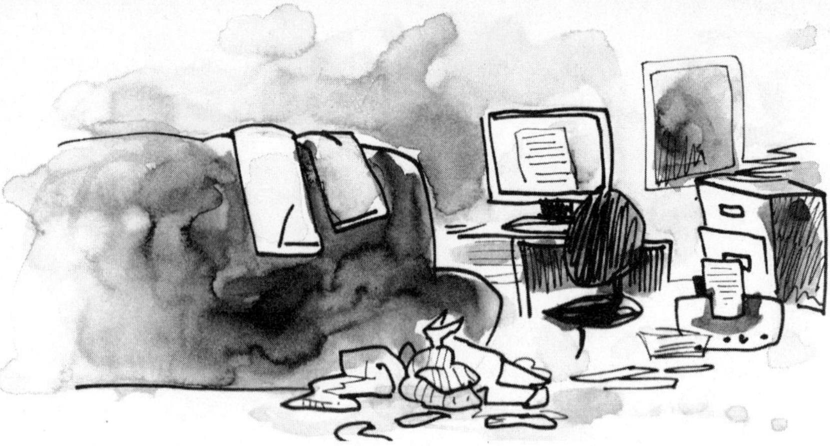

We didn't pour out our hearts or anything. I wasn't expecting to. But I could see in the way he carried himself that he was a different person. Trying to rebuild, I suppose. I wonder if that's in my eyes and body, too.

"I had my first drink," I confessed. I had a list of things to talk about in case we were too quiet.

"I was about your age when I had my first drink. How was it?"

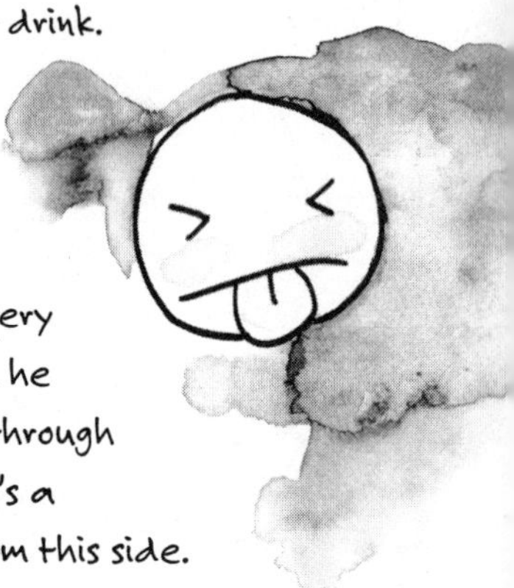

"It was pretty gross. I don't know how you do it."

Dad laughed. "Remember that." He was very charismatic when he wanted to be. When he grinned that big grin of his and laughed through that beard, you had to laugh with him. It's a really powerful tool, the smile, seeing it from this side.

I took my sketch journal out of my bag to show Dad, and I asked him not to read it too closely since it's all pretty personal. I asked Chloe not to look, too, though she got really curious as it was out. A year and three months since he bought it for me and nearly a year since I filled in my first page, and here it was, just about full.

"Wow," he said, flipping through the pages. "You've gotten really good.

When did you get this good?"
He gave my arm a nudge with his
elbow.

"I don't know," I said, impressed with myself.

"I wish I could read it," he said. "Too personal,
though, huh?"

"Yeah, kinda . . ."

"Good, it's not worth writing if it isn't." I thought of
what Mom said, about Dad writing her into his books.

"Who's this?" he said, pointing to one of the pictures of
Gretchen.

"That's my friend Gretchen," I said.

"All right, pretty foxy," he said with a
laugh, shaking my hands.
It would have been less
embarrassing without
Chloe there, though she
did have a smirk on
her face.

"Looks like you've been keeping busy,"
he said. "That's good. I'm real proud of you."

I'd pretty much fallen apart very publicly, lost most of my friends,
and have practically failed out of all my classes. At least I have
something someone says I can be proud of.

"So Mom let you drive that?" Dad said, referring to the Corvette.

"Yeah, it was sitting out there for a pretty long time," I said.

"Still looks like new. You're going easy on her, right?"

"Yeah, this was the first time I drove it, actually."

"No, I meant your mother. Are you going easy on her?" I hadn't been. Not at all.

"Yeah," I said.

Dad took me outside to show me how to treat the car. I thought about asking him more questions like I had with Chloe and with Mom, like how he could leave me, and if he'd ever get back with Mom. I mean we really didn't get that deep at all. But it probably would have entailed some adult answers like "Someday you'll understand," or "I did it for you, you know," and really I'd rather just enjoy the moment.

If being Happyface is my mask to hide away my insecurities, then Dad must have the Fort Knox of masks. Pretty impenetrable. For the guy who once said, "You're a sincere guy with feelings and that's nothing to hide," I think Dad hid quite a bit.

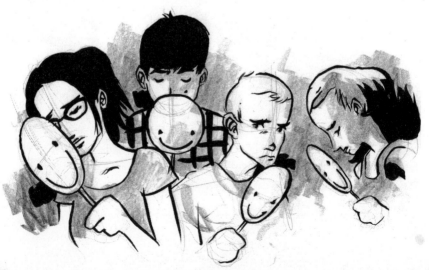

I thought about all the other Happyfaces I'd met and gotten to know on the way home, each with their own masks. Whether it was Gretchen and her mysterious past, hiding her boyfriends from her parents, her drinking parties and books and boating magazines, or if it was Trevor's braggadocio hiding his lovelorn self, it seemed to be more common than I'd thought. There was Mike and his sneaking cigarettes and stressful life; even Chloe was as insecure as I ever was inside. Even Mr. Molly had trouble just saying he was worried about me and wanted to help somehow. It made me respect my mom especially, for really putting everything out in the open and not hiding anything. When she was sad, she cried, and when she was angry, she'd throw me up against the wall and let me know, but she's always been honest with her emotions. Not very many people can say that.

I've hid everything I am to my new friends and lost them all. I lied to them and I wasn't a friend myself, and I was angry when they didn't buy it. I was lying to them clear as day, red face and all. I lied to myself, which is probably worse than all the other stuff.

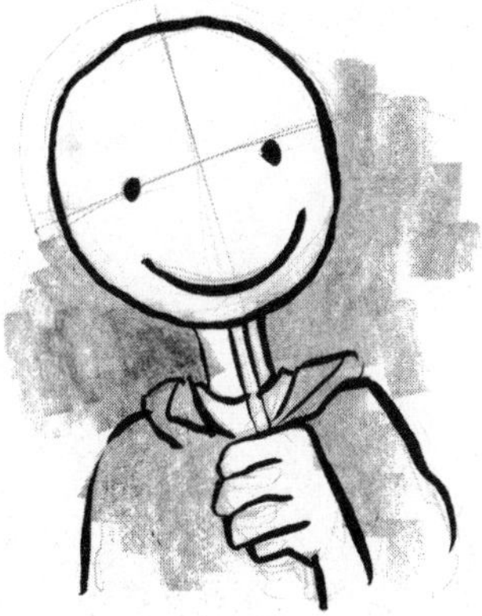

It was the same mask though, wearing this smile even when I didn't mean it that opened me up to talk and act how I felt inside but wasn't always able to show. In some ways it made me actually more genuine. After all is said and done I'm more comfortable being myself than ever was before.

Maybe with a little self-improvement and definitely a few apologies I can still mend a few burned bridges. Maybe someday I can even make up with Frog and Oddly. Maybe we all need to mature a bit. But first I have to put this journal down. Almost done . . .

OH HAI, ITZ HAPPYFACE: THE WEBCOMIC-IN-PRINT
Time with Chloe Edition!

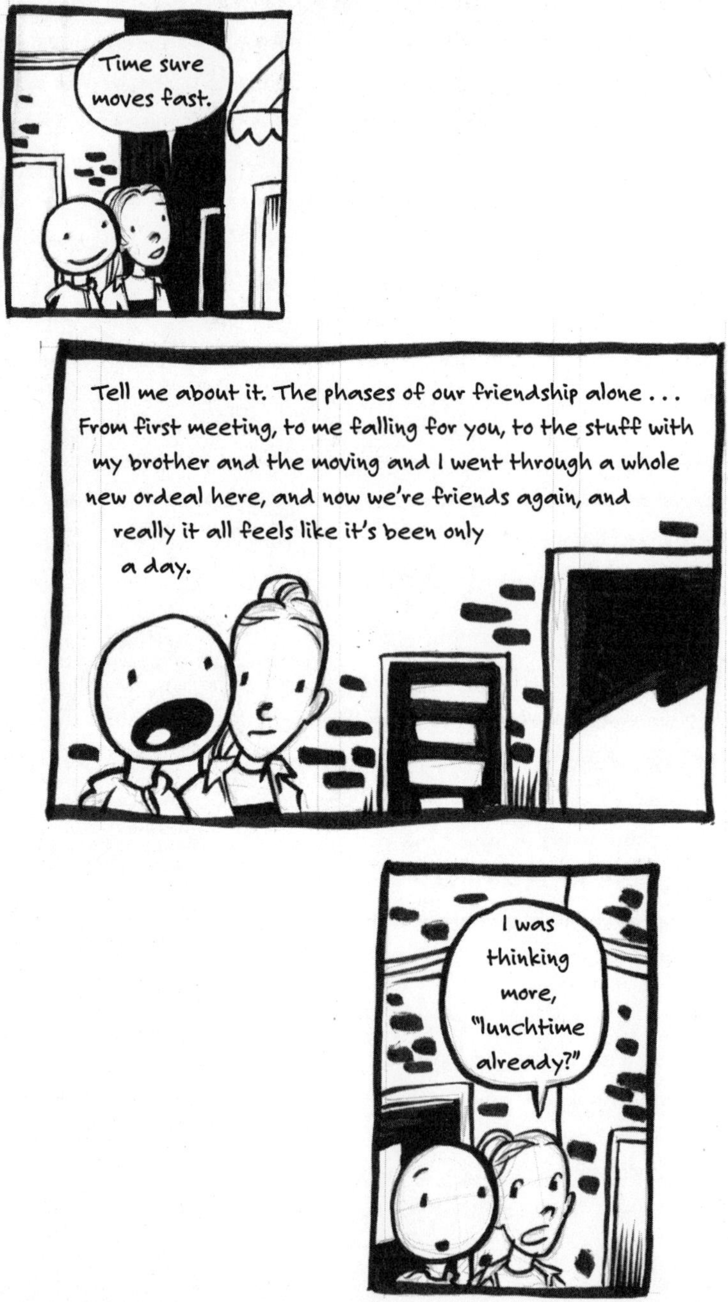

Time sure moves fast.
Tell me about it. The phases of our friendship alone . . . From first meeting, to me falling for you, to the stuff with my brother and the moving and I went through a whole new ordeal here, and now we're friends again, and really it all feels like it's been only a day.
I was thinking more, "lunchtime already?"

OATH

TAKE TWO

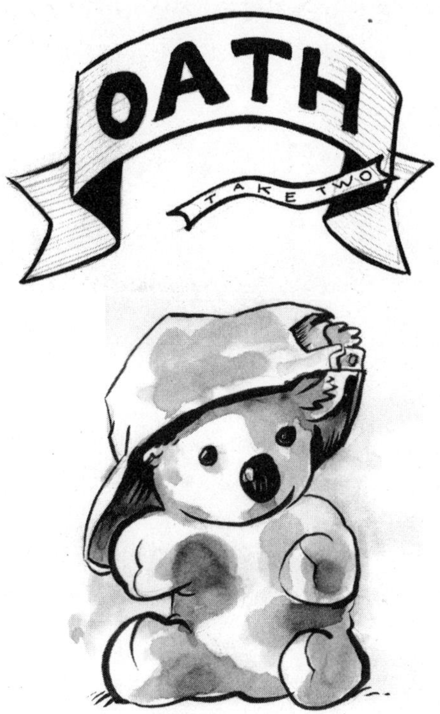

I swear, with Chloe Bear once again as my witness . . .

That my problems and failures will not stop me, nor will they dictate who I am.

That I will continue to be my own person.

That life is too short, and I will live every day as the best person I can be.

That I will grow and that I will change.

That I will smile and hold my head high.

That this is a new start and a new day.

That I will allow myself to cry or sit by myself when I need to.
That I will find things to really smile about.

From: CartoonBoy@hooray.com
To: KarmaKameleon@geemail.com, MistyMoon05@geemail.com
Date: 03/18 17:02
Subject: Apologies

Reply

Forward

Spam

nize

box
afts
ent
ash
pam
ries
dar

tions

Hi guys, sorry if I've been a less-than-optimal friend. I've been through a few things, but I am working on it and hope you'll stick with me through it!
Your friend,
Sorryface

From: KarmaKameleon@geemail.com
To: CartoonBoy@hooray.com
Date: 03/18 17:40
Subject: Re: Apologies

Alright Sorryface, but if you do it again, I'll cut you!

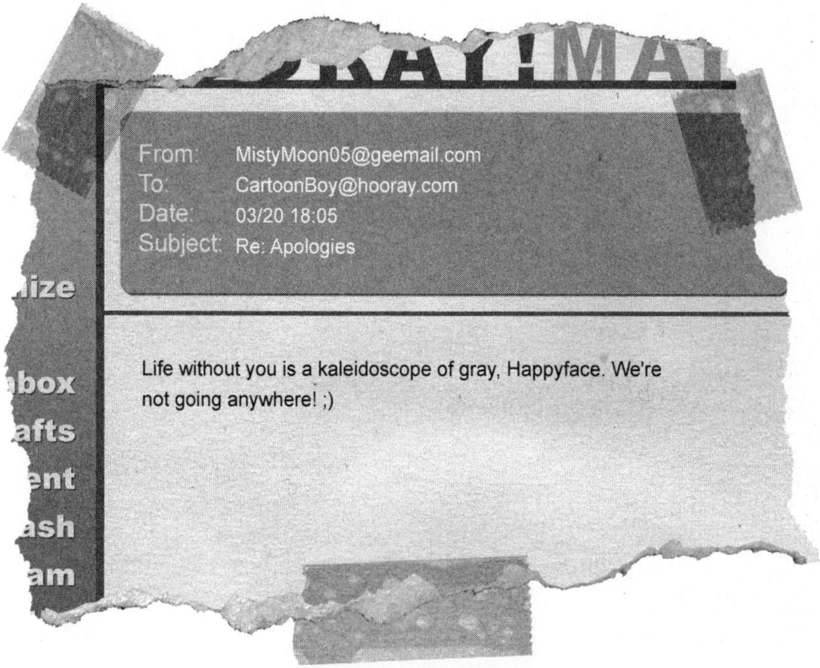

RAY!MAI

ize

box
afts
ent
ash
am

From: MistyMoon05@geemail.com
To: CartoonBoy@hooray.com
Date: 03/20 18:05
Subject: Re: Apologies

Life without you is a kaleidoscope of gray, Happyface. We're not going anywhere! ;)

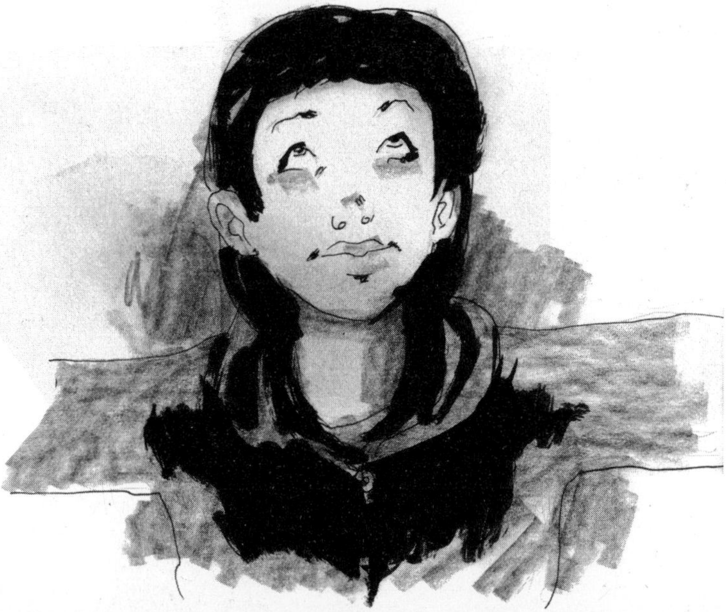

HOORAY!MAIL

Delete

Reply

Forward

Spam

Organize

Inbox
Drafts
Sent
Trash
Spam
Categories
Calendar

Options
Log Out

From: CartoonBoy@hooray.com
To: TrevorsTheMan@hooray.com
Date: 03/18 17:05
Subject: Apology

Sorry again about everything, Trevor. Maybe we can start fresh.
See you around?

From: TrevorsTheMan@hooray.com
To: CartoonBoy@hooray.com
Date: 03/18 19:31
Subject: Re: Apology

Happens to the best of us, no problem. Hope everything
is alright.

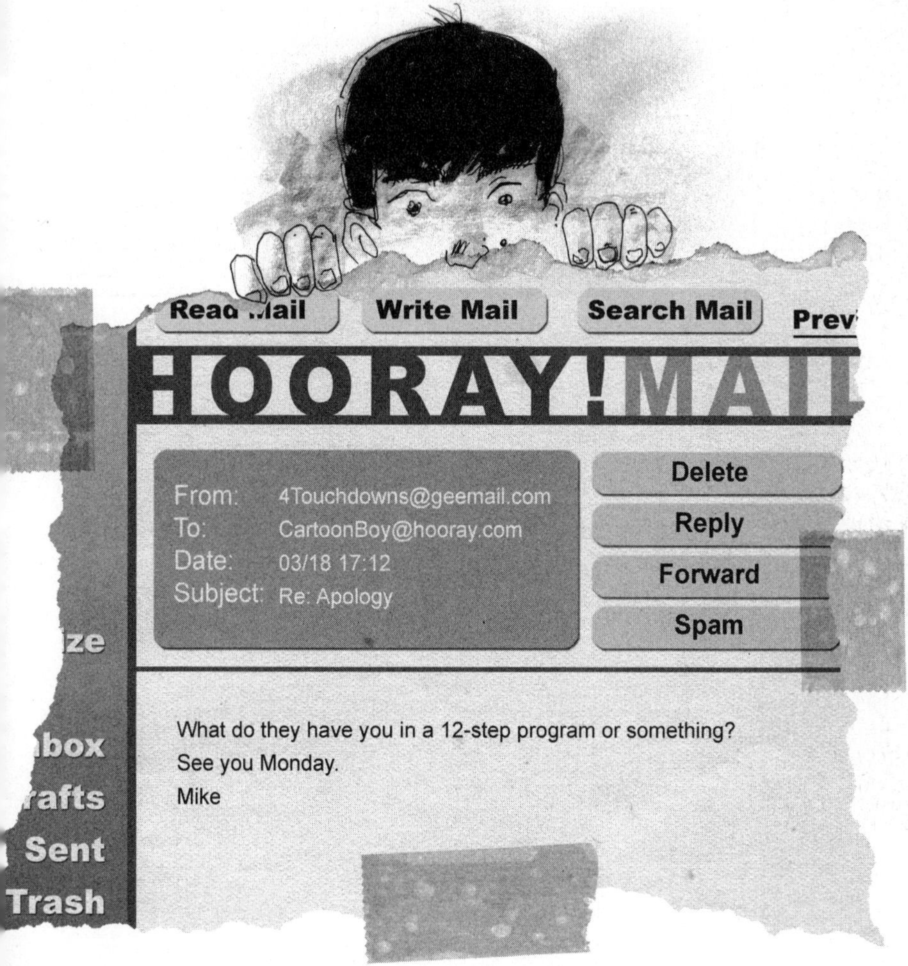
Read Mail
Write Mail
Search Mail
HOORAY!MAIL
From: 4Touchdowns@geemail.com
To: CartoonBoy@hooray.com
Date: 03/18 17:12
Subject: Re: Apology
Delete
Reply
Forward
Spam
Sent
Trash
What do they have you in a 12-step program or something?
See you Monday.
Mike

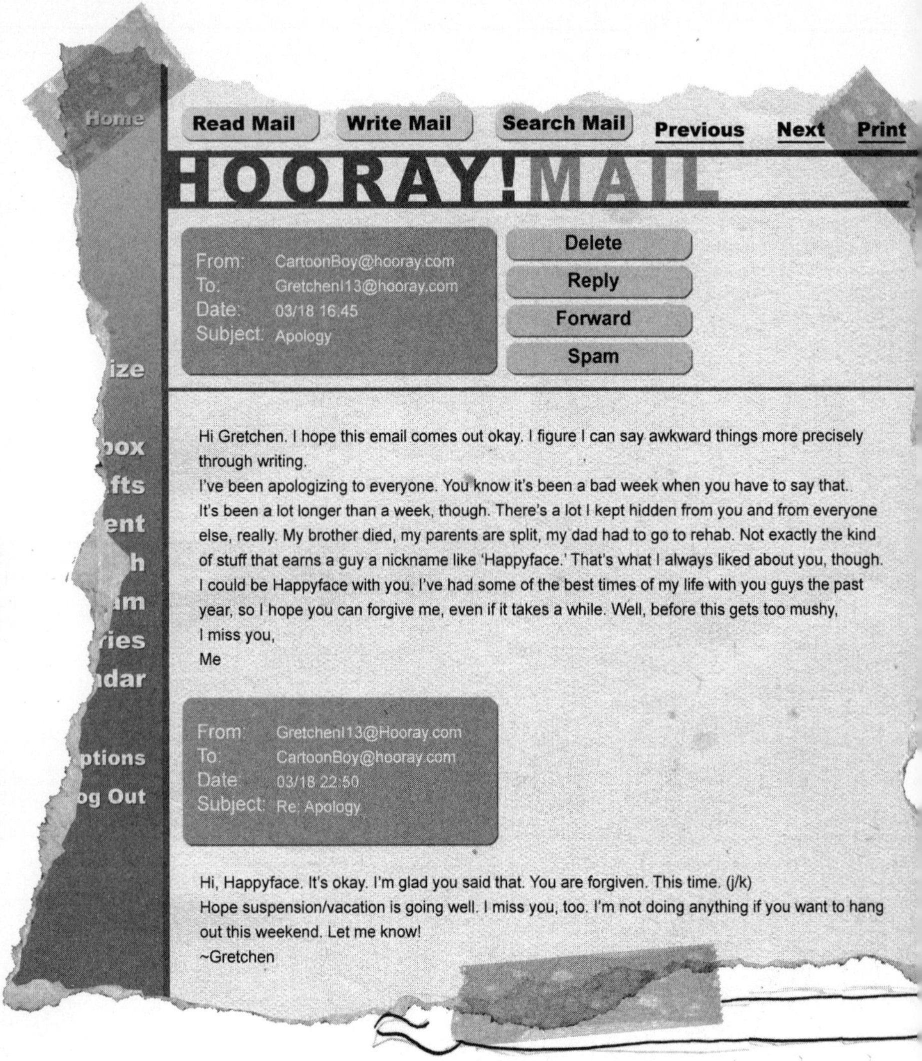
Home

Read Mail | Write Mail | Search Mail | Previous | Next | Print

HOORAY!MAIL

From: CartoonBoy@hooray.com
To: Gretchenl13@hooray.com
Date: 03/18 16:45
Subject: Apology

Delete
Reply
Forward
Spam

Hi Gretchen. I hope this email comes out okay. I figure I can say awkward things more precisely through writing.
I've been apologizing to everyone. You know it's been a bad week when you have to say that.
It's been a lot longer than a week, though. There's a lot I kept hidden from you and from everyone else, really. My brother died, my parents are split, my dad had to go to rehab. Not exactly the kind of stuff that earns a guy a nickname like 'Happyface.' That's what I always liked about you, though. I could be Happyface with you. I've had some of the best times of my life with you guys the past year, so I hope you can forgive me, even if it takes a while. Well, before this gets too mushy,
I miss you,
Me

From: Gretchenl13@Hooray.com
To: CartoonBoy@hooray.com
Date: 03/18 22:50
Subject: Re: Apology

Hi, Happyface. It's okay. I'm glad you said that. You are forgiven. This time. (j/k)
Hope suspension/vacation is going well. I miss you, too. I'm not doing anything if you want to hang out this weekend. Let me know!
~Gretchen

Life awaits!

Acknowledgements

Acknowledgements are hard to write. If I were naming who influenced and helped the writing of this book, it would be almost everyone I've come in contact with! I guess that's the problem with writing a personal work.

A lot of this book sprang from my own mid-high school move and my first relationship thereafter, so I thank my grandparents, Mary and Vinnie, who I moved in with, and I thank Briana for all the story fodder. :) Really, all of my relationships found their way into this book, so thanks to Elaine and all of my ex-girlfriends and crushes. I'm a famous author now. *Cough*

Also thanks to Cori, whose friendship provided lots of story ideas and whose endless enthusiasm for my work keeps me writing.

Thanks to Sara for being a super friend and for listening to me ramble on endlessly about all of the challenges in writing a novel. Thank you for so much laughter when I was really stressed.

Ultra-mega thanks to Connie Hsu, Alvina Ling, Ben Mautner, Amanda Hong, and everyone else at Little, Brown. They gave me so much encouragement and helped me through all the dark corners of this story that I just couldn't see. They had me out for visits and workshopping ideas for hours and hours, and great lunches, and they even sent me books and gifts for no reason at all. It is so awesome to be working with them. My grandmother still can't get over the stories I tell of how nice and supportive they are. I can't either.

Thanks to my mom, Mike, and my dad. Monkey and Hermie, but especially Monkey for not snubbing me all the time.

Thank you to Taryn. You're a big part of this book.

I could go on but I should probably be working on my next book.

Oh, and thanks to everyone who bought this book and read this far! Visit me on stephenemond.com and say hello. :)

BONUS SECTION!

Here's some behind-the-scenes fun stuff.

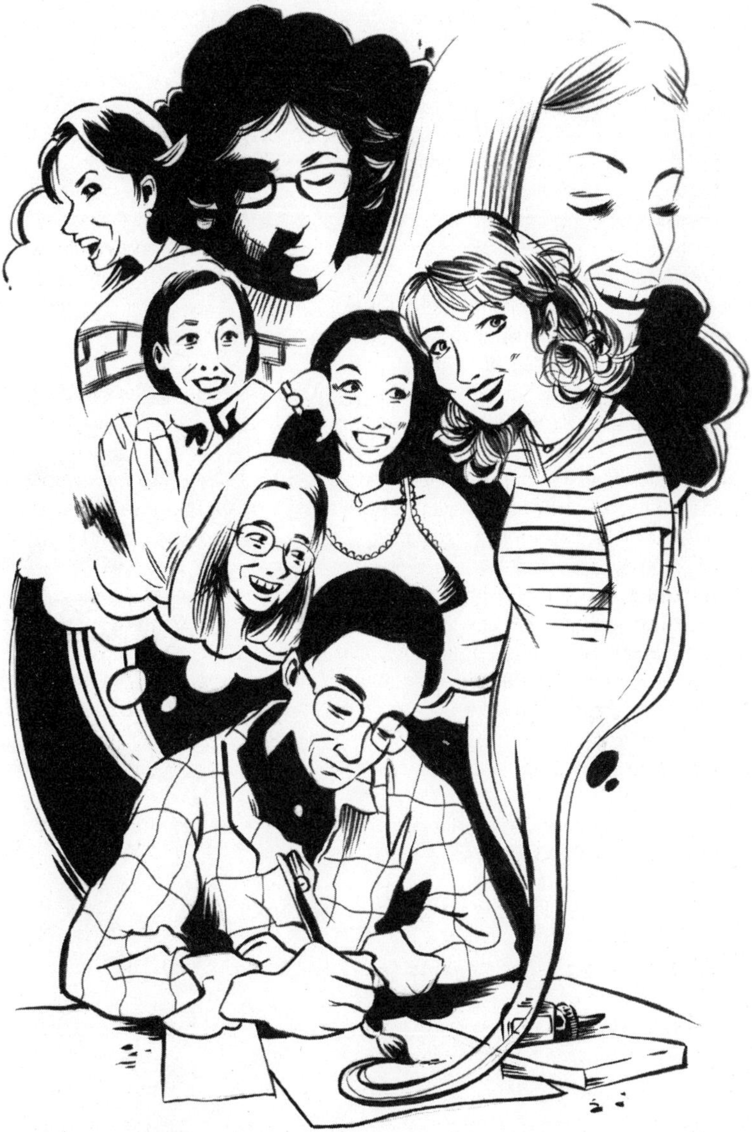

Right up above is teenaged girl-crazy me, writing and drawing away my own sorrows!

Here's a look at the sketchbooks I used for the writing and art in this book. The first pages of the first book were very text heavy as I struggled to figure out what the story was going to be. As the early chapters evolved, I was able to dig into the art.

CDEFGHIJKLMNOPLQRSTUVWXYZ
CDEFGHIJKLMNOPQRSTUVWXYZ
cdefghijklmnopqrstuvwxyz
cdefghijklmnopqrstuvwxyzz
cd
CDEFGHIJKLMNOPQRSTUVWXYZ
CDEFGHIJKLMNOPQRSTUVWXYZ
cdefghijklmnopqrstuvwxyz
cdefghijklmnopqrstuvwxyz
CDEFGHIJKLMNOPQRSTUVWXY
CDEFGHIJKLMNOPQRSTUVWXYZ
cdefghijklmnopqrsrstuvwxy
cdefghijklmnopqrstuvwxyz
BCDEFGHIJKLLLMNOPQRST

I tried to make a font of my own handwriting.

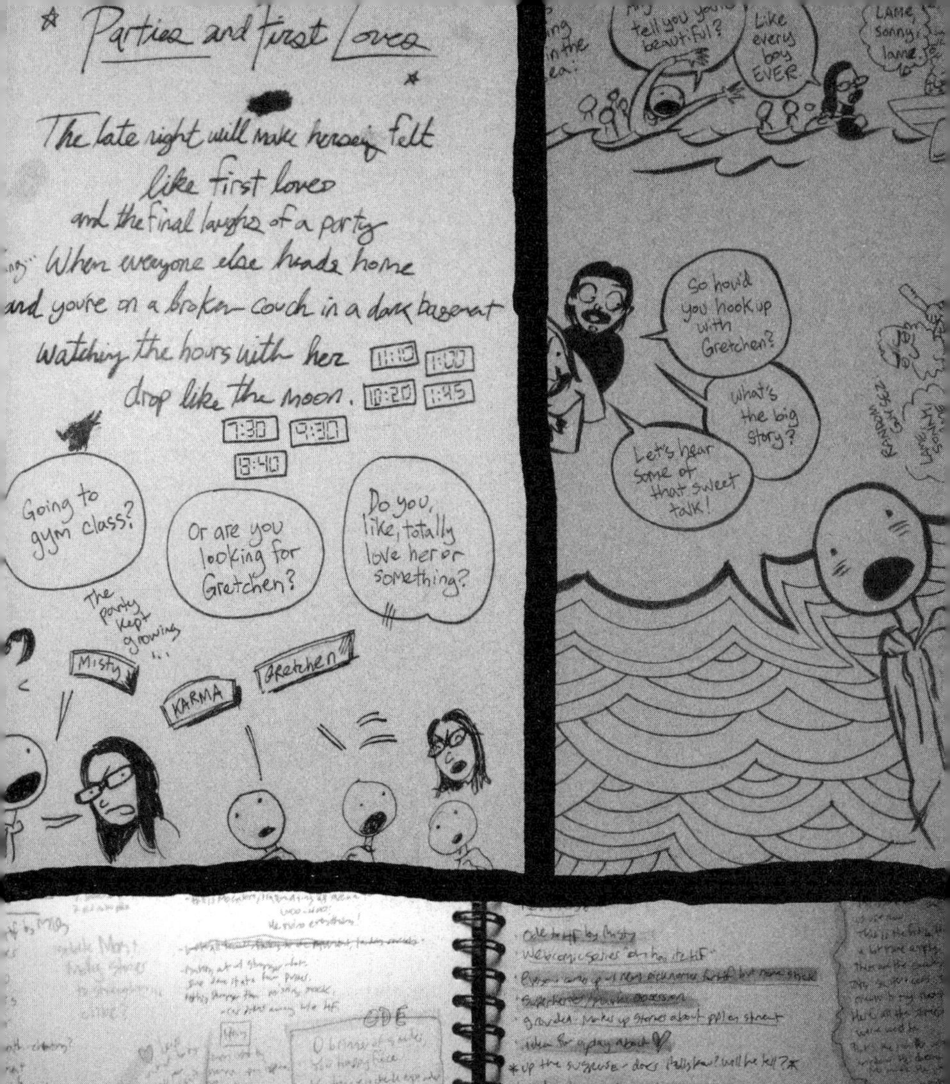
Parties and First Loves
The late night will make herself felt
like first loves
and the final laughs of a party
When everyone else heads home
and you're on a broken couch in a dark basement
watching the hours with her
drop like the moon.
11:10
1:00
10:20
1:45
7:30
9:30
Going to gym class?
Or are you looking for Gretchen?
Do you, like, totally love her or something?
The party kept growing...
Misty
KARMA
Gretchen
tell you you're beautiful?
Like every boy EVER
LAME, Sonny, lame.
So how'd you hook up with Gretchen?
What's the big story?
Let's hear some of that sweet talk!

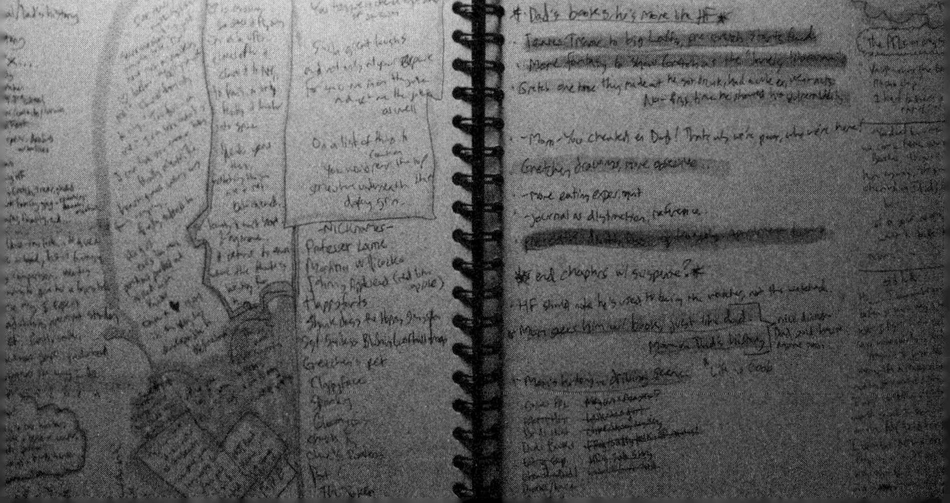
ODE
-Nicknames-
Professor Lame
end chapters w/ suspense?

I had to thumbnail some of the more complex sequences, to make sure everything would flow nicely and so two-page spreads would have an even, balanced look.

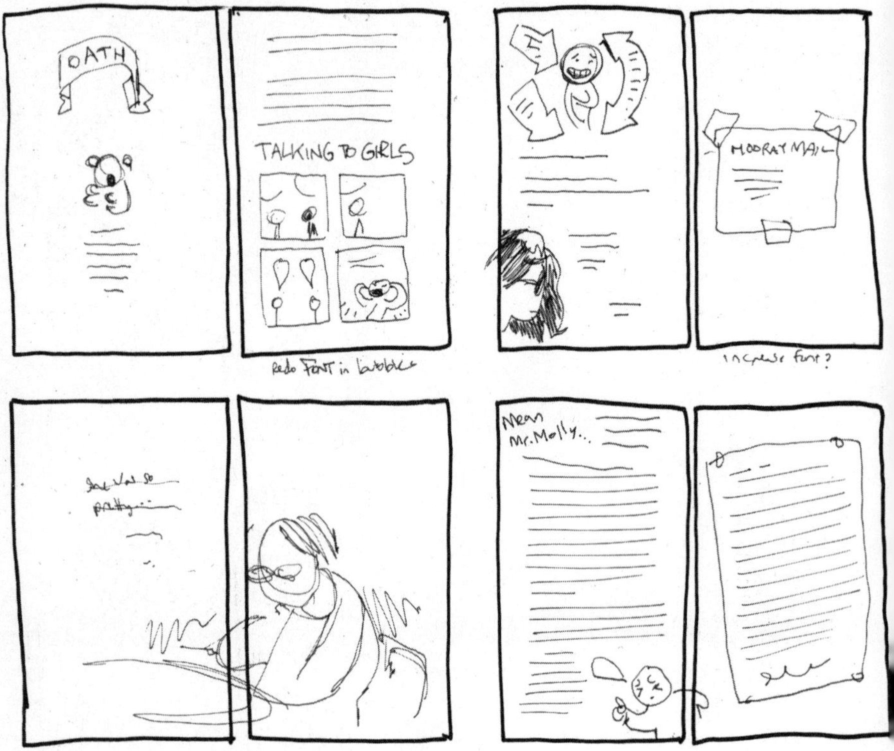
OATH
TALKING TO GIRLS
Redo FONT in bubbles
HOORAY MAIL
Increase font?
Mean Mr. Molly...

There was a lot of art I did that didn't make it into the final book. Most often I just didn't have enough space when all the text was in and had to make some edits. But at least I can show them to you here!

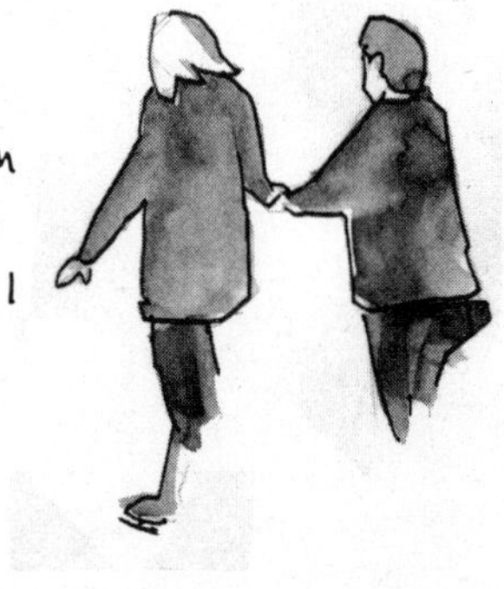

I liked all these little skater guys I drew for the ice skating chapter, but didn't have room for even one of them in the end.

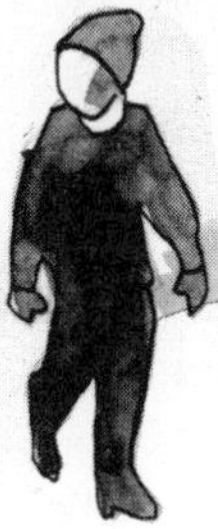

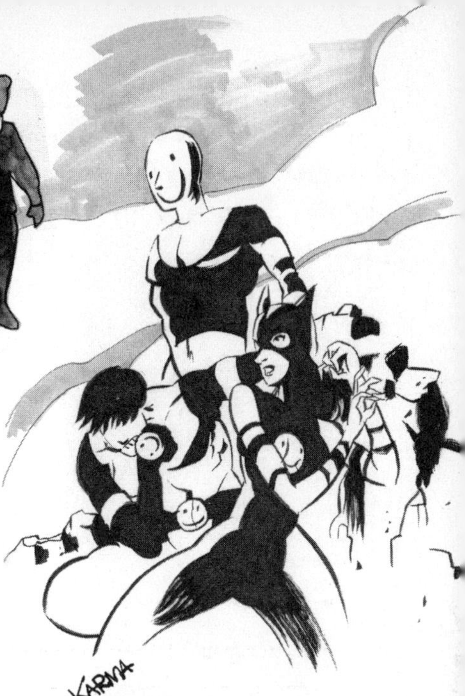

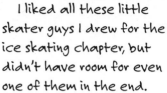

This was a full-page comic book picture I did for when Happyface first meets Mike. I tried a few of these full-page art sections, but they had a tendency to stall the reading experience.

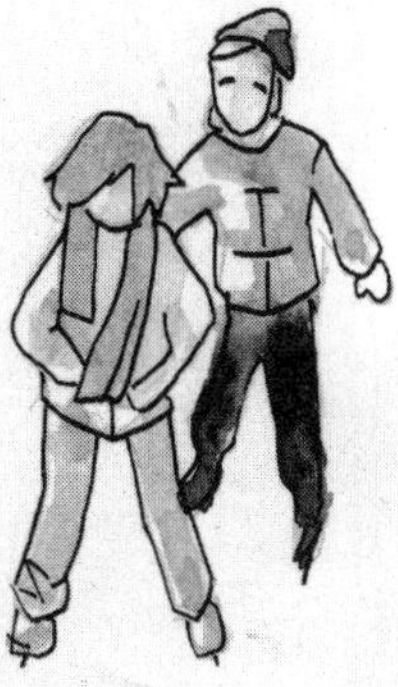

Here's the first Happyface-related drawing I did, of the Moon sisters.

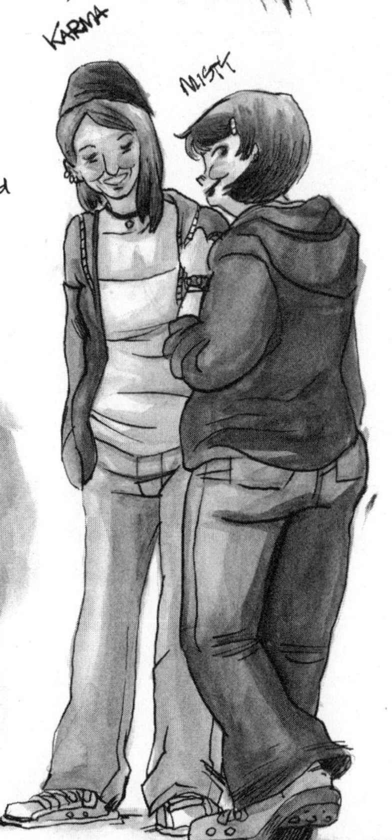
KARMA
MISTY

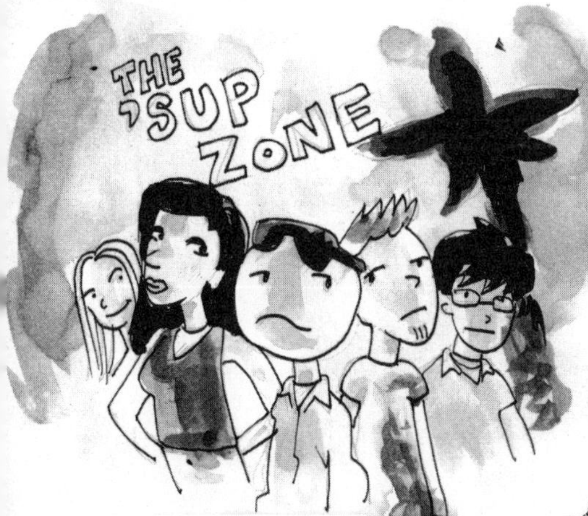
THE 'SUP ZONE

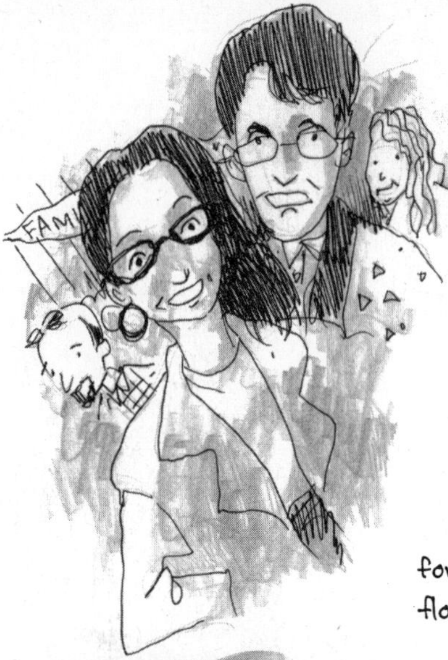

Originally I wanted Happyface's story of how he met Gretchen to be that they met at a _Family Ties_ party; she was dressed as Mallory and he was Skippy. It was an in-joke between a friend of mine and me, but we decided it wasn't really age-appropriate for a teenager. A childhood without _Family Ties_, how tragic!

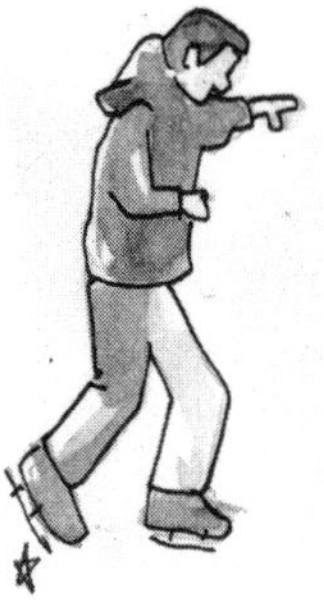

I reworked this sequence for the final book to help it flow a little better.

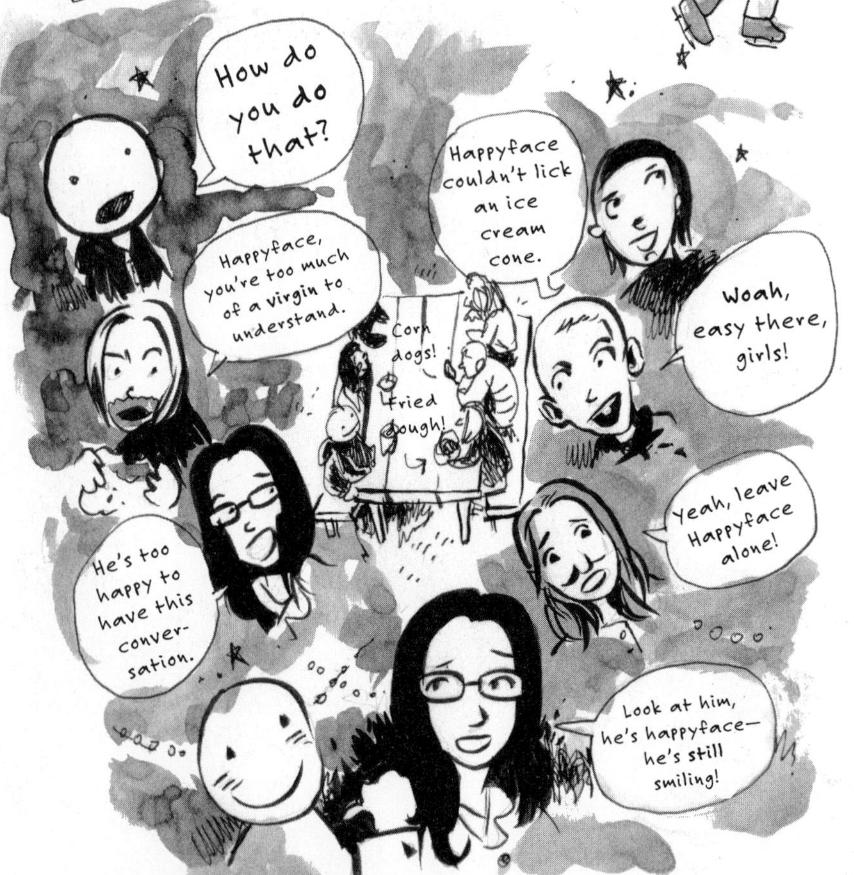

How do you do that?
Happyface couldn't lick an ice cream cone.
Happyface, you're too much of a virgin to understand.
Woah, easy there, girls!
Corn dogs!
Fried dough!
Yeah, leave Happyface alone!
He's too happy to have this conver-sation.
Look at him, he's happyface— he's still smiling!

Another of my "Happyface draws hundreds of portraits of Gretchen!" attempts. It just didn't have any real need to be in the book.

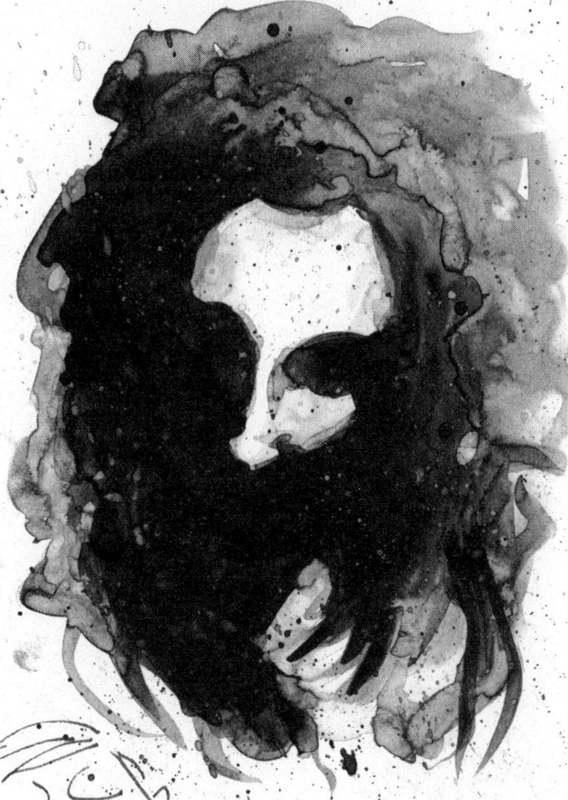

Some unused Mr. Molly doodles, and a Misty Moon drawing that didn't feel very "Misty Moon." She just works better in a more cartoony form.

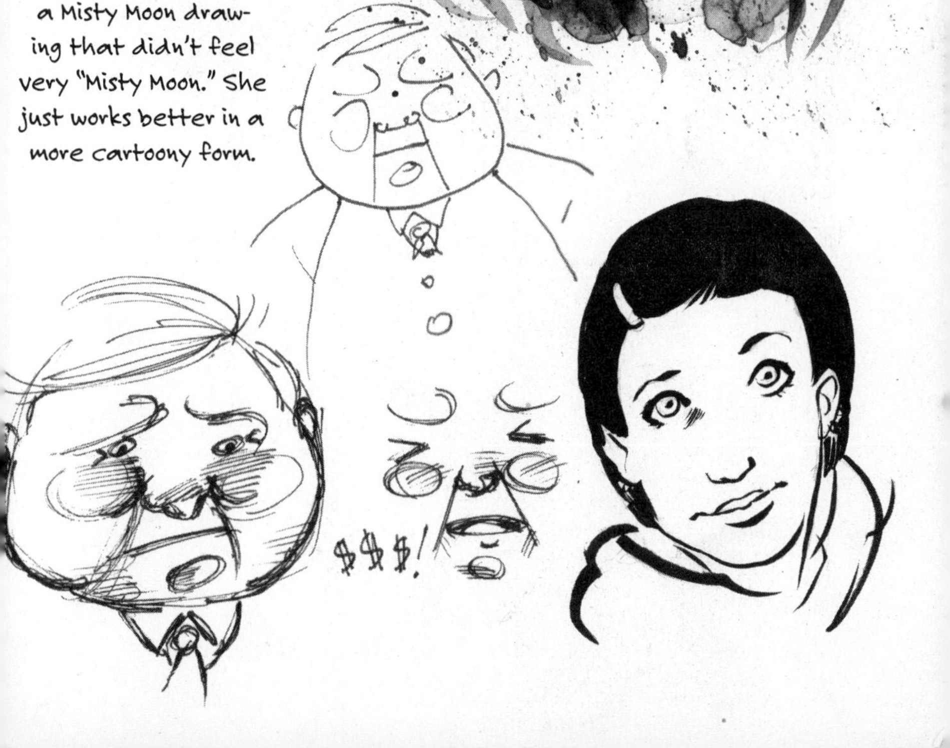
$$$!

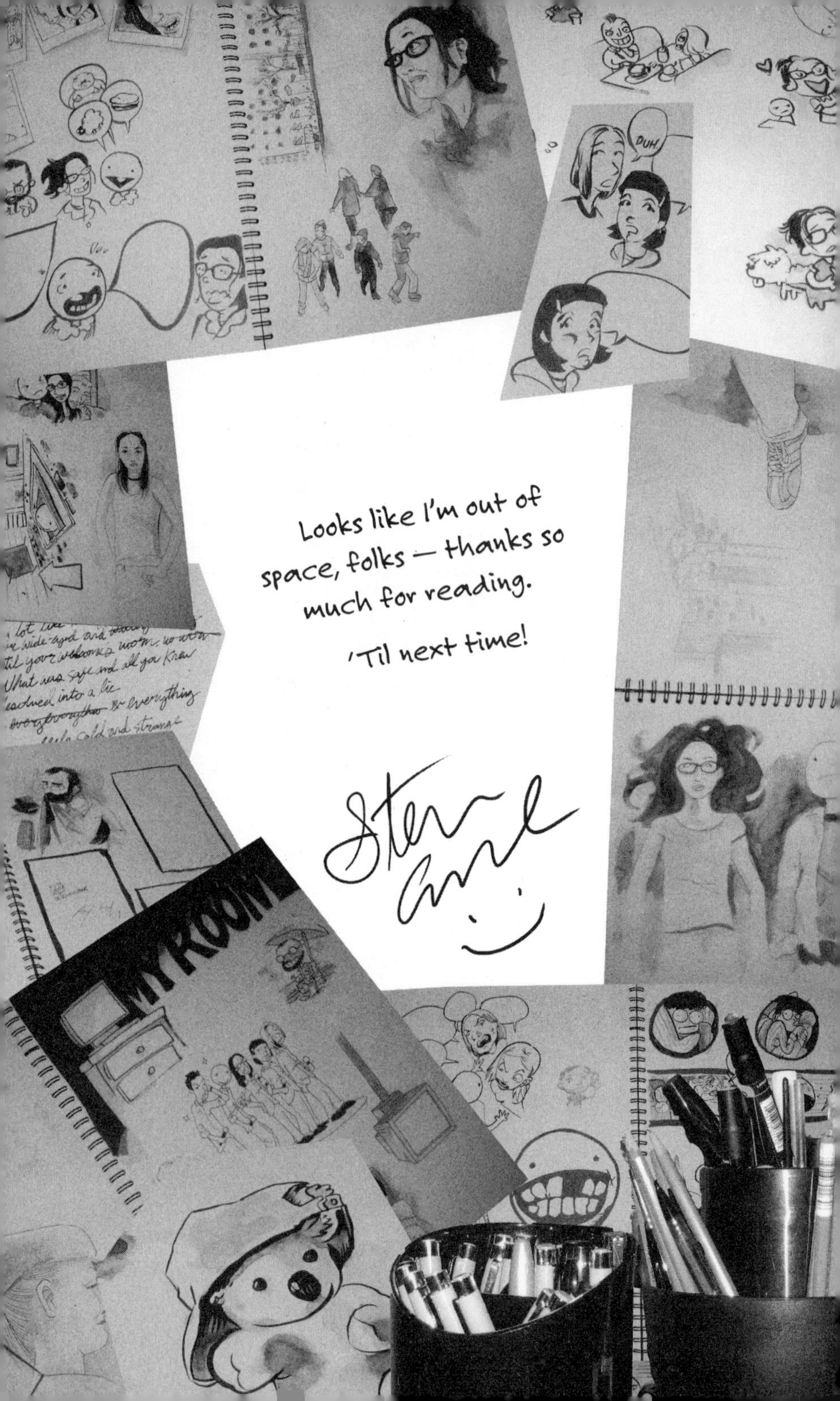
DUH!
Looks like I'm out of space, folks — thanks so much for reading.
'Til next time!
MY ROOM